I0614063

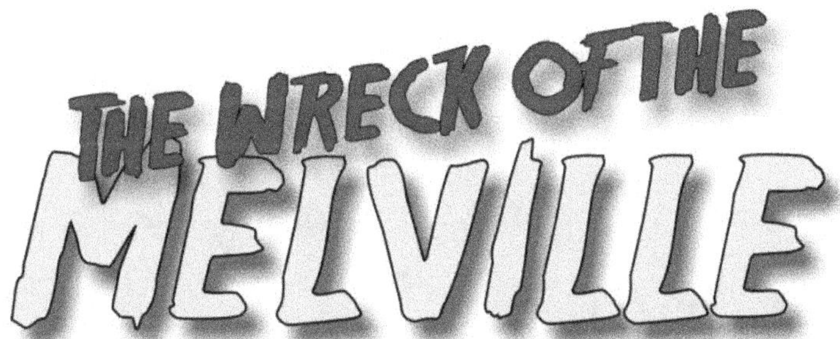

MARK SMELTZ

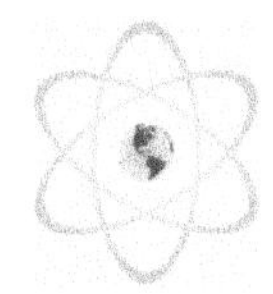

2021, TWB Press
www.twbpress.com

The Wreck of the Melville

Edited by Terry Wright

Cover design by Terry Wright
Cover image from pixabay.com by Comfreak

ISBN: 978-1-944045-80-7

Table of Contents

Introduction

The twenty-first century has seen remarkably few works entered into the literary canon. School curriculums and college courses are largely set in stone; it is a given that students will read Steinbeck in high school and Austen at university. More modern pieces, if indeed they are taught at all, are relegated to "alternative" classes, which seldom offer critiques as thorough as those applied to the classics of English literature. Since the academic culture has fostered this environment in which only an established subset of authors are treated with serious attention, there has been a resulting search for the unpublished "lost" works of these authors. It is often only by the discovery of such pieces that the literary canon, at least as it exists historically, can be appreciably expanded.

There are many such examples: *Wild Fruits,* ostensibly the last of Thoreau's body of work, was discovered and published over one hundred and thirty years after the death of its author. While perhaps not altogether revelatory, the inclusion of this "new" work in the literary canon has allowed us to develop a fuller understanding and appreciation of this influential thinker. For an even more recent example, we need look no further than Conan Doyle's *The Narrative of John Smith*—written in 1883, it was not rediscovered and published until 2011. That a subsequent frenzy of scholarship surrounding this title would soon follow was a foregone conclusion.

However, discoveries of this significance are few and somewhat far between. It is widely acknowledged that any further rediscovered manuscripts will be of lesser and lesser importance; the great literary legends have been discovered already—or they are presumed lost. Even the most diligent scholars have been unable to unearth Stevenson's first draft of *The Strange Case of Dr. Jekyll and Mr. Hyde*, for example, and no one has produced the entirety of Melville's *Isle of the Cross.* The well, in other words, is running dry. Many academics now despair of finding a major diamond in the rough and have instead turned to the realm of *history* in an attempt to shed light on the lives of classic authors, thereby influencing the way in which their masterpieces are interpreted.

For example, discussion of American author Henry James' repressed homosexuality has completely and irrevocably altered the way in which we view his work. The impression of James as a timid man who feared to express intimacy in his private life has largely been swept aside in favor of an altogether different analysis—one in which sexuality necessarily opens his every sentence to a new and productive interpretation. Entire volumes have since been written on the subject. In this way, the discovery of *biographical* details can have tremendous impact upon the way in which classic literature is evaluated and appreciated.

That is why the following manuscript, if indeed its authenticity is independently verified by the academic community at large, must necessarily force us to reevaluate both the lives and works of its principal actors. Found in a collection of sea stories belonging to (but not written by) the obscure novelist Charles Romyn Dake, whose own career was cut short in 1899 when the writer took his own life[1], it is a journal quite unlike any of its contemporaries. Were it simply a piece of fiction, as at first its fantastic and horrifying events might suggest, it would remain a fascinating story in both the macabre and *bildungsroman* traditions, and one well worth further literary analysis. However, after many months spent in the laborious task of digitizing the original volume and transcribing its narrative, I have come to believe that it can be nothing but genuine.

This is a conclusion which has serious ramifications for the literary canon. Particular attention will need to be addressed to the bibliographies of Jules Verne, William Hope Hodgson, and William Clark Russell. Many of the fantastical moments in their stories, it will now be seen, may have been inspired by true events.

---

[1] While macabre-minded readers might be tempted to draw a parallel between the novelist's suicide and this volume (as though he were driven mad by its contents), there are textual indications that it was actually written after Dake's death. How it ended up in his collection is unknown but is only a curiosity in the face of the volume's larger implications.

It would be difficult to overstate the magnitude of the reinterpretations which will be forced upon our understanding of these authors—to say nothing of our understanding of the natural world itself—as a result of this manuscript's discovery. As such, I am excited to present this not only to the academic community, but also simultaneously to a more general readership; the discoveries herein truly belong to the entire world.

With this broader audience in mind, I have in certain sections of the text provided my own notes and observations, which I believe will demonstrate relationships to the works of the authors herein, offer evidence to support the authenticity of the manuscript itself, and generally allow a modern non-academic readership to more fully grasp the implications and significance of the piece. I have also engaged in the minor indulgence of inserting a passage from Herman Melville's body of work (with a single exception) at the outset of each chapter; while these quotations are not always strictly related to the text itself, I believe they are in keeping with the spirit of the memoir, and I do not think that its author would have disapproved.

However, it must be said that in the task of preparing this narrative for the modern reader, I have had only the most cursory hand in the presentation of its content. Serious scholarship of this text must fall to others more qualified than myself—and will, perhaps, belong to the historian and naturalist rather than the literary critic. In the end, of course, the sole credit for the following pages must belong to their author: a singularly courageous young man who, unless further data is eventually brought to light, will be known to history only as "Gordon."

TELLS HOW I FIRST SIGHTED THE *MELVILLE* AND DETERMINED TO OBTAIN PASSAGE ABOARD HER

"For in tremendous extremities human souls are like drowning men; well enough they know they are in peril; well enough they know the causes of that peril;--nevertheless, the sea is the sea, and these drowning men do drown."
-Herman Melville, *Pierre; or The Ambiguities*

The voice first came to me, as best I can remember, when I was a boy of perhaps ten years. The voice was nothing unnatural, indeed nothing outside the realm of ordinary experience, and I imagine that nary a young man or woman exists who does not, upon occasion, hear its call. It was the voice of restlessness, the voice of wanderlust, the voice that always seemed to ask me—most often in the midst of some unpleasant chore or another—wouldn't I rather be engaged in some *other* activity? If I were to be found working in the yard beneath the hard eyes of my father—would I not rather join the boys playing in the street? If I were playing with those same boys, engaging in the idle but wholly engrossing activities, which are an art belonging, I am convinced, only to our youth—would I not rather aspire to greater things? To be in *greater* company? And if I were at my desk in England, with an ocean betwixt myself and the house of my father, applying myself to my studies—would I not rather be somewhere else, *achieving* instead of learning? Without belaboring the point, I would make it known to my reader that I was a fundamentally unhappy soul, never to be satisfied, continually yearning for something different, something *more.*

By the summer of 1890 I had attained twenty years, most spent in the dreadful confinement of formal education, and the voice was louder now than ever before. I wanted to move on and to find something new. That I would find it will no doubt be confirmed in your mind by the time I finish the telling of this tale, if in fact I can, or if indeed such a tale can ever truly be told in its entirety. Do not life's momentous occasions resound within us for eternity? Indeed such an echo was sufficient remembrance of the horrors I had endured, and I had previously determined not to record the narrative which I now begin; the events that followed the embarkation of the *Melville* on her fateful voyage had wholly altered my intentions to pursue a life of journalism, for I could scarcely lift a pen without thinking of the travails of that adventure.

The cause of my lapse in determination now can be attributed to the failure of my colleagues to record the details of our travels with their own infinitely more artful pens. It is true that the men with whom I sailed have written many volumes since our brief time together, some of which contain certain elements of the truth under the guise of fiction, but to date a complete record of the events that befell the *Melville* and her crew is absent their bibliographies. Perhaps their hesitation to record the truth was a reflection of the fear that their stories would not be believed, and that their reputations would suffer in the wake of any published confessional. Or perhaps their reticence stemmed from an undue modesty; reluctant to claim the heroism of that voyage for their own, my friends (I feel justified in addressing them as such) chose instead to project their finer qualities onto characters of their own imaginations. But seeing that I have little reputation to protect and few valorous deeds to call my own[2], I feel no such compulsion to refrain from relating the account which follows.

And so I begin the record of the extraordinary circumstances which befell me in the year 1890, with the caveat that I hope the reader will forgive the antiquated nature of my prose; for truly I had abandoned my passion for the written word following the events that took place aboard the *Melville,* and as such it might be said that I never developed my voice beyond a style which has since fallen into some degree of disuse.

I have already alluded to the fact that it was my good fortune

[2] The author's modesty is a recurring element throughout his memoir; despite the legitimate heroics in which he later engages, he is inclined throughout to attribute the best qualities to his elders.

to attain that most lofty of academic aspirations: an English education. I returned from university at the age of twenty, believing myself prepared to begin an honest American career in journalism. However, I had discovered something extraordinary during those long weeks spent in crossing the Atlantic: with the ocean before me, the crest of every wave seemed to represent an infinity of possibilities, the wind rippling a ship's canvas seemed to whisper a thousand untold futures, and the voice in my head—that damning, all-consuming voice—had fallen silent.

I must confess that my program of study was literary in nature, and that the intricacies of the human psyche are wholly outside the realm of my educational experience. Any conjecture I make concerning the cessation of that voice in my head is therefore merely that: conjecture. But I found that so long as I remained near the sea, even on the coast, that the restlessness in my soul was more or less quiet. I suspect that the answer to this riddle has less to do with the sea itself than with the prospect of adventure it represented in my mind; with the ocean in sight, it seemed to me that *some great thing* might arrive on the very next ship to make berth, or that such a ship might carry me on to something grander. And so I found myself unable to settle farther inland than the isle of Nantucket.

I convey this information now because it is critical to the development of an understanding of how I came to be at the *Inquirer and Mirror*, that worthy newspaper which accepted my apprenticeship and will, perhaps, publish this account upon its completion.[3] It will also perhaps prove useful to provide an understanding of my state of mind during the period in which the *Melville* made berth in Nantucket.

The subject of the arrival of the *Melville* and the subsequent voyage she was to make were to be featured in the newspaper, and the coverage of these noteworthy events had been assigned to me. This was to be the first real story upon which I had the honor of reporting, and I intended to do so with the greatest enthusiasm.

---

[3] The *Inquirer and Mirror,* which dates back to 1821, did not ever publish this memoir in whole or in part. Certain language in its final chapter leads me to believe that its author chose never to submit it for consideration in the first place.

Such enthusiasm was not hard to muster upon learning the purpose of the ship's voyage. She was not destined, as so many ships out of Nantucket once were, to be a whaler. Instead she was to be a ferry for passengers, although this description does inadequate service to her splendor. The *Melville* had been assigned the singular honor of being chosen to transport the greatest literary minds of the day upon a brief sojourn along the eastern American seaboard, during which time these authors were to engage in a writing session which was, as was made plain to me by my superiors at the *Inquirer and Mirror,* perceived to rival even that meeting between Mary Shelley, Percy Bysshe Shelley, and Lord Byron, which in 1816 generated the seed that had eventually matured into the legendary *Frankenstein.*

This meeting promised to be no less extraordinary, for on board the *Melville* would be none other than the eminent French author, Mr. Jules Verne, and the master of the rousing sea story, the incomparable Mr. William Clark Russell. Only Herman Melville himself was to be missing from this great meeting of minds. It must be duly confessed that this last writer was somewhat unappreciated at the time of our adventure and has only since come into some degree of well-deserved posthumous fame (for he was fated to pass away only shortly after the conclusion of our adventures), and as such an invitation was not extended to him.[4] Nonetheless, the captain, whose description will presently be furnished, professed a great admiration for the man and so named the ship in his honor, unwittingly ensuring that the man's name would forever be associated with our time aboard the vessel.

It is useless to describe the excitement which I felt upon learning that I would be reporting on the business of such great men, both of whom I had read during my time in England. In anticipation of the work to be done, I had bent the ear of a sympathetic customs man at the harbor in advance, who saw that I was promptly notified upon the arrival of the *Melville.* Thus I found myself approaching the docks on the unusually foggy evening of the ship's arrival. Dusk was falling and the light was

---

[4] Of course, one may speculate whether Melville, by 1890 a retiree working on his ultimately unfinished *Billy Budd, Sailor*, would have accepted such an invitation even if it had been extended.

failing, and the sounds of the workday had begun to fade, to be replaced only with the lapping of the waves and the reluctant cries of the gulls, which were loath to give up the day.

The crewmen were said to have gone ashore, seeking carousal and merrymaking prior to spending several weeks more at sea. This suited me, for I had intended merely to observe the ship with the aim of securing some description of her for my story. I did not anticipate any special need to interact with her crew. While such a description of the ship indeed shortly follows, it is colored with the realization that presently overcame me: the *Melville* was the finest sight upon which I had ever laid my eyes, and that I would do anything, indeed I felt that I would make any sacrifice, to walk her decks and again feel the salt spray of the Atlantic upon my face. Such is the draw of a great ship, and such is the allure of the sea upon all men. Melville himself has said, and with more brevity and eloquence than I might summon were I left to my own devices, that “there is magic in it.”

The ship named for him was not lacking in such magic. She was a glorious square-rigged three-masted sailing vessel, without perhaps the utilitarian practicality of a modern steamer, but surpassing any such ship in sheer imaginative grandeur, rising at least fifteen feet from the water and looming out of the evening mist as a Biblical leviathan. Well over a hundred feet in length, I could see that she was thirty feet in breadth if she were an inch. The mere sight of her called to my mind all of the most daring sea stories I had read, most of which originated from the pens of the authors who were shortly to board her.

To think that these great authors would be gathered together! To imagine what stories might be conceived as the ship cleaved her way through the waves! The romance of the idea seized my mind with such force that I found myself possessed of a sudden irrational desire to participate in this adventure by any means necessary. For the first time in months, that damning voice was speaking to me again, and it seemed that during its absence it had grown swollen and pregnant—for now its bubble burst with unsurpassed loudness and urgency in my mind.

“Wouldn’t you like to go along?” it cajoled. “Wouldn’t you like to leave this dull fishermen’s town behind you?”

Indeed the fancy struck me so powerfully that I moved down

the docks at that very moment, forgetting for a time any idea of recording a description of the ship herself.

I found the harbor nigh deserted but espied a lantern glowing aboard the ship which had so caught my eye. I approached as far as the end of the docks, where the black ocean was deep enough to harbor the vessel and certainly deep enough to swallow me (I confess to being no great swimmer). Therefore, with my feet firmly planted upon the planking, I cupped my hands to my mouth and uttered the loudest “halloo!” I could muster. Initially it appeared as though my call would go unanswered, but at last I perceived the motion of a second lantern onboard the ship, glowing only dimly through the fog. I distinguished that a figure held the lantern aloft, moving across the deck to lean upon the rail to make my acquaintance. I found myself unable to see the man with any real clarity, but I determined that he had large build and possessed a most unusual tangle of hair. This lent a decidedly lion-like character to his silhouette as it appeared through the veil of mist, which cloaked the ship in twilight.

“What’s this? What brings a boy to call upon an hour so late?” In the man’s other hand, illumined by the lamp in his raised fist, I thought I detected the presence of a bottle. My suspicion was further evinced by a slur to his tongue and the general rudeness of his manner, though, as I would learn, this latter was as much a fixture of his personality as it was a byproduct of his intoxication. “Be damned or be gone, or both, if it suits you, for I’ve nothing to say to you.”

“I have come to negotiate terms of passage.”

“I’ve no taste for passengers, and less use. Again I say be gone.”

“I beg you hear me. I mean to write of your ship.”

I had no opportunity to further explain my intentions, for the man perceptibly straightened, and he called out in an altogether different tone of voice.

“A writer, is it?”

“The same, sir.”

“No doubt you are aware of the purpose of the *Melville*’s voyage.”

“It is to be the finest adventure in literary history,” I declared, tasting on my tongue for the first time the words which I had already devised to be the headline of my story.

At this the man laughed. It was a harsh, nasal sound, not unlike the barking of a dog, but there was a rueful note in it, which I believed to be absent in any species, save for man. It is our unique providence in the natural order to experience mirth in communion with despair, and such a combination I sensed in the laughter of this strange man from the first.

"Indeed," he said, "it is a voyage to exercise the minds of great men. Doubtless you would like to study with them, and have so approached the captain of the ship to plead your case."

I suspected that this praise of his passengers was somewhat less than genuine, if his intonation were any guide, but I thrilled at my luck in stumbling across the skipper with such ease. It must be admitted that perhaps I should have been turned from my scheme upon the acquisition of the knowledge that it was the *captain* who was in his cups, and that such an inauspicious encounter might hardly bode well for the journey to follow, but it must also be admitted that I was young, and rash, and felt no such apprehension—and indeed I persisted in my entreaties to be heard and understood.

"I am to report on the voyage in the employ of the *Inquirer*-"

"Ho! A reporter, then? You'll do well to keep away from my ship!"

He turned his back to me, and once more his strange laughter rolled across the still water to reach my ears. At this, I shouted to clarify my position, but the captain had begun to move away, swinging the lantern in his hand and roaring the tune of a bawdy sailor's song, the words of which are perhaps not altogether suitable for inclusion in my narrative here.

The reader would be correct to surmise that my blood had thoroughly risen upon the receipt of so abrupt and unjust a dismissal from the captain, without having first been given the opportunity to explain my intentions and so make a reasonable case for enlistment as a passenger aboard the *Melville.* My account may well have ended upon receiving such a discharge, save for a story I had once read as a boy. The tale in question was written by an author whose name I find myself unable to recall—but it concerned a young man who sneaks aboard a sailing ship and only reveals himself to the crew once the journey is sufficiently underway to prohibit his return to shore.[5]

So inspired, I began to entertain thoughts of likewise sneaking aboard the ship and acting as a stowaway, and indeed I immediately began to put this ill-conceived plan into effect. I moved away from the pier at the end of which the *Melville* was anchored and proceeded to walk along the harbor in the hopes of finding an amenable soul who might be persuaded to ferry me alongside the ship. For I was now determined beyond all reason to circumvent the skipper's admonitions and to gain passage aboard the *Melville* at any cost.

Would that I had obeyed the captain! What tragedies might I have been spared were it not for the presence of a stubborn streak in my heart, which chose to assert itself at that very moment! Each step along the docks, unbeknownst to myself, was bringing me closer to that strange circumstance of fate which was to transform my life, hitherto a promising and successful enterprise, into a trial of horror and anguish!

But all things seem clear on the further side of experience, and in any case it must be admitted that there are times when even I grow restless with the predictable routines of life ashore. It is during these times that I look back upon my adventures with some degree of fondness, tempered as it must be with lament for those who were irrevocably lost. And so I do not altogether regret that my life was full enough to include experiences which lent to me a greater understanding of human nature and of what is possible on this earth, and which perhaps even gave my life some semblance of meaning. But as I am not particularly given to philosophic digressions, I will dispense with further such discourse and get on with my tale, plainly as I am able to tell it.

Now, I have said that night was falling and the docks had become largely deserted. Still I chanced to come across a lone fisherman who was in the process of mooring his fishing boat and tying up his day's catch. Without further hesitation, I decided to

---

[5] While there are many such stories that the author may have read, one possibility is *The Narrative of Arthur Gordon Pym of Nantucket* (1838) by Edgar Allan Poe. This is Poe's only novel, and it is doubly interesting for our purposes here. The story prompted Jules Verne to write his own sequel, *An Antarctic Mystery* (1897), which may in turn have also been inspired in part by certain events that transpired aboard the *Melville*.

seize upon this opportunity so afforded to me by Providence, and I approached the fisherman presently. He was a thin and wiry sort of fellow, with a face tanned by long exposure to the sun and wrinkled into a semblance of leather with the unyielding force of wind and wave to which his occupation relentlessly exposed him. And yet, for all his time spent upon the sea, he was as far removed from the station of a true mariner as myself. For as the mariner wanders across the oceans of the world, on one ship or another, here was a man who possessed a home to which he would return at the close of day. Though I was distinguished by no great powers of deduction, I needed only look at him to place him as such; he was marked with no tattoos and carried no sea-chest aboard his little boat. No, this was a man who went to sea by day and returned to shore ere nightfall—the true mariner was a man who carried all his earthly possessions with him, though they might consist only of a Sou'wester and a housewife.[6]

This is not to suggest that this man's station was in any way inferior to that of the seaman; indeed, it might rightly be said that the fisherman enjoyed an altogether higher standard of living on the whole. I illustrate the difference only to demonstrate to my reader, who may be as unfamiliar with life at sea as I once was, those particulars which made my companions especially suited for the trials with which we would soon find ourselves confronted. For the mariner is of a unique constitution, and peculiarly hardened to face the ever-present dangers supplied by an ocean whose temperament changes upon the slightest of whims. It must furthermore be acknowledged that he has few enough defenders at shore, where he is widely perceived as an errant drunkard—and so I feel compelled to make a case for his bravery here. Let those who live their lives in comfort ashore experience for a moment the harrowing fury of the sea, the crash of her mighty combers on deck, which have washed many a man overboard ere they drain through the scupper-holes, only to be succeeded by a yet mightier cascade of water, to say nothing of the rigid discipline enforced upon those who live their lives before the mast, and witness how they too would seek comfort in liquid libation and seize any moment of relative safety as an occasion worthy of celebration!

---

[6] A rain hat and a small sewing kit, respectively.

It is my fervent hope that the reader may forgive this digression into the character of the sailor, as it is not without its purpose. Many a man has died at sea without knowing the why; I illustrate the manifold dangers here so that the pluck of my companions might shine out all the brighter in the pages to follow, more especially when contrasted with my own cowardice. For truly I exhibited such fright as would shame a child (and I thought myself a man!), and which certainly shames me in the admission. So let the reader not be deceived with my apparent exhibition of disregard for the security of my own future as I approached this fisherman with the aim of sneaking aboard the *Melville;* 'twas a flight of impassioned fancy and little more, and it was as far removed from bravery as the earth and stars. Consequently, it will come as no surprise to learn that I experienced some inward relief when my scheme was presently foiled.

"Sir," I began, "May I beg a moment of your time?"

The fisherman, a creature seemingly composed of raw muscle and sinew, did not stop in his work, but did lift his head and cock one gray eyebrow at me as I clumsily attempted to explain why I had accosted him.

"I am a reporter, and I should very much like to get a closer look at that ship." I gestured to the *Melville* as I spoke; the fisherman could hardly have remained ignorant of its arrival, which had caused quite a stir in the harbor.

"So feast your eyes," the man said to me in a voice that was as flat as the still night air. "I won't stand in your way." He hauled his net, nigh bursting at the seams with the slick, scaled bodies of his catch, some flopping feebly about in the salt air which was life to us and death to them, over his shoulder, and he pushed past me.

"I should like to do it under the cover of darkness," I continued, only slightly raising my voice to retain his attention as he moved a few paces from me. When I saw that he looked back at me, I lifted a change purse from my pocket. "And I would be pleased to see that you were duly compensated for your time."

For the first time since I spoke to him, the fisherman's composure wavered. Though I have already contrasted his vocation favorably with the hard station of the mariner, it bears mentioning that his life was not an easy one. A purse full of coins could well represent a week's worth of wages. I watched, fascinated, as a battle of emotions waged open war across his tanned and lined countenance in the evening light. My hopes were momentarily raised as I began to suspect that he would succumb to my proposition, but were summarily dashed when his face settled back into its previous disinterested scowl.

"I don't know what you're up to," he said slowly. "And truth be told, I don't much care. But I've heard tell of the man that sails that ship." He fixed me with a dead stare. "And you won't catch *me* sneaking up on him in the dark."

I suppose he must have considered me duly warned, for he turned to go, but I was not to be discouraged so easily—foolish youth that I was! I shouted to him one final query, desperate though it seemed. For having been rejected by both the captain and this worthy, I had no one else to whom I might turn.

"Do you know where I can find the crew?"

He stared at me for several moments, as though deciding whether to reply, and finally sighed. "Do you know the Green Pelican?"[7]

I indicated that I did.

"You may find them there."

Without another word, he moved away and rolled into the rapidly darkening evening with the unmistakable gait that is peculiar to those who spend much time on the water. As he was lost to my sight, lightning flared somewhere over the sea to my back, briefly illumining the evening with the light of day. And before that light had fully departed from the sky, a boom of thunder rattled the heavens.

For the first time, I felt some misgivings about the course I was pursuing. A vague, unspecific apprehension lifted the hairs about the back of my neck. But as the first of the night's rain began to fall, I pushed my doubts aside and left the harbor, heading for the Green Pelican: a pub well-known for the crowd of ill repute it attracted.

---

[7] Though Verne places his fictional "Green Cormorant" in the Kerguelen Islands, it seems likely that he took inspiration from this small Nantucket inn when writing *An Antarctic Mystery* (1897). Like the crew of the *Melville,* Verne's characters spend time at this inn before embarking on an eventful voyage at sea.

IN WHICH I ENCOUNTER THE CREW AND ATTEMPT TO INGRATIATE MYSELF TO THEM

"But who can forever resist the very Devil himself, when he comes in the guise of a gentleman, free, fine, and frank?"
-Herman Melville, *White Jacket or, the World on a Man-of-War*

Though it could scarcely compare to the force of an out-and-out gale upon the sea (a spectacle with which I would soon have the dubious pleasure of becoming fully acquainted), the rain which fell upon the isle of Nantucket that evening was of an unseasonable cold. My clothes were presently soaked through as I approached the doors of the Green Pelican, and it came as no small relief to enter the inn and behold the warmth of a crackling fire, the jovial laughter of men "in their drink," and the intoxicating aroma of stews and chowders boiling upon a greasy stovetop.

The inn had wholly embraced the whaling culture which had once lent it prosperity. Behind the bar were arranged broken and rusted whaling lances, most of which doubtless originated with the sailors who were oftenest found in places like the Green Pelican betwixt times spent at sea. The wood upon which the bar matron served her "deliriums and death," to again borrow from Melville, was etched by so many sailors' knives with countless depictions of scenes of the mariner's life. Some of these were quite enough to turn my stomach with their grotesque depictions of the butchery of those leviathans of the sea upon which these hard men had once earned their bread.

Rare then was the whaler that left from Nantucket rather than New Bedford, and rarer still will be the whaler which departs from anywhere on the east coast before my days are done, unless I am much mistaken. But let it be said that the Green Pelican had not forgotten her heritage. Indeed, the general atmosphere was such that I felt as though I had stepped not merely into the inn and out of the burgeoning storm, but rather somehow through time. My frame of mind was sufficiently disposed to entertain romantic thoughts of literary heroes and fine adventures—the result of which was that I was more determined than ever to make my acquaintance with the crew and bring my plan to board the ship into fruition.

I settled upon a bench and caught the eye of the bar matron, a buxom woman who looked back at me and seemed to be attempting to ascertain whether I represented another wild mariner upon whom she must needs keep her eye in the event that fisticuffs should occur. I seemed to meet with her satisfaction, for her features soon relaxed and her eyes moved on to search out more likely troublemakers. Plainly, I was dismissed. This prompted me to ponder the difficulties of maintaining peace in a setting fraught with men who had been denied the opportunity to carouse for weeks at sea and were only now, and only for a brief spell, truly free men again. I doubted whether I should be up to the task. Indeed, I was sufficiently intimidated by the mere prospect of *introducing* myself to any of the patrons of the Green Pelican, all of whom appeared to represent a rather rough breed of man.

Take, for instance, that wild ruffian who I would soon learn to be the ship's carpenter. Standing at seven feet tall if he stood an inch, this brawny and bearded man roved about the bar with all the pent-up aggression of the lion (if little of its grace). He downed mug upon mug of ale, slapped his fellows on their backs, and knocked aside tables of cards when it appeared that his luck at the game had turned sour. But he did not despair! Having thus lost his wages at the game, he would turn to competitions of strength, at which he accumulated enough handfuls of coins to make him forget his prior ill fortunes and return to the cards with hopes renewed. I watched as he conquered yet another opponent by slamming the smaller man's fist upon the tabletop, belched, and loosed a roar of victory that again brought to my mind the fury of some untamed beast. The reader will understand that to approach such a man with my request hardly appealed to me, and will perhaps forgive me for continuing to look around the inn for another crew member with whom prolonged interaction might prove to be somewhat less daunting.

Such a search was by no means easy, for the crew of the *Melville,* easily identified by their appearance and behavior, were altogether a raucous lot of sailors. In hindsight I might have wondered at this. The voyage of the *Melville* was to be, at its heart, a recreational cruise—however it turned out in the end. And given her noteworthy passengers, I might have expected the crew to be comprised of mariners who were rather more disposed to appreciate the culture and literature of the day. Put plainly, had I been possessed of a clear head at the time, I might have wondered why the *Melville* would need such a hard crew for what amounted to a leisurely voyage.

But alas, I was fixated with my desire to gain passage aboard the ship, and I gave little thought to the manner of her crew other than to decide which of the men seemed the most approachable. Eventually I settled upon a small-framed man who sat quietly apart from his compatriots, hunched over a drink upon his stool. In truth, there was little to mark this man as a member of the crew, were it not for the fact that occasionally one of his burlier fellows would entreat him to join their camaraderie, at which the small man would invariably respond with a curt shake of his head.

I ordered two mugs of ale and bade my time, sipping at my drink and watching this small man until it seemed that he had finished his own. Then I hastened to my feet and sat myself beside him, sliding one of my mugs across the hardwood to him. He accepted the ale graciously enough; his noncommittal grunt may even have been intended as a form of thanks. But when I glimpsed his eyes, staring over the rim of the cup at me, and when I sensed the sober, calculated intelligence in them, I felt a pang of misgiving that I had selected this man to approach. Perhaps I'd have done better to choose one of the brawnier men, more threatening on the surface, admittedly, but perhaps more open and relatable than this somehow shrunken man. He now seemed somehow cloaked in the shadows thrown from the fireplace, and he radiated a sense of quiet danger. But I had already come this far, and there was nothing for me but to carry on.

"You belong to the *Melville?*" I ventured.

"Inasmuch as any man may be said to belong to his ship."

"I would belong to her as well."

A smile broke across the man's face, a smile that spoke not of warmth and light and humor, but of fogbound winter mornings in a churchyard cemetery, where a rime of frost crept over the headstones, and of cold, freshly turned earth. He extended a hand across the table, and for a fleeting moment that nonetheless seemed to stretch to eternity and back again, I was certain that his hand would be cold and wet, slippery and limp as though it were a fish pulled from the sea by one of Nantucket's countless anglers.

I shook his hand. It was warm and dry.

As he loosed his grip, his smile seemed robbed of malice. For the moment he appeared just a sailor; a hard man without question, but no worse than his fellows. "I am Jeremy Fairchild."

I introduced myself in turn. "My friends call me Gordon."

"So you wish to run away to sea, is it, boy? You seem fit enough, and if it's honest work you're after, I've little doubt you'll find it. But it strikes me as you can do a spot better than the *Melville*, at that."

"And yet no other ship offers the prospect of tutelage under Mr. Jules Verne or Mr. William Clark Russell."

"Ah," said Mr. Fairchild[8]. "So it's not work you're after."

"Yet neither am I opposed to it. I am of sound body, as you yourself have noted, and I intend to carry my weight to the satisfaction of both the captain and his crew."

"Have you ever been to sea, boy?"

"Yes."

"In what capacity?"

"As a passenger."

"A passenger! Well, we've little need for one of those, though it's not my place to say so. And a cabin boy we already have—though he's worth about as much as a passenger, for how often he's his nose in a book.[9] No, boy, I don't see as you're any use to

---

[8] Historically, only the officers on a merchantman would be addressed with the title "Mr." This tendency of Gordon to address all sailors as such might reflect on how reverently he treated them, or his ignorance of nautical customs. I have followed his example in my own footnotes for the sake of consistency.

[9] Mr. Fairchild appears to be referring here to the *Melville*'s cabin boy, William. Though the author gives no last name to William, he is unmistakably a young William Hope Hodgson (1877-1918), an Englishman who went to sea as a boy and later became a prolific author of nautical and weird fiction. Further evidence to support this identification comes up later in the memoir and will be

us, but as I've said, it's not for me to say yea or nay. That'll rest with Captain Carrig."

I noticed that he said this with a slight twist to his lip, as though with disdain. "I fear the captain has already summarily dismissed me."

"Then there's little help for you. Have another drink, lad, and go home. I expect we'll be back in this pub in a fortnight—with precious little to show for our time, like as not. I'll tell you all about it for another round of ale."

And then, though Mr. Fairchild did not stand or even truly lean back from the table, he seemed to somehow withdraw into the shadows of the inn. I understood that I had been dismissed and that no further help was likely to come from this corner. In any case, my empty spirits were matched by my empty mug, and it appeared as though my efforts to persuade this man were destined to be in vain. I stood from the stool in a torrent of despair that belongs exclusively to the young, who seem to feel all emotion more keenly than their elders, and I took a step toward the doors, hoping that the storm had abated and that I would not be caught in a deluge on the long walk home. It was at this moment that I first caught sight of a piano standing unattended in the far corner of the Green Pelican. Its scrimshaw keys shone warmly in the firelight, seeming somehow resplendent with invitation.

Now, I have referred to receiving an English education, and it must be said that rarely does a student escape such an education without some indoctrination into the classical arts. My tutors had been delighted to learn that I was possessed of a natural aptitude for music in general and the piano in particular. For a moment I must put all humility at risk, and venture to suggest that I considered myself something of an accomplished musician. Seeing the way in which the piano in the corner seemed to call itself to my attention, I considered how I might utilize my talent to attract the attention of the crew. It was immediately clear that neither march nor waltz would suffice; I cast my mind back to those regrettable days at university in which my colleagues and I had the predictable misfortune to discover alcohol—and of the bawdy songs we were wont to sing.

---

addressed as it arises.

A vague plan was taking form in my mind, you see, and before I had quite realized that I had come to a decision, I found myself turning from the door and threading a path through the crowd toward the piano. I seated myself at its bench and allowed my fingers to engage in an exploratory run along the ivories. A trill of music followed the motion of my fingertips; the atmosphere of the inn wavered slightly, responding to this sudden intrusion of noise, before stabilizing to its prior level of volume. I realized that I still had the opportunity to abandon this plan—which was surely the height of foolishness—or to instead abandon caution and make a final desperate ploy to gain the acceptance of the crew. I trust that the reader will, even at this early juncture in my narrative, recognize that I was possessed of little enough in the way of good judgment, and will therefore be able to surmise that I chose to forge ahead. My fingers fell into an old rhythm, seemingly of their own accord, and I began to accompany the music with a coarse university song, the regrettable content of which is reproduced here:

O'er forest, field and fen,
Come all ye drunkards, ye glorious men!
All over town, from street last to first,
We'll fill every tavern and quench every thirst!
Suffer not the teetotaler and his damnable think,
Instead indulge Bacchus and his venerable drink!
Neither king in his tower, nor salt on the brine,
Would e'er turn from his whisky or wine!
The Macedonian's[10] approval is endorsement for me,
We're all free to drink, though none drink for free!

To my great surprise, several men in the bar joined their voices with mine in the completion of this verse! But what could be more natural? Here were seafaring men who, if they had not come from distant shores themselves, had sailed with many who had. As sailors are ever wont to sing in an effort to coordinate their work and resist the stagnation of their spirits, they belonged to a lot which delighted in the proliferation of new and entertaining

[10] Possibly a reference to Alexander the Great.

minstrelsy. And while my own "pipes" may not have rivaled the skill of my fingers upon the keys, I was met with no small degree of gratification upon receiving a thunderous round of applause from the patrons of the Green Pelican. I gave a little seated half-bow, flushed with pleasure.

A strong hand fell heavily upon my shoulder and another hand was thrust into one of my own, as a cadre of wild seamen descended upon me. The owner of the hands in question was none other than that unlucky gambler of a man whose antics I had so recently observed with unease: the very same Barbary lion of a brute whose physical prowess had intimidated me into turning to the chilly company of Mr. Fairchild. As it turned out, I had done better to approach him from the first.

"That's a fine song, lad, though it's sore mistaken on one point."

"Which is that?"

"Anyone as can play like that, *does* drink for free!"

At that, his hand in mine was replaced with a mug. Ale sloshed over my fingers and onto the piano's keys as the giant of a man slapped me upon the back.

"How now, Mr. Derrick?" came a flat voice, giving name to my benefactor. "Is he to play us another song with one hand, then?"

The speaker was a short and squat fellow with a rather toad-like face; his body resembled nothing so much as that of a normal man compressed to half its height, resulting not in obesity but in a dense frame of compacted musculature. His eyes narrowed as they took me in, and there seemed little warmth in their depths. And while his smile seemed genuine enough, the lines around his mouth spoke of cruelty. Such was my first impression of the boatswain, Mr. Harris, and though I am no physiognomist, to this day I hold to its general accuracy as an appraisal of his character.

Not to be deterred at this critical moment, however, I seized the opportunity to down my drink in a single quaff (to another scattering of applause) and return my hands to the piano. I reprised my original tune and prepared to deliver another verse, but was interrupted by Mr. Derrick.

"Hasten that melody," he commanded, wrapping an arm around the boatswain, who scowled but seemed unable to shake the great mass of the man's arm from his shoulders. "Mr. Harris and I'll take up the tune."

I duly obliged, doubling my tempo and adding a little flourish here and there; my fingers danced across the keys, and Mr. Derrick, true to his word, sung in a voice which reflected his character—which is to say that it was deep, sonorous, and exceedingly cheerful. After an encouraging blow was delivered to Mr. Harris's ribs by the elbow of Mr. Derrick, the former also joined in, harmonizing with Mr. Derrick in a surprisingly mellifluous voice, which belied his generally unwholesome appearance. Their own song, even more jaunty and robust than my own, proceeded as follows:

Oh, tireless and brave are the men
Of cantank'rous old Captain Glen!
We had better not fail
To run up that sail,
'Fore the old bugger counts up to ten!

Oh, hearty and hale are the men
Of lecherous old Captain Glen!
He says jump! And we run,
And who else has such fun,
Without complaint first now and then?

Oh, thirsty and poor are the men
Of pennywise old Captain Glen!
At sea six weeks more,
For one night ashore,
And like fools we'll do it again!

At the lively conclusion of this last verse, the voices of its chief authors dissolved into raucous laughter. I soon found my own voice echoing amongst the general din as I parsed their lyrics, which, while simpler than those of my own song, were unexpectedly subtle in the specific aspersions they cast upon the character of the *Melville*'s captain. I recognized at once that this was the sort of song into which any captain's name could be inserted, and it must have therefore been a particular plague to many a skipper's ear. The thought made me laugh even harder. My fingers slid from the keys in my good humor, and I found my hand crushed in many calloused seamen's handshakes as I was congratulated for my music, which more than one sailor pronounced was "fit to beat the devil."

In regards to my subsequent conversations with the crew, it should perhaps be said that the dialect of the men was somewhat less refined than proper King's English—and yet I have transcribed it as such without making any real attempt to reflect the staggering array of foreign accents and creative pronunciations with which I was confronted. No doubt some of my friends are of a different mind concerning this representation of the mariner's vernacular, and indeed some have portrayed it in a stylistically quite interesting fashion.[11] But I must trust that the adventures I experienced will stand upon their own merits and will not unduly draw the reader's attention to my own deficiencies as an author.

In any case, no criticism can be applied to the singing of the crewmen; their diction and form were faultless, and my own conviction and bigheadedness were increased in equal measure as their words and humor wrapped themselves around me, and I began to believe myself positively destined for this meeting in the Pelican. And who can say that I was not? For destiny can be cruel as well as kind—a fact with which I would soon be confronted and learn to regret.

"Gordon, my boy," said Mr. Derrick, after ascertaining my appellation. He wrapped an arm about me and wrested me from the bench. "I see in you something of myself, as I once was." His voice had begun to take on the slur of intoxication, and his strength seemed to have doubled without his taking notice of the fact. I struggled to keep from spilling another drink, which had without warning appeared in my hand.

"Nonsense," intoned the flat timbre of Mr. Harris, who in contrast sounded as though he were entirely in possession of his faculties. "You were never so young!"

---

[11] It seems likely that the author is referring most especially to William Hope Hodgson, whose novel *The Ghost Pirates* (1909) contains lengthy passages of phonetically written dialogue between characters. This is a technique commonly used in the "sea story" genre by authors such as John C. Hutcheson and, to a much lesser extent, William Clark Russell himself.

"Nor so untested," came a third voice. I looked up and saw to my surprise that Mr. Fairchild had joined our company at the piano. His eyes met mine, and in them I saw a species of considered calculation.

"Though an idea comes to mind," he continued. "A way in which we might evaluate the boy's merit…if he is to sail with us." Mr. Fairchild looked around at his small audience and raised his eyebrows in what I intuitively understood was a mockery of the expression it purported to be. "For such is his wish."

Alas, to hear my own aims so baldly stated! I feared it would go badly for me now, as I did not believe that my companions were yet sufficiently intoxicated to entertain the notion. But I was to be surprised.

"Oho!" said Mr. Derrick. "I warn you, Gordon, we've no piano aboard ship!" He and Mr. Harris fairly roared with laughter, though I noticed that the boatswain's eyes were untouched by mirth and remained steady upon me. Mr. Fairchild again managed that grim upturn of his lips, which was intended to approximate a smile.

"What must I do?" I queried, seizing upon Mr. Fairchild's suggestion. Though I was loathe to trust the man, I was ready to accept the aid of any ally.

"A seaman must be prepared to run the rigging in the swiftest gale, at heights for which his farm boy's life has left him woefully unprepared."

The reader will have gathered that this account of my youth was not entirely accurate—but I abstained from objecting. I thought that maybe I could surprise him.

"And while we have not a gale for practice," he continued, "we have a little rain, and I do believe the boy's deep enough in his cups." This he said with another of those ghastly smiles. Mr. Fairchild turned to Mr. Derrick and Mr. Harris. "What say you?"

"Aye, it's true enough," said Mr. Derrick slowly and with evident reluctance.

I felt my first prickle of foreboding as I studied his face.

"Sankaty Head?" Mr. Harris said, his voice devoid of the emotion it had so richly held whilst singing, though something of a grin still lingered about his lips.

"Sankaty Head," confirmed Mr. Fairchild. It sounded as

though he had pronounced a sentence upon me—in retrospect, it is conceivable that he thought he was doing precisely that. Yet I was not to be deterred. Was I not familiar with that stalwart Nantucket landmark, the Sankaty Head lighthouse? None better, I fancied—though the jovial camaraderie I felt with the inanimate structure at the time was perhaps bolstered by my consumption of alcohol, as in truth I had never done more than view it from a distance. Nonetheless, I determined to rise to this occasion and seize this opportunity that seemed to have been afforded me.

I soon found myself outside in the rain-lashed night, surrounded closely by the dark-obscured forms of Mr. Derrick, Mr. Harris, and Mr. Fairchild. I became aware of the sensation of my feet plodding along the walk beneath me, though they seemed to move without any specific direction from their owner. It felt as though my head were floating above the rest of me, with one object in my sightline: the intermittently flashing beacon of the lighthouse, just visible from the inn. My feet moving of their own accord, I bumped against the squat figure of Mr. Harris and was repelled more by his grimace than by his hand, which gave me an unceremonious shove and sent me tottering laterally across the road and into the grassy verge which bordered it.

This development was just as well, for it so happened that we needed to leave the road and cut across a broad field in order to realize the most direct route to our goal. The high grass, which was of course soaked through, quickly achieved the same condition in our clothing, but it must be stated that I did not feel the chill through the armor of inebriation, which provided an additional layer of illusory protection from the deluge above.

As we stumbled (for there is no more apt descriptor of at least mine own gait) through the dark, I fixated upon the lighthouse as a migratory bird is fixed upon the southward arc of its flight. It came only distantly to my attention that Mr. Fairchild and Mr. Harris had fallen somewhat behind and were engaged in a low conversation of unintelligible words, punctuated occasionally with a short, staccato laugh from the toad-like Mr. Harris. I found myself walking farther ahead with Mr. Derrick, who in any case appeared to be the most benevolent of my companions. Possessed of a newfound confidence, I decided to frankly address the carpenter with some of my nascent anxieties. "What sort of trial is in store for me?"

"What sort of trial indeed?"

In the episodes to come, I would learn that such opaque responses were a habit of Mr. Derrick, who considered himself something of an amateur philosopher.

"And whose trial may it be, at that?"

"How do you mean?" I asked, not without hesitation, struck by the subdued mood that had befallen the previously ebullient man.

"We all must face a trial at some juncture. A judgment, or so the clergyman tells us, though for my part I wonder whether he is any more qualified than you are to tell me the nature of such a judgment."

"It's the captain's judgment which worries me," I said, looking down.

The carpenter barked laugher. "And right you are to worry! And yet even the captain's judgment may prove transient in the end. Japes notwithstanding,"—this presumably a reference to the song he had performed in the Green Pelican—"I fear the captain's eyes are clouded of late. He is a steadfast man, none moreso, and I think that the crew would follow him whithersoever he sails—and yet, it is not the captain who will call us to account in the end, is it?"

I felt a chill penetrate the fog of my intoxication, but I said nothing. Eventually, Mr. Derrick seemed to recover himself somewhat.

"A cheery conversation for a cheery evening, eh, Gordon?" His hand briefly touched my shoulder, correcting my course as I veered drunkenly from our route. "Your own concerns tonight are of a more immediate and, mmm, *corporeal* nature." He stressed the word, as though proud of knowing its definition and employing it correctly. But he was right: we had arrived.

The Sankaty Head lighthouse towered above us at a height of over seventy feet. Though the completeness of my memories of the latter portions of this evening is inversely proportional with the escalating level of my inebriation, I recall stopping in order to crane my neck at the structure far above. As its light flashed out, a wave of dizziness washed over me; though I had certainly seen the lighthouse on many previous occasions, never before had I comprehended its grandeur, nor how astutely it was designed to lead a desperate mariner to shore. Mr. Derrick laughed at the expression upon my face, which surely was one of wide-eyed wonder and which would have spoken to my utter naivety—but he encouraged me forward with a gentle push.

A small double wood-frame building abutted the lighthouse, but in drunkenness and excitement it did not occur to me so see whether anyone were inside. At any rate, the crew was wholly unconcerned with any such possibility, and they ushered me past the dwelling and to the door set into the base of the tower itself. Mr. Fairchild produced a key from his overcoat with a flourish before putting it to the lock and opening the door. A narrow stair of iron spiraled into darkness before me. Mr. Fairchild made a grand gesture.

"We're right behind you, my boy."

Indeed, the other men were pressed so closely behind me as to effectively force me to climb the stairs. This I would have done regardless, for I was intent to impress upon the crew my conviction and ability. So they thought to intimidate me by installing me in a high place? I thought, rather smugly, that in my present state I was afraid of little enough, and such a trial after all would scarcely be anything I could not endure.

And yet upon reaching the apex of the climb and approaching the edge of the tower, for one moment my conviction deserted me. I swayed upon the rail; nearly six dozen feet of empty space yawned up at me. I gasped aloud as a heavy hand gripped my shoulder; it was none other than Mr. Fairchild. As he bared his teeth at me in the sporadic flashing of the lighthouse, for the first time I believed that his smile expressed genuine amusement—albeit at my expense.

That weight on my shoulder seemed to intensify as Mr. Fairchild's hand squeezed upon my collarbone. Struggling to maintain the security of my footing, I looked over my shoulder at him, certain that he must not fail to appreciate the plea in my eyes, were there anything of human spirit left in him. Had I misjudged this situation, after all? What sort of scoundrels had I fallen in with?

"What do you say now, Gordon?" said Mr. Fairchild through a mouthful of teeth—too many teeth. In my delirium, I fancied that row upon row of pointed incisors filled his widening maw, until it began to resemble that of a shark. "Do you have a head for the heights, or not?"

As I reeled upon the rail, I surprised myself once more that evening by flashing my own smile in answer to that of my accoster. This memory returns to me with the utmost clarity: the voice that had brought me this far, that had encouraged me against all odds to find a way aboard the *Melville*, to seek some unknown destination in a desperate bid to cure the restlessness of my soul—that voice emerged from the confines of my own head and passed richly, confidently, exuberantly through my lips.

"Judge for yourself, you great elasmobranch," I declared, aware but not especially concerned with the fact that the comparatively uneducated Mr. Fairchild was not likely to appreciate this allusion to the shark family. But he responded to my unexpected assurance; for a moment, his grin faltered, his petulant lips closing over gnashing fish teeth. Delighted, I shifted my balance to one leg and lifted my other out and over the rail, over the great expanse of night and open air beneath us, and spun three times in a circle. My balance and poise were flawless as I executed this daring pirouette, and the voice in my head laughed merrily at Mr. Fairchild's obvious surprise.

This accomplished, I came to a halt, my vision spinning around me (a condition on which alcohol, contrary to what may be supposed, was not wholly to blame) and arched an eyebrow at Mr. Fairchild. What I saw on his countenance was not what I had anticipated. Rather than surprise or approval (I was yet newly acquainted with Mr. Fairchild, it must be remembered, and had not yet learned to expect only disapproval and discontent from him), his expression indicated only a grim sort of satisfaction, as though he had expected to find me wanting and had been confirmed in his expectation. But I continued to smile, for I knew that his silence meant he could raise no objection—I had demonstrated my resilience in the face of his hastily conceived trial. The damnable voice in my head had seen me through; it had brought me here.

But it could bring me no further this night. As I attempted to perform a sweeping bow to cap my heroic performance, I experienced a sudden lurch. The lighthouse floor rose to meet me, I felt the burn of bile in my throat, and blackness took me.

IN WHICH WE SET SAIL

"There is no folly of the beasts of the earth which is not infinitely outdone by the madness of men."
-Herman Melville, *Moby-Dick or, The Whale*

I awoke to a strange sound and the familiar aggravation of a tremendously sharp pain behind my eyes—any drunkard will recognize its particular pang. I would later come to learn that the sound was the creaking of the catheads and the raising of the anchor as the crew prepared the ship for embarkation; judging by their industry, they had recovered from the night's celebration altogether better than I had. But at this precise moment I was more occupied with the immediate issue of my discomfort. Slowly coming to my senses, I perceived that I lay in a hammock in a darkened space. I have since been told that a hammock is preferable to a bunk at sea, for it sways with the movement of the ship upon the ocean, whereas on a bunk one's body is inclined to slide around with the rise and fall of the waves. I doubt I would have appreciated the information just then, however, owing once again to the considerable state of physical distress in which I found myself.

But as the noise of the catheads had indeed awoken me, disrupting the relative silence of the room in which I found myself, I regretfully lowered my feet to the floor and attempted to stretch. This movement revealed to me that my quarters were decidedly close. My body was quite sore, and together with my headache such soreness might well have caused me to return to the hammock, but I knew that any attempt to obtain further rest would be futile. You see, I am not entirely devoid of curiosity (even if my imagination pales in comparison to those of the authors I hoped to meet), and even then I had begun to understand that I was in the forecastle of a sailing ship. Could it be, then, that I found myself aboard the *Melville* at last? As though perceived through the haze of a dream, memories of the previous night filtered through my addled head. I had certainly met and entertained the crew. But had they really agreed to take me aboard? It occurred to me that there was nothing for it but to find out.

I climbed the few short steps and opened the door topside. I was gratified to recognize the rewarding sight of Nantucket harbor pulling away astern. But then a sudden tapping on my shoulder diverted my attention from this receding shoreline, and I turned to face the interruption. I was greeted with a fresh-faced, dark-haired youth of some thirteen years. He was small in stature, yet he stood with the sort of easy, enviable grace that so often accompanies those individuals who feel secure in their own standing amongst their peers.

"You've awoken," he said.

A radiant smile broke open across his face. The very warmth in his expression seemed to chase some of the fog from my head. His smile was the utter antithesis of Mr. Fairchild's grimace back in the Green Pelican; it seemed inconceivable that both expressions could fall under the same appellation.

"Is this the *Melville*?" I was ashamed to ask, but I counted myself lucky that my complete naiveté was exposed only to whom I correctly assumed must be the cabin boy.

"She is," he said. "My name is William.[12] Let me be the first to welcome you aboard."

"Gordon," I said.

We shook hands.

I patted the pockets of my trousers and was pleased to discover my pen and journal. It seemed as though I would be able

[12] This is the earliest identification for William that the memoir provides. His age coincides with that of William Hope Hodgson, who would have been thirteen years old in 1890 – the age at which he first ran away to sea. Furthermore, the author's description fits Hodgson to a tee; he has been described historically as a feminine sailor who often attracted the bullying of his shipmates. Nevertheless, Hodgson developed an interest in fitness and bodybuilding, and was more than capable of fending for himself. The events described herein certainly would have inspired him to pursue the art of self-defense and physical prowess as necessities for surviving life at sea.

to record the journey of the ship for the *Inquirer and Mirror*, after all.[13] Despite the aftereffects of the previous night's indulgence still clouding my every thought process, I determined to waste no time in taking steps to achieve my goal.

"Are Mr. Verne and Mr. Clark Russell aboard?" I asked.

William's eyes widened slightly, and then narrowed in a look of suspicion, which seemed somehow absurd upon his honest face.

"You know of them?" he asked. "Most of these other brutes would fail to recognize their names, let alone the men who belong to them." He waved a hand to indicate other members of the crew, who were presently bustling about the deck.

"Know them?" I protested. "I should think every literate American should!"

"And Englishman," William said, patting his chest to indicate his own origins. "And yet if literacy is the barometer by which we judge the capacity of one man to recognize the artist in another, then I confess that our crew comes up wanting." As he said this, the beginnings of that sunny smile began to play about his lips once more.

"Well, man, are they aboard or aren't they?" I was charmed, but I was determined to have my answer directly.

"They reside in a private cabin; they have not yet shown themselves on deck. I imagine they will make themselves seen at some point or another, though I for one doubt if I shall have the pluck to introduce myself to them."

"I have little choice," I said. "I am here to write a newspaper story of their journey."

William nodded, seeming impressed with this duty. As I would eventually come to learn, he was rather literary-minded, and he regarded the act of writing with a sort of respect, which sometimes bordered upon reverence.

"And has the captain given you no other duties?" he asked.

"The captain is not aware of my presence aboard this ship," I said, forced at last to admit this rather uncomfortable truth.

When he heard my confession, all traces of humor washed

---

[13] The journal mentioned here does not appear to be the same volume in which this memoir was written. Gordon's story is told here as a retrospective; it seems likely that any real-time notes were ultimately abandoned.

from William's face.

"Then I advise you to stay hidden from sight," he warned. "Captain Carrig is a tyrant of the first order. He will toss you overboard and expect you to swim home, should he discover a stowaway whilst still in sight of shore."

"But many of the crew members themselves are known to me-" I began. I did not finish, for William caught my arm with a strength belied by his youth and small frame. He steered me back toward the forecastle and hauled me bodily down the steps.

And so I found myself returned to the quiet of the sailors' quarters. Nor did William linger to allay my lonely vigil, for he stated that he would shortly be missed on deck. He scurried through the hatch with a nimbleness of body which I am not sure I ever possessed, even at his young age. I reflected on this fact for some time, as my unabated headache and general discomfort had combined to suggest to me the idea that perhaps I was not physically suited for a voyage in these conditions. My own previous experience at sea had been as a passenger, and my berth had enjoyed certain advantages over the rather Spartan nature of my current accommodations.

I was soon to be distracted from my melancholy, however, for it was not long before a burly figure descended into the forecastle and took notice of me. It was none other than the carpenter, Mr. Derrick.

"Why, if it isn't the ship's musician?" he teased—though, as before, I sensed no particular malice in his words.

"He is bereft of his instruments and is a musician no longer," I rejoined.

"More's the pity. I had hoped that you might play us out to sea and perhaps put some spring into the crew's steps—none needs it more than that louse, Mr. Fairchild." He heaved a theatrical sigh and sat down on a nearby chest, fishing a pipe from a jacket pocket and packing it thoughtfully. "I suppose we'll have to put you to some other use."

"I'm not afraid to work with my hands. But the cabin boy fears I'll be discovered and sent ashore."

"William?" Mr. Derrick struck a match, and the bowl of his pipe bloomed with a warm red glow. "A good lad and a good worker himself, providing you can pry him from his books."

"That may be an affliction I share with him," I said with a smile, though in the gloom of the forecastle and the haze of my headache, I am afraid it may have looked more akin to a leer—for Mr. Derrick started slightly before speaking.

"Well, as you've managed to set sail without so much as a purse to your name, you should have few enough distractions."

"I did not intend to come aboard without my belongings, you understand. But it seems I must have rather taken leave of my senses. Perhaps it has something to do with my recent acquaintances? I seem to remember many a cup pressed into my hands."

Mr. Derrick laughed. "I don't recall you protesting overmuch, at that." In the dimness, the visibility of his countenance waxed and waned with the intermittent luminosity of his pipe. Tendrils of smoke curled past his beard and obscured his face, though I perceived that it had grown suddenly pensive. Such was the habit of Mr. Derrick—at the slightest provocation or the merest jest, he would lapse into a mood of meditation and utter the most cryptic remarks. This was one such occasion: "And yet, had it not been for the drink, or the encouragement of men who ought to have known better, would you still find yourself here?"

"Please suffer no guilt on my account, sir," I said, mistaking the nature of his musings. "For I had every intention of gaining passage; indeed, I would have done so by any means necessary." But I need not have worried; it was as though I had not even spoken.

"What man could lay claim to his own actions?" the philosopher continued. "Is not every man acted upon by some outside influence? Be he intoxicated with drink or with passion—or merely with the strictures of a family or a career which was chosen for him—whose motivations are truly his own? Is there any among us who can say clearly how he chose a course of action, and why? What I mean to say is: can any man truly act for himself in this life?"

Somewhat taken aback by this unexpected flood of rhetoric, I nonetheless responded without premeditation, guided by instincts formed from years of debate practice at university. "I think every man acts for himself," I said. "Should we excuse the criminal his crime because of the influence of his peers?"

Mr. Derrick's eyes lit up, his eyebrows raised. "Aha! We are to the point already, I see—to cast blame on those other than the perpetrator of a crime is the commonest tool of those who seek to escape the proverbial noose—except perhaps for those who allege to be of unsound mind. But might it not be that there is some truth in the matter? I do not wish to absolve the blackest scoundrel of his guilt, of course, but it may be that there is something useful in casting a wider net when fishing for the guilty party. Wouldn't you say?"

The little forecastle was now fairly filling with the sweet-smelling smoke issuing from Mr. Derrick's pipe. I stifled a cough, unused to the closeness of the atmosphere. Mr. Derrick's face had begun to seem to change, its features shifting and realigning themselves until the man looked like another individual altogether. I blinked, dispelling the illusion, and saw that Mr. Derrick seemed to have also come back to himself—for he was staring at me intently.

"I say, Gordon—you look altogether unwell."

I waved a hand, as though I could push away his concern and his smoke together. "Merely the aftereffects of our recently concluded revelry."

Mr. Derrick's brows drew closer together. "I'm not so sure. As it happens, there are two of us among the crew with precious little to do at the outset of this journey. As the carpenter, I'm afforded some measure of leisure until my skills are needed in the repair of some object or other. The second is the doctor[14], whose time is his own, provided that he is not needed to administer to the crew. I shall fetch him presently."

He stood to pursue that errand, and I half-rose to restrain him, provoked by a sudden anxiety that my weakness should become known to the crew and that I should suffer in their estimation as a result. But the great brute of a man used one hand to absentmindedly force me to return to my seat. This task was easily accomplished, as I could scarcely hope to contest him in matters of physical strength. He gave a small chuckle and climbed from the forecastle.

---

[14] On many ships, the "doctor" is just a nickname for the cook. Here, though, the carpenter refers to an actual physician.

I sat for some time on the sea-chest, swaying unconsciously with the motion of the ship and listening to muffled song and shout from on deck. The smoke in the enclosed space must have gradually diminished, but it was supplanted in equal measure with a sort of psychological smoke that seemed to expand to fill my own head. At length, I became aware of a peculiar rapping noise echoing throughout the room. I started, fixing my gaze upon a chest some ten paces from me, and the room seemed to swim around me. As the sound persisted, I slowly became convinced that the knocking was issuing from this chest. It was a small thing of simple and plain design; certainly not a receptacle in which even the most eccentric sailor might store a living thing. But the noise increased in intensity, and I found my hands clenching of their own accord as I nervously began to expect that there could be no great delay before whatever was trapped inside would burst through the wood in its bid for freedom. I leaned forward, despite my growing apprehension, when I caught sight of my own foot below me tapping faster and faster against the floor.

I sat up, chagrined at my foolishness. The sound had been nothing but the convulsions of my own impatience. I passed a hand over my brow in an effort to clear it of confusion. I was forced to admit, after all, that perhaps Mr. Derrick had been right: I was not simply suffering the natural result of my overindulgence from the night prior. Could it be that I was afflicted with something altogether more serious? Visions of hospitals and—dare I admit it?—morgues suddenly danced before my eyes. How would it go when I perished in this dismal forecastle, when none ashore could guess where I had gone? It occurred to me, in this sickness-induced panic, that not a soul aboard could even identify me positively. I had not given so much as a surname to any of my newly-acquired companions! If the uncaring Captain Carrig (as I had been given to believe was his disposition) were to find me deceased aboard his ship, would he not simply toss me to the waves? And would my grim corpse then be left for the unnamed creatures of the deep to dispense with in their own singular fashion? I shuddered with the thought, feeling the cold drops of perspiration begin to bead my forehead.

Mercifully, my fevered ruminations were presently interrupted by the return of the carpenter, now with the doctor in tow. The latter proved to be a stout man, who appeared to roll rather than walk down the few short, steep steps into the gloomy interior. He had the appearance of a once-handsome man whose countenance has been pushed into unlikely contortions by the accumulation of excess weight. A monocle perched over one eye was held tightly in place by the swollen flesh of his face. I do not intend to be unkind in my recollection of the man, but only to present an accurate impression of what I observed upon the occasion. I trust that the reader will keep in mind that I was experiencing certain sensory abnormalities at the time, and in no way was I uncharitably disposed toward the good doctor, especially as he had arrived to see what could be done about my condition. Presently he took my hand and introduced himself. I felt my own hand consumed by his fleshy appendage as he did so, and I suppressed a wince, though his touch was, after all, quite gentle.

"Dr. -----,"[15] he said brusquely, dropping my hand after detecting that my handshake was something less than enthusiastic. "Let's examine this *kopf.*" Immediately, his hands took hold of my head, and I felt his probing fingers part my hair to reach the scalp beneath. I experienced a startling spasm of pain which caused me to inhale sharply, and the doctor chuckled to himself, muttering in his own language as his fingers traced the dimensions of what felt like a distended protuberance somewhere just beyond the crown of my skull.

"Have you perhaps experienced a recent fall?" he demanded in what I perceived as an unreasonably curt tone of voice. "Or have you struck your head in this close space?"

"I may have done so," I offered in response, hesitant to fully describe the circumstances of the previous evening and the unceremonious conclusion of my trial in the lighthouse.

"*Ach,* the patient, he is always reluctant to admit his folly,"

---

[15] The doctor's name is omitted from this page in the original manuscript, and he is referred to thereafter simply as "the doctor." I posit several hypotheses for this decision. First, as the doctor was a private gentleman, Gordon may have wished to respect his privacy and identity when submitting the manuscript to the *Inquirer and Mirror*. Further, in light of the man's fate, the absence of his name may have been designed to spare the grief of any surviving relatives. Finally, an element of discretion may have been preferred concerning the nature of the doctor's relationship with the ship's captain.

the doctor said, casting a suspicious eye in the direction of the observing Mr. Derrick. "But it may be that I am not so easily fooled." He lit a match and passed it before my eyes, bidding me to follow its flame. Next he touched my wrists and pressed upon my fingernails. He grunted in satisfaction before leaning away from me, concluding his brief examination.

"It is, I think, only a small concussion," he diagnosed. "Have you experienced any perceptual irregularities or hallucinations?"

"None," I lied.[16]

"Then the matter is settled," he pronounced, clapping his hands together with finality. "I will prepare an infusion for your headache, and you will remain at rest for some days, though I do not wish that you will sleep overmuch." He looked at Mr. Derrick again and then back at me. "I have gathered that your presence here is to remain, ah, inconspicuous?"

The carpenter and I both nodded, though for my part, I did so reluctantly. I was beginning to feel that it were best to make a clean breast of my stowing away and to face the captain as soon as I had made a sufficient recovery. I reflected that any anxiety I felt on the matter may even have been contributing to my indisposition.

"*Sehr gut,* you shall remain in these quarters." The doctor repacked his small bag of medicinal supplies; though he had used nothing but a match from its contents, he had managed to strew a surprising amount of detritus atop the surface of an overturned barrel next to him. Having collected his belongings, he did not linger to exchange pleasantries or even a farewell, but simply nodded to Mr. Derrick and marched from the forecastle.

"Is he a good doctor?" I asked the carpenter, who had stayed behind.

---

[16] Given that Gordon had clearly already experienced hallucinations and was not inclined to admit them, one may well wonder whether his later experiences were not hallucinations resulting from a more severe concussion or injury than was diagnosed. I am disinclined to accept this explanation, for reasons which I attempt to make clear throughout these notes. I would preempt the argument which will surely be suggested by a skeptical readership—namely, that *none* of Gordon's subsequent observations are to be trusted. However, one may find that such a reading may be of some limited interest as an intellectual exercise.

He did not reply immediately. His pipe, now cold, was clamped between his teeth, his bearded jaw clenched. When his reply came, I must admit that I did not find it particularly reassuring.

"May we never have to find out." The giant of a man stood and pocketed his pipe, his hair brushing the forecastle's ceiling. "I will have William bring the doctor's brew," he said, "if it can be arranged without arousing any suspicion. I recommend sleeping while you have the opportunity, as peace and quiet can be hard to come by once we're under full canvas."

Though Mr. Derrick's advice was contrary to that of the doctor, I felt that it came from perhaps a more genuine place of concern. And so once again I had the dubious pleasure of solitude. Some may yearn for such aloneness, but to find it unsought is without doubt one of life's many small tragedies. Here I was, in an alien environment and in a state of poor health, my very presence a secret to the ship's captain. The company of another man, however coarse, would have been of some comfort to me. Instead I was forced to languish with only my own doubts and insecurities for company. In the absence of conversation, I turned my mind to a question which weighed on me: how would I reveal myself to Captain Carrig? Surely I should wait until I had recovered my vigor; presenting myself not only as a stowaway, but also an infirm one, would hardly endear me to the man. But if I must wait, what was there to be done in the meantime?

Rescue came from a most unlikely source. Bereft of actual human conversation, I found that the voice in my head, at whose feet I laid the blame for my present circumstances, had something to say. I trust that the reader will not find my representation of this exchange to be excessively facile. I have striven to represent my condition, with all its attendant absurdities, as accurately as my recollection allows.

"Are you content here?" the voice said.

"Certainly not," I snapped, irritated.

"Is this not what you wanted?"

"Rather say what *you* wanted, I think. I desired merely a measure of adventure. Now I am no more than a concussed drunk, and a stowaway to boot."

"Your actions are your own."

"Mr. Derrick might say otherwise," I said with a small snort, recalling that philosopher's musings on the subject.

"Mr. Derrick did not bring you here."

"Indeed not; the blame for that falls squarely upon your shoulders."

"My shoulders are your own. Why do you insist on burdening them with this scheme?" Now I thought I had begun to detect an accusatory tone in the voice, which was something I found myself unwilling to tolerate. I would not abide being scolded from within my own head.

"Now listen here," I admonished. "I won't have that kind of talk. We both know that it was your damned insistence on *change* that brought us here. You are never satisfied; well, now look where it's led us."

"Change! Now you've hit upon it."

"Change?"

"Precisely."

"Out with it, man. What do you mean to say?"

"You are not happy in your current situation. *Change it.*"

With that, my brief conversation with myself was concluded. I attempted to elicit further clarification upon the question of what exactly was in my power to change about being stuck belowdecks in a ship that was already under sail, but the voice was unwilling to participate in further debate. My entreaties were met only with a maddening silence; I reflected that I might well be the first man living to be abandoned not only by his fellows, but also by himself. Needless to say, the thought did not provide any great measure of comfort.

But I considered the question of change—and at length, I began to devise a plan. I had been advised by the crew to avoid the captain, which could only be accomplished by remaining in the forecastle, and I had been advised by the doctor to avoid sleep, which could hardly be avoided in the forecastle at the onset of evening, when the natural rhythms of my body would demand rest. The only way to satisfy both requirements would be to occupy myself at night by properly exploring the *Melville*. I could thereby avoid sleep whilst remaining concealed from the captain, who would presumably be confined to his own cabin. If he happened to be awake and roaming the deck at night, I thought that perhaps I could trust to the darkness to conceal me. And if such a plan also served to incidentally satisfy my own curiosity regarding the layout of the magnificent ship, as well as her situation upon the ocean, well, what of it?

I sat back and felt a slow smile begin to spread across my face.

A CONVERSATION BY STARLIGHT

"The catalogue of true thoughts is but small…the truest poets are but mouth-pieces; and some men are duplicates of each other."
-Herman Melville, *Mardi, and a Voyage Thither*

At last the hour had arrived. Throughout the day, members of the crew had filtered in and out of the forecastle. In this manner, I gradually became acquainted with most of those on board. Of course, I had already met with William, the cabin boy; Mr. Derrick, the carpenter; Mr. Harris, the boatswain; and Mr. Fairchild, who turned out to be the quartermaster—and the less said about this unlikable fellow, the better. The doctor was also part of the crew, though he held himself somewhat apart from the rest, and he would certainly make his own particular contributions to the events which follow. But there were other sailors whom I had occasion to meet during my prolonged sojourn belowdecks: Mr. Taggart, the mate; Mr. Lawrence, the helmsman; and Old Cedar; the cook.

This lattermost made a severe impression upon me. To begin with, Old Cedar was a woman of advanced age. To have a woman serving as a member of a ship's crew was remarkable by itself; but then, it was hard to imagine a setting in which she would have belonged. You see, one of Old Cedar's eyes was clouded with rheum and was presumed blind by her shipmates; the woman herself never responded to any inquiries on the subject. But her other eye compensated for its counterpart's deficiency with a cold blaze of startling blue; indeed, the sharpness of that eye seemed to peer not at me but straight through me, perhaps straight through the timbers of the ship herself—almost as though it would cleave in twain the waters of the ocean and pierce the very veil of the world which lay beyond. She preferred to let this eye perform the functions of communication, where possible—and when she did deign to speak, her remarks rivaled even Mr. Derrick's most esoteric musings for their puzzling obliqueness. I confess that I was somewhat in awe of her, and despite her relatively low rank among the other sailors, it seemed that they, too, were content to give her a wide berth.

How the crew had been persuaded to keep quiet about my sudden appearance on the *Melville* was something of a mystery to me. Granted, much of the crew had been present at the Green Pelican and were in fact complicit in my recruitment. But for those sailors who had been unknown to me, I only surmised that they must have felt no great loyalty to the allegedly tyrannical Captain Carrig and felt no compunction to report a stowaway—or perhaps they forbore at the influence of Mr. Derrick, who seemed amused by having me aboard and had, after all, managed to convince the doctor to conceal me. Regardless of the reason for their discretion, I was grateful for the opportunity to remain hidden while it was still possible to do so.

But my thoughts were rather more occupied with the ship herself than with her crew this night; once the last man had dropped off to slumber, I crept from the forecastle with equal parts haste and caution. Being unfamiliar with the routine of a ship at sea, I could not predict how many men might yet be patrolling the decks in the course of their duties. While I had previously crossed the Atlantic, it must be remembered that I had done so as a passenger, and my nights were spent in circumstances altogether more comfortable; my privileged status had left me happily blind to the rhythms of the working men aboard. I wished to remain undetected in case the captain should be on deck, but fortune favored me in that watches aboard the *Melville* were changed every four hours, and I had crept from the forecastle shortly after two bells.[17]

Before I had even gained the top of the stairs, I detected movement behind me. I turned to discover a small form slipping between the bunks in the darkness. The diminutive size and furtive

[17] Depending on the timing scheme implemented on the ship, this would've been about 1:00 AM, giving Gordon at least an hour to explore before the watch changed.

movement of the figure should have proved at once that it could be none other than my recent acquaintance, William—but for a fleeting moment, the dim impression of his silhouette creeping in the blackness reminded me forcibly of my earlier hallucinations while left alone in this very forecastle; my mind conjured a fancy of some mad, unknowable form escaping from a seaman's chest and pursuing a lurching and malevolent course towards me with unnatural speed!

"Where are you going?" spoke William in a low whisper, dispelling the unsettling illusion with jarring rapidity.

I pointed above, blinking in mute surprise. I was loath to wake any of the sailors, for one thing, but I also did not trust that I would be able to communicate anything intelligible; I was grateful for the darkness as my cheeks flooded with embarrassment at my failure to recognize the closest person to a friend and peer I had on board. I gestured for him to follow me, that we might speak more safely on deck. With the cold night air on my face, words came more easily to me. "I mean to explore the ship."

"To what purpose?" William's tone was not accusatory, but simply curious.

I extracted my journal from a pocket and brandished it in the semidarkness. "If I am to write about the ship, I must know something of her. And as I am still a stowaway…it may be best for me to learn in secrecy."

I was gratified to see that William's peculiarly cheerful smile was not limited to the hours of daylight, and in fact his expression even did something to alleviate the darkness itself, which was otherwise penetrated only insufficiently by a lamp placed near the wheel—though even this minor source of light shed a startling degree of illumination across the deck. Whilst making these observations, it occurred to me that I was fortunate to have gained the company of a knowledgeable member of the crew. Perhaps he would be able to provide some firsthand information; I opened the as-yet blank journal and poised my pen above its pages. "Is it quite usual for the entire crew to sleep at once?"

"Not the entire crew," William replied, with a surreptitious gesture towards the lamp that I had observed at the wheel. "The helmsman has not abandoned his post. He could be relieved, of course, but Mr. Lawrence is very particular about his duties. He doesn't like to relinquish them if he can still keep his eyes open."

We crept closer to the helmsman. The spectral glow of the lamp lent his face a sinister air, which, having already met him in the forecastle, I understood to be an illusion. In reality, he was neither excessively friendly nor especially menacing; he seemed to go about his duties with an unflappable sort of equanimity, taking all things as they came to him in stride. His face was cleanly shaven, which at a distance made him appear younger than his middle years; but upon closer inspection, I could make out an array of deep scars across his countenance: perhaps the result of a troublesome complexion in his youth. He stared straight ahead from underneath a brow thatched with hair the color of sand, unmoving but for the constant minute adjustments of his hands upon the wheel.

Though I would like to think that we moved quietly about the deck, it is entirely possible that William and I could have made a considerable din without raising the attention of Mr. Lawrence. This is not to suggest that he would be derelict in his duty of watching the ship at night, but rather to (perhaps somewhat facetiously) reinforce the impression that I would desire to give of the stalwart man: namely, that he was possessed of an imperturbable nature. Indeed, my reader shall soon see that in the troubles to come, he kept his head altogether better than the rest of the crew—however little it abetted him in the end.

"Where is the captain?" I asked, once we had moved away from Mr. Lawrence's earshot. "Does he too sleep at night?"

William took a shallow breath before answering. "The captain keeps his own hours." Now there was some reluctance in his voice. "On the passage from England, he could be found awake and alert at any time of day, in any part of the ship. He was—and is—agitated and impatient. But since we have collected our authors[18], a change has come over him. It's almost as though he were waiting for some momentous...*thing* to begin, and he could

[18] Apparently Verne and Russell also boarded at and embarked from Nantucket; specific historical records of their known whereabouts are difficult to reconcile in the face of the events depicted herein. It stands to reason that concrete evidence of what transpired in 1890 would have been suppressed by the parties involved.

not rest while it was yet undecided; now that we are properly underway, he seems relieved." William held up a hand to preclude any interruption from me, though his eyes had grown far away. "I do not mean to say that he is less troubled, but rather, he seems ready to confront those troubles now."

Oh, my friend! How perceptive you were, had you only credited your powers of observation and intuition. Would that I had paid heed to your words! Instead I sought to find in them some confirmation of my own desires: to witness something great aboard that fated ship.

"But I have digressed," William continued presently, his eyes returning to mine. "The helmsman is, in all likelihood, the only wakeful soul aboard, save ourselves. We lessened the sails before the fall of darkness: the high sails, the forestaff, the royal, the topsail...in this manner we are less vulnerable to the wind, and the crew may enjoy some rest. This is not possible aboard a particularly troubled sea, of course, but at the outset of a journey it has been the captain's policy to allow us respite while we can yet afford it."

Alas, any furtherance of my nautical education was destined to wait, however; for at that very moment, the door to the passenger's cabin opened with a creak that rent the silence of the night air like the truncated sawing of a summer cicada. And what august personage should stride forth from the cabin but one of the very authors upon whom I had designs to report? The memory of my first sight of the man is sublimely clear to this day; perhaps even clearer than my recollections of the dreadful scenes in the days to follow, for it is untainted with the lingering dregs of loss and regret.

Mr. Clark Russell was a slight man who nonetheless gave the impression of a robust presence; though his years as a midshipman had left him permanently infirm, I perceived at once that there remained a strength of constitution about him that would manifest itself in physical terms if called upon to do so. His hairline was quite high, drawing my attention to that noble cranium from which issued the stories that had led me to sea; but his prominent mustache and the intent, amused look in his eyes lent a balance to his face that would have been lacking in a lesser man. As he turned to stare at the night-black sea, I observed that his left hand clutched a small lantern tightly, as though he were in the grip of some consternation. His right hand hung loose and open at his side; it was there that his arthritis struck him most acutely—indeed, I learned that at times he even had some difficulty in holding a pen with this hand, and he was forced to resort to dictation in order to complete his last novels. In the fullness of time, I would have occasion to observe that this disability also forced him to shoot a pistol with his left hand—though I never suspected that such an action would prove to be necessary upon a voyage ostensibly designed to further the literary pursuits of its passengers.

Hidden from his sight with William at my side, I was enraptured with the mere sight of this legendary "seafarer."[19] The Englishman hefted his lantern to see more clearly, passing by Mr. Lawrence and nodding once at him. The helmsman, true to his nature, returned the nod without so much as turning his head to look at the newcomer. It seemed that Mr. Clark Russell did not perceive this as a slight but only as his due reception; he did not pause in his walk to the rail. It occurred to me that I was watching Mr. Clark Russell move across the *Melville* as an actor moves across a stage; and indeed at that point in time I knew the man no more than the audience knows the actors in a drama.

But behold! Mr. Verne was himself a study in the dramatic—and he emerged from the passenger's cabin mere minutes after the appearance of Mr. Clark Russell. The Frenchman was possessed of a high and commanding hairline which lent a sense of weight to his eyebrows—which were at the moment furrowed in a forbidding look of intense concentration. This was his usual expression, although his eyes were no stranger to an occasional twinkle that belied his essential good nature. His whiskers were no smaller than those of the captain, if decidedly more silver with age, though this latter feature only further distinguished him with the dignity of his

[19] William Clark Russell, while generally well-reviewed, had certainly not possessed a "legendary" reputation in 1890. It seems that Gordon's admiration for the author, which undoubtedly approaches hero worship, may have inflated Russell's status in his mind. Since Russell also began writing as a journalist, it is tempting to speculate whether Gordon may have imagined parallels between the author and his own rising star. In fact, Gordon's use of quotes around the term "seafarer" may refer to Russell's pseudonym when writing for *The Daily Telegraph.*

years. This dignity would have been compromised in any other man by the pronounced limp which Mr. Verne exhibited (owing to a pistol shot received from his disgruntled nephew four years prior). But in this stately man, it suggested instead a certain breed of dogged tenacity. As he dragged his leg slightly behind him when especially animated by stress or excitement, he gave the impression of a fellow who had been stricken but not beaten by the world—in short, a survivor. And he would soon have a great need for this quality, as even now we rapidly approached an unprecedented series of calamities which would see the *Melville* reduced to splinters and the lives of her crew snuffed out like so many candle flames.

But I cannot allow this narrative to proceed out of turn. At the moment, normalcy reigned on the deck—as close to such a state as was possible when two great minds were meeting at the rail. For Mr. Verne had positioned himself next to Mr. Clark Russell, arriving at his side with only the mildest trouble from his aggrieved leg. The two men stood in companionable silence for a time, each having undertaken the voyage despite the significant disabilities they were experiencing as a result of their injuries. I thought that this comparison should serve me very well when the time arrived to compose my article, and for one romantic moment I fancied that perhaps they too reflected upon the similarity of their conditions. Alas, I should have known that men such as these would arrive directly at more practical considerations.

"The human mind delights in grand conceptions of supernatural beings," said Mr. Verne without preamble. "And the sea is precisely their best vehicle. I propose to explore those superstitions which lie at the heart of every mortal man upon the water."

Mr. Clark Russell shook his head. "I should rather exhume the darkness inherent in those same mortal hearts. I too have written of the supernatural, and I do not believe that it is necessary for the telling of our tale. Might we not rely upon the conflict of men in the invocation of suspense?"

I remained crouched in the shadows, scribbling at my notebook in a decidedly feverish state. I had never learned proper

Pitman's shorthand[20] at university; I had always been able to rely upon my own dexterity and ability to write more quickly than my peers. I sensed rather than heard a faint exhalation of breath from my young companion as he stifled laughter upon observing me at my work, but I heeded him not. I could scarcely credit that I was so lucky as to be observing the authors at the creative process on my very first night aboard. This was history playing out before my eyes. No—more importantly, it was *art*!

"I see no reason why we should not do both," was Mr. Verne's reply. His tone had now taken a decidedly frostier note, and my pen paused in its erratic track across the page of my journal.

"I should not be surprised at your insistence," said Mr. Clark Russell sharply. "Your characters are rarely complex enough to generate meaningful conflict."[21]

"I beg your pardon?" Mr. Verne said stiffly.

My pen was now quite stationary; I watched with wide eyes and my heart in my throat. Surely this enterprise was not so fragile as to fall apart before it had even begun?

"Forgive me," Mr. Clark Russell said after a long moment, his demeanor softening in the starlight. "I spoke with undue haste. Please remember that I have only read your works in English, which are at the mercy of the translator's pen and undoubtedly suffer in comparison to the original. But it is more than that. Something about this vessel sits badly with me, I confess."

I expected the Frenchman to react with further hostility, but I was surprised to hear agreement in his voice, along with a peculiar

---

[20] Sir Isaac Pitman developed a shorthand method in 1837. It is still taught today in conjunction with a method devised by John Robert Gregg in 1888.

[21] A criticism often leveled at Verne. Omitting the notable exception that is *The Survivors of the Chancellor* (1875), much of Verne's fiction features little in the way of conflict between protagonists. A typical example is the seminal *The Mysterious Island* (1874), in which five individuals find themselves stranded on an island for a period of years. In this timeframe, the characters not only avoid virtually all conflict with each other, but also manage to find and rehabilitate a criminal in the process. It is, however, worth noting that some of Verne's early work was rewritten at the behest of his editor and publisher, Pierre-Jules Hetzel, resulting in more "optimistic" versions of Verne's original stories.

note that I can only now, in light of all that transpired subsequently, describe as relief. "It is not the vessel herself. She is sound, if rather old-fashioned. It is her crew."

"Yes," said Mr. Clark Russell. "They are a hardened lot, and of a shade rather coarser than I would expect to find on a merchantman."

I exchanged a look with William in the near-darkness. I had now met most of the crew, and while they were hard men, I did not have a sufficient frame of reference to determine whether they were exceptionally so. But certainly neither Mr. Fairchild nor Mr. Harris had struck me with an especially favorable impression. I arched a questioning eyebrow at my new friend; surely he was better poised to confirm Mr. Verne's doubt. And after only a brief hesitation, William nodded.

"Certain among them have a military bearing," continued Mr. Verne.

"Say rather former military," corrected Mr. Clark Russell. "For it seems to me as though their discipline has lapsed, though they remain strong as a team of oxen."

"A stampede of wild bulls, more precisely."

Despite experiencing a degree of anxiety over the near-dispute between the two authors, I smiled to myself as I observed this exchange; it was my first exposure to their habit of continually attempting to surpass each other in their craft, even when it came to turning a neater phrase within the realms of verbal simile and metaphor. Some would have called it pettiness; some pride. I have found that the two are often indistinguishable, and they are to be found within men both great and small.

Their talk soon returned to literature. For some time, the men spun various premises and beginnings of tales betwixt themselves. I abstain from recording the minutiae of these conversations here, for many of the seeds sown that night eventually germinated into the published works of the authors and are both well-known and well-regarded in the present day. Their much-anticipated collaborative work, of course, was simply not to be—and I regret to say that the two authors never made a second attempt to write together after the conclusion of our voyage aboard the *Melville.* It occurs to me that, had they attempted to do so, the weight of the shared memories of the catastrophes we endured may simply have been too much to bear.

But we scarcely anticipated any such misfortune at this juncture, and the various tragic stories of hardships and survival proposed by the authors remained wholly, for the moment, within the realm of fiction. And what fiction it promised to be! Surely whatever tale was decided upon would be a thing to shake the foundations of the publishers' houses; doubtless it would be celebrated in London, Paris, and New York alike! And for my own humble part, what acclaim might be attributed to the savvy journalist who was intrepid enough to cover the very conception of the story? My blood fairly thrilled with the possibilities, and for a self-defeating moment my pen fell slack in my hand.

Staring intently at the two authors standing at the rail, I was absorbed in the act of hanging onto every word spoken from the mouths of these learned men, and so I chanced to be unaware of the figure creeping to my side until a hand was placed suddenly upon my shoulder. I started violently, jarred from my reverie, and nearly shouted aloud with alarm at so sudden an intrusion upon my thoughts. I stifled my outburst, however, so as not to alert the men to our presence on deck. Instead I turned as quietly as I was able and beheld the open countenance of the ship's carpenter, Mr. Derrick. His eyes were aglow in the far-reaching light of Mr. Clark Russell's lamp, and they danced with good humor—doubtless at my expense.

"What do you want?" I demanded with a great scowl, forcing more irritation into my voice than I truly felt, hoping that it might disguise my consternation from Mr. Derrick's eye. Alas, I fear he saw through my bravado with relative ease: his grin only widened at being so rudely greeted.

"Tell me, lad, what do you see in these men?"

I perceived that William was taken aback by the question; being quite as literary-minded as myself, he probably would have liked to mount a defense on behalf of the authors. Yet he remained silent, as was his wont in the presence of his more senior shipmates—which is to say, all of them.

"What do you mean?" I asked, taking up the mantle. I was reminded by Mr. Derrick's question that there were those among the crew who did not venerate these authors as William and I did. And yet I suppose that it is so in all walks of life; are there not heathens in the employ of the Church, though they might keep their lack of faith to themselves? Are there not fishermen who cannot abide the taste of flesh from the sea? To enter into a career is not necessarily to transform one's ideology or taste; it can be merely a way to fill one's coffers—and so it was with Mr. Derrick, at least at the start; he had shipped as a carpenter, with little choice (and less care) in which vessel would take him aboard.

"Why do you skulk in the shadows and listen to their conversations? What can they say that is worth hearing when you might otherwise be asleep in your bunk?" He gestured to the forecastle.

I was still considering the fact that Mr. Derrick could not immediately comprehend the influence these gentlemen had exerted upon the literary world, and so my attempts to enlighten him were perhaps less articulate than they might otherwise have been. I had already observed how Mr. Derrick prided himself on his rhetorical skills; I have little doubt that he noted the lack of eloquence in my own argument.

"They are…the finest storytellers of our day," I said haltingly. "I stand here in the hopes of witnessing the fruition of a *new* story, a collaboration born at sea. What could be more exciting?"

"There *are* no new stories," the enormous man said with good-natured contempt. "These men have nothing to say which has not been said by many better men before them."

I admit that his attitude shocked me to my core. No new stories! Better men! And this from a sailor who could, by his own admission[22], not even read!

"Absurd!" I fairly sputtered.

"He is not wrong," came a sudden slow baritone from behind us.

I spun around in haste; imagine my surprise to discover that Mr. Verne and Mr. Clark Russell had overheard our conversation and were now standing next to us! My face flushed with shame for

---

[22] This appears to be an allusion to an unrecorded conversation between Gordon and Mr. Derrick. It may be a useful reminder that this memoir, while sequentially complete, cannot possibly contain every snippet of dialogue which must have occurred between the members of the crew.

the second time that night; surely the writers had realized that I had been eavesdropping upon their conversation. I chided myself for allowing myself to be surprised in so unpleasant a manner not once, but three times in a single evening.

"There *are* no new stories," continued the speaker.

I saw to my relief that Mr. Verne did not look greatly perturbed. He wore an indulgent, almost paternal expression, and I was encouraged to voice my objections to what I perceived as a very disturbing line of thought. "There are new stories every year," I said. Then I thought of my own fledgling career at the *Inquirer and Mirror,* and I amended my statement: "There are new stories every *day!"*

Mr. Verne only shook his head, while beside him, Mr. Clark Russell broke into a wide and knowing smile.

"They are the same stories," the Frenchman declared. "Adventures had, loves won, lives lost. The human condition has not fundamentally changed in thousands of years. There is nothing truly original left to be said."

"Then why write?" I ventured.

Mr. Verne shrugged. "If a story is worth hearing, it's worth hearing more than once. These stories have all been told. What of it? That doesn't mean they aren't worth retelling. The same ideas resonate with us because they mean something to us. Giving an old idea a new lease on life is not such a bad thing."

Silence settled over the deck. Mr. Verne had neatly countered the arguments of both myself and Mr. Derrick, and I must admit that his convictions have stayed with me these many years. Indeed, though the voice of restlessness which had led me into my forthcoming predicament aboard the *Melville* has now fallen silent, the voice of Mr. Verne still speaks regularly in my ear as I record this narrative.

"In any case," interrupted Mr. Clark Russell, little knowing that I should pick up the pen several years hence and in the process put a lie to his words, "No stories are in the offing tonight. What say we retire?"

His sentiments were met with unanimous approval, as they so often were, and I realized suddenly that I was quite tired indeed. I would scarcely have been able to continue an intelligent conversation with these men, even if they had been willing to entertain my sophomoric ideations of literature any later into the evening. As it was, I passed into quiet oblivion in the forecastle that night feeling largely satisfied with the proceedings of the *Melville*'s journey thus far. I had already made the acquaintance of Mr. Verne and Mr. Clark Russell, and the foundations for my story were already being laid in my mind. While the prospect of my imminent meeting with the captain (for I could not postpone that engagement indefinitely) did cause me some vague unease, I certainly experienced no presentiment of the fate which would soon befall the crew in a rapid succession of unspeakable tragedies!

TELLS OF MY AUDIENCE WITH THE CAPTAIN AND MY SUBSEQUENT INTERACTIONS WITH THE CREW

"Why, that fellow has all your lives and eternities in his hand."
-Herman Melville, *Redburn: His First Voyage*

Some years later, I had sufficiently recovered from the horrors and adventures to which I was subjected and had begun to display a renewed interest, however incremental, in the goings-on of the world at large once again. It was during this time that I came across a passage in the literature of the day which reminded me forcibly of Captain Carrig. It bears quotation here for the impression it gives of the man: "he...had the weather-beaten appearance of one who has spent most of his time in the open air, and yet there was something in his steady eye and the quiet assurance of his bearing which indicated the gentleman."[23]

While this description will not by itself suffice to furnish an adequate portrait of the captain, I believe it speaks to those qualities of the man which particularly suited him to his chosen vocation. To this description I would add mention of his long-limbed figure, aggressive gait, and mass of fiery orange hair which called to mind comparisons to the African lion or perhaps an especially wild horse (indeed, I had been stricken by a similar notion when I first encountered the captain by the glow of his lantern on the docks of Nantucket, before I ever set foot on the *Melville*'s deck). And yet this wildness was belied by certain other, more thoughtful characteristics: the way he paused before

[23] *The Hound of the Baskervilles* (1902) by Sir Arthur Conan Doyle. Such an unusually specific reference provides a useful clue towards determining when the memoir was written; it also disallows any connection between the memoir and Charles Romyn Dake's suicide (see introductory footnote).

speaking, as though to collect his thoughts, even when speaking in anger; the slow, considered strokes of his pen when recording the ship's log; the fatherly hand he laid upon William's shoulder as he taught the boy to navigate by the stars. These qualities suggested a man of some culture, perhaps even of some education, and indeed I sometimes spied in his eyes an unexpected cast of what I can only describe as a sadness, or perhaps a species of regret, deep as any ocean upon which we sailed.

Such nuances of character did not present themselves immediately upon my official introduction to the captain, however. Instead, I saw him at his two most polar extremes: complete lethargy and utter wrath—and he moved between the two at a speed for which I was entirely unprepared. Of course, my reader will soon recognize that I was quite unprepared for *any* of the situations into which I had managed to implicate myself. While Mr. Derrick and William did their utmost to prepare me for this meeting, it would fall to me to win him over if I could. My actual presentation to the captain is therefore given here without further prevarication.

It was the very next morning when I found myself hauled to within an inch of the door to the captain's cabin. The oversized hand of the ship's carpenter guided my steps as he had once guided my drunken path to the Sankaty Head lighthouse; now, however, his grip was firm and a grimace was plastered upon his face. He rapped heavily upon the door with his knuckles, his every movement suggesting scarcely-contained furor: for my stalwart companion had his own part to play upon that morn.

The door opened slowly and noiselessly; for had not Mr. Derrick himself oiled its hinges? Indeed, though the *Melville* would be torn asunder within the space of a fortnight, not an ounce of blame could be placed upon the shoulders of that honest carpenter. Behind the open door, all was shadow. I discerned a figure bent in earnest concentration upon his work.

"Mr. Derrick," the hunched figure said with a nod. The voice that escaped from that den of blackness was languid and sibilant. I had the impression of a great beast wakened from its winter-long hibernation. I gathered the dim impression of an outstretched leg; the captain must have kicked open the door with his foot.

"Captain," said the carpenter.

And so my second sight of Captain Carrig was taken in scarcely less shadow than my first, for he appeared to be working in virtual darkness. Only a single guttering candle flame lit his work space; the surface of his desk was cluttered with navigational charts and handwritten scraps of paper. At the moment, he was engaged in the application of a compass across a map of the eastern seaboard. Even this limited glimpse allowed me to see that his fingers did not seem quite steady; moreover, his movements had a halfhearted quality to them, and he stared down at his maps with his hair hanging in his eyes.

"Who's this, then?" The captain finally looked up from his desk. His eyes were bloodshot and bleary, his face blanketed with orange stubble. I felt Mr. Derrick's hand give an involuntary twitch as it tightened around my shoulder; it seemed even that fearless fellow quailed somewhat in the face of his skipper—even when the latter existed in a state very far from sobriety.

"A stowaway," the carpenter replied, according to the scheme we had concocted between us. You see, I had no desire to implicate the crew in my crimes; for one thing, I was grateful to them for their assistance in getting me aboard, and I did not wish to repay that kindness by bringing the ire of their captain upon their heads. For another, I knew that I was quite at the mercy of my shipmates and that I would suffer tremendously if they felt that they had any grievance to hold against me. I had no doubt that the likes of Mr. Fairchild or Mr. Harris would visit punishment upon me to such an extent as to exceed any that was inflicted upon them.

"I found him in the hold."

"Indeed?" drawled the captain. He pushed aside an empty glass decanter with a clumsy hand, frowning at Mr. Derrick as though daring the big man to call attention to its emptiness. His unfocused eyes gradually cleared, and he turned his attention to me. His whole manner changed in that instant; I felt as though I were rooted to the deck upon which I stood, so squarely had I been pegged by his formidable gaze. There was a brief pause in which I could feel myself being assessed; for a moment, I was as an insect pinned to the naturalist's board. Then the captain stood with a sudden movement, his tangled hair whipping about his head, and abruptly all traces of drunkenness vanished from his demeanor and were replaced with the fierceness which I had been led to expect.

"The writer, or I'm very much mistaken!" he bellowed. He covered the distance to me and elbowed Mr. Derrick aside without so much as a second glance. He leaned into my face and sneered; waves of vinous breath washed across my face, and I strained to the utmost to maintain my composure. "Didn't think I'd recognize you, eh?" the captain demanded. "Thought old Carrig's eyes had turned a bit dim, did you?"

I refrained from jeopardizing myself further by delivering the obvious retort, which was of course that it was not his ability to recognize me which I held in contempt, but rather his capacity to remember me after first encountering me in a state of obvious inebriation. Instead, I took the altogether safer course of action (which in fact had been recommended to me by both Mr. Derrick and William) of merely shaking my head and gazing silently at my feet while being thus berated.

"Well, these eyes are still sharp enough to see Nantucket," he snarled. "Do you think your arms are strong enough to get you there?"

I turned my head in alarm; I recalled William's warning that the captain might very well pursue this precise course of action, but I had thought that by now we were safely beyond the reach of shore. I certainly could not see land astern of us, but in my consternation it seemed suddenly possible that Captain Carrig was quite capable of such a feat. I turned back to the captain, who was now clutching at my shirt with knotted fingers. But before my very eyes, though his gaze lost none of its alertness, his face softened and his grip loosened. That tense hand released my bunched shirt and began patting it smooth. He straightened himself and touched me lightly on the shoulder before abruptly turning his head to stare across the waves. When he looked back at me, I thought that I detected a telltale shine to his eyes.

I was utterly flummoxed by this change in temperament. For some days I confess that it led me to perceive the captain as someone who, in addition to carrying an obvious vice in the form of alcoholism, was perhaps not quite sane. Not for the last time, uncertainty stabbed at me—what sort of contract had I carelessly entered when I had decided to join this ship?

However, I had done him an injustice in doubting his sanity. With the benefit of hindsight, I can now see his anger and its sudden abatement in a different light. While he may well have felt a stab of instinctual rage when confronted with the fact that I had defied his orders and slipped aboard his ship without his leave, I believe that the bulk of his anger was directed at the fact that another innocent soul had now been embroiled in the perilous course he intended to set for the *Melville*. For I now understand that the captain was possessed of a kindly heart, despite his ruthless exterior, and when his fury melted away it was replaced, not with the vague confusion of a mind gone soft, but rather with a keen sense of regret and a grim resignation when he realized that there was, after all, no possibility of reversing course at this late juncture. And so I would not sully his memory by casting him in an unfair light; instead let him be remembered as a man ordained to navigate extreme straits under the influence of tremendous familial obligations; would that we all might fare so well in such unenviable circumstances!

Presently the captain turned from the sea. His eyes alighted upon me once more, with altogether less sheer aggression in his gaze and something more of appraisal, though I am not sure that I can say which was the worse.

"Well, writer. What can you do?"

"I can write." The words escaped my lips before I had conceived of them consciously. I can say nothing in defense of this flippancy other than to suggest it may have been the fault of the voice that had placed me in these circumstances in the first place. I felt my face redden as soon as the words had been uttered, but it seemed that fortune was willing to smile upon yet another fool—for the captain turned out to possess a sense of humor, after all.

His lips twitched unmistakably as he suppressed a smile. "Can you sail?"

"I have a head for high places, as the expression goes. I believe I could be of some use in the rigging."

"Indeed?" The captain arched a bushy eyebrow. "And can you run up a canvas? Can you trim a sail?"

I opened my mouth to reply, but the captain did not allow me to answer. In truth, I do not know what reply I might have offered.

"Can you weigh anchor? Can you stand watch, or keep steady the wheel? Hell, boy, can you *cook*? No, I suppose you're of less use than a fellow—" he looked me up and down "—maybe five years your junior."

By now I was fairly spluttering with indignation. No, perhaps I could not perform any of the duties which he had described—but surely it was my prerogative to say so! Having my own qualifications so summarily dismissed by another who was not even my acquaintance proved to be a deeply galling experience. I had every intention of laying my frustrations out before the captain, consequences be damned, but it seemed that even now he was not genuinely soliciting my input on the matter.

"But I don't suppose it can be helped," he continued. "After all, what trouble is a third writer when you're already saddled with two? And maybe there'll be a story to tell here before the end. But look here, lad." He fixed me with a stern eye. "If you're to be of any use at all, you'll not get in the crew's way. And you'll keep that pen handy, for it may be that you'll see a thing or two worth writing down. But stick to the facts, and keep it simple. We have enough, ah, *creativity* to deal with from the two old busybodies I was fool enough to hire."

"You cannot mean Mr. Verne or Mr. Clark Russell?" I protested in astonishment.

"The very same. You can't rely on creative types, lad. They've always got an *agenda*." This time he made no effort to disguise his smile, and it was a terrible and awesome thing. "But they may find that I've got an agenda of my own, and each man has his place, it's said. At least aboard the *Melville* that still holds true. Now I suggest that you find your own place, and keep to it. Don't give me cause to regret such a charitable decision."

And so it was that I found myself with remarkably free reign of the ship's decks. I could scarcely believe my good fortune in this matter; not only had I escaped punishment at the hands of a purported tyrant, I had also received express permission to pursue the very course of action upon which I had been set. I avoided the captain's quarters, naturally, and my own reticence forbade me from dogging the footsteps of Mr. Verne and Mr. Clark Russell too closely (though this latter reservation was relaxed with the passage of time). Instead, I contented myself with explorations of the ship's decks and holds. I interviewed the crew at mealtimes or when I perceived that they were amenable to the interruption of their work. I conflated them all to actors in a grand play; I daresay even

Mr. Fairchild was cast in something of a heroic light in my initial, somewhat idealized first notes—though this particular fantasy was quickly corrected. A few illustrative examples of my encounters with the crew will presently be supplied so that my readers may gather some sense of the development of relations aboard the ship. This may also serve to convey the general mood that characterized the crew before the onset of the strange disasters which rendered our fate wholly unique in the long annals of seafarers across all the oceans of the world.

One such encounter occurred between myself and the ship's mate, Mr. Taggart. Though I had exchanged the briefest pleasantries with the mate while I was confined to the forecastle, it was not until after my meeting with Captain Carrig that we entered into any substantive discourse. To own the truth, I felt some apprehension about interacting directly with Mr. Taggart. As his authority was second only to the captain's, his will represented a direct extension of the captain's own will—and if I had the captain's reluctant blessing to interact with the crew in the course of writing my story, well, it was his very reluctance that suggested that I should avoid running afoul of those seamen who wielded any authority. The best way to remain in their good graces, as far as I was concerned, was to make myself scarce. Yet eventually it occurred to me that I could hardly furnish a comprehensive review of the *Melville*'s voyage without speaking to the ship's officers. So I finally gathered the courage to approach Mr. Taggart at the wheel as he conversed with Mr. Lawrence, the helmsman.

"What qualifications do you possess which made you eligible for the post of mate?" I asked. At this point in the conversation, we had already dispensed with our pleasantries (such as they were—the men of the ship were not generally known for their courtesy) and had settled into the business of conducting my interview. I rather think that Mr. Taggart viewed the whole affair with a sort of tolerant good humor—if he thought the exercise was a waste of time, he at least had the good grace not to say so. My pen was poised to record his answer.

"The Royal Navy this is not," answered Mr. Taggart, revealing that he was an Englishman. "I daresay the skipper ought to have appointed anyone he deemed fit for the job, regardless of his age or service record. But as it turns out, I did serve, as did our friend the helm[24] here." He thumped Mr. Lawrence on the back; the man only scowled and gave a little grunt by way of reply. "Now, if the end of our military duty was not entirely satisfactory to either party, what of it? Evidently the captain recognized something of our better qualities, as he's seen fit to appoint us accordingly."

"And what are your responsibilities as the *Melville*'s mate?" I asked, glossing over the uncomfortable question of how exactly Mr. Taggart may have been discharged from the Navy. "Is it not usual for there to be a second mate, as well?" It did occur to me that I could have been better prepared for this particular reporting assignment; I really knew very little about the command structure on a ship. But I felt that it would be productive to direct these questions to the parties they concerned; in that manner, I might receive answers more specifically tailored to the particular circumstances of our voyage. And indeed, to a certain extent my efforts were rewarded—though the mate was somewhat more ambiguous than I might have preferred.

"Would that I had a second mate!" Mr. Taggart exclaimed dramatically. I thought I saw a long-suffering smile creep over Mr. Lawrence's face at this proclamation. "Someone to help me shovel the shit, if you understand my meaning. As things stand, I have to watch over the crew—both in matters of discipline and welfare—on my own, while the captain attends to his own business. We have our own boatswain and quartermaster, lad, but make no mistake, I perform both of those roles, in my turn. At the end of the day, I serve to execute the captain's wishes in whatever scheme he's concocted. It's up to me to make his plans work…even when he's hired this lot of hard-headed oafs who can scarcely distinguish aft from stern."

"Do you have reservations about the crew's competency, then?" I asked, my budding journalist's instincts activated by this cryptic remark. The mate did not answer immediately, though, and a change came over his features. He appeared cautious now, as though perhaps he sensed that he may have spoken out of turn or revealed more information than he had intended.

"Do not trouble yourself with the ability of the crew," he said

[24] i.e., helmsman

finally. "I have them well enough in hand. If you need something to turn over in your mind, might I suggest the events that occurred in that lighthouse instead?"

"Sankaty Head?" I asked, bemused by this abrupt change in the course of our conversation. "I hadn't realized that my trial was known to the rest of the crew."

"His *trial*, he calls it," Mr. Taggart said. Ostensibly this was an aside to Mr. Lawrence, but the mate's eyes never left my own, and he watched my face intently as he spoke. "You made quite a commotion in that bar with your music, lad. I did not fail to notice that a few of my men left with you shortly thereafter, though they may not have noticed me. And you may be sure that I questioned Mr. Fairchild closely on the following morning, for I detected at once that it was his particular brand of mischief at play. Did it occur to you that he may not have had your best interests in mind? Did you stop to question whether he would have been at all remorseful if you had plunged to your death that night? It would have been a simple thing indeed to characterize your death as a drunken accident; the whole Pelican had seen you drink more than your share."

"You cannot mean to suggest that Mr. Fairchild meant to have me killed?" I asked, flabbergasted at this accusation. "I cannot deny that he is a slimy fellow, and I don't doubt that he meant for me to lose my nerve—he would have reveled in the dashing of all my ambitions—but I cannot seriously believe him a murderer. What's more, Mr. Harris and Mr. Derrick were also present, and it is quite outside the realm of possibility that they could have all conspired in such a nefarious scheme."

"Have you really not gotten the measure of them yet?" Mr. Taggart asked. "Harris is as sinister as Fairchild ever was, and Derrick is a good-natured fool. For all of his philosophical pretensions, he cannot but see the good in everyone. I'm starting to suspect that it's a quality he shares with you."

I opened my mouth to protest further, but the mate overrode me.

"I am not interested in debate on the subject, for I am not particularly concerned with anything that happens when the *Melville* is not at sea. If I should witness a repeat of this incident while the men are on duty, you may rest assured that I will see the appropriate punishment enforced." A dangerous gleam rose in Mr. Taggart's eye. "In the meantime, I only suggest that you exercise a bit more caution henceforth."

Though the course of the conversation had diverted wildly, and most of my questions regarding the duties of the mate remained unanswered, it was clear to me that my interview was now at its conclusion. I recognized that I must employ a new tactic to gather the information I wanted. Over the next few days, I had the opportunity to speak with Mr. Taggart now and again, and I let slip a question or two when I perceived that he might be willing to answer them. In this way, I began to acquire a more fully-realized view of the role this man played aboard the *Melville*, which was largely to function as the captain's right hand. But the specifics of the mate's functions would be interesting, I suspect, only to a very small percentage of my readership, and so I will not subject them to a full enumeration of these responsibilities. Instead, I would turn to a subsequent conversation with another member of the crew. For it was not long before I ran across Mr. Fairchild again, and I could hardly be expected to refrain from raising the issue of the lighthouse and the true nature of his intentions therein.

"And what are some of your own duties?" I asked the quartermaster. I had enough sense to arrive at the point obliquely rather than to rush in with the questions which I really wanted to pose. Persuading Mr. Fairchild to agree to an interview had been difficult enough; I could scarcely afford to get into a confrontation with him right away. "In what ways do they differ from those of the mate?"

Jeremy Fairchild spat on the deck. "Did you know that the quartermaster was a role to be coveted one hundred years ago?" He nodded sagely, as if he were in possession of some arcane knowledge which he would now impart to me. "Aye, the pirates knew how it was to be done. The quartermaster was second only to the captain. He could even succeed the captain if something, ah, happened to him. And the quartermaster was in charge of meting out punishments. Believe me, boy, there are a few on this ship who I'd flay to the bone, given half a chance." He spat again; his phlegm was viscous and tinged with blood. It glistened on the deck between us in the dull sunlight of an overcast day at sea. Mr. Fairchild frowned. "Nowadays a quartermaster doesn't have the power God gives a babe, especially in the merchant service. Maybe if I were still with the Navy I'd have a scrap of authority[25]. On this tub I've got nothing better to do than count our biscuits and make sure there's enough water in the casks to see us home."

"It seems as though the men follow your example," I said, appealing to his selfish nature and slowly trying to steer the conversation towards the topic I truly wished to address. "From the moment we met, it was clear that they accepted your guidance. That would suggest to me that you wield some authority."

Mr. Fairchild scowled. "I am undermined at every turn. Oh, it's true enough that I can generally encourage the crew to see things my own way; there's hardly a brain among them. But put me up against Taggart or Carrig, and you'll see how quickly that facade of authority crumbles."

It was time to strike. "I'm not so sure. The men followed you to Sankaty Head readily enough, and no one tried to stop you—not even Mr. Taggart, who I know for a certainty was present at the inn. Or maybe he guessed your purpose in going there and already approved of it?" Now, I knew this was not the case, for Mr. Taggart had already told me that he had reprimanded Mr. Fairchild for his deeds on that night. But I had calculated my words to show my hand, so to speak, and now I would see whether Mr. Fairchild would show his own by admitting to any wicked intent.

To his credit, he did not lose his composure. Instead, his mouth twisted into a familiar leering expression, and his eyes danced with a sort of mocking delight. I actually rather think he was impressed, despite himself. "So you've been talking with the mate, then," he said slowly. "I don't doubt that he's put an idea or two into that head of yours. But before you make any accusations which can't be taken back, let me give you another idea to think on. You might wonder why I took you to that lighthouse; ascribe any ulterior motive to me that you will. I'll freely admit that I have no use for you as a member of this crew. But what happened that night is that you got what you wanted, and any hypothetical design of mine to the contrary was duly thwarted. And so I'll give you a

[25] Even had Mr. Fairchild still been employed by the Navy, he would have been unable to exact his preferred form of punishment; flogging was prohibited in England by 1881.

piece of advice: leave well enough alone. Don't give me any reason to make a second attempt, as it were, and mayhap we'll get along just fine." He flashed another grotesque shark's smile at me; it seemed to be comprised entirely of teeth.

Looking into that ghastly face, I felt an unexpected rush of defiance. Had I not already beaten this man once before? Surely I could do so again; and moreover, I instinctively recognized that it was important not to show weakness before this predatory sort of scoundrel. "You are right on one important point, Mr. Fairchild," I said in a pleasant tone of voice. "I *have* been speaking with the mate. What's more, I've been welcomed into the captain's cabin, and I now enjoy the privilege of having his ear." If this were not strictly true, I trusted it was close enough to reality to jar the quartermaster from his self-assured poise, and to stand up to at least a bit of scrutiny if he chose to investigate the claim. "You've lamented that you cannot flog the men of the *Melville*; I wonder what would happen to a man who was found to attempt murder aboard the selfsame ship? I fear it would go very poorly with him. And I say 'attempt,' for what has slipped once through your hands is likely to do so again. Keep that in mind, and you'll be right on a second point, as well—we'll get along just fine."

The quartermaster's smirk tightened in displeasure, and he turned away from me without another word. I smiled at his back; that would put paid to the question of Mr. Fairchild, I thought. Like any bully, he needed only to see that I would not be cowed by his threats, whether they were veiled or overt. I congratulated myself on eliminating this potential source of ongoing conflict; little did I suspect that I had made a permanent enemy whose ongoing machinations would cause me no end of grief!

At any rate, another chance encounter during my first week at sea proved somehow even more unsettling in nature, and to this day I remember it with a vague feeling of uneasiness, even in light of those altogether more explicitly horrifying circumstances which were soon to follow. The encounter in question consisted of a conversation between myself and Old Cedar, that strange woman who was placed in charge of the ship's vittles. I had been assiduously recording the day's events in my little journal, though they had been decidedly mundane thus far, and was in fact so intent upon my task that I did not hear the cook's approach until she was upon me. She alighted just over my shoulder and announced her presence by clearing her throat. To be frank, the sound most closely resembled the death rattle of an invalid upon her sickbed.

"Come, woman," I fairly snapped, irritable and embarrassed at being so startled. "You ought to summon the doctor for that cough."

Old Cedar was entirely unfazed by this admonishment. She merely stared at me, or perhaps rather through me, with her single clear eye. She breathed in and puffed out her air in an exaggerated fashion, her chest rising and falling with the intake and expulsion of breath. For a moment I was reminded of a fat robin on a late fall morning, its breast swollen with worms—an impression enhanced by the uncanny, birdlike stare with which she affixed me. When she finally deigned to speak, her words were entirely unrelated to my own.

"You've been speaking to the men," she said. It was not a question.

"I am a writer," was my reply, though it was not yet strictly true at the time, and has really only come to pass with the composition of this very account. "Of course I have interviewed them." I am afraid to say that I was rather cross with the old woman, on account of being so surprised while concentrating on my work—to say nothing of the feeling of revulsion that her rather frightening aspect stirred in me.

"Hmm," she said, and the lines on her weathered face deepened as her brow furrowed, creating a shifting landscape of creases that turned into small rivers and tributaries as beads of sweat dripped from her thin bundle of hair. "And have they been entirely forthcoming with you?"

I was somewhat taken aback by what represented, for this woman at least, a startling instance of verbosity. "I've been given no reason to doubt their candor," I replied. Even as I said this, though, I bethought me of Mr. Fairchild's mocking eyes and the twist of the lips that served for his smile. But I was still under the spell of the ship's allure, you see, and I pushed aside this memory of the treacherous quartermaster. Still, I was forced to amend my statement, even if I could hear that my voice took on something of a defensive tone: "At least, no specific reason that I can identify. I am surprised that you would call the character of your betters into question."[26]

"Maybe so," she said, breaking into a wide and genuine smile that somehow did nothing to set me at ease. "And yet matters of position and status prove inconsequential and are swept aside by the long arm of the Father Ocean."

Despite my annoyance, my own literary curiosity was roused by such an inscrutable statement. "I have always known the sea to be romanticized in the feminine pronoun," I said. Almost unconsciously, I poised my pen above the page, prepared to transcribe whatever mysterious wisdom Old Cedar was about to dispense. But she was not to be distracted by my sudden interest, returning instead to her original discourse regarding the honesty of the crew.

"I advise you only to heed what you are told with caution," she said. "For it may be that the *Melville*'s prow points not in the direction you have been promised. Or have you not observed that her course has gone askew? Indeed, we may now move under the auspices of a compass hitherto unknown." She tipped a wink at me when she said this last, and when she winked, it was her clear eye that she closed, leaving me with the discomfiting sight of that blind milky orb floating alone in a miniature sea of broken blood vessels. She shuffled off across the deck without so much as another remark, her coat swaying just above her ankles. For the first time I took notice of how heavily she was dressed, and this despite the heat of the midday sun and its dazzling reflection upon the still water.

Still, I gave but little thought to her appearance and probable discomfort, for my head was fairly spinning with what Old Cedar had intimated to me. I need scarcely explain that at this juncture I possessed only the most rudimentary understanding of the intricacies of sail or the means by which a sailor navigates. In short, I was supremely unqualified to discern whether the *Melville* were following her prescribed route along the Atlantic seaboard.

[26] If this seems especially uncharitable, it may be useful to remember that the position of cook was the only role that a disabled (in this case, half-blind) person could hope to obtain on a ship. Gordon may have already begun to exhibit the prejudices of the social environment in which he found himself.

To be sure, no land could be seen from our position, but that was hardly to be wondered at. Could the old woman's words be true? And why should she have taken me into her confidence? A great many things which had seemed innocuous at best and only eccentric at worst now began to take on a decidedly sinister hue. I recalled the eaves-dropped conversation between Mr. Verne and Mr. Clark Russell, during which the two authors discussed the military mien of the *Melville's* crew. I reflected upon my recent audience with Captain Carrig and the way his personality seemed to vacillate between two extremes, and I wondered if he too did not have some nefarious scheme figured into his plans.

But then the perpetually sunny countenance of William, whom I already considered to be a friend, sprang unbidden to my mind. Surely his motivations were both transparent and honest, and he would hardly be a willing party to any such deception. There was also Mr. Derrick to consider. The carpenter had shown naught but care and concern for my injured condition, even going so far as to summon the doctor to my side in secret and to present me to the captain in as favorable a manner as could reasonably be contrived. Even the doctor himself, for all his brusqueness, gave me no reason to doubt his essential kindness. Last, there were the two venerable authors to consider. It was not within the realm of possibility that such learned men would fall prey to any sort of trickery regarding the purpose of the *Melville*'s voyage, and it was equally inconceivable that they would enter into any dubious purpose of their own volition.

And in such a manner I sought to allay the concerns that Old Cedar had planted in my mind. For the most part my effort was successful, and I was able to occupy myself with the duties of a burgeoning journalist on his first assignment. Life aboard the *Melville* proceeded in this manner for a period of some days, and I became more fully acquainted with my shipmates. Together with William, I planned how I might get closer to Mr. Verne and Mr. Clark Russell in order to record the progress of their collaborative efforts. But after about a week had elapsed upon the open sea, it so happened that the progress of the *Melville*—whatever her course—was impeded by the unexpected formation of a tremendous storm just over the horizon. As I saw the darkening clouds coalescing in the dusk of the day, I thought for a fleeting moment that they resembled an outstretched human hand. I heard the words of Old Cedar invoking the name of the 'Father Ocean,' echoing in my head as distinctly as though the enigmatic old woman were speaking directly into my ear. I even went so far as to seek her out as she served the men their evening meal. But something quailed within me—call it an uncertain presentiment of doom—and I turned back before ever reaching her post, forgoing even my own supper. I only wish now that I had availed myself of this final opportunity to obtain her counsel.

IN WHICH THE SHIP IS BESET BY STORMS, AND WE FIRST EXPERIENCE A LOSS, AND THEN MAKE A DISCOVERY

"From the peculiar time of your call upon me, I suppose you purposely select stormy weather for your journeys."
-Herman Melville, *The Lightning-Rod Man*

The storm coalesced with such rapidity that it was just as well that I had skipped my dinner. The crew's repast was interrupted by the captain himself, as he was evidently sober enough to identify the coming squall and to direct the men in the task of preparing the vessel to weather its oncoming blows. I knew nothing about storms—let alone experiencing a storm at sea—but it was evident from the first that Captain Carrig expected the approaching gale to be a veritable Shakespearean tempest. The captain brought the crew out onto the deck, leaving Old Cedar to hurriedly clear the men's plates of half-eaten supper and to stow their cups in the galley. Some of the crew immediately dashed off to various corners of the ship, their duties already understood. For the rest, they awaited their orders from the captain.

The preparation of a ship to withstand a gale is a matter of no little technicality, the specifics of which I do not expect my audience to especially appreciate; for a fuller understanding of the process, I would refer the interested reader to Dana[27]. But that is not to say that I shall forego a description of the crew's efforts entirely, for it reflects admirably upon their character that they were able to perform these duties in the midst of the looming threat presented by the black clouds massing quickly over our heads. The men first donned their oil-cloth suits and tarpaulin south-wester caps to better protect themselves against the rain, and then they

[27] Henry Dana, *Two Years Before the Mast* (1840).

sprang aloft to begin executing the captain's orders.

The first of these orders was to reef the sails, which was done in a sort of reverse order to prevent the *Melville* from slewing sideways with the force of wind. The sailors risked the most precarious handholds and footholds to accomplish this job, ascending to dangerous heights to furl the royals and top-gallants and to take in the flying jib. Some of the men anchored themselves with ropes when they clambered into the rigging, but most did not—I am sorry to say that time was valued rather more strongly than safety when it came to carrying out the captain's orders. Next came the back sails and lower courses, before the crew could proceed to take in the foresail and mainsail and finally the headsail. Taking down all of this canvas would allow the ship to more safely ride out the weather, you see; too much wind pressing on her sails could risk snapping the yardarms or masts—which would have been nothing short of disastrous in the middle of a storm. When the ship was finally ready to fly "under bare poles," as the expression goes, Captain Carrig ordered Mr. Lawrence to direct the ship into the oncoming waves.

"Is that not especially dangerous?" I protested feebly, still somewhat lost for something to do as the rest of the crew busied themselves in the rigging. I became aware of my hands twisting nervously together.

"I shouldn't say so," replied the helmsman, his sandy hair already beginning to stick to his forehead as the first few drops of rain started to fall. He squinted into the binnacle and turned the wheel just as indifferently as you can imagine; just as though he had not a care in all the world. "The prow is the sturdiest part of her, and the best to handle the hardest of the waves. You'll not catch me running before the wind." Even as he spoke, the ship dipped into the trough of a swell much larger than we had experienced thus far. "The real difficulty," he grunted, "is keeping the rudder in the water so I can properly steer. It takes a bit of skill to steer a close-hauled ship in a storm, lad, and even a little carelessness will wreck her. We've got to get up a measure of speed before it'll get any easier."

"How can we do that if we've just struck the sails?"

"Aye, you've got to the heart of it," the helmsman grinned.

His levity was undercut by a peal of thunder, heralding the

first truly earnest efforts of the storm. The rain, which had heretofore been a gentle patter, began to come down in heavy sheets. Somewhere over the bow, a bolt of lightning briefly illuminated the unnatural darkness that had been brought on by the gale's forbidding black clouds.

My eyes seared by its flash, I turned back to Mr. Lawrence. A thought had occurred to me which, in the safety and ignorance of my passenger's berth, had not presented itself when I last found myself at sea. "Have we anything to fear from the lightning?"

"Don't trouble yourself on that account," came the helmsman's steady reply. "It's true enough that a direct strike might shiver a mast or catch the rigging alight, but that's nothing that a decent carpenter and a sharp crew can't handle." He spun the ship's wheel deftly in his hands as we crested another wave. "But most strikes'll be caught in their tracks by our thunder rod, or else on the rest of the iron throughout the ship." He took his eyes from the ocean and spared me a glance, looking up and down at my increasingly sodden appearance. "I'd concern myself with my own health, if I were you. You'll pardon my saying so, but I don't think you're used to this sort of weather, and I can't imagine you'll be missed if you skip off to the forecastle."

Well, for all my foolishness, I was smart enough to recognize the wisdom in this advice. I thanked the helmsman for the skillful execution of his duties and wryly excused myself by observing that he seemed to have all well enough in hand—at which he gave an ironic little salute—and then I set off in the general direction of the forecastle. The storm did its best to hamper my efforts; for a moment, the rain was even replaced by hail. These balls of concentrated ice stung my exposed hands and beat insistently upon my brow, forcing me to duck my head as I shuffled across the deck; I marveled that the crewmen could continue to work in these conditions. But the hail did not persist for long, much to my relief—though the rain was scarcely an improvement. It soon became so heavy that the deck became difficult to traverse. I resorted to pulling myself along with the aid of handholds provided by the ship's rail.

Presently a full six inches of water were washing about my boots; the flow was running up against the scupper-holes, which now proved unequal to the task of draining the sheer amount of water which was thrown at them, and sloshing back to transform the deck into a sort of shallow pool. I could now see nothing; the force of the wind had turned the rain horizontal, stinging my eyes and changing the world into a sheet of gray monotony. I staggered through this alien environment, wondering that the world could be so completely changed within the space of just a few hours—and very much wishing that I had had the sense to remain belowdecks. In my blind wandering, it was perhaps inevitable that I should have run up against some trouble. Had I been struck by a loose pulley block or some bit of flying tackle, it would have been no more than I deserved for my thoughtless behavior. But the trouble which I encountered was of a different and rather more sinister nature, and it occurred as I stumbled perilously against the port rail, which I could barely discern through the driving rain and its attendant mist.

My body was thrown without warning right up against the rail; so sudden was the attack that I thought I had stumbled with the pitching of the ship and had fallen of my own accord. But then I was hoisted partway off the ground, and I felt the unmistakable sensation of two fists clutching the front of my shirt. I sputtered incoherently in an indignant sort of panic, swatting ineffectually at the hands that held me steadfastly in place.

"And who should chance to be caught wandering on a night so dim?" came a hissing voice. A leering face loomed into my view from out of the murk of the stormy atmosphere; it was the boatswain, Mr. Harris. His ugly countenance nearly brushed right up against my own, so closely did he lean in to me in order to be heard. "A man could wash right overboard in a gale like this, and he would not be missed until morn." His grin widened. "I would say that you should be more careful in the future, boy, but I somehow think that you shalln't have the chance."

"Release me at once," I commanded, summoning more authority and confidence into my voice than I felt. Was this to be a crime of opportunity, or had the boatswain planned all along to corner me at night, using the storm as his cover? I was terrified, and I understood that he meant to put a scare into me, but I did not even now seriously imagine that Mr. Harris had any real design on my life. I hammered upon his forearms with my fists, but the toad-like man was made all of wiry muscle and seemed hardly to notice my blows. I even managed to connect a kick directly with his abdomen, but the sensation was very much like striking a wall. Nonetheless, he grimaced when I landed this blow, and he lifted me higher. My posterior was now well above the top of the rail, and it would take very little indeed to send me to my death in the churning water below. "For God's sake, man, this prank has gone quite far enough."

"A prank, is it?" Mr. Harris scowled. "Was it a prank when you threatened the quartermaster? No, boy, I've known men like you, and I cannot abide your kind. You might think your status[28] gives you the prerogative to walk all over the common sailor—and on shore maybe it even does, after a fashion—but things stand a little differently at sea. I shalln't stand idly by while you jeopardize the livelihood of a good man by whispering despicable lies into the captain's ear."

Sudden understanding crashed upon me, just as the storm-tossed waves crashed upon the *Melville*'s hull even as we spoke. "Dress it up however you like," I shouted to be heard over the ongoing crack of lightning. "But it is murder. I see now that you and Mr. Fairchild have concocted this scheme between you; failing to do away with me on Nantucket, you mean to try again here." I renewed my struggle, though my efforts were too little and too late. All the boatswain had to do was release his grip on me, and I would be doomed.

But suddenly a small shape crashed right into Mr. Harris, and he toppled sideways with the unexpected force of the impact. Suddenly freed, I fell heavily onto the rail and flailed about wildly, scrabbling against the slick wood in sheer desperation. A friendly hand clasped my own and pulled me to safety; I cannot begin to express the relief which I felt when I placed my feet upon the deck once more. Wiping the rain from my eyes, I stared incredulously at my rescuer: it was none other than William! But to my surprise, he was not looking at me; instead, his gaze was resting steadily upon the form of the treacherous Mr. Harris, who was picking himself up from the deck. Though the rain was as unstoppable as ever before, I thought that I recognized unmitigated fury on the boatswain's face.

---

[28] As an educated man in society, presumably; certainly Gordon held no formal status as a member of the crew.

"Oh, but that was a mistake, cabin boy," Mr. Harris growled. "And I'll make you pay dearly for it, too; I'll just as soon toss the pair of you over the rail." He took a threatening step towards us, and his utterly sodden appearance cut a very intimidating figure indeed, with his lank hair hanging wet and monstrous over the anger-contorted planes of his face.

"You may try," said William evenly. "You may even succeed; but the attempt will cost you. For I will fight back, and I will hurt you, before we are through." Apparently undaunted, he took up some sort of a fighting stance, raising his fists and turning his feet just so. Inspired by this show of defiance, I stepped up behind him. I was not much of a fighter, but I liked to think that any man would think twice before attacking two others. And in fact Mr. Harris hesitated, apparently calculating whether the odds were still in his favor. He plainly wondered how the situation had turned against him so rapidly.

But I was not to see whether he would have chosen to proceed with his attack, for a sudden commotion rang out on the deck. The sound of shouting reached us even through the all-encompassing din of wind and rain, and it almost came as a surprise to be reminded of the presence of other members of the crew—such was the isolating effect of the storm and the preoccupying nature of my conflict with the boatswain. But as this disturbance escalated in volume, it became impossible to ignore; all three of us turned our heads to see the gray shapes of men running about the ship's stern. With a final, terrible glare at the two of us, Mr. Harris turned and trotted off in the direction of the fray.

"Thank you," I said to William; I fear it was an insufficient expression of the fact that I owed my life to him, but it was all I could manage at the time.

He grinned at me, and even in the midst of the unending cascade of water pounding the ship and plastering our clothes to our bodies, his expression seemed to crack a window in the storm; for a moment I felt an unaccountable levity in my breast. "That was a lucky break. I only regret that I didn't get the chance to give him what for," said William, "but maybe I'll catch up with him yet; I daresay the captain won't be too pleased with this latest development. But what say we investigate whatever is happening astern?" He jerked his thumb in the general direction of the commotion.

As we approached the source of the sound, it was clear that the main thrust of the drama had already concluded. Five or six men were clustered around the mizzenmast with their necks craned upward, and one or two others were climbing down the rigging therefrom. But others were already jogging off to other parts of the ship, resuming their duties as the storm continued to rage, and they were soon lost to sight. This was not heartlessness, but cold logic: no one man's tragedy could be allowed to disrupt the business of keeping us afloat in the middle of such a terrible storm.

And a tragedy it was. For as the men touched down from the mizzenmast, those of us still gathered there—including Mr. Harris—came closer together to hear what they had to say, and presently the whole affair was made plain. The first to speak was Mr. Taggart; apparently the mate had been working high in the rigging with some of the more experienced seamen, and—

"Though it's hardly my place to say so," Mr. Taggart said, and he cast a furtive look around the deck before continuing. "The cook had no business being up the mast." There was a general murmuring at this proclamation, though it could scarcely be heard over the fury of the storm.

"You cannot mean that Old Cedar was ordered into the rigging?" cried William, aghast. "What has befallen her? Is she not blind?"

"Close enough, I should say," demurred the mate. "Aye, the captain ordered 'all hands' to the mast, though even that might've exempted the old dame, but for the captain's specific direction to the contrary—and a queer thing it was, at that." He looked around again, as though making absolutely certain that Captain Carrig was not present and could not possibly overhear him. "'Cook,' he says, 'Seeing as you've led me into this damned tempest, get up there with the mate and see if you can't spot a way through.' Now what that might've meant I'm not prepared to guess, but the old dog moved right quick, and I had a bit of trouble to keep up with her. Now that's quite enough gossip; there's work to be getting on with, and there'll be time to say a word for the old biddy once we've seen the end of this storm."

"To say a word for her?" I protested. "Do you mean to say that she perished?"

"Aye," said the mate. "She slipped from the rigging and fell straight into the sea."

"That's not what I saw," said another sailor. I cannot now recall his name, but I remember his wide-eyed face and the sparse beard which blanketed his red cheeks like a threadbare rug. "She slipped on the ropes, sure enough, but then she spread her arms and flew right off into the rain like a bird."

"Now that really is quite enough," said Mr. Taggart quickly. "We've entirely too much work to indulge in absurd superstition. Get to it!" He clapped his hands for us to disperse. "Mr. Harris, where had you gone off to? I've been looking all over for you, not that I can see a damned thing in this rain. Go and lend the men a hand with the headsail—we'll get through this yet. William, I'll need you at the wheel with Mr. Lawrence; I fear he's got more than he can handle with these waves. All right, then? Work together, lads. We'll see each other on the other side of this thing."

The mate ran off midship, presumably to examine the reefing of the sails on the mainmast, now that the mizzen was addressed to his satisfaction. I felt the acute sting of having been assigned no work; even on a day when the half-blind cook had been ordered into the sails to do her part, I had not been deemed worth the trouble. And it must be said that the weather did nothing to alleviate my situation: the storm was now truly punishing the *Melville*, with wave upon wave pummeling the deck. The water would have been up to my waist had I been foolish enough to labor in the lee scuppers, and with the crest of each swell the ship tottered, pitching the masts to a forty-degree angle from the vertical. No matter the skill with which she had been assembled in the shipyard, it was inevitable that the ship should suffer some damage under these circumstances.

I did not, however, foresee the dramatic development that presently transpired. With a tremendous cracking sound that I distinguished even over the unyielding boom of thunder and the constant dull roar of rain, the foremast staysail simply exploded, shredded to scraps by the scouring of the wind! Bits of storm-tossed canvas whipped about in the air, blowing past our faces before vanishing into the heart of the storm. I looked around; dismay and alarm were writ large upon the faces of those men whom I could see through the rain. Clearly they had not had the opportunity to take in the staysail before it was destroyed by the storm—we could only count ourselves fortunate that the mast itself remained undamaged. As it was, I supposed that repairing the sail would have to wait until the storm had ceased its fury; it had been about to be furled, in any event, and I thought its absence could hardly impair us now. But it was not so.

For behold! Striding from the mist like an apparition from another, stranger reality came Captain Carrig. He emerged from the occlusion of rain-washed atmosphere with a purposeful cast to his gait and a permanent scowl affixed to his face. Though the storm had soaked him as thoroughly as any of us, he affected not to notice that his wild shock of hair now lay lank and listless on his brow or that the tops of his boots spurted little jets of water with every step he took. He cast a roving eye over the assembled crew.

"Mr. Harris!" he shouted.

"Sir?" said the deceitful boatswain, standing straight. He was suddenly the very picture of obedience and tact.

"Take in what's left of that staysail."

"Sir?" There was a tremor of hesitation in his voice now.

I must admit to taking a savage sort of pleasure from his obvious discomfort.

"I won't have this ship sailing in poor repair—not for a moment. There are eyes on us, you understand, and if we are to be deemed acceptable then it simply won't due to present an unworthy aspect. I shalln't ask you again, Mr. Harris."

A sudden nudge in my ribs alerted me to the presence of William, who had drifted from his post at the wheel to get my attention. He gave me a dark look which communicated what none of us dared to say aloud: the captain seemed to be speaking the plainest nonsense. Had the storm robbed him of his senses? It seemed hardly credible; surely a man as experienced as Captain Carrig had seen a worse storm than this. Could it be guilt over the loss of Old Cedar, whom he had ordered into the rigging? Or could the ugly mask of alcohol be rearing its head at this most inopportune moment? Whatever the cause for the skipper's strange pronouncement, Mr. Harris quickly decided that the most prudent course of action was to follow his orders. He sprang onto the ropes of the foremast and began to effect the necessary repairs.

The captain's decision to have Mr. Harris in particular take in the scraps of sail was curious. As the boatswain, he was responsible for the *Melville*'s rigging, cables, anchors, and sails—but these duties were typically executed in an administrative fashion. He was a master of inventory. But then every son of Neptune[29] was expected to carry his weight, and Mr. Harris could haul-to with the best of them. Indeed, he scurried about the rigging in a way that belied the shape of his squat body. Much like the way in which the quality of his voice did not seem to match his appearance, the boatswain moved with the agility and dexterity of a much more athletic man.

Naturally, the foremast is the mast with the most complicated array of clewlines, buntlines, and leechlines, representing a veritable spider's web of rigging that each sailor is expected to know like the back of his own hand. Mr. Harris's maneuvers began as he stretched himself out on the bowsprit, whereupon he began to gather the bits and pieces of sail still attached to the lines. A few crew members joined him at the captain's behest in order to help with the installation of a replacement sail. Together, they attached the tack, sheets, and halyards before making sure that the new sail was securely furled. Throughout the entire operation, I couldn't help but marvel at the uselessness of it all. Why should men risk life and limb to run up a new sail during a heavy storm, only to take it in immediately? The whole prospect was incomprehensible to me—but the captain seemed intensely gratified when the task was complete.

"Well done, Mr. Harris. I daresay we all owe you our hides, though I expect it'll be some time before the rest of this lot comes around to appreciate it." He clapped the sodden sailor on the back with an exaggerated, excessive breed of enthusiasm. I exchanged another glance with William; it was becoming apparent that the boatswain's usefulness in this bizarre exercise had greatly raised his estimation in the captain's eye. It was now very doubtful indeed whether Captain Carrig would credit our account of the villain's treachery and his assault upon me.

I have taken the time to relay these conversations as I best I can recall them. But these words in their written form are insufficient to express the manner in which they were conveyed.

[29] i.e., a sailor.

Each syllable was shouted to be heard over the roar of the weather; every routine movement was contested by the adamant will of the wind; and it must not be imagined that the storm had relented throughout this episode. The tempest continued to blow as strongly as ever—in fact, circumstances were soon to become very grim indeed. I cannot begin to estimate how long we had been toiling under the influence of these bleak and sunless skies, as I had by now lost all sense of time. The attempt on my life, the loss of Old Cedar, and the captain's erratic behavior had the cumulative effect of rendering me dizzy with one shock piled atop another. And so I scarcely reacted when Mr. Taggart came stumbling from the hold in a panic.

"Captain!" he said. "I've just been below. We've a leak of some size in the hold—I fear we've struck some object, or else some object has struck us. We're taking on water."

For his part, the captain handled this news better than I might have expected. "Aye, we're all taking on water," he muttered. Then his voice boomed out over the storm: "Where is the carpenter? Mr. Derrick! You know your trade—you have your tools?—then get to it! Boy, go along with him, for I'll need the rest at the pumps, and it may be you can be of some small use to Mr. Derrick." Here he indicated me, much to my own surprise. Was I to be given some work to perform, after all? I accepted a lantern from the captain's outstretched hand and hastened to obey his harried gesture to follow Mr. Derrick into the ship's hold. Within this subterranean environment, the roar of water against the hull was amplified and sent back in layered echoes, bouncing from the countless crates and barrels which populated every spare corner. We were forced to make a few turns in this warren of cargo and equipment, but it was not long before the object of our search made itself apparent. A hole some fifteen inches across was yawning in the side of the hull. It was above the waterline, but with each wave more water washed into the ship. Already there were several inches of water sloshing about our feet.

"How can it be helped?" I asked in despair. For although the hole was scarcely more than two feet wide, I could not see how it could be patched whilst the water continued to pour through. I struck my lantern alight and held it aloft to illuminate the damage, and the light also revealed Mr. Derrick's strained grin. The big man shook his hairy head.

"This is not so terrible, lad," he said, rummaging through his supplies, "and I might even venture so far as to say that the mate has blown it out of all proportion." He paused in his activity and tilted his head to the side, considering. "It's no more than his nature, I suppose, though it may prevent him from ever ascending to the command of his own ship. Let it be a lesson to you, Gordon, for even the truest servant may stagnate in perpetuity, though he executes his duties with perfect faithfulness. Better to be the quickstart[30], the trouble-maker, who is remembered by the captain and makes an impression with the ship's owner, so long as no great harm is done along the way. At the conclusion of a voyage, even the most irascible fellow may be remembered fondly if he's done his duty—by some means or another—at the day's end. That's the path to success, I think."

I could see that there was a very real risk of Mr. Derrick continuing along these lines indefinitely, and all the while water would carry on rushing into the hold. "Quite right," I said, "but what about this leak?"

"Mmm," he said, producing a wedge-shaped length of wood from somewhere amongst the tools and supplies which lay scattered half-submerged in the water before him. "Don't fret; our ship is not so easy to sink—wood floats, after all."[31] He took this lopsided wooden block and hammered it into the hole in the ship's side until it was snug. I could see at once that it was an imperfect seal: though it slowed the water to a trickle on either side, it would not suffice to stop the leak altogether. I said as much to Mr. Derrick.

"Ah, but you've not accounted for the swelling of the wood," he said, raising a finger as though he'd anticipated this objection. "It will grow in size and plug up this little hole pretty nicely indeed. Don't worry, now; I know my trade, and I've got this quite in hand. Give me that lantern and see if you can't help with the

---

[30] This appears to be a neologism coined by the carpenter.

[31] This is something of an oversimplification. A wooden sailing ship displaces an amount of water greater than its mass. This would keep the *Melville* afloat, but if the hold and other hollow parts of the ship were to fill with water (e.g., from the leak in question), sinking would quickly become a real possibility.

pumps." For while we worked to stop up the leak, a great commotion had arisen on the deck somewhere above our heads, as of many men all talking at once and thumping their heels upon the wood. I picked my way through the hold at Mr. Derrick's suggestion, still eager to be of some use (for I had not really been very helpful to the carpenter), and I ascended back into the furor and gloom of the storm. The majority of the crew had gathered around the ship's two Downton pumps. These were operated by great wheels not unlike the ship's own wheel, and it was sometimes necessary for two or even three men to work together to effect their operation.

Working the pumps was not such a difficult job when contrasted with many of the sailors' regular duties; in fact, there was a good deal less risk involved, which you might expect would render this assignment particularly attractive to the worn-out crewmen. But as the pumps pull water from lower in the holds—including the bilge—and spew it out carelessly onto the deck to be washed away through the scuppers, it represents one of the most undesirable jobs one can imagine. For my own part, I was horrified at the thought of wading through the filth that now intermingled with the water rushing about our feet. But there was to be no reprieve; the captain had ordered all hands to work in rotation, and it was such a slow process and required so many shifts that I could not hope to be excluded from my turn.

Hours passed; I cannot now say how many. I took my turn at the pumps and was duly relieved. I relieved William in turn and took another round of duty for myself. The rain, the wind, the unending turning of the pumps' wheels now chafed raw my hands; all conspired to reduce my world to shades of dim monotony. Though it seemed that morning should have come, the dark clouds let slip no herald of its arrival. I think that I ceased even to become aware of my own physical body as this time-out-of-time rolled on in such a manner; only distantly did I note the rocking of the ship as she shuddered upon some sea-borne object or particularly stiff wave. I think this most recent impact only really caught my attention when Mr. Derrick came stumbling onto the scene, the lantern which I had given him now faint and guttering in the wind as he emerged into the open air. His eyes were wild.

"Captain!" he fairly barked. "You felt that, I don't doubt?

We've got more holes knocked in us! It's all I can do to keep them plugged, and this time, well, I think I've seen what put them there."

"And what did you see?" the captain responded. His quiet voice somehow cut across the din of the storm, and a look of intense interest now crossed his face. He seemed to be keeping his calm about the new leaks, which I suppose was well enough in order to keep the men from panicking, but he also seemed to be genuinely more concerned with what—to me—was the altogether less important question of whatever object had damaged the hull.

"I saw…well, I don't think I shall say what I saw, if it's all the same to you, captain," he said with a nervous look around the assembled crew, who were obviously hanging on his every word. The carpenter appeared now to gather himself before continuing, twining his fingers into his matted beard in the midst of his distress. "What's more, I've measured the water in the hold, and I'm afraid there's nothing good to report on that front, either."

Those readers who are interested in nautical matters may appreciate the manner in which this check was performed. In order to calculate the amount of water we had shipped, Mr. Derrick was obliged to lower an iron rod, graduated by inches and feet, into a pipe that ran from the upper deck of the *Melville* all the way to her hold. Drawing up this rod with a line, the carpenter was then able to ascertain the total amount of water we had taken on. Though it did not afford a perfectly accurate measurement, it was accomplished quickly and did serve to give a general impression of the straits in which we found ourselves. And these were desperate straits indeed: "I'm afraid the pumps simply aren't up to the task," the carpenter reported in frustration. "Unless we get a break in the weather, the *Melville* cannot ride out this storm."

"The men must work harder," said the captain. "Mr. Taggart! Put some spirit into these sailors—by any means necessary."

The mate was himself working at the pumps, and he had to step aside to catch his own breath before he was able to muster a reply. "It won't do," he panted. "They are exhausted. I am exhausted. No man here will quit the pumps while he still breathes…but neither can we work a miracle."

At Mr. Taggart's pitiful words, my spirit quailed within me. Had we been abandoned by God, to perish so miserably upon a sea so dark? The voice in my head which inspired my participation in this foolish adventure suddenly sounded—but it did not speak. Instead, all that I heard was mad laughter, ironic laughter, echoing and spiraling within me until my entire consciousness seemed wrapped in the insane contradiction of it all. Suddenly my boredom and dissatisfaction with life seemed an attractive alternative to the current situation! A real laugh almost bubbled from my lips; I suppressed it only at the very last instant.

It was a good thing I did; the captain's eyes were fire as he absorbed the report from Mr. Taggart. I shudder to think how things might have gone without the intervention which soon followed. I remembered the captain's terrible reputation, and I remembered Mr. Fairchild's wish that flogging were still in practice. Could it have gone that far? My understanding of Captain Carrig's character makes me think that he could not stoop to such brutality…and yet I do not know whether he was fully in control of his actions even at this early stage of our troubles. It may be that some malign influence was already beginning to work its evils on the *Melville* and her crew.

But much to my relief, a sudden interruption postponed the question. For Mr. Verne and Mr. Clark Russell had arrived on deck! Whether they were drawn by the general commotion or simply could not abide the severity of the storm any longer, I cannot say. Whatever their prompting, they arrived together, dressed in their best foul-weather gear, and quickly took stock of the situation. It was clear at once that they were both natural leaders. "Why the long faces?" Mr. Verne said. "There are a couple of men still left with untapped strength in their arms," he announced, acknowledging that he had overheard the preceding conversation and intended to contribute to the efforts to save the ship.

This was really quite extraordinary. The reader may think it only natural that everyone on a ship should help in the attempt to save their own lives, but in the merchant service it was entirely unheard of for passengers to so much as speak with the crew—let alone to assist with their labor. Moreover, neither author was an especially young man (indeed Mr. Verne was verging on elderly, though his prodigious strength was undiminished by his years). Their participation therefore lent a palpable increase in energy to the crew: if these old landsmen could find the strength to turn the wheel, where did that leave an able-bodied sailor? And so when Mr. Verne approached the first pump in his typical half-limping fashion, a ripple of vigor seemed to pass through the *Melville*'s crew. The wheels began to turn with a newfound drive.

Demonstrating his natural understanding of the mariner's character, Mr. Clark Russell also led the crew in a rousing sea song, even as he relieved a man at the second pump and began to take his own turn at the very same labor. His song was of the sort which is meant to encourage hard, synchronized work and to inspire even the most fatigued of men to perform to the best of his ability, and it was quickly taken up by the rest of the crew working the pumps. I wonder now whether the treasure trove of this writer's mind had ever been fully revealed to another, or whether all of the collected songs and clever rhymes he carried within were ever committed to the pages of his novels. I can only attest to the knowledge that this song has not appeared in his published repertoire. I give it now in its entirety:

Bells ring and the helmsman cries,
Weary men rise from light slumber,
This storm-tossed ship their only redoubt,
Though binnacle's dark and sky is umber.
Wheels turn and buckets rise,
Drowned men toil in black weather,
To thwart the devil whatever his guise,
These men must all pull together.
Timbers creak and sharp winds wail,
Exhausted men will soon tire,
But none on this ship would ever turn tail,
Though the masts be limned with St. Elmo's fire.
Waves crash and thunder roars,
Careless men now slip o'er the side,
The rest do their duties and chores,
Though song is their only guide.
Day breaks and the sun slips its bonds,
Beleaguered men raise a cheer,
The ship gleams now all golden and bronze,
Though none can say when a new storm draws near.

Seas stretch to the horizon,
Watchful men now look landward,
For the prize they must keep their eyes on,
Though there's nary a gull nor shorebird.

The effect that this song had upon the crew was remarkable. Men broke out in spontaneous cheers, calling for the song to be sung again for the benefit of those who did not know its words during the first go around. I felt a renewal of hope within my own breast, for it seemed suddenly within the realm of possibility that we could yet prove equal to the task of surviving this storm. I lent my own voice to the swelling impromptu chorus, surprising myself by volunteering for another turn at the pumps. Though my arms were sore and weak, new life was granted to them by the collective energy of our replenished morale. As I pulled at the wheel with the best of them, I wondered that my mood had been so transformed. Perhaps we had not been abandoned after all! Perhaps, like the archetypal sailors in the song, we would find our way through this weather and arrive at last upon sunnier seas.

Indeed, as my reader must surely have surmised, this possibility was eventually borne out; though we labored for many hours more, and the captain ordered multiple adjustments to our sail as the weather began to clear (necessitating many of the men to abandon the pumps for the rigging), at long last I spied a rift in the clouds, with the faintest suggestion of daylight behind it. I stopped what I was doing, wiping the water from my eyelashes, and felt another swell of optimism: could this dreadful episode finally be approaching its conclusion? My ruminations were brought to an abrupt halt as one of the crewmen struck me (more or less good-naturedly) on the back, reminding me that there was still pumping to be done. I gripped the wheel with hands raw and red; our work was not finished.

But it was not long before the weather began to clear in earnest, and even if the sun did not exactly shine as in Mr. Clark Russell's verse, there was some suggestion that the very worst of our turmoil might be at an end. Even as the rain began to slow and the ocean began to quieten, though, we were confronted with a new curiosity on the water: morning had brought us within sight of another ship! Alas, this was not a colleague of ours passing by chance upon the wide sea, nor was she another survivor of the storm: she was a tremendous merchantman galleon which had been utterly wrecked, ripped apart by some unknown calamity and left to float in separate, scarcely connected halves upon the heaving waves. As the men rushed to the rail to get a better look at her, I felt the moisture evaporate in my mouth. This was an ominous portent indeed.

TELLS HOW WE ENCOUNTERED A DERELICT IN A STATE OF SINGULAR RUIN, AND HOW OUR SUBSEQUENT TROUBLES BEGAN

"Better to sink in boundless deeps, than float on vulgar shoals; and give me, ye gods, an utter wreck, if wreck I do."
-Herman Melville, *Mardi, and a Voyage Thither*

The vision of the wreck loomed large before us; it was as though the storm had carried us along, wave upon terrible wave, precisely to arrive at this queer desolation. For no sooner had we come within sight of the ship than the churning agitation of the water began to relent and the inexorable buffeting of the wind began to recede. Still, the derelict was disguised by a shroud of rain, and I could not ascertain much in the way of detail—nor the manner in which the ship had been broken. For the first time in hours, however, I felt as though I might walk about the deck without risk of being swept overboard. I seized upon this opportunity to approach the wheel, where a number of the crew were gathering. Even as I stumbled in that direction, I saw the bedraggled shapes of exhausted men sliding down the ropes, from which positions they had still been battling with the wind to secure the sails in the face of the tremendous tempest. The men were gathering in a nervous huddle as I approached, though the captain stood a few paces apart and could now be seen peering through the eye of an ornate brass spyglass.

"It is a ghost ship," spoke Mr. Fairchild, and he made the sign of the cross upon his breast—thus demonstrating to my increasingly disillusioned self that no link need necessarily exist between the pious and the virtuous. But I expected Mr. Fairchild's pronouncement to elicit a sharp reprimand from the captain, at any rate; sailors are famously superstitious, and the captain would certainly not want to risk his crew descending into a scrum of panic and dread at the mention of such a spectre. To my surprise, however, Captain Carrig did not visibly react to the quartermaster's suggestion. Instead he remained focused on the derelict through the lens of his spyglass, a very grim expression fastened upon his rain-lashed countenance.

Now a brief treatise upon "ghost ships" must be furnished, for it is "a belief in which all mariners are united," as Mr. Clark Russell has told me, and no reader will fully appreciate the apprehension with which we viewed the derelict unless he possesses some understanding of the legend itself. The very idea of a ghost ship is eminently disconcerting, even before any element of supernatural origin is brought to bear upon the topic. Such a ship is found to be entirely bereft of its crew; whether the sailors have succumbed to disease, starvation, mutiny, or some other more mysterious ailment, the end result is a ship which drifts about the seas according to its own whims, without so much as a living hand to guide its course. The annals of history are rife with examples[32], and the fear they engender in even the stoutest mariner is hardly to be wondered at. Practical considerations alone would dictate that one should not have liked to come into contact with a ship infested with disease, to name a single example, lest he be infected. But practical considerations alone are not foremost in the mind of the average sailor.

Mariners have long held that ghost ships are entangled with those unnatural forces which are widely supposed to haunt the seas. The agent of the supernatural varies according to the teller of the legend: it may be a burning merchantman that appears annually as a bright flame upon the horizon on the anniversary of its wreck; it may be an old pirate galleon crewed with the dead souls of those still lusting after untold riches; it may be a drifting French privateer with corpses nailed to its masts and its decks jellied with congealed blood. The infamous account of the *Flying Dutchman*

[32] The *Mary Celeste* was discovered in the Azores in 1872 after a month at sea. The crew was completely missing, though the ship was in good condition. Many theories of supernatural calamity were put forth to explain their disappearance; this is just one of several such "ghost ships" that would have informed Gordon's understanding of the legend.

even holds that its captain is doomed to roam the ocean for all time, and that to behold the ghastly light of this ship at night is as a portent of tragedy.[33] Now, the reader may ridicule such wild tales as nothing more than fantasy, but it is easy to dismiss them as such when one can take the light and comfort and warmth of land for granted. It is an altogether different matter upon the water. There the howling wind can ratchet into the scream of a banshee as it whips through the sails; there the creaking of the ship's timbers can sound as a man in his final agony; there the sea and sky fuse into infinity at the horizon until all the world seems an illusion; and there the scudding clouds can obscure the moon at night to such an extent that one wonders whether the day will ever come again. In these circumstances, even the basest superstitions begin to acquire a dreadful credibility, and the prospect of encountering a ghost ship in some unknown tract of ocean is enough to chill the blood of the stoutest skeptic.

Such was the mythology which weighed heavily upon the minds of the crew, and what little I knew of the legend served to send a ripple of apprehension down my own spine. I looked to the captain, still expecting that if anyone were to scoff at these stories, it would be him. But he continued to regard the derelict in an altogether very serious manner, and his steady gaze did not waver. Little did I suspect that he might know the ship for what she really was; his severe expression suggested no more than a sailor's innate wariness of the supernatural. But any such circumspection did not seem to affect the captain's decisions about our next course of action, at any rate; with a frown and a shake of his hairy head, he turned to face us at last. "We will approach her. There may yet be men alive."

"Alive?" repeated Mr. Fairchild in a tone of incredulity. He had gone as white as any ghost. "Look at her, captain. She is a ruined hulk. This is no recent wreck; none aboard can remain alive."

The captain looked hard at Mr. Fairchild, and suddenly there was a flame in his eyes which matched the fiery hue of his hair. He took two quick steps toward the defiant mariner and cuffed him

[33] William Clark Russell's own *The Death Ship* (1888) offers one treatment of this story.

hard across the face. Mr. Fairchild collapsed to the deck at once, crumpling with the force of this unexpected blow. He rubbed his cheek and glared at the captain with undisguised murder in his eyes. The captain took note of the quartermaster's expression and moved closer to his prone form.

"Well, then, Mr. Fairchild, if you mean to have a go at me, don't waste any time!" he roared. The prostrate seaman lowered his eyes, and the captain snorted. "If I say there may be men yet alive aboard that ship, then to that ship we go. I am not a heartless man—except perhaps to the very worst scum scraped from the bottom of my boots." He spat on the deck next to Mr. Fairchild, leaving us in no doubt to whom he was referring.

"Mr. Lawrence!" he barked. "Alter course and bring us around! We'll get a bit closer before we launch the boats." And here, unexpectedly, he turned to me. "Writer! I believe you suggested that you had some head for high places? Scamper up the rigging, if you would be so kind, and sing out the name of this wreck if you can discern it. Take my glass along, for it may be that even your young eyes will need some aid. But take care—for you will be repaid in equal measure for any damage inflicted upon it."

Having seen how quick the captain was to knock Mr. Fairchild to the deck for a simple objection, the reader will surely understand that I dared not disobey the captain in his current temper. I tucked his spyglass into a pocket of my jacket and made haste for the mainmast. Despite my inexperience, I really did have a knack for this sort of thing, and climbing the netting was less daunting than might be expected. Nonetheless, I very nearly managed to make a poor job of it, owing to the wetness and slickness of the ropes—for the storm had only recently subsided in the fullness of its intensity, and a light rain still fell. The spars and crossbeams were just as treacherous, and though I used them gratefully to haul myself higher, there was more than one occasion upon which I very nearly slipped into the open air. My hands were already chapped and raw, and the abrasive fibers of the saturated ropes dug into them cruelly. My breath soon came in heavy gasps as I subjected my unconditioned body to the exercise of climbing. At one juncture, about halfway up the mast, I made the dreadful mistake of looking down to the deck. It need hardly be said that the sight turned my stomach, for at this point I was approximately at the height of a four-story building on land. And yet I swallowed my fears and persevered, for this was just the sort of trial for which I had been tested at the Sankaty Head lighthouse, and it was just the sort of task I had rather bragged about being able to achieve—though I had underestimated just how difficult the ascent would prove, particularly when factoring in the nauseous rolling of the troubled sea.

Presently I reached the crow's nest; I clambered inside, where I was very grateful to be surrounded by a railing to which I could cling. The sensation of standing on one's own two feet at this extreme height, rather than clutching the rigging with four limbs, is one which I cannot altogether recommend, though I will say that it was absolutely unique in my experience. I still felt the rocking of the ship beneath me, but the impression was somehow reduced by the tremendous height of the mast, as though I were standing at the end of a long lever which was serving to reduce the gyrations of the ship below me. Looking down, I was surprised to see just how small the other men appeared to be; whether they were gazing up at me or looking across to the wreck was impossible to discern from this vantage. The perspective from which I viewed my surroundings had a queer flattening effect; the men seemed to be robbed of all height and were as but insects scurrying about the deck, obscured by a veil of mist and rain. The sea itself presented something of a singular aspect, as well; it stretched featureless from horizon to horizon just as it did from the deck of the *Melville*, but from this outlook even the white-capped waves to the west, where the storm still blew with unabated fury, appeared now flat and diminished.

It was a heady, dizzying sight, and it filled me with unprecedented emotion—a full description of which would require me to exhaust several more pages in the telling. Alas, I had not been ordered to the top of the mast to take my leisure or to collect my thoughts, but rather to accomplish an identification of the wreck. Accordingly, I removed the (thankfully undamaged) spyglass from my pocket and set about surveying the ship astern of us. I quickly perceived that the captain had been wise to turn this vantage point to his benefit; the height of the mast allowed me to see more of the ship than had been possible from below. Indeed, with the aid of the glass, I could see more detail than I would have wished. For the derelict was wholly wrecked, and not recently; whatever had caused the ship to flounder, it had since been pummeled by the relentless pounding of the waves and wind and now lay upon the ocean in two great halves. Peering between these halves and across a landscape of splintered wood, I wondered what unthinkable force had split the ship in twain. But wait—I fancied that I could see a bright streak upon the monochrome uniformity of the ruined deck, even withstanding the curtain of rain which obscured my view and served to mute all colors. I surmised that this must be some bit of sailor's cloth that was as yet unbleached by the weather, or perhaps a growth of coral rising through the ship's beams—after all, was it not likely that the ship had wrecked on some reef or shoal? Consequently, I dismissed this incongruity and resumed my search of the ship, scrutinizing the wreck for anything which would name her. At length, though the condition of the ship was pitiable, I discerned that I could only just make out some lettering on her stern. I squinted hard enough to hurt my eyes, for it was not easy to be sure of what I had seen, owing to the interference of the persistent rain. Despite my best efforts, a few letters remained obscure—but those which I could identify left me satisfied that no other interpretation of the ship's name were possible.

"She is the *Veronica!*" I shouted to the men below me. How the captain heard me I shall never know, but I perceived that he did by the way in which he suddenly spun around and leaned over the railing, as though this would afford him a better view of the wreck. Picking him out amongst the rest of the men was no difficult task, owing to his especially vivid orange hair. With the terrible knowledge I now hold, I should very much like to have seen his face when all his intermingled hopes and fears were thus confirmed. But having accomplished my mission, I did not linger in the crow's nest; I took a final sweeping glance across the ocean spread out before me, trusting that the memory would serve as a souvenir of my adventure—which I did not care to repeat. I then began my descent through the rigging, which proved to be more difficult than the reverse, for the downward momentum of my progress made me feel each slip of the rope all the more acutely. My ordeal passed without incident, however, and I soon found myself standing securely upon the ship's deck once again.

I quickly learned that the captain had not been idle while I had taken the time to effect a careful descent from the mast. The men were busy running to and fro, outfitting two of the ship's four boats in preparation for departure. Captain Carrig himself was shouting out orders, and I could see Mr. Lawrence's arms straining to bring the ship around to achieve an advantageous position for launching the boats. Presently we came to within a cable's length of the wreck, and as the captain began to verbalize his plans, I realized that it would be critical for me to be amongst the men sent over to the *Veronica.* How could I miss the chance to report firsthand on whatever might be discovered there? Though I felt a pang of uneasiness flutter within my breast, I determined that it would not affect my resolve.

"Mr. Derrick! Mr. Taggart!" the captain ordered. "I want you both in one of the boats. And take Mr. Craft with you; we may find some use for him yet." I don't believe I have mentioned this lattermost sailor in my narrative until this juncture; he was an especially dull-witted fellow, but one of enormous stamina and stature. Had I been thinking more clearly, I may have wondered what the captain expected to find on the *Veronica* that would necessitate the participation of this man and his brute strength. Alas, I was entirely too occupied with ensuring that I myself had a place on one of the boats. "Mr. Lawrence, I leave the *Melville* in your care; I trust that I will not be gone long enough for you to sink her."

"Captain!" I interrupted, and I perceived from his utterly flummoxed expression that he had not expected any input from me in this business. He arched a bushy eyebrow at me, and I fished rather lamely for an argument that would convince him of my aim. "I would accompany you to the derelict, if I am to record—"

"Very well. You shall be in the second boat with me. It may be that this adventure will find a paragraph or two in your journal. Besides," he added with just a hint of a smile, "You would very likely stow away if I told you no." The reader can well imagine my surprise at being so neatly preempted, but the captain's mind was already moving on to other matters. "And William!" he said after a pause for consideration, very nearly as though it were an afterthought.

"Sir!" my young friend said, jumping to attention, his face lit with excitement.

"Find that damned doctor, will you? I want him with me, too."

His hopes dashed, William nonetheless dutifully ran off to look for the doctor, who had not been seen abovedeck since the storm first began in earnest. To own the truth, I rather suspect that he was sea-sick—why he had ever agreed to ply his trade on the ocean presented a fine paradox indeed. Nevertheless, William returned within a few minutes with the doctor in tow, the latter looking decidedly green about the gills. And thus the boarding party was now fully assembled, with three men for each boat. I daresay that we could have done with a single boat, but I guessed that the captain was saving space in the event that we encountered any living men aboard the *Veronica*—though privately I did not think this very likely. We clambered into the vessels with our hoods pulled down tightly over our heads, for it seemed as though the wind had kicked up, lending the storm some measure of its former fitful passion. The lowering of the boats was supervised by Mr. Lawrence, with the assistance of several other crewman, and it was only moments before we found ourselves bobbing about in a decidedly choppy sea. In my own boat, the task of rowing was taken up by the captain and the doctor—though the doctor did not seem especially suited to the task, he made a better job of it than I could have done, for my own limbs were still shaking with exhaustion from my climb up and down the mainmast.

The aspect presented by the sea from the perspective of a ship's boat cannot be compared with my vantage point from atop the crow's nest. Indeed, it seemed hardly possible that I had climbed so high and come so low in a single day. My time for reflection upon this contrast was limited, however, as Mr. Lawrence had really done a commendable job in bringing us about, and we had but very little distance to cover. I resolved that I would thank him profusely for his efforts, as traveling in the boat was an altogether less comfortable mode of transport than on the larger ship; here, one feels every dip and swell of the waves, and there is no question of escaping the spray of salt about one's face or the water that fills one's boots. And so I was quite pleased when we reached the wreck; Mr. Taggart's boat had arrived first, owing to the vigorous rowing of Mr. Craft, and I watched the mate make his boat fast about the *Veronica*'s hulk by looping lengths of rope about the cleats ranged along the ship's loose timbers. Mr. Derrick and Mr. Craft, meanwhile, helped to pull our own boat in, whereupon the captain began at once to secure our own boat as I clambered out with the doctor. When the boats had been anchored to the captain's satisfaction, the six of us clustered closely together, and shouted to one another in order to be heard over the pounding of the rain.

"Mr. Craft!" the captain thundered. "You will stay behind and watch over the boats. I do not like the look of these planks, and shouldn't trust that they won't rot away and snap cleanly off behind our backs. That should leave us in a pretty pickle indeed."

He looked around, taking stock of our situation, his hair and beard slick and matted with rainwater. "The *Veronica* seems to have split nearly in half, and as we have landed on the bow end of her, we've a treacherous trek ahead of us. We'll check the forecastle first, naturally enough, but it is my intent to proceed all the way to the cabin and the officer's quarters in the stern. If we are to find any…survivors, that is where we will find them. Depend upon it." I imagined that he had been about to say something else, but there was no time for speculation. With a final admonition to "step carefully," the captain led us off across the deck of the derelict. I cast a look back at Mr. Craft as he stood watch over the boats, his hand resting upon the gunwale of the foremost, and he gave me a brief word of encouragement; I hardly suspected that it was the last time I should speak with him.

My attentions were soon occupied by the difficult task of finding sure footing across the deck of the *Veronica.* Due to the nature of the wreck, each half of the ship had sunken partway into the water and now presented a challenging angle of some thirty-five or forty degrees. The way was not made easier by the slickness of the wood, which had been pummeled by the corrosive action of salt and water until it was just as slippery as if it had been painted with grease. We turned our feet sideways and took only short steps; our progress was slow, and at times we were forced to crawl up the slope on hands and knees. Presently we reached part of the ship where the foremast shrouds had collapsed onto the deck; the mast itself was snapped off and bobbed about the water to the port side of the wreck, still partially entangled in the netting.

The ropes were of some use in gaining traction as we continued to climb, and within the space of about ten minutes we had reached the closed hatch leading to the forecastle.

As the carpenter, it was determined that Mr. Derrick would be best qualified to determine whether we could risk a descent into the crew's quarters. He flipped open the hatch and peered into the dark interior of the forecastle, borrowing a lantern with which the captain had been leading us through the early morning dimness. Looking over his shoulder, I perceived that the steps were crooked and that at least a few of them had become partially detached. I felt confident that Mr. Derrick would pronounce them as unsafe, and a wave of relief washed over me at the prospect of avoiding a trip into that black cavity in the bowels of the wreck.

"The steps will serve," Mr. Derrick said shortly. "But I should only be comfortable sending the lightest amongst us, for I judge that they will not bear the weight of a man fully grown." He turned to me. "I believe that uniquely qualifies you, my boy." I could scarcely credit it, but he was even smiling at me.

"I couldn't possibly," I protested at once, turning to the captain with this entreaty. "You have said that any survivors would be found in the captain's cabin, or else in the officer's quarters. Surely this is but an unnecessary risk."

The captain's hand fell heavily on my shoulder. "I have also told you that each man has his place aboard my ship. It may be that today you have found yours; I will readily concede that you have not been entirely useless this morning." Here his eyes narrowed, and I fancied that I perceived something of a monomaniacal fury smoldering in their depths—though it were as yet banked to embers. "Should you wish to remain useful, you will not argue with me any further. I will leave no hold of this ship unexplored until I am satisfied in my search, and any man who frustrates me in that effort should find the remainder of our time together very unpleasant indeed."

Needless to say, I found this speech to be neither particularly encouraging nor motivating—but I dared not balk any longer before a direct order from so fearsome a personage. It seemed as though any kindliness and sentimentality which I had seen in the captain had been utterly replaced with a singular intensity; indeed, the transformation could be traced back to the first appearance of the wreck off our stern. And so I accepted the proffered lantern from the outstretched hand of Mr. Derrick and, without further equivocation, began my descent into the black depths of the *Veronica*'s forecastle. My steps were tentative, and I braced my hand not holding the lantern against the wall in order to steady myself—though I do not think that this should have prevented me from falling, had the steps really broken. Nonetheless, it offered some illusion of security, and if the planks beneath my feet did creak and groan something horrible, as well as shift alarmingly under my weight, at least they did not come apart and plunge me directly to the bottom. And so at length I reached the floor of the forecastle safely enough, whereupon I held out the flickering glow of the lantern before me. In truth, it did very little to penetrate the utter blackness that pervaded the living quarters of the men before the mast. The bunks and cots of sailors loomed at me out of the pitch as I carefully stepped through the forecastle, checking each plank of the floor before placing my feet. But they were only intermittently visible, appearing briefly in the tiny corona of light which emanated from the lantern before fading back into the murk as I passed by.

I soon became aware of a crashing, churning sound that puzzled me greatly. I thought right away that it must be the sound of some liquid, for such was its character, but I was at a loss to explain its source. As it happened, I was not long to be kept in suspense; passing the sea-chests arranged along a far wall, I observed a large black patch upon the floor which did not resolve into the familiar wood of the forecastle as I approached with my lantern. Ever wary in this forbidding environment, I ceased my forward movement and crouched down, bringing the light nearer to the strange space, devoid as it was of all feature and color. Imagine my surprise to discover that it was a great hole rent in the wood! The cavity was some fifteen feet across and was ringed with splintered, twisted beams; these ruined bits of floor were oriented directly upwards in the direction of the main deck, immediately leading me to the inescapable conclusion that the forecastle had been punctured from below by some tremendous force. Fascinated despite myself, I leaned forward over the hole, only to discover that it carried all the way through the half-deck below and ultimately into the roiling sea. I could even discern bits of white-flecked foam below as they caught the paltry glow of my lantern from afar. This, then, was the mysterious liquid sound I had heard: the sound of the very ocean itself, for the forecastle was now connected directly to the water by this empty shaft punched through the *Veronica*'s hull.

It need hardly be said that I did not like to think how this hole should have come to be. I stepped back and was suddenly overcome with a violent tremor borne of the fear and peculiar loneliness of this empty ship—for I was utterly convinced that we should find no living man aboard. My convictions were reinforced by my subsequent discoveries as I stepped around the ship's great wound, giving it a wide berth, and continued to explore the forecastle. Still trembling, I reached the far side of the hole and found a scattered collection of tools arranged in the queerest fashion. It was as though they had been dropped at random, rather than arranged or stowed for storage; and in the act of looking more closely, I perceived that the collection was comprised of such a random array of implements as to defy any sense of organization. There were many tools of the carpenter's trade, which no doubt Mr. Derrick would have been better qualified to identify. Those which were familiar to me included the following: a broad axe, a cutting axe, an assortment of mallets, several adzes, and even a chisel or two. But there were other sailors' tools scattered amongst this array: a drawing knife, an iron square, two or three boat-hooks, and even a much-splintered and broken oar, which must have originated with one of the *Veronica*'s boats.

A terrible picture began to coalesce in my mind's eye. The astute reader will no doubt have already reached a similar conclusion. This image sprang to my mind with a sudden presentiment of horror, and I would have turned away from this unwanted knowledge, but the revelation was as undeniable as it was unbidden. Though the forecastle was now empty, it would not have been so when the great hole was first hewn into the ship's hull from below. I could see a half-ring of sailors assembled around this hole, as plainly as though they stood before me now, crying out amidst the flying bits of wood and clutching whatever implement was to hand. Perhaps the ship's carpenter had had time to raid his sea-chest and provision the other sailors with his own tools; perhaps they had merely scrambled for whatever weapons their grasping fingers could clutch in the dimness and the sudden chaos. But it was certain that their hammers and their axes, their hooks and their oars had proved futile against whatever unknowable *thing* had risen from the sea and into the forecastle with locomotive force—for not a body remained in this forlorn and desolate hold. I could see weapons dropped from nerveless fingers; I could hear the screams of bewildered, terrified men as they were pulled from their feet and dragged into the water waiting below; I even fancied that I could feel the cold, hard shell of the abomination that had manifested itself here not so very long ago.

I was bathed in a cold sweat, and before I had gathered my wits about me, I was running through the forecastle. I tripped and stumbled on the broken bits of floor that ringed the great hole, all semblance of caution cast aside, and I sprinted for the steps as quickly as my trembling legs would permit. I climbed the stairs out of the forecastle after the manner of a beast, using all four limbs, and the lantern bounced senselessly in my hand and sent a wild cascade of light and shadow across the wall with the passage of each step—before finally winking out just as I came gasping and shaking into the dim mid-morning light of the main deck and the bewildered company of my shipmates. They accosted me with a barrage of questions, but I only half-heard their voices, so thickly was my heart pounding in my ears, and it was some time before I had recovered sufficiently to answer them. The explanation which I furnished must have been incomplete and fragmentary in nature, for I was met only with confusion and—incredibly—amusement, particularly from Mr. Derrick and Mr. Taggart.

"We'll make a sailor of you yet, with tall tales like that," said Mr. Derrick. "But whence did this vision come? How can a few scattered boat-hooks have led you to such an inconceivable conclusion?" His eyes were not unkind, and if he were amused, I do not think it was at my expense. But his disbelief was writ plainly upon his face.

"I cannot say whence it came," I said. Though as I record this now, I have my own particular suspicions—as will my reader, I think, when my tale has been told in full. "I can only say that I was seized with a sudden certainty which was not to be denied, and I was filled from head to toe with dread, and I cannot doubt but that the men of the *Veronica* have met with a violent end."

"Now here," said the doctor, and it occurred to me that he must be remembering how he had diagnosed me with a concussion, and how it followed that he would attribute my recent experience to an hallucination. I could only hope that he would not mention it aloud, for his examination had been conducted before Captain Carrig had been made aware of my stowing away. I did not like to think how the captain would react if he discovered that he had been duped. "You must appreciate that we live in a material world," the doctor continued. "It is true that certain members of my profession have begun to give weight to dreams and visions; to place these experiences under the banner of science and to draw quite radical conclusions from them. But this practice belongs more appropriately within the purview of the *Wahrsager*—you would call them fortune-tellers or mystics. The wise doctor does better to concern himself with the practical world, and premonitions do not enter into it. I would suggest instead that you are experiencing nothing more than a nervous reaction to the circumstances of this wreck—which are altogether quite dreadful enough without bringing anything *unnatürlich* into it."

"For my own part, I am not so sure," said the captain unexpectedly.

I turned to him in surprise, but his eyes were hooded and distant, and he was not looking in my direction.

"I rather think, on the whole, that it is a good thing that we have left Mr. Craft to watch over the boats." I followed the line of his gaze even back to where the boats were moored, dipping and nodding restlessly against the splintered hull of the derelict. Mr. Craft himself was just visible; he appeared to be prowling restlessly between the two boats. "We shall continue nevertheless, though I will caution each of you to avoid complacency; I know not what we may find here."

I had begun to feel a bit better at this juncture; though I was not convinced that my vision was hallucinatory in nature, I was at least comforted by the presence of such obviously capable men as the captain and Mr. Derrick. And so I voiced no further protest as we continued our traversal across the *Veronica*'s main deck, though our progress was slow and halting, owing to the perilously slick surface of the wood beneath our boots.

At length, we reached the point at which the merchantman

had been cloven in twain. The deck here was canted to such an angle that remaining upright was nearly impossible, but I felt drawn by some strange need to creep closer and peer over the edge of this unnatural precipice. Call it the curiosity of a journalist, perhaps, or merely the whim of a boy too careless to know better. But when I reached the cracked and broken beams, crawling on my hands and knees, and peeped down into the great rift that had wrecked the *Veronica*, I felt my stomach drop precipitously inside me. I do not think that I had really appreciated the size of a sailing ship until I saw the interior of the *Veronica* exposed and laid bare to the elements. The wreck had been split open in the middle of her hold; I could see directly into the cavities of these compartments; I could see countless casks and chests and supplies rocking about with the agitation of the waves acting upon the ship. Even as I watched, a cracked wine barrel rolled through one such compartment, catching briefly on a lip of ruined wood, and made its final plunge into the greedy ocean below. The splash that it made was infinitesimal, and it was this, I think, more than anything, that brought home to me how very small I was, and how very great the scope of the tragedy that had befallen the *Veronica*.

As I was occupied with the humbling experience of understanding my own insignificance for the first time in my young life, the other men had busied themselves in the altogether more productive task of determining just how we were to bridge the gap between the stern and bow halves of the wreck. The distance we had to accomplish was not especially great: perhaps ten or twelve feet at the outside. The problem was in the sheer fragility of the deck. As one approached the edge, one's footing grew increasingly unreliable, and it would have been foolhardy to trust the rotten, waterlogged beams to hold any great weight. I watched Mr. Derrick pace back and forth, to the extent that he was able to do so upon the dramatic angle of the deck, while he pondered this conundrum. For you see, the captain had left this matter in the hands of the carpenter; it seemed that he had chosen his companions wisely, after all. The big man ran his hands through the tangled mass of his beard as he grappled with the problem. Finally, it seemed that he had reached a solution, for he turned to us with the light of an idea dawning bright upon his countenance.

"Gordon, do you fancy another trip into the forecastle?"

"I most certainly do not."

The carpenter chuckled. "I'm afraid there's no help for it, lad. I'll need you to cut down three or four sailors' hammocks for me. There's rope all about this damned ship, but the forecastle is about the only place where it'll be halfway dry." He rummaged about in a bag slung over his shoulder and produced a small hand-axe, passing it to me by the handle. "But be quick about it—and take the doctor with you, for you can pass your cuttings up the stair to him as you go. In the meantime, I'll do my own part of the job here." He removed another, larger cutting axe from the bag and cast a glance around the deck. I was again reminded of a lion surveying its domain and looking about for a likely meal; I daresay I will always remember Mr. Derrick for this enormous vitality which characterized his every movement.

But I hefted the smaller axe in my own hand doubtfully. "Surely there is rope of a better quality aboard our own ship? I should not like to trust my life to the *Veronica*'s hammocks; they are as likely to be rotted through as not." I hoped that this feeble protest did not completely betray my cowardly reluctance to reenter the dark domain of the wreck's long-vanished sailors. To my dismay, though, it was here that the captain stepped into the conversation—and a manic, eager look was on his face.

"I will not postpone any longer, boy, nor will I waste my time in returning to the *Melville* when every minute may be of critical importance. Furthermore, in matters of carpentry, we will trust to the ship's carpenter. I have every confidence that his plan will be quite practicable." He turned to the doctor. "Escort our young friend to his task and see that you assist him where you can. Time is of the essence now more than ever." He turned his back to us, our compliance assumed, and began to make plans with Mr. Derrick and Mr. Taggart. I found myself meeting the doctor's eye; he gave me a rueful smile and a sort of futile half-shrug. I sighed and began picking my way slowly back down the wildly tilted deck in the direction of the forecastle hatch.

"The captain, he is *eigensinnig*," said the doctor as he followed behind me. He grunted as his feet slipped. Steadying himself, he continued: "There is nothing to be gained from a contest of wills with that sort of fellow." A fondness in his voice belied the criticism his words might otherwise have represented.

"I am grateful that you did not mention my concussion," I said honestly. "I don't know whether I could have withstood the captain's wrath piled atop the dread which I already feel for this job."

"Make no mistake," the doctor said, drawing abreast of me as we reached our destination (for our progress was much faster in this direction). "There is no phenomenon aboard this ship or anywhere else that cannot be attributed to a natural explanation. I am quite certain there is nothing for you to dread."

I will spare the reader the tedium of recounting my second fearful descent into the *Veronica*'s forecastle. Suffice it to say that, while the experience was sufficiently frightening, I did not experience a recurrence of the specific vision which had left me so recently aghast and trembling. The crew's quarters were a lonely environment which had taken on something of a sad and tragic character, but they did not press a second premonition of doom upon my senses. I was therefore able to carry out Mr. Derrick's orders with relative ease, for his axe was oiled and sharp, and the fibers of the hammocks were actually reasonably dry, owing to the fact that they had been sheltered from the rain in this mostly-closed environment. I sent each hammock up the stairs to the doctor as I finished with it; in total, we retrieved four of them from the forecastle. We staggered a bit under their weight, for they were cumbersome to carry, but it was not overlong before we returned to the captain and the carpenter with our prizes in tow.

By this point, Mr. Derrick had already cut and pried a number of choice planks from the wreck's main deck. Even as I watched, he was engaged in the use of a small hand-saw in order to trim them and fit them neatly together. He looked up as we approached, and his teeth flashed from beneath his beard in a grin. "Well done, boys. Now lend me a hand with this beam." Though the carpenter's strength was prodigious, it required all five of us to hoist the bridge that he had constructed. The beams salvaged from the deck had been cunningly fit and locked together in such a way that each piece exerted pressure upon another, and none could slip from its fittings. I do not pretend to understand the method by which this was accomplished; I can only say that Mr. Derrick had chosen his vocation well. Once we had laid this contraption across the gap between the halves of the wreck, we had quite a serviceable bridge indeed. But Mr. Derrick was not satisfied with what, to him, represented a rudimentary effort. He proceeded to cut some thinner beams from the ship's rail; taking these and an armful of netting from the hammocks, he took a first step onto the bridge.

"A carpenter should always be the first to test his work," he said around a mouthful of nails. But the bridge held, as he must have known it would, and he quickly set about the installation of a makeshift rail on either side of it. To this rail he attached the hammocks, which he skillfully tied off at both top and bottom. I must admit that I was somewhat awestruck at the way he scampered nimbly across this precarious bridge of his own construction, hammering and tying and stepping back to assess his work. In the space of an hour, it was complete: an entirely respectable bridge, complete with two rails and a safety netting, made only from components retrieved from the very wreck upon which we stood. And so my reader will understand that even I, a self-confessed coward, did not experience an undue degree of apprehension as the five of us duly filed across the bridge—even as I passed ten feet of open space with the sea boiling and frothing beneath me. Such was my faith in Mr. Derrick's work; a faith which was echoed by the rest of the company.

"I say," said the mate. "You've done a fine job indeed, Mr. Derrick. Lord knows you've had little enough to do on this voyage so far, and I don't mind admitting that the quartermaster has been driven very near to apoplexy at the thought of the wages you've been earning without putting in the commensurate work. But I daresay this job (not to mention your work on the hull) pays for all!" Mr. Taggart thumped Mr. Derrick heartily upon the back, causing the carpenter to stumble into the rail of his makeshift bridge and very nearly put the soundness of its construction to the test. The mate pulled him back to center and grinned a little sheepishly. Mr. Derrick scowled at him, but it was a good-natured scowl, and I could see that he was proud of his accomplishment.

"Now, what's this?" said the captain presently.

We had crossed the bridge safely and were now gathered at the top of the stern half of the wreck, which presented a similar aspect to the bow half in that it also rested at an oblique angle, sloping dangerously down to the captain's cabin and officers' berth below. I could see at once that which had attracted the captain's attention: a broad furrow of some garishly bright purple substance had traced a path neatly down the center of the main deck. This path ran all the way down the ship, even to the cabin. I crouched next to Captain Carrig, who was already bent in examination of this unusual sight. The purple substance made an uneven line across the wood; it was better than four inches in width. It presented a furry, mossy sort of aspect and was comprised of uneven clumps, with fine filaments of a hair-like substance sprouting from them. It was splotched throughout with little white blooms, which somehow seemed to suggest the unfurling of flowers and the speckling of mold simultaneously. I recognized that this must have been the patch of bright color I had spotted from the mainmast of the *Melville.*

"How very curious," I said slowly, and for some reason my own voice sounded strange and distant in my ears. I reached out a finger to touch the spray of purple growth upon the wood. To my surprise, I found my wrist grasped in the iron grip of the captain's hand. He met my gaze and very slowly shook his head at me.

"Doctor," the captain commanded, without breaking eye contact with me. "Now is the hour for your expertise. I would know what manner of substance is before us, and whether it is the same."

Well, I thought that was rather a strange thing to say. The same as what?

But the doctor seemed to take his meaning, for he presently crouched beside the two of us. "It is the same, and no mistake. Do you not recognize it?"

"I fear I did."

"It is not a doctor which you require, but a surgeon." He extracted a small glass vial from an inside pocket of his jacket. Then he rummaged about in a shoulder bag and removed a set of gleaming instruments wrapped in black linen. From this bundle he selected a small scalpel, which shone with a luminous light even in the rain and gloom which hung heavily about us. Unstopping the vial, he lay both the tube and cork aside on the deck, far enough from the violet substance to avoid any risk of accidental contact. Then he slipped on a pair of gloves, which he obtained from the same shoulder bag, and very carefully excised a small amount of the purple growth using the tiniest, most precise movements of the scalpel. I could see that he had chosen a piece of the material which contained both the purple mold and the pale blooms, as well as the short, slender hairs which sprung from both. The doctor turned towards me unexpectedly.

"Tongs," he barked.

I complied wordlessly, handing him the indicated tool from his linen-wrapped collection. As I watched, the doctor used the tongs to gently place the sample of fungus into the vial. Then he stoppered the tube, placed it down on the deck, and removed his gloves in such a fashion as to wrap the scalpel and tongs within them. Thus shielded from contamination, the instruments were replaced within their wrappings and bundled back into the doctor's bag. As for the vial, he held it up to one critical eye—the eye which was not aided by his monocle—before replacing it into his jacket pocket. All told, the operation was over within the space or two or three minutes, though it felt rather longer, owing to the delicacy of the proceedings.

The doctor stood. "There are a few singular qualities to this substance—even now it squirms and moves inside my vial—but we will learn no more until I am given the opportunity to study it in detail. But I cannot say how long it will remain, ah, fresh, once removed from the main body." He looked about the wreck with a skeptical eye. "If we have further investigations to conduct, we would do best to effect them with all due haste."

"You know that we do," the captain said evenly. "Now: I can plainly see that the growth terminates at the door to the captain's cabin ahead. What's more, there are a few instances along its path where it seems to swell into the shape of an unusual mound, which I should like to examine. I may even require you to take another sample, though I rather think I already know what we should find." Standing, Captain Carrig turned to face the rest of us. "In accordance with the doctor's wishes, we will henceforth move a little faster. Mr. Taggart and Mr. Derrick will proceed directly to the officers' quarters to determine whether any crewmen remain alive. Keep your wits about you and do not touch any of this violet growth. I will expect a thorough report of what you find. The doctor and the boy will come with me to examine one of these mounds before searching the cabin." When no one moved immediately, the captain gave a great scowl. "Unless you'd rather pass the rest of the day on this godforsaken hulk?"

With rueful grins and downcast eyes, Mr. Derrick and Mr. Taggart hurried off down the deck toward the officers' berth, moving as quickly as they could manage along the steeply pitched deck. I accompanied the captain and doctor as ordered, stepping carefully to avoid any collision with the brilliant moss. I did not wholly understand what contamination we had to fear from the unknown substance; it was curious, to be sure, but it did not seem especially sinister. Nonetheless, I followed the captain's example and stepped widely around the trail of fungus and any of the multiple tenuous offshoots which extended an inch or two from its main course.

Presently we reached the first of the peculiar mounds where the moss had accumulated in a sort of great deposit; there must have been four or five of them in total scattered across the *Veronica*'s stern. It was as though some unknown coagulating agent had caused the substance to build up in these particular spots. The mound we examined was perhaps two feet in height and thrice as long. It resembled nothing so much as a heap of coral which had somehow amassed itself on land; the tiny threadlike filaments which sprouted from the moss in uneven clumps waved in the misty air like so many sea anemones casting about in an ocean current. I cannot say that I experienced any presentiment regarding the identity of the object, even in light of the term which the captain had chosen to describe it. To me it seemed a mere curiosity, and I was eager that we should be done with it and return to the *Melville* as soon as could be arranged.

"It is not altered in structure," said the doctor, leaning in closely to the mound with his hands clasped behind his back. He squinted, fixing his monocle more firmly in place. "Maybe it is denser, maybe not." He looked at the captain. "Shall I extract a second specimen?"

The captain did not reply immediately. He was bent over, examining the far end of the mound, where it sloped abruptly back to the deck and rejoined the main trail of much thinner moss, progressing in what was very nearly a straight line to the cabin. He stared for several moments, his head inclining by a measure of degrees as he followed the path of the alien bloom. At length, he looked back at the doctor. "No," he said finally, and the tone of distraction in his voice matched with the faraway expression upon his countenance. "I think we must proceed. Better to let well enough alone, I think, lest we come to regret prying too deeply."

Well, this was another strange thing to say! Until now the captain's curiosity had been insatiable; why otherwise should we have set foot on an obviously desolate ship in the first place? It was almost as though the captain had reached some foreboding conclusion about the nature of the peculiar mounds, or even about the nature of the very substance which formed them, and had decided that it was better that we should not share in the knowledge. My reader may begin to wonder how I could be so dim; how I, who had already experienced a terrible vision in the forecastle of the wreck, could fail to make the obvious and horrible deduction regarding that which rested beneath the lilac-colored growth. I can only plead youth, and maybe inexperience, as I have so many times already—though as things turned out, there were elements to this puzzle that no sane man could have been expected to predict. Would that I could now return to this state of innocence!

But it was not to be; our investigation was destined to march toward its grim finale. The captain presently led us past the first mound, and then another, and then another. Their placement caused the trail of the mold-like substance to divert from its direct course, as the heaps were not arranged all in a row, but the strange stuff always returned to a line leading right to the door of the captain's cabin. Approaching this door, I saw that it was recessed slightly into the bulk of the deckhouse. To my surprise, the captain rapped smartly upon the door with the knuckles of his left hand; it was as though he legitimately believed, or maybe hoped, that he might receive an answer from therein. I supposed it may have been the simple courtesy which one captain extends to another before entering his berth; even if the second captain is almost certainly deceased. It may also have been one final hesitation before breaching that threshold; in light of what we discovered inside, I am inclined to accept this explanation for his unexpected gesture: it afforded him one last moment of ignorance before all terrible realities must be confronted and accepted.

Needless to say, no response answered Captain Carrig's

knock. And so he eased open the door with a push of his hand, and we filed into the cabin, being careful to avoid the violet trail which crossed the doorstep and led into the gloomy interior. Although the light was dim, the cabin was possessed of large stern-facing windows which extended from the floor to the ceiling. The windows were grimy and cracked, and in some places the panes of glass were missing altogether, but they admitted a certain amount of murky, filtered light into the room. A quick scan of the quarters revealed furnishings that were somewhat more comfortable those that Captain Carrig himself enjoyed aboard the *Melville*: there was a bed along the port wall, a dressing table with numerous cabinets and shelves built into its base, and a writing desk with various inkwells and charts still scattered across its surface. There was even a section of the cabin partitioned by a dividing wall which, I surmised, was meant to serve as the captain's own private toilet. Were it not for the room's gruesome centerpiece, our own captain might well be forgiven for envying the spaciousness and luxury of this cabin. But none amongst us could appreciate these features, astounded as we were by the sight which greeted our horrorstruck eyes.

Two corpses sat in the center of the berth, their skeletal arms thrown about one another in an eternal embrace. They were clad in simple clothes that had been rotted away by the humidity of the saltwater atmosphere. I could see at a glance that the dead were once man and woman; one wore the remains of a gray cotton dress after the country style, the other a maroon waistcoat, its buttons rusted and dangling by the thinnest of threads. Of their flesh, only scraps had endured the indeterminate time of their postmortem vigil: a bit of skin clinging to the exposed cartilage of the man's nose; the pale white wrist of the woman's arm protected beneath the shelter of her wristwatch; a sprout of wiry hair protruding from the man's trouser cuff. The rest of them was bone, and my eyes were held by their wasted skulls: all gaping eye sockets and leering jaws, capped with terrible wigs of dead hair that had long since turned green in the cold, wet wreck of the *Veronica*'s cabin. The corpses sat with their legs crossed beneath them, as though they had seen the agent of their death approaching and had decided that it were better to await it with dignity intact.

To my shock, Captain Carrig loosed a sudden gut-wrenching

howl of anguish! I do not believe I shall ever hear a sound containing more hopelessness and despair than that man's cry. Even as I watched, he made to rush forward to the bodies—but he was swiftly restrained by the doctor, who seized one of the captain's arms and began chastising him loudly in the German tongue. As a contest between the two men could only end with the captain's superior strength winning the day, I stepped forward and laid hold of the captain's other arm. Together, we wrestled him into compliance, though it was no easy task, and I shouted again and again to remind the captain that he could under no circumstances be permitted to touch the corpses.

For the two bodies' bones were covered—indeed, completely encased—in the bright purple moss that had led us here. The growth snaked into their open mouths, whereupon it trailed visibly down the delicate bones of their throats and into their ribs, which poked here and there through the mask of mold and fabric. It shook and pulsated with animation which I could not wholly attribute to the wind blowing through the broken windows of the cabin; it trembled upon the outstretched fingers of the dead man and upon the tips of the dead woman's shoes. It was a brilliant bloom, a tropical riot, an unbelievable profusion of color—and the danger it represented finally, irrevocably, pressed itself upon me.

"This substance is death," I said softly.

"We have our report," came the sudden voice of Mr. Taggart. "Though there's little enough to be said. The officers' quarters are utterly barren…" he trailed off into a stunned silence. I was jostled from behind as the mate and the carpenter forced their way into the cabin from behind me, but I did not turn around. I was unable to wrest my eyes from the deadly splendor of the moss which had enveloped these unfortunate souls on some distant, fearful day. For a moment, utter silence reigned in the chamber; the only sounds were the occasional gust of wind, now almost spent of its fury as it rattled the window panes, as well as the gentle creaking of the ship's timbers as its weight shifted and settled upon the sea which had spelled its doom. And in truth, what was there to be said? What light could this handful of sailors shed upon so dreadful a scene? Even the captain himself was speechless, his entire body trembling with suppressed emotion—and, admittedly, I was baffled by his severe reaction to the scene. It was horrible enough, to be sure, but it was as though Captain Carrig was personally aggrieved by the death of the unknown persons. I should have liked to dissect this problem and puzzle over its connotations, but at the moment I was altogether more concerned with escaping the wreck and leaving these tragic figures behind us.

"I say," spoke Mr. Derrick, the first of us to break the heavy silence. "What is that?" He pointed a thick, callused finger in the direction of the corpses, and I realized that there was an element to their configuration which I had overlooked in my initial revulsion, owing to the advanced state of their decomposition. I have said that the bodies were entwined in one another's arms; to be more specific, one arm of each skeleton was slung about the shoulders of the other. In their free hands, though, was clutched an object which had hitherto escaped my notice. It was a queer device of carved wood, spherical in shape and cleverly comprised of interlocking panels. It was about the size of a large melon and was inscribed all over with many strange characters and runes. Though I had studied several languages while attending university abroad, and though the light in the cabin was dim, I felt sure that these figures represented a language wholly unfamiliar to me. "It is a thing of exceedingly great workmanship," the carpenter breathed.

But as Mr. Derrick was illiterate, his own fascination with the object could hardly be attributed to these unfamiliar inscriptions. Instead, I perceived that the carpenter recognized the skill and artistry with which the device had been wrought. It was, in other words, the activation of his own professional interest at play. Even as I watched, his fingertips twitched as though he would have liked to hold the object in his hands and admire its craftsmanship. But to approach the corpses and lay hold of the device would be to commit an act of lunacy; none could deny that the bizarre fungal growth had been the instrument of death here in the *Veronica*'s cabin. Or so I thought.

"Mr. Derrick," said the captain, a tremor in his voice.

"Sir?"

"Empty your bag. We have found none alive on this wreck," and here the captain swallowed audibly, "but neither shall we depart empty-handed." He turned to face the carpenter, who obeyed this order without objection, wordlessly unslinging the bag and upending it over the floor of the cabin, sending a variety of nails and tools clattering across the planking. He handed the empty receptacle to the captain, whereupon the latter shook free of the hands that restrained him (I had not even realized that I still clung to his arm, so spellbound was I by the macabre circumstance of the corpses) and advanced through the room, studiously avoiding the spray of purple growing along the floor. The captain pulled a sailor's fid[34] from his belt and used it to gently wrest the wooden sphere from the skeletons' grip. Freed from the clutches of the dead, the ball rolled directly into the outstretched bag. Captain Carrig dropped the fid in after it, pulled the ties on the bag to close it, and turned to us. His face was a mask of grief.

"Lead on, then, lads," he said heavily. "Mr. Taggart will show us the way, and I will serve as rearguard."

The four of us were eager to comply. For my part, I was only too glad to put the tomb that was the captain's cabin behind us. Our departure across the stern half of the *Veronica* was not swift, it must be said, but neither was it especially eventful. We passed the mysterious mounds of moss, avoiding the trail which arrowed its way up the deck, and eventually came to the bridge which Mr. Derrick had so skillfully installed there. It was here that we received a very unpleasant shock. While we had been exploring the *Veronica*'s stern and staring in disbelief at the wasted corpses of the strangers, it appeared that the queer purple growth on the ship had not been idle. There was now a thick rope of it extending along the planks of Mr. Derrick's bridge, working its way between the crevices of the boards and joining the other half of the ship. I took a step closer so that I might see across the bridge and down the bow of the wreck, and what I saw did very little to cheer my spirits: the substance had already progressed to such a degree as to approach our boats. I leaned in to examine it more closely and saw that its filaments and blossoms were now writhing vigorously throughout the violet mass. I recoiled in disgust.

"*Die pilze,* it is so swift," the doctor said, and there was something of awe in his gruff voice as he patted his breast pocket. "My sample was not inert, but never in all our trials did I suspect *this* degree of activity." I remembered his staid assurance that there

---

[34] A kind of wooden peg used by seamen to splice rope and untie tangled knots.

could be nothing supernatural on the *Veronica* or, indeed, in the world at large. I wondered whether he was still entirely certain.

"I need hardly say that caution is more critical now than ever before," warned the captain. "For we have seen that which the moss is capable of performing—and make no mistake, gentlemen, lest you think that the growth consumed the bodies in the cabin sometime *after* their death. No, it was the very agent of their expiration, and now we have some indication of the speed at which it is able to operate. If you should so much as brush your shirtsleeve against this substance, you will disrobe and cast the shirt overboard posthaste. Or you will be left behind." He looked at each of us individually, and his eyes were clear. He was still under the influence of some tremendous emotion, but it seemed that he had found something of his old resolve.

Naturally, not one amongst us found reason to voice any protest. I privately wondered, in the event that one of us stepped inadvertently into the substance, whether the captain would not have the offending limb amputated altogether. This was a question I did not fancy having to answer, and so I exercised extra care when we crossed the precarious bridge. The quivering purple substance ran neatly down the center of the structure, forcing me to place my feet on either side of it. As I walked across the gap, I scarcely noticed the crashing of the ocean below me; the nearness of the terrible growth occupied my entire concentration. I almost imagined that tiny tendrils of the moss would suddenly send out exploratory shoots and stems; that they would, in a sort of blind, groping quest, seize upon my feet and infect me with whatever unthinkable ailment they carried. But although my imagination carried this scenario through to its awful conclusion, I was relieved to reach the other half of the wreck without coming into contact with the substance. There, I was able to step aside from the purple trail and onto a comparatively safe portion of the deck.

We passed the forecastle, and the memory of the bizarre experience I had undergone in those dark quarters before the mast flashed once again before my eyes—but, strangely, I had now seen enough horror in reality that the vision was robbed of some of its power. We did not stop at the forecastle, having learned everything which we were likely to learn from its gloomy depths, and we soon reached the part of the bow which was littered with the shrouds of the foremast. I gratefully clung to this waterlogged rigging and used it to assist my downwards momentum. All the while, our progress was accompanied by a robust trail of the violet moss, which pulsed and undulated as though it were alive. This uncanny path led directly to the ship's submerged prow, where the boats of the *Melville* were bobbing about in the water. As we drew near, I suddenly realized that I could see no sign of Mr. Craft.

Now, you may think it incredible that I had not noticed the man's absence until now. I can only offer as a defense the fact that my attention was consumed with the dangerous nature of our journey across the wreck; a danger which was enhanced by the spectral presence of a deadly alien substance. Had I stopped to think about it, in any case, I would have been just as likely to assume that Mr. Craft had simply taken a rest behind the foremost of the boats. I think I have already said that Mr. Craft was not the cleverest amongst the crew, and it would have been entirely in keeping with his character to shirk his duty as our watchman and fall asleep "on the job," so to speak. Indeed, such was my first thought when I ascertained that he was nowhere to be seen. But I was soon disabused of this notion. For as we approached the boats and observed with relief that they were not as yet afflicted with the mysterious growth, I spied a new object on the deck.

"It's one of those mounds!" shouted Mr. Taggart, all discipline forgotten in his evident—and wholly understandable—consternation. For indeed it was one of the lumped hillocks of accumulated moss, situated neatly between the boats and therefore almost invisible until we were nearly upon it. The captain rushed forward—I do believe he already had some inkling of what must have occurred here. The rest of us followed in his wake, experiencing equal parts curiosity and dread at what we would find. As we drew nearer the boats and the mass which lay between them, I felt something drop in the pit of my stomach. The mound, for the first four feet or so of its length, did not differ greatly from the others. The moss which comprised it seemed considerably more active, with its sprouted tendrils moving about in an excited state of agitation, but in form, shape, and color, it appeared just as any of the others which we had already examined on the other half of the wreck. But as I stepped up to the mound, its true horrifying nature was suddenly revealed to me.

The mound was nothing else but the body of Mr. Craft! He lay prone on the deck of the ship, his head turned feebly aside to prevent the water sloshing about the wood from interfering with his ability to breathe. It was impossible to say whether he had fallen asleep or been knocked down forcibly, but breath was now the least amongst his concerns. For the purple moss had utterly consumed him from his feet to his shoulders, wrapping him in a deadly cocoon of suffocation and death. Even as I watched, I could see questing lines of the violet substance stretching from his shoulders to his neck, knitting together by the means of some terrible unknown agency. It would be only minutes before he was enveloped entirely in the appalling stuff; already I could see bits of the fungus reaching for his mouth and extending to plug his nostrils.

"The other mounds, then," said the doctor, his voice but a whisper. "We did find the crew of the *Veronica*, after all."

"Never mind them!" shouted Mr. Derrick, rushing to help his fallen shipmate. His hands fumbled at his belt but came up empty. "Someone fetch me an axe—I abandoned my tools in the captain's cabin, but if we can only scrape away some of this damned moss, I daresay we can-"

"Belay that," Captain Carrig's voice cut in quietly. We all turned to look at him; the faces of the other men reflected the hopelessness and fear that resounded within my own heart, but the captain was equanimous. "We have lost Old Cedar. It is plain to me that we have also lost Mr. Craft. I will not lose another soul if it stands within my power to prevent that loss. The boy was right: to touch this substance is to condemn oneself to death, and it is better that one man should die than that all of us should perish in the attempt to save him."

This was a cold calculation, to be sure, but even I could see the wisdom of it. I was only thankful that Mr. Craft appeared to be entirely comatose; had he been able to hear this rational decision to let him die, it would only have compounded his suffering. As it was, I do not believe that he suffered long. The fungal growth continued to stitch itself together over the sailor's head, becoming as a shroud within the space of ten or fifteen minutes, and we stood silent in vigil to witness our shipmate's final passage into whatever realm waits beyond this one. I watched, resigned to my own quiet horror, as the filaments of moss entwined themselves into the thick nest of Mr. Craft's hair, weaving and braiding together into a tapestry of madness which I do not think I shall ever be able to forget. In time, the alien mass was all that remained to be seen, hunched upon the deck like a loaf of risen bread, and there was no sign of the man that had once been a simple-minded but stalwart member of the *Melville*'s crew. The heap of moss had become a burial mound, a living tomb from which its occupant would never again rise.

"Dr. -----," the captain said. "You may abandon your sample."

That stout fellow turned to regard him, and I am sure that he was shaken—but whether from the gruesome death of Mr. Craft or from the captain's sudden order, I cannot say. His hand strayed to the pocket of his coat, where the vial of moss had been stowed. "Are you quite certain?" he asked. His voice was small.

"We have no further need of it. The evidence is plain to see before our eyes, and I will not have that substance transported to my own ship."

The doctor tossed the little glass receptacle onto the deck in quiet obedience; it did not shatter but rolled directly into the water where it was swallowed from sight by the hungry waves.

The rest of us continued to gaze at the unlucky Mr. Craft.

"We cannot even commit his body to the deep," observed Mr. Derrick. "If there are no objections, I should at least like to speak a few words over his grave, such as it is."

I nodded; it seemed only appropriate that some gesture should be made. Mr. Taggart and the doctor also indicated their approval of this sentiment, and for a moment Mr. Derrick looked heartened at the prospect of commending the fallen sailor to his Creator.

"No," spoke Captain Carrig suddenly. "This man has strayed from the sight of God." He held up a hand to forestall any objection to such a radical statement. "I do not say that Mr. Craft in particular has fallen from grace. But it is clear to me that we have all been abandoned. Any Lord, whatever His nature, who has allowed such blasphemies to exist"—here he indicated both the hardening shell that had completely enveloped Mr. Craft and the devastated wreck in its entirety—"is not one to whom I will pray."

After the expression of this extraordinary sentiment, the

captain turned his back on us and made to climb into the first of the ship's boats. The remainder of our party followed with some reluctance, exchanging glances and casting a few final looks back at what was left of our crewmate. There was very little conversation as we began to row our way back to the *Melville*; a few shouted orders to coordinate our efforts were all that could be heard echoing across that dismal stretch of water which roiled between the wreck that was and the wreck that was yet to be.

IN WHICH THE CAPTAIN REVEALS HIS INTENTIONS

"For in this world of lies, Truth is forced to fly like a sacred white doe in the woodlands; and only by cunning glimpses will she reveal herself."
-Herman Melville, *Hawthorn and His Mosses*

The captain was the last of us to climb aboard the *Melville.* He had lingered in the second of the ship's boats, staring back at the wreck of the *Veronica* as though he would imprint the sight of that doomed ship upon his memory indelibly. When he returned to our own vessel, he had a familiar parcel tucked under his arm. I recognized it at once for the strange device that had been clutched between the desolate skeletons in the cabin of the wreck, now free of the bag in which it had been wrapped. Though I felt some stirring of curiosity at this development, I was altogether too exhausted to pursue this line of inquiry. Instead, I contented myself to sit with the rest of the crew, who were scattered about the deck in various postures of repose. My hands were trembling visibly as I joined the men at their ease, and I took note of William's pale face as he sat himself down beside me. I remember thinking to myself that it would be some time before the marks of the morning's events would fade from our psyches—if indeed they ever would.

The captain hastened to his own cabin, and Mr. Taggart and Mr. Derrick began the process of tying up the second boat with obvious fatigue. The reader may be surprised to learn that there was very little in the way of conversation in the immediate aftermath of the events that occurred aboard the *Veronica.* The crew who had not been selected to accompany us were obviously consumed with curiosity, but they ascertained from our faces that we were not yet prepared to share our dreadful experiences. For those of us who had escaped the wreck together, a weary sense of camaraderie prevailed about the deck—there was no need to discuss the things we had seen, for we had seen them together. It was not until Captain Carrig emerged from his cabin, some twenty or thirty minutes later, that conversation prevailed.

When the captain did make his appearance, I perceived at once that some enormous transformation had taken place within his constitution. He was cleanly shaven and freshly dressed; his eyes were clear and bright; his posture was calm and confident, without any of the flickering rage that had characterized him until this stage. He paced back and forth for several minutes without speaking, his back straight as he collected his thoughts, and then he turned finally to address the sailors gathered before him.

"It has occurred to me that, as my crew, you are owed some degree of explanation for the chain of events which have led us to this peculiarly ill-fated derelict. Those of you who accompanied me to the *Veronica* need hardly hear a review of what we discovered therein, but as that company comprises but a select few of our men, I will ask you exercise some degree of patience during the summary to follow. The rest of you will have already observed that we have returned one fewer in number." The captain then proceeded to outline the circumstances aboard the wreck, including the unnatural death of Mr. Craft, as well as those two strange corpses locked into an eternal embrace. I observed, however, that he did not mention the queer container which he had retrieved from that ship. I attempted to catch Mr. Derrick's eye, for I knew that as a carpenter he had been especially interested in its construction, but that worthy's full attention was for the moment latched firmly onto the captain.

"The truth of this affair is that we did not run across the wreck as a matter of chance. Indeed, I have been searching for this very ship for a long time now—and its discovery was our purpose on this voyage." Several voices were raised in protest at this startling revelation, but the captain shot such a fierce scowl in their direction that they quickly quieted. "I will thank each of you to listen closely to the tale I have to tell, for it is not a short one, and its contents have direct bearing upon what we have seen and done on this day. But if I am to tell this story in its proper fashion, I must first tell another. It begins when I returned to Ireland after a stint at sea, nearly two years ago now. You see, I had only just arrived at my own home after my first commission as a captain. And waiting upon the hearth, just as though it were the most innocent correspondence in the world, was a letter from my own sister. I shall read it to you presently."

The captain removed a creased bundle of crinkled papers from the pocket of his breast; I observed that his hands were not shaking as he unfolded its pages. These are the same pages which I now tuck betwixt the leaves of my own journal, in the hopes that the last known words of Colleen Carrig may be preserved hereafter.[35] I have copied them here with the aim of offering as complete a narrative as possible, although something of their original character and immediacy is lost when transcribed by another hand. It was in the rough but steady voice of the captain that I myself first heard them, and I would encourage the reader to imagine the following words spoken in his rich, deep timbre, inflected with alternating bouts of tender emotion and visceral aversion, for it was in such a manner that I listened with a growing sense of disquiet.

> My dearest Brother,
>
> So much has transpired since you first went away to Sea that I scarcely know where to begin. I trust that my letter will find you in good health and humor and that you will not take it amiss when you discover that I have gone. I suppose I must prevaricate no longer—I am to be married! Now please withhold your protestations, for neither will I leave any question unanswered, which I can anticipate, nor is my Husband wholly unknown to you. He is none other than Roger Lundamere, your most stalwart boyhood companion. While I do not specifically recall him from our youth, he remembers you and has recounted many of your wayward adventures with abundant glee. You may therefore be surprised to learn that he is no longer that vigorous urchin of the streets; he is grown uncomfortable with the press of the pavement, the great crowds in the

[35] Some of the pages of this remarkable letter were still folded neatly within the journal when I came into its possession; please refer to the Appendix to see a photograph of the document as I found it.

town square, and the social niceties that dictate public behavior. He now prefers to spend a morning watching fish leap and splash in the brook; to take his evening constitution in a forest glade at dusk; and to revel in the all-encompassing music of the crickets as evening settles her cloak at last upon the world of men. One might even say that Roger has a marked connection with the natural world, and it is this quality of his with which I have become most enamored.

But allow me to explain: our present acquaintance was born of the merest chance, for we encountered one another only whilst sharing a hansom cab. One conversation was enough to pique my intellectual curiosity as well as my romantic interest, and I was delighted that Roger should ask whether he were permitted to call upon me once more. Our subsequent engagements were held in the absence of a chaperone, and each was more mentally and spiritually intimate than the last.

I shall describe one such engagement for you in detail, for it was striking in several particulars. Roger had escorted me on a short trip to the countryside on an early morn, whereupon we ventured some ways from the road and into a great field of heather. Settling himself upon a tussock, Roger looked at me, the smile slipping from his face. "You have told me all about yourself," he said to me quite seriously. "It may be that you should know something more of me." But he did not speak—instead he bade me to follow him farther from the road. Allow me to set the scene for you, my Brother, who has a head only for ships and sails and the rolling sea. The forest is as different from your domain as you can imagine: instead of a waste of salt in every direction, there is greenery and life! Even on the outskirts of town, the twitter of birdsong quickly overwhelms the din of humanity, and the wind whispering between the hazel and rowan speaks of mysteries older and greater than even those which are intoned from the pulpit.

At length, we reached a clearing in the wood ringed by yew and juniper. Roger knelt and lowered his head, bidding me to do the same. He began to speak in a curious language wholly unfamiliar to me; it was certainly no dialect of Ireland or Scotland. The soft rise and fall of its vowels and the harder clatter of its consonants summoned to my mind the thought of a stream running over rocks in a forest older and wilder than the one in which we knelt. I suppose I should have been alarmed at the sheer alien quality of this speech, but for a certain soothing effect that the words had upon me. I began to relax and to grow introspective, and I cannot say with certainty how much time elapsed in this fashion. My next distinct memory is of hearing the sound of footsteps upon the dry grass and dead leaves of the clearing. Despite Roger's admonitions to the contrary, I could not help but raise my head to identify the origin of this sudden intrusion. Imagine my shock to discover that we had been encircled by a party of forest ruminants!

There were five or six animals in total; in addition to the familiar red deer, there were elk or reindeer which I had not known to occur on our Island. But chief amongst our Visitors was an overlarge Black Goat, which approached us directly. Its pelt was grown long and tangled with briar and thorn, and the hair on its legs reached down to its hooves to drag upon the ground. As it advanced I looked down in some haste, for I suddenly understood that to gaze upon its face would have been to see something which could not subsequently be unseen. The animal stepped to within a hand's breadth of us before coming to a stop, and I could feel its breath in my hair as it snorted and stamped with impatience. All the while, Roger continued to speak softly in that strange language, and I began to feel that for a moment the entire world had drawn its breath.

The peculiar, mournful vocalization of an owl sounded abruptly in the limbs of a willow somewhere above our heads, and it seemed to be the signal for which our Visitors were waiting. The animals seemed to heed its call, and they melted back into the trees from which they had so suddenly materialized. We remained on our knees in the glade until the sounds of the forest returned one by one. Roger stood, and he dusted his knees with his hands in an uncharacteristically fastidious gesture. “Were you not afraid, then?” he asked me. I replied in the negative, for I had found the experience wonderful rather than frightening. Roger appeared to consider my response for a space of several moments, before finally replying. “I should be grateful if you were to accompany me home, my dear Colleen, for it occurs to me that there is yet far more which I can now safely share with you.”

I accompanied Roger to his house forthwith; it will not surprise you to learn that his is a country home set somewhat apart from town. Roger led me into a room at the rear of the building, which was enclosed entirely by glass after the manner of a greenhouse. I perceived at once that the contents of this room would be hidden from without, as the home’s rear was also encircled by buckthorn hedge. This was prudent, for arranged on long tables throughout this greenhouse was spread such an array of the bizarre as to draw the prying eye of any curious neighbour.

For a time, I forgot Roger’s very presence, and the whole of the world seemed to fall away from me as I examined the objects laid upon these tables. My eyes landed upon weird and misshapen artifacts; potted plants strangely entwined with each other; sheaves of parchment covered in indecipherable script and tightly bound and fastened with detachable padlocks; stone tools and adzes still embedded in untidy clumps of excavated earth; and a great collection of skulls, some of which belonged to common animals but others of which were quite unknown to me. Among the items which especially caught my eye were a leather-bound journal (etched into its cover was a phrase: The Devil in the White Mountains[36]); a large brass vessel carved with Arabian script and stoppered with a plug decorated with strange cabalistic symbols; a perfect golden glass sphere with a number of red stars floating suspended

---

[36] I have since come into possession of a copy of this curious volume, which is written in several different hands in both Hindi and Nepali scripts. I am working with several translators and hope to have a version of it made available at some later date.

within it by way of some clever workmanship; and a brilliantly-colored purple flower enclosed within a glass-topped display case, as is typically used for jewelry. I paused at this last, daring to allow my finger to trace the contours of its petals through the glass. Here was an object of Transcendent Beauty, I thought then as now; here was something which evoked the same inescapable sense of the divine that had enveloped me when I knelt before the Black Goat in that clearing in the woods.

"I see you have come straight to the jewel of my collection," Roger said. His gentle voice shook me from my reverie. "I should expect no less from my Beloved than to arrive directly at the heart of this matter. For you must understand, my Colleen, that I have not been entirely forthcoming with you." He clasped his hands behind his back and turned to face me, allowing his eyes to rove over the assortment of curiosities that filled the room before settling at last upon my face. "For many years, certain unexplained Phenomena have led me to believe that there is some truth in the old stories of the world, but it was not until my twentieth year that the Black Goat first showed itself to me. You cannot imagine my shock when I looked upon its face and saw my own features reflected back at me! It was just as though I were staring into a mirror; I could plainly recognize my own aquiline nose; my own uncommonly dark eyes; and the twist of the lips that approximated my own rueful smile. This animal wore my face as its own, and it beckoned to me—and it was then that I received the Errand which has since represented the great labor of my life."

Roger now approached the wooden case which held the luminous purple flower. He unclasped a golden catch on its lid and gently opened the box; at once I became aware of a sweet, delicate fragrance wafting from inside. I observed also that the flower was not planted in soil; it rested on a bed of cloth and yet seemed as full of vigor as if it had just been plucked from the stem."I have been assigned to return this singular bloom to the land from which it was removed, some hundred years or more. I have chartered a ship to America, though I am given to understand that this will not be its final destination. It is thus with a heavy heart that I make my final confession: our Romance cannot continue until this act is done and I have ferried my charge across the Sea, beyond the reach of the Father Ocean at last." He closed the lid of the box and turned away from me in despair.

Dearest Brother, you may marvel that I did not interrupt this speech, which was hardly to be believed. But was not the evidence arranged carefully before my eyes? Was it not catalogued and tagged after the manner of a scientist? And had I not so recently shared an encounter in the wood which would stymie the protests of even the most ardent skeptic? No, disbelief was hardly what held my tongue. I seized Roger's arm with sudden violence and spun him around to face me. I became aware that tears were now spilling from my own eyes as I reprimanded him with the harshest vehemence I could muster. "Do not act as though matrimonial bliss and your particular brand of scholarship are mutually exclusive," I fairly spat. "Have you not already inducted me into the strange rites of your obsession? For I too have been approached by the Black Goat, though I dared not meet his eyes, and I know from whence the knowledge of your Errand comes. Therefore I will accompany you, and we will be married in America, or wherever your ship makes berth, or on the very Sea itself if needs must, but you, Roger Lundamere, shall not be rid of me so easily."

We wasted no time in making the necessary preparations for travel. Perhaps the most exacting chore was the packing of the mysterious flower. It has now been sealed in a unique device of Roger's own design, which he has manufactured according to certain principles identified in the course of his researches; I do not presume to understand its function. We are scheduled to depart Galway Harbor on the 21st of March—accordingly, I will be at Sea by the time you hold this letter in your hands. As one Carrig returns from the Sea, so shall another venture forth upon it. When the Veronica leaves her berth in two weeks' time, it shall serve to mark the beginning of a new chapter in my life. I urge you to wish me only the swiftest success in this undertaking. I expect to return before the year's end, whereupon you may finally reacquaint yourself with my Husband-to-be. I know that Roger can scarcely wait to re-establish your mutual Friendship.

Your loving Sister,
Colleen

At the conclusion of this marvelous oration, a thunderous silence reigned on deck. The captain carefully folded the pages of the letter, creasing and smoothing them between this thumb and forefinger, and replaced them in the pocket of his coat. A slight tremor had returned to his hand, but I gathered that it was a mark of his suppressed emotion rather than the lingering effects of drink, for he seemed wholly consumed with resolve. The captain surveyed his audience with an accusatory stare, but he did not immediately speak. I can only surmise that he must have been gauging our reaction before deciding the manner in which to proceed. I cannot think that he found the faces of the men especially receptive; though I have said that sailors are famously superstitious, this was a tale to test even the most credulous of their ranks. For my own part, despite what I had seen firsthand that morning, these matters of the supernatural were not foremost on my mind. Or, more precisely, the question of whether I found them credible was not. Instead, I was inwardly thrilling at how exciting my story for the *Inquirer and Mirror* had just become. I knew that I would have to fill many pages of notes in my little journal just as soon as this remarkable interview was concluded.

"There are many singular aspects to the story which you have just been told," the captain said presently. "Some of these aspects I have confirmed independently; some of them have been verified before your own eyes as recently as this morning. But for our present purposes, I would request that you disregard them all, save one. You will recall, I am sure, that this Roger Lundamere"—his distaste was evident— "professes a childhood friendship with me. Gentlemen, I have never cared overmuch for the judgment of God, but I will attest here today before the eyes of men that I have never known anyone to whom that name belongs, be he boy or man. And if I name the lie to that earliest association by which he began to win my sister's heart, it follows that every subsequent utterance that passed his deceitful tongue should be called into question.

"So I do not ask you to consider whether stories of black goats, faery languages, and animals who wear the faces of men can possibly fall within the confines of reality. As far as I am concerned, these are elements of an elaborate fiction which Roger Lundamere has constructed around a single kernel of truth. Regrettably, that kernel of truth involves the departure of my sister aboard the *Veronica*; you can imagine how quickly I set about the business of retrieving her from his grasp. Verifying the existence of the ship was simplicity itself, though it had already been at sea for several months by the time that I returned to find my sister's missive waiting for me. Tracing its passage was an altogether more difficult matter; for though the ship was destined for America, I need hardly tell you that she did not arrive on those shores. And so I began my own investigations into the unknown." He flashed a wry smile upon the sailors assembled before him. "I assure you, the irony is not lost upon me. My inquiries took more than a year to come to fruition, and I spent a great deal of time in the most disreputable of places as I ferreted out the information I sought. At length, I came across a person who professed to be capable of finding the *Veronica*. You knew her as Old Cedar."

I cannot really say that an audible gasp ran throughout the crew of the *Melville*, but this unexpected surprise was writ large across the face of every man present. Given the benefit of hindsight, I wonder that we should have been surprised at all. For I could hardly deny that the cook had exuded a mysterious, inscrutable aura from the first. I recalled the cryptic warning that she had given to me regarding the course of our own ship and whether the sailors were being entirely honest with me. In a way, some of the supernatural mystery of that warning was now stripped away; yet it did not explain why she should have chosen to share that information with me. Not for the last time, I felt a pang of regret that she had been lost at sea.

"I will not say where I found her, or what her help has cost me, for I do not foresee that any good can come of it. But Old Cedar placed certain restrictions on our voyage," the captain continued, "which she stated would be critical to our chances of success. For one, that is why we are in a sailing ship, rather than a more modern steamer. There are forces in the world, she suggested, which are older and wilder than the marvels of man, and which would fail to reveal themselves to a vessel of engines and smoke. And were she not lost to us now, I would shower her with praise. For she has led us unerringly to the storm by which we have passed into these waters; and if it has extracted its toll in her own blood, it was no greater a price than she was prepared to pay. Second, she stipulated that the crew should be comprised of men who would be uncommonly useful in a scrap, which is why most of you were recruited from the streets and the taverns rather than the dockyard. I am pleased to say that she was correct in this estimation, for I do not think that a lesser crew should have escaped the *Veronica* so cleanly. And we may yet see further action in which your particular skills will continue to be of use." He paused. "Now, the recruitment of Mr. Verne and Mr. Clark Russell, I confess, was my own idea."

Mr. Verne's face was as a thunderhead. "I should very much like to hear the line of reasoning that led you to this stroke of brilliance."

"It is quite simple," Captain Carrig replied. "I trusted to the wisdom of Old Cedar, such as it was, as far as I could. But I reasoned that I must also prepare for the potential of disaster." He cast a shrewd eye over the two authors. "I ask you now: how many stories of shipwreck have you written? How many ingenious methods of survival have you concocted within the pages of your books? Have you not taken your characters to the very limits of what the human body can endure, and have you not discovered where those limits lie? In the event of a catastrophe, I should very much like to have your cleverness in my corner. If this upsets you, I suggest that you pray your ingenuity is not needed."

"This is an unspeakable outrage," Mr. Verne said, fists clenched. He had gone very red in the face.

"You will be ruined," Mr. Clark Russell said simultaneously. "I gather that this is but your second captaincy; you may rest assured that it will be your last. What you have done is tantamount to abduction."

"In light of what we have seen today, and in light of what I have learned about the fate of my sister, you are suffering under a delusion if you think that I should care one whit about my career as a captain once this voyage is concluded," the captain said—uncharacteristically, there was no anger in his voice. "I do not expect that you should be pleased with this state of affairs, but I would remind you that you shipped with me so that you might collaborate on a novel. Well, novelists, you may proceed with that endeavor, for it matters very little to the story whether we sail the Atlantic seaboard or the tract of the ocean upon which the *Veronica* has perished. It may even be that you have found something here to inspire the scratching of your pens.

"As for the rest of you," and here the captain's voice resumed something of its natural hardness and vigor, "I will not solicit your input upon these matters. You have all received your advances, and you will collect what is owed to you upon our return to Nantucket. I have satisfied the object of this voyage today, and its results were largely what I had feared them to be, though I had of course hoped for better. We shall ride out the last of the weather here this evening, and I will determine our further course in the morning." He looked at each member of the crew directly in turn, and I wondered what he saw in their faces. "Now you will retire, but for Mr. Taggart and Mr. Lawrence, who I will require at their stations. I do not ask you to believe what you have heard today, but I trust that you will believe the evidence of your own eyes. The more swiftly we complete this business and put an end to the whole sordid affair, the better."

True to his word, Captain Carrig did not entertain any questions or grievances from the men. They shuffled to the forecastle in a sullen line, with much in the way of muttering and dark looks. The captain watched them go, but he did not comment upon their evident disgruntlement. It occurred to me that he was sending all of them together to their quarters, bereft of leadership, where they would certainly discuss in the dark those matters which they had been prohibited to discuss in the proverbial light. Even then, with all my wealth of inexperience, I recognized this for the mistake it was.

MUTINY!

"Evil and good they braided play / Into one cord."
-Herman Melville, *Clarel*

It was perhaps inevitable that the crew would react badly to the captain's startling confession. Even the most fanciful sailor would find the tale hard to credit—and those who were inclined to believe in its veracity could hardly be expected to appreciate being made into potential victims for the malicious supernatural entities which had ostensibly come to be involved in our fates. I do not think that this absolves the men of the crimes they conspired to commit, but it does prevent me from condemning them wholly—with the exception, it must be said, of Mr. Fairchild. From the first, it was evident that this particular miscreant was interested in stirring up trouble for its own sake. Maybe it was that he nursed a particular need for vengeance against the captain after being unceremoniously struck down after the storm, or perhaps it was only his natural inclination for mischief at play. Whatever his motive, it was with Mr. Fairchild that the *Melville*'s mutiny began.

I came to learn of the plot when I followed the men into the forecastle after being dismissed by the captain. I trailed them at a distance, lingering behind with reluctance. You see, I had hoped to overhear something of the argument that was now developing between Mr. Verne and Mr. Clark Russell. They were plainly very upset about being tricked into shipping with Captain Carrig, and I was keen to see how they would handle the situation. But their voices were pitched too low for me to discern, and I was obliged to join the rest of the crew lest my attention be noticed. So it was that I found myself caught in mid-descent upon the stairs when the conversation had already begun.

"Now, gentleman," came the voice of Mr. Fairchild, and I

should not have been surprised had I seen the shine of his silver tongue flashing in the dark. "It need hardly be said that this is a delicate business."

"Aye," said another voice, which took me but a moment to recognize as the honeyed timbre of Mr. Harris. A chill ran up my spine as I crouched there in the dark, recalling how that man's designs upon my own life had very nearly been carried out during the cataclysmic storm. "For all the captain's faults—and they are many—he is a shrewd cove, and no mistake. I should not like to be caught out before we've a chance to cement our plan. Many a mutiny has been snuffed out ere it ever got well and truly underway."

Mutiny! The very word was enough to strike trepidation into the heart of the stoutest sailor; the reader may well imagine the effect which it produced upon me. I was but a passenger, really, who understood so little of the ways of the sea—but I understood that my life would be placed at great risk if the command of the vessel were to be contested by the likes of that great villain Mr. Fairchild and that blackest of rogues, his companion the boatswain. I was plunged into a state bordering upon panic, and I found myself caught between immediately fleeing the forecastle and charging down to assert my objection to their plan. My indecision led me to indulge the better part of valor, as the saying goes, and to do nothing. So it went that I was able to witness firsthand the debate which presently followed.

The first to protest was Mr. Derrick. "I should not like to question the legitimacy of your complaints, Mr. Fairchild," he began. Hearing his voice, I inched closer, bringing the carpenter into my field of vision. "For it is without question that we have been deceived and ill-used, and indeed I share your grievances in a general sense. Yet there are certain particulars here which are worth a closer examination, I think." He paused, seeming to gather his thoughts as he packed tobacco into his pipe. As I came to know the man more closely, I recognized this as a sign of his characteristic pontification. I forced my rigid muscles to relax: it was likely that Mr. Derrick would go on at some length. I thought that I may as well make myself as comfortable as possible under the circumstances.

"First and foremost amongst these considerations is whether

our objections to the captain's conduct are appropriate," continued Mr. Derrick. He held up a finger, forestalling protest from the crewmembers, who were now listening intently. "I do not say that they are invalid, exactly, but rather I question whether it is our prerogative to make them in the first place. For is it not so that the captain is granted absolute authority over his vessel and the crew which mans it?"

"He has exposed us to unfathomable danger!" snarled Mr. Fairchild. "He has abdicated his responsibility for the welfare of ship and crew alike, and in my estimation that is more than sufficient to renegotiate the terms of our engagement with him."

"Aha!" returned Mr. Derrick, sounding just as satisfied as if the quartermaster had made his point for him. He lit his pipe and took a first draw upon it, savoring the smoke and expelling it from his mouth with obvious satisfaction. I could see that the carpenter was now truly in his element and was warming to his theme. "Yet the very condition of the sailor is that of exposure to unfathomable danger. Was it the captain's fault that Old Cedar was swept into the sea? Is she any less dead than if she had been killed by some unnatural agent? Danger is danger, gentlemen, and the manner of death matters very little to the dead man."

"It matters to me," Mr. Harris said in a grumbling tone.

"And to me as well," agreed one Mr. Allen, a wiry and youthful sailor who I understood had been a particular friend of the late Mr. Craft. "I should not like to encounter anything unnatural." This was met with general agreement; heads nodded in the gloom, and a chorus of "hear, hear," was heard throughout the forecastle.

"That settles that, then," said Mr. Fairchild. He nearly spat the words. "Or do you have any other *considerations* to which we must be subjected?"

"Indeed I do," said Mr. Derrick. I heard more than one sailor groan, but the carpenter pressed on unperturbed. "But they are considerations of practicality, which may perhaps appeal to those of you who are less inclined to, ah, my particular brand of subjectivity. Now, listen. The captain has dismissed us and robbed us of the opportunity to exert any control over our own fates. This much is true. But he has not yet reached his *own* conclusion, either. I remind you that his last words were to tell us that he would decide our next steps in the morning." He leaned back, exhaling, and his keen eyes glinted through the smoke. “I ask you, is it not possible that he will determine—on his own—that to continue our present course is folly? And if he should chart our course for home in the morning, what use is a mutiny tonight? I am a practical man above all else, gentlemen, and I would posit that it is wiser to wait and see. If the captain should come to his senses, we will let the matter rest, collect our pay, and consider ourselves well rid of him. If he should choose to persist in his efforts, well, we may revisit this conversation upon the morrow.”

Mr. Derrick looked around the room, eyebrows raised. His reclined posture somehow conveyed the impression that he was not supremely concerned with the reception he would receive. I am not certain whether this was an affectation meant to calm the men or whether his philosophical inclinations truly allowed him to view the situation as though he were removed from it. For my own part, I found myself nodding along with the merits of his argument. I silently willed the men to take heed of the carpenter’s words; surely any reasonable man would have been swayed by his sound logic! Alas, we had certain agitators in our midst who were not reasonable men. I could see at once that Mr. Fairchild would not consent to letting things stand even for another night.

“Mr. Derrick offers sage advice,” the quartermaster now began, speaking not to the carpenter but to the room at large. “And we are indebted to him for rendering it to us with such eloquence and grace. But we are merely men, and we all know what must be done. Should we delay until the morn, who amongst us will retain the necessary resolve? We would do better to act while our tempers are hot. Mr. Derrick may think me rash, but I say that decisive action must be taken rashly—lest none be taken at all.”

Well, it turned out that Mr. Fairchild was a fine orator, I thought. A liar and a would-be murderer, to be sure, but one who could turn a phrase. I could see his words having an effect on the men closely gathered in the semi-darkness. Heads nodded, faces drew down in grim resolve, and for a moment it seemed that no voice of reason would speak against the quartermaster. But then a clear, young voice sang out.

“You did not board the wreck,” said William. The quartermaster’s head turned sharply in his direction, and my young friend swallowed nervously—but he did not desist. “You did not see what was found there. You did not see what claimed the life of Seth Craft."

"Nor did you," said Mr. Harris, waving a hand in dismissal.

"But Mr. Derrick did."

All eyes turned to the carpenter. For a long moment he was silent, leaning back against a crate and puffing away on his pipe with a distant, troubled expression. A profound change seemed to have come over him. Where now was his previous loquaciousness? Was he only now allowing himself to remember the inexplicable events of the *Veronica?* When he finally spoke, his voice came as from far away. "I did board the wreck," he said softly. "I saw Seth Craft entombed alive in a shroud of some living alien substance which even the doctor declined to identify. I saw a ship wrecked by some tremendous force. And I saw—or thought I saw—something which nearly consigned the *Melville* to a similar fate." He hesitated, sitting forward and staring at William. "I shouldn't like to put a name to it, lad, but I shouldn't like to see it again, either." He cast his eyes over the entire forecastle, and when he spoke, his voice was full of regret. "I would like to give the captain the chance to make things right of his own accord…but if this is your resolve, then I suppose I will stand with you."

"I'm afraid there is little chance of the captain reconsidering on his own," came a sudden voice from behind me. It was Mr. Taggart, and I nearly jumped from my own skin when I heard him! I had been so focused on the conspiracy unfolding belowdecks that I had failed to detect the mate's arrival. Shamefaced, I was ushered impatiently into the forecastle proper as he came down the steps behind me, followed closely by Mr. Lawrence.

"Aha, our little stowaway is caught once again," said Mr. Derrick as I stepped into the circle of men. A sad smile briefly lit the carpenter's face. Though he had ultimately lent his voice to support the mutiny, I think that he spoke with genuine regret. I think he would have spared me from getting involved in this dreadful situation had it only been within his power to do so.

"Never mind that," said Mr. Taggart. "We have more pressing concerns. I've listened to your talk for some moments and I gather that you've already spared us the trouble of bringing you around to our own view on the matter." With a nod at Mr. Lawrence, he continued. "The helmsman and I've come to the conclusion that Captain Carrig is unfit for command."

"You don't say so," said Mr. Harris in a dry sort of tone.

"Pray tell us what you've observed," Mr. Fairchild interjected smoothly. "We've independently reached the same conclusion—as you know—but we would value the impressions of the captain's own right-hand man."

"He has renounced all reason," said the mate simply. "He saw Mr. Lawrence to the wheel and ordered me to stand watch until eight bells[37], at which point I was to rouse the crew. I asked him what he intended to do, but I could make no sense of his reply. It seems that he has failed to rescue his sister and has now vowed vengeance on something he called the father of the sea, or some such nonsense. I understand that Old Cedar is somehow mixed up in his grand delusion, but I'm no longer entirely certain that he can discern reality from fantasy. He mumbled something about damning the old cook's warning and opening the infernal device on his own. He retreated to his cabin before I had the chance to make him explain, but I now believe that he means to continue in this madness. I do not believe the morning will bring him a change of heart."

I watched as the crewmen absorbed the words of Mr. Taggart, and I paid special attention to whether Mr. Lawrence was in agreement. Thus far the helmsman had remained silent, true to his essential nature as a steady man who was not susceptible to the temperamental mood now pervading the forecastle. But it was his reaction to the captain's erratic behavior which particularly worried me. It had occurred to me that as the navigator, his approval would legitimize the entire seditious enterprise. The quartermaster must have had the same thought, for he turned to the helmsman—and I had the unshakable impression that he was carefully playing the politician.

"Mr. Taggart," he said, "do you concur with the mate's interpretation of the captain's behavior? It is a weighty decision we make here today, and I should like to hear from all parties." His words were fair, but I still could not shake the impression that he was putting on a show of political theater.

To Mr. Lawrence's credit, he received the question in his

---

[37] i.e., midnight.

typical unhurried manner: his scarred brow furrowed, his lips pursed, and he did not utter so much as a word while he gave the matter his full measure of consideration. But then he looked about the forecastle and met the eyes of each man in turn. Finally he gave a slow, solemn nod and returned his attention to Mr. Fairchild, who seemed to take the helmsman's agreement as the ultimate vindication and the right to proceed.

"Then the only thing for it is to call a vote," Mr. Fairchild said. "The resolution before us is whether to take command of the ship and thence return to Nantucket. Let any man here who is opposed to this course make himself heard by raising a hand."

This, then, was the moment at which I must choose whether to make a stand. How had I found myself in this situation? What string of circumstances had led to this unenviable predicament? Could my folly be traced back to the embarkation of the *Melville,* when I had rashly determined to stow away? Or could it be traced even further, to the point at which I had entered the Green Pelican to make the acquaintance of the crew in the first place? No matter where it started, one consequence had led to another until I found myself buried beneath the burden of my ill-considered decisions. And now I had come to the point where a decision must be made. In desperation I turned to the voice in my head, seeking guidance from that part of me which I blamed for the greater portion of my recklessness. To my chagrin, I found that it had deserted me utterly. And yet, much as when I had stood in opposition to Mr. Fairchild before the tempest had wracked the *Melville,* I found some hitherto unsuspected reservoir of courage within me. I looked upon the face of Mr. Derrick, the kindly carpenter who was so recently cowed into submission by his fear of the unknown. I looked upon William, my friend and confidant who dared not raise a hand for fear of his shipmates' retribution. And then I experienced a dim feeling of surprise when I discovered that my own hand was rising into the air seemingly of its own volition.

I am afraid that I did not make for an especially triumphant figure as the sole dissenter to the mutiny that was now brewing below the *Melville*'s decks. My hand shook, and I did not trust my voice for fear that a verbal tremor would undermine the confidence I would have preferred to convey. But I am proud to say that I objected nonetheless—and it does give me some small satisfaction to recall how Mr. Fairchild's face darkened with anger when he saw me. But it was Mr. Harris who spoke first.

"Gut him and be done with it," he growled. "The boy is more trouble than he's worth." As if to reinforce his threat, the boatswain's hand strayed to finger a knife which was clasped to his belt.

"Very well," I rejoined at once. It seemed for the moment that my mouth was moving faster than my mind. "I would only remind you that I have slipped through your fingers not once now, but twice. A third time pays for all, I suppose, but I think you'll find that I shall sell my own life rather dearly." No weapons being immediately available, I curled my hands into fists and prepared to engage the boatswain. I could not allow his squat physique to fool me, for I had seen him move nimbly amongst the rigging and knew that he was a deceptively lithesome man. The trick would be to avoid the strokes of his blade and to win the fight quickly, if I could manage it, before the other mariners had the opportunity to determine whose side they fell on.

"Now, now, my friends," Mr. Fairchild said. His tone was conciliatory, but I sensed that steel lurked just beneath. "We wouldn't want to deprive any member of this crew the opportunity to speak his mind. And whether we like it or not"—his expression left me in no doubt as to his own preference—"he is, for the moment, a member of our crew. And I for one have little doubt that he can be made to see his error." A predatory grimace crept across his countenance as he raised his body to a half-crouch, as though he too were preparing to spring upon me. I blanched; this was a most unwelcome addition to the equation. I did not rate my chances of survival very highly now.

And then the carpenter stood. He towered over the other men as he stooped to keep from striking his head against the forecastle's smoke-darkened rafters. One outstretched arm was sufficient to impede the threatening advances of the quartermaster and the boatswain alike. They sank back onto their haunches with obvious reluctance, but there was no gainsaying Mr. Derrick's massive frame as the carpenter glowered at them, cracking his swollen knuckles. For the moment, the rest of the crew watched silently.

"If we're going to do this thing," Mr. Derrick announced, "I should like to do it without violence." I am still not certain what exactly compelled him to mount this defense of me, but I remain eternally grateful for his unexpected intervention. However, his advocacy for me was not entirely unconditional: the carpenter next turned his attention to me, his hair hanging over his shadowed eyes and rendering them unreadable. "Now, boy, I don't want to see any harm come to you. But I'm not ashamed to say that I value my own life rather more dearly. I would see us all home safely, if we can manage it—but I think our best chance would be to make as little trouble as possible, eh?"

"Have you no principles?" I said ungratefully. "How can we betray the captain?"

The carpenter only shook his head. "You, at least, signed no ship's articles. And as for the rest of us"—he encompassed the mariners assembled in the forecastle with the sweep of a massive arm—"principles are all well and good, but dead men can have none. I'm not enthusiastic about what we're doing here, but I'm less enthusiastic about dying." He held my gaze. "No loyalty is worth your death."

Only then did I truly understand what the carpenter was doing: offering me a way out of the situation into which I had so heedlessly charged. Perhaps this amateur philosopher was an even greater politician than Mr. Fairchild, in his own way! And if part of his politician's repertoire included the threat of brute force, what of it? No carpenter worthy of his trade would fail to use every tool at his disposal. And so it was with only a little regret that I lowered my trembling hands to my sides. My objection was withdrawn; the mutiny would proceed.

"Yes, well, very good," said Mr. Taggart. "I could not have abided the murder of an innocent even in the direst of circumstances." He did not sound especially convincing, but he clapped his hands, clearly eager to move the plot along. "Now, gentlemen, as your new commander I should like to propose a few rules of conduct—"

"What? Our new commander?" said Mr. Harris with a low chuckle.

"I don't believe as that's been decided," said Mr. Allen.

"No indeed," said Mr. Fairchild. "And with all due respect to the mate, I would posit that one so closely associated with the captain should have learned his true intentions before now. Perhaps Mr. Taggart is not the most qualified amongst us to lead."

I had the sinking feeling that I was witnessing a rehearsed performance; I could have guessed what would happen next. And so it transpired, the carpenter playing neatly into his hands.

"And whom would you propose?" said Mr. Derrick, returning to his seat and drawing deeply on his pipe. "Yourself, I presume?"

Mr. Fairchild gave a sort of mocking little bow. "I can think of none better qualified. As your quartermaster, I have some passing familiarity with the ship's navigation, with her provisions, and, of course, with her crew." He turned in a slow circle, making eye contact with each of us. "Does it not fall to your quartermaster to settle disputes in the absence of leadership?"

"I should say it falls to me," returned Mr. Taggart. "What you are proposing far exceeds the bounds of mutiny, Mr. Fairchild—it completely upends the order aboard this ship. And in a crisis of this magnitude, order and leadership are of paramount importance. Need I remind you of the legal consequences we stand to face upon our return?[38]"

"And yet I do not see anyone rising to your defense," said the quartermaster. "Perhaps the men feel that they do not need *your* leadership. After all, you have shown yourself unable to protect us thus far. Why should the future prove to be any different?" He pivoted again, giving each sailor another chance to meet his eyes. "Gentlemen, did we consult the mate before we made our decision here today?"

He was met with silence.

"And do we now call upon him to lead—he who lacks the strength even to defy a man who would lead us into certain death?"

Still no one spoke, although William fidgeted in clear discomfort and Mr. Derrick busied himself with repacking his pipe. Mr. Taggart turned to Mr. Lawrence for support, but even the

---

[38] While punishment for mutiny in the military service was far more severe, the men of the *Melville* could still expect serious repercussions for partaking in a mutiny even in the private or merchant services. However, established law in the United States in the 1800s did hold the caveat that a crew was not bound to obey unlawful orders. The mate's argument here seems to be that the crew should have preserved some semblance of law by adhering to the chain of command in the face of the captain's inappropriate conduct.

helmsman averted his gaze. At length, the mate tossed his hands into the air in total exasperation.

"I sailed with each of you across the Atlantic," he said. "You know my character to be true. Would you really prefer to follow this man instead of me? He knows only how to taunt and divide, and he lacks the strength to lead. Was I the only man on deck when the captain struck him to the sternsheets? I did not see any leadership from him then. I did not see any purpose or any determination. I saw only weakness and cowardice."

What happened next I can scarcely credit. In one swift gesture, the boatswain tossed something to the quartermaster; it shone briefly in the darkness as it flipped end over end before landing firmly in Mr. Fairchild's grasp. Before anyone could react, Mr. Fairchild was on his feet with his body pressed closely against the mate's—and the haft of a long-handled knife was suddenly protruding from Mr. Taggart's throat. Blood welled and bubbled around the wound, and the mate's eyes went wide with surprise. He did not speak—he could not speak—and he only turned an incredulous expression on his attacker as though he could not quite believe how things had gotten so serious so quickly. He pawed weakly at the foreign implement which had so abruptly rent his windpipe; dark arterial red spattered his hands in staccato bursts, and the mate slumped against the foot of the stairs as his strength began to desert him. Still he did not speak—and still the quartermaster did not release his grip.

"And what do you see now?" said Mr. Fairchild softly. His voice was almost a whisper as he drove the knife deeper into the mate's neck, crouching atop his fallen body for leverage and leaning into his ear to speak. "Do you still doubt my purpose, my determination?" The mate's head lolled back on his shoulders as he finally expired, and the quartermaster pulled the knife free with a horrible sucking sound. Standing, Mr. Fairchild wiped his hands on his trousers and began to clean his weapon in a similar fashion. He seemed entirely untroubled by the crime he had just committed.

"And so our pact is sealed in blood," the quartermaster pronounced lightly. To my shock and dismay, he leered at the assembled coalition of mutineers in an appalling parody of good humor. In retrospect it seems incredible that this event did not cause an uproar—and yet I cannot stress too strongly the rapidity with which the murder occurred, or the severity of the fear which now rippled through the forecastle. A line had been crossed, you see, and now there was no going back. A man had been killed—the *mate* had been killed—and no sailor party to this mutiny could now ever expect clemency in the eyes of the captain or the law.

TELLS HOW I SOUGHT ANOTHER AUDIENCE WITH THE CAPTAIN, AND OF THAT MAN'S FINAL DESPERATE GAMBIT

"Who in the rainbow can draw the line where the violet tint ends and the orange tint begins? Distinctly we see the difference of the colors, but where exactly does the one first blendingly enter into the other? So with sanity and insanity."
-Herman Melville, *Billy Budd, Sailor*

The next twenty or thirty minutes passed in a sort of blur, and I was only dimly aware of the preparations which were now being made. Mr. Derrick and Mr. Lawrence wrapped the limp form of Mr. Taggart into an extra bit of sail canvas and sewed him up with big, looping stitches. Their hands shook. I understood vaguely that the mate would be given a burial at sea, which is to say that he would be simply tossed over the side. Somehow I did not imagine that our new leadership would allow for the proper ceremony and reverence to be paid as he was folded into the ocean's final embrace. While they worked at this grim task, William made some effort to scrub the blood from the sheets of the forecastle—until, that is, Mr. Fairchild ordered him off with a look of disgust. There was business to arrange, it seemed, and the quartermaster would prefer to leave some evidence of the cost associated with crossing him. Somehow this was almost more horrible than Mr. Taggart's actual murder: cleanliness and discipline are so deeply ingrained into the mariner that to cast them aside is akin to casting aside one's very humanity.

This, more than anything, convinced me that I could not let matters rest. It was all too easy to imagine how conditions aboard the ship would deteriorate into brutality if Mr. Fairchild were truly allowed to assume command. I had little doubt that he would even implement the abhorrent practice of flogging as punishment for any perceived threat to his authority or that of the boatswain—he had said as much himself. And I had no reason to believe that the murders would stop with Mr. Taggart. It was perhaps now that my life was in its greatest jeopardy to date!

Fortunately, one path to rescue still remained to us. As the men cemented their plans to take control of the ship, I tried desperately to catch William's eye from the fringes of the assembly. Surely he could be counted upon as an ally! When he finally happened to glance in my direction, I held his eye and surreptitiously mimed the act of writing into an open book. Then deliberately I pointed a single finger above our heads at the ship's deck, willing him to understand my coded message.

I need not have worried. After only a moment's confusion, his countenance cleared with understanding and he nodded swiftly. In the event that my meaning remains unclear to the reader, I shall make myself plain: I had seized upon the idea of turning to the writers for help! Mr. Verne and Mr. Clark Russell were possessed of a wealth of world experience at which I could only guess. Was that not the very reason for which the captain had selected them to sail on the *Melville*? Their combined ingenuity would surely be able to devise a solution to the madness which now gripped the crew. While I do not mean to justify the captain's decision to deceive the authors, it occurred to me that we could perhaps turn the very same idea to our advantage in order to facilitate our own redemption. The trick would be to reach them in secret, before any other members of the crew thought to apprehend them first.

In this, we experienced an unexpected stroke of good fortune. It seemed the plan was to delay the mutiny until eight bells, when the captain had originally planned for Mr. Taggart to wake the crew. Well, they would be awake, to be sure, and they meant to storm the captain's cabin as one in order to catch him unawares. Mr. Fairchild made some vague promises about preserving the captain's life and safety, but I did not rate his credibility very highly. Even then I could see Mr. Harris trying to suppress a grin of anticipation and doing rather a poor job of it. Nonetheless, the men were to be left to their own devices until such time as the plan would be put into action. For most of them, that meant returning to their hammocks—even in the midst of a conspiracy and the wake of a murder, the chance to catch some genuine rest aboard a busy sailing ship was not one to be passed by. I realized that I would now need a good reason to leave the forecastle without arousing the quartermaster's suspicion. This meant that I would be forced to swallow my pride and exercise what little cunning I had.

"Mr. Fairchild," I said as I approached him. "I know we have not exactly seen eye to eye on every occasion, but the carpenter's advice has made some impression on me. I would like to preserve my own life, and I can see that will require following my head rather than my heart. I've made no secret of my distaste for the idea of a mutiny, but I understand now that it is our only way to see the men home safely. What I mean to say is that you can count upon me as your man, so far as that goes."

"And how far does it go, I wonder?" he said slowly. His eyes were chips of ice, and his voice was no warmer. "Well, boy, you've run up against me once or twice already. I'd just as soon dispatch you as shake your hand...but I may be able to use you. Just do your damndest to stay out of my way until you're needed."

"Very well, sir." Everything would hinge upon what happened next. "I should only like your guidance on a few particular points, if I can trouble you just a moment further."

The quartermaster only arched an eyebrow. This close to his face, I could see that he was tired. No doubt he would have preferred to take to his bunk like the rest of the crew, but as the chief conspirator he was not to be afforded this luxury. He would be forced to stay alert to ensure that the mutiny was put into effect at the right time. And from what I knew of his character, he would have been loath to go to sleep for fear of waking with a knife in his own throat. It's what he would have done to another, after all. Such is the curse of evil men: they cannot conceive that other men are better, and so they exacerbate their own misery by anticipating betrayal at every turn.

Well, in this instance at least he would not be disappointed. "You see," I continued, "I think it would be in our best interests to give the appearance of nothing untoward until we strike at eight bells. During the interim, all must appear to proceed according to the established routine."

"A novel idea," returned Mr. Fairchild. "How did I incur the good fortune to enjoy the company of such a learned shipmate?

I'm sure we would be sunk without you." His voice was rich with sarcasm, but he was distracted; he started to turn from me almost before he had finished speaking. "I've already sent Mr. Lawrence back to the wheel. That will suffice to establish the appearance of normality. Remember that I told you to stay out of my way."

"My point, sir, is that I am not typically to be found in the forecastle at this time of night." I was gratified to see that he paused, though he did not look back and so I could not see his face. The only thing for it was to press on. "I have become accustomed to roaming the decks and talking with Mr. Verne and Mr. Clark Russell, and I would be remiss to say that they haven't begun expecting me. Remember that I am only on this ship to report on their doings—I fear my absence will be noted this night."

"And you would have me release you now, when you will run straight to the captain? Or even try to gather the writers into some little rebellion?" He laughed, and my heart sank—I hadn't imagined he would guess my purpose quite so quickly.

"Send me with him," came a new voice. It was William. "I may only be your cabin boy, but I am a member of this crew all the same, and I would not see any harm come to my comrades. I too have taken to speaking with the authors of an evening, and my appearance on deck will be very natural indeed." He gestured in my direction. "I will not allow him to put our plan in jeopardy."

Mr. Fairchild did turn back to me now, and his tired eyes were narrowed with suspicion. "Do you think me blind? The two of you are thick as thieves, and no doubt share some common purpose." But then he paused and appeared to think things over. "Nonetheless, while I cannot trust you, I did say that I could use you. There is some truth to what you say. But I do not think I shall send you alone." He turned to the sailors making themselves comfortable in their hammocks.

"Billy!" he called.

Grumbling, Mr. Allen rolled out of his bunk and onto his feet with the smooth, practiced movements of an experienced sailor. He weaved through the dim forecastle and approached our little party.

"Eight bells already, is it?" he grumbled.

Mr. Fairchild frowned at him. "I need you to stick to these two. They want to speak with the *authors.*" He fairly spat the word. "Let them do as they will, but take care that they don't peep a word of our plan. We'll take the authors when we take the captain; I expect they won't object. The Frenchman at least will join us, likely as not. I daresay that fellow was as mad as a bull."

"Aye, sir," said Mr. Allen. He yawned and waved us on ahead of him. I exchanged glances with William; he inclined his head in the scarcest of nods. And so we found ourselves escorted from the forecastle under the sleepy but watchful eyes of Mr. Allen. He followed closely behind us, muttering softly to himself about being roused from his slumber. I pushed open the hatch and emerged onto the deck. It was a clear night, with a swath of stars shining radiantly in the dark firmament overhead. A beautiful night for dark business, I thought. And now we had the additional complication of Mr. Allen to overcome. Would it be possible to slip away from him to alert Mr. Verne and Mr. Clark Russell? On such a bright night, that seemed unlikely. Could we perhaps count upon the unhappy mariner to fall asleep of his own accord? Maybe if we talked with the authors long enough, he would find some comfortable rail to lean upon…

I could see that the two authors were standing together at the stern, leaning over the rail and talking quietly, as was their wont. In happier times I should have been thrilled anew at the prospect of hearing them discuss the creation of their new stories. After spending the days with their heads bent over their writing desks, their diligence broken only by the occasional stroll on deck, the evenings were the writers' opportunities to step back and fully digest the new worlds and characters brimming in their fertile imaginations. While I was not so privileged as to watch them at work, the chance to speak with them while they decompressed from the labor of creation was truly one to savor. Even now, a little thrill coursed through me at the thought. But we had an altogether different errand to accomplish this night—and in any case, I rather thought that the two men would be discussing a different topic this night.

But first I had to focus on solving the problem of Mr. Allen. As we approached Mr. Verne and Mr. Clark Russell, our chaperone yawned loudly. I was very much on edge and my every nerve ending was tingling with fear and anticipation, but I found his yawn contagious nonetheless. When was the last time I had slept? Perhaps I could turn our mutual exhaustion to my advantage.

I began to turn to Mr. Allen with some vague idea of suggesting that he might as well make himself comfortable, since our talks with the writers tended to drag on into the wee hours of the night. But to my utter shock and dismay, Mr. Allen was already falling to the floor! His face hit the deck with a muffled smack, and standing behind him was William, still holding a belaying pin[39] in his upraised fist. He flashed me a sort of sheepish grin as his victim gave a soft groan on the deck and stirred feebly.

"Quick now, help me with him," William said. "I hit him as hard as I was able, but I wouldn't like to gamble on how long he'll stay down."

"What have you done?" I cried, aghast.

"Keep your voice down and take hold of his legs."

"There'll be no saving us now!" I hissed. "What are you going to say when he wakes?" But for a long moment, William just looked at me.

"Take hold of his legs," he repeated finally.

And so, trembling all over but scarcely knowing what else to do, I hoisted the comatose mariner's legs while William strained to raise the man from under his arms.[40] My friend led us to the rail, and a terrible understanding washed over me. I risked a backwards glance to where the writers were clustered on the other side of the ship. So far our struggle had gone unnoticed, and there were none of Mr. Fairchild's men on deck to raise the alarm. I looked back to the rail and the waters churning beneath. The white crests of the waves shone faintly in the glow from the heavens.

"You cannot mean us to…?" I left the thought unsaid. I was also short of breath—Mr. Allen was heavier than he had appeared.

"It's him or us." William's face was uncharacteristically dark. "I don't need to tell you that things won't look very good for us under the command of the quartermaster. On three, now," he said, brooking no further argument.

If it seems impossible that I could have gone along with this, I can offer no argument in my own defense. I would like to say that

[39] Usually made of metal or wood, a belaying pin is used to secure the lines of a ship's rigging.

[40] William Hope Hodgson would become a bodybuilder later in his life; this episode suggests some natural talent for the sport.

I acted according to my better nature, seeking at all costs to prevent a mutiny which would result in an even greater loss of life. I would even like to say that I acted from self-preservation after realizing that only by taking a life could I save my own. Both arguments would perhaps carry some merit in a court of law, but both are falsehoods. I acted only because William had caught me by surprise, and I did not know what else to do. This is one of the great truths of the human condition: our most defining actions are all too often born from nothing more than cowardice and opportunity. At least, this is how it seems to me when I remember how we swung his body back and forth in time with William's count, and how we loosed him over the rail together. And this is how it feels when I recall his limp form striking the waves, scarcely making a splash as the ocean greedily sucked him down. I am sorry that we did not kill him first, because I can scarcely imagine the terror and confusion he must have felt when he entered the frigid water with a shock before drowning in a state of semi-consciousness.

"We therefore commit his body to the deep," muttered William.

I'm afraid I did not let him get any further with this sailor's prayer. It seemed an affront to me that we could now beseech God's grace after betraying Him so thoroughly. "We are damned," I said, turning from Mr. Allen's silent, churning grave to meet the eyes of my friend in consternation and hopelessness.

"Maybe so," he said. "But we are alive, and I will try to keep it that way." He retrieved his belaying pin from where he had left it on the deck. "Now we must move quickly." What transformation had come over my cheerful companion? He was possessed now of a grim determination which I could scarcely credit. I began to realize that he was made of sterner things: unexpected planes and sharp edges. He now gestured to the two writers across the ship. It seemed miraculous that they could not have observed what transpired some thirty yards from their backs. What had transformed my soul into an agony of anguish had gone entirely unnoticed! This, too, is a shared experience of the human race: what reduces one man to despair is beneath even his neighbor's notice.

The writers turned to watch us approach; we had not taken

special care to move quietly now that we had so dramatically escaped our chaperone. As we drew near, I was struck at once by the severe expression on Mr. Verne's face in particular. His eyebrows drew together and his mouth dropped open in surprise. In the flickering glow of their lantern, the gravity of his countenance was multiplied tenfold. A similar appearance of shock soon passed over Mr. Clark Russell's face. I wondered at their ability to detect the change which had come over us—only later would I realize that there was some spatter of blood on William's shirt. Evidently he had thumped Mr. Allen altogether harder than I had realized.

"What is it, boy? You wear a mask of distress," the Frenchman said, seizing me by the forearm to arrest my movement. Even in this state of agitation, it occurred to me to admire the way in which Mr. Verne casually commanded language to such great effect. In school we are taught that the great writers of our time are closer to popular heroes or legends than mere intellectuals or simple entertainers. And what man or woman can meet their heroes and still imagine that they share the common yoke of humanity? This is perhaps not altogether a good thing—but understanding where I stood on the matter will help my reader to understand how I was only too happy to give up control of the enterprise to those whom I viewed as my superiors. I trusted that the authors would be able to grasp the entirety of the situation and to predict all of its possible outcomes. A life spent telling stories about men acting and reacting in extraordinary circumstances had surely furnished the authors with a thorough understanding of those things which motivate a man to pursue one course of action over another. If a satisfactory solution were to be found, it would be these men to find it.

And so I did my best to convey how things stood, recounting the conversation which had passed between Mr. Fairchild and the rest of the crew and what it portended: a violent seizure of the ship at the tolling of eight bells. When I had delivered this dreadful news, Mr. Verne's face grew very forbidding indeed. He nodded with impatience as I spoke, seeming that he would prefer to absorb the information directly from my head than to wait for it to be delivered with the altogether slower efforts of my tongue. But as my jumbled narrative drew to its fitful conclusion, Mr. Clark

Russell only studied my face intently. To my surprise, neither of them immediately pronounced judgment upon our murder of Mr. Allen.

"And why alert us to the mutiny now?" said the Englishman.

"Well," I said, momentarily flummoxed. "Hasn't the captain made his intentions plain to us when he might have kept his motivations to himself? I think he acted with his own kind of loyalty, and I would like to repay him in kind." I paused. "And I would see no more bloodshed this night."

"Indeed not," said Mr. Clark Russell dryly. He flicked the fingers of his left hand against William's shirt before turning to his colleague. "Well then, Jules? Let's hear your opinion. I think we'll have to act soon, before one of the rascals starts looking for their missing sailor."

Mr. Verne gave an abrupt shake of his head. "Of course," he muttered. "In an age of madness, to expect to be untouched by madness is itself a form of madness."

I thought this was rather a circular argument, but it seemed that he meant it only for himself. When he next spoke, I fancied I could see his mind working actively behind his eyes.

"I think we can agree that it would be unwise for us to approach the captain all together," he said.

"Why is that?" I asked.

"Consider the captain's situation," Mr. Clark Russell said. "When he last spoke to us, Mr. Verne and myself were not exactly in his camp."

"I do believe you threatened him," said Mr. Verne.

"I did," returned the Englishman. "And I intend to make good on it. But we'll see if we can spare him the capital punishment." He looked at William and me. "You see, the captain has no reason to believe that we have his best interests at heart. If we take the matter to him, I'm afraid we'll only cause him to dig in his spurs. It may even come to a question of force. No, I think a gentler approach is called for—if we've any chance of bringing the old man around."

"We've another problem to sort out," said Mr. Verne. "Even if the skipper hears us out and credits our tale, how do you think he'll respond? Unless I'm much mistaken, he's apt to charge into the forecastle with pistols blazing. We'll be lucky then to greet the morning with a captain *or* a crew."

"We could deal with the chief instigator ourselves," said William quietly.

"Mr. Fairchild," I realized.

My friend the cabin boy only nodded. To think that he was contemplating a second murder! It would have been the third on this ship in as many hours. And for a moment I feared that the writers would go along with the idea, for Mr. Clark Russell's face transformed momentarily into a mask of fury that I had little suspected lurked behind his perpetually kind appearance.

"I need but to catch him by the scroff and breech," the writer said, "and bring his spine to my knee to kill him. That'll put an end to things quick enough."

"I'm not so sure," I said slowly. "There's Mr. Harris to consider, for one. He's as villainous as the quartermaster, and he's more careful. And the rest of the men didn't exactly leap to the mate's defense when Mr. Fairchild stuck a knife in his throat." My stomach roiled with the memory. "I think killing one of them might actually make matters worse."

"What would you propose, then?" said Mr. Verne softly.

I hesitated, unsure of myself. I had meant to turn matters over to the writers to handle, and here I was arguing with them! But I felt some responsibility for turning the tide of the conversation, so to speak. A mantle of duty seemed to have somehow settled itself around my shoulders, and while I did not relish its burden, I knew what must be done next.

"I will speak with the captain alone." I expected an outcry—surely I was the least qualified man present to undertake the mission. The authors had years of experience and authority on me, and William at least was a member of the crew. I was no one! But there was no outcry; there was not even a halfhearted objection. My companions only looked at me. Could it be that they, too, sensed the inevitability, the *rightness* of my decision?

"I must be the one to convince him," I said, defending myself against no one. "Mr. Clark Russell is correct—the captain will not listen to either of you. And he will not listen to his cabin boy, but for some reason he tolerates me. He didn't precisely welcome me onto the *Melville,* it's true, but he has accepted my presence. He called upon me to spy out the *Veronica,* and he permitted me to board her. I was with him in the cabin of that wreck when he espied his sister's corpse, and I bore witness to his naked grief. He may never call me a friend, but I think that maybe some bond now exists between us." I drew a deep breath and let it out. The wind hitched in my throat. "If there's a chance of persuading him to reverse course, I think it lies with me."

When I had finished speaking, Mr. Verne did something unexpected. He stooped slightly, the better to reach the level of my gaze. He laid a heavy hand on my shoulder and gave it a squeeze. "Twelve years ago, I published the story of a boy named Dick Sand[41]. Little did I look for him to come to life before my very eyes."

Well, my reader can surely imagine the effect that this kind of praise had on me! And this, in the face of the confession that I was a murderer! I looked away, lest my hero see a tear springing to my eye. Keeping my gaze at my feet, I nodded once, twice, stiffly.

"I had better get on with it, then."

I willed myself to approach the captain's cabin with some reluctance. Frankly, I harbored some doubt about whether I would even be able to rouse the man, for he must have taken to his bunk after all of the excitement aboard the *Veronica* (the mutineers were surely counting on the same premise!). Nevertheless, I drew near to his door and rapped upon it several times with my knuckles. It was a bad job I had, to be sure, but I had volunteered for it, and there was no sense in putting things off.

To my surprise, I was answered almost immediately.

"Away with you, Mr. Taggart!" came an abrupt shout from behind the door.

"It's Gordon, sir."

There was a long pause, and then I heard the sound of a bolt unlatching. The door creaked open to reveal just a sliver of light from within, and the captain's face slid into the gap. He looked at me suspiciously, as though he did not quite believe the evidence of

---

[41] *Dick Sand, A Captain at Fifteen* (1878). The titular protagonist of this novel rises to the occasion of captaining his own ship during a crisis at sea, before going on to rescue multiple victims of the African slave trade. To be identified with one of Jules Verne's most heroic characters must have been a tremendous honor.

his own eyes and expected me to transform into the mate without warning.

"The journalist, is it?" He continued to squint at me in the darkness, but I was pleased to observe that there was no evidence of alcohol upon his breath. Perhaps he hadn't given in to despair just yet. "Haven't you had enough horrors for one day, lad?"

"Captain Carrig," I said simply. "The crew means to mutiny."

The suspicious eyes widened, and before I knew what was happening I found myself tugged bodily into the cabin by the collar of my shirt. The captain shut the door behind me and stared at me imperiously, waiting for an explanation. His hands were curled into fists, and for a moment I doubted the wisdom of my plan.

"Well? Out with it, then."

I will spare the reader the particulars of our conversation; suffice it to say that I apprised the captain of the mutiny brewing belowdecks and the appointed hour of the uprising. I intimated strongly that perhaps—just perhaps—if he acted promptly, he might be able to put the whole thing to bed before it really got started. The trick of it was to make sure he felt as though he were coming to the right conclusions on his own. This was not a man who would respond to being told what to do by someone like me. But as my tale progressed and I attempted to steer the captain around to my own view—that a peaceful resolution was still possible—his face only grew darker and darker.

"We must needs gather those of the crew and passengers upon whom we can place our trust," said the captain immediately. He was rallying, and I feared that the situation was already at risk of getting away from me. "Can you shoot a pistol, lad?" He rummaged on a shelf near his desk. "I have some faith in Clark Russell, at least, if only he can be brought around to my way of seeing things," he continued. "Can the Frenchman also be trusted to handle his own? He's not young, although neither am I, exactly. And are there any in the forecastle who might go against the plans of this rascal Fairchild?"

"There is the cabin boy," I said, staggering somewhat under this frantic barrage of questions. "And there is Mr. Derrick. He is wild, but he seems a good fellow at bottom—though I can't see how to separate him from the crew. I trust none of the others." I thought of their dark, glittering eyes aglow with the idea of taking command of the vessel, and shuddered in the gloom of the cabin.

"Very well," said Captain Carrig with a sigh. He turned away from his desk to face me once more. "It is an unlikely enough group: one real mariner, two old men more comfortable with a pen than a knife, and two green boys. But never fear, lad." His eyes glinted dangerously and his mouth twisted in a smile. "Your captain still has a shot in the locker."

Well, this is where things truly took an unexpected turn. The captain checked the lock on his door and then hurried to his bunk. From beneath it, he withdrew a small sea-chest outfitted with a sort of combination lock. He hunched over the chest, jealously guarding the combination from my view. Then he stepped back, holding a mysterious round object in his hands. I recognized it at once: it was the strange spherical device taken from the cabin of the *Veronica*!

Now that I could see it in better light, I was overcome with the same sort of reverence which had beset the carpenter when he first laid eyes upon its workmanship. The device resembled nothing so much as a small wooden globe, comprised entirely of interlocking panels. Each finely-grained panel was carved with cabalistic symbols resembling hieroglyphs, as well as short words or phrases transcribed in a language which I still could not identify. When I had first seen the globe, I had imagined it to be about the size of a large melon—but now it looked smaller in the captain's hands, fitting easily within the grasp of his fingers. Whether this was a trick of the light or some property inherent to the strange device, I cannot say.

"Do you know what it is?" I asked.

"I believe it to be Roger Lundamere's greatest treasure."

I perceived plainly by the look on his face that it was now the captain's greatest treasure, too. His eyes fairly shone with worship as he turned the object gently between his hands. It seemed it would fall to me to bring him back to reality.

"You said you didn't know Roger Lundamere," I reminded him.

"I knew him well enough," confessed the captain, sparing me a sideways glance. "Though I believe he was deceived, and I believe he captured my sister's heart with a lie. But I also believe that much of Colleen's narrative has the ring of truth. As I've said, I have worked with Old Cedar to independently verify as much as we were able." He turned towards me fully now and lowered the device so that I might get a better look at it. His voice became distant. "Our investigations took us into dark corners of old Europe and into a nefarious sort of company still clinging to existence only on the fringes of civilized society. We paid a price, to be sure, but it was no more than I was willing to pay—and we met with some success. It fell to Old Cedar to instruct me in the meaning of these symbols. Alas that she is not here—I'm sorry to say that I proved to be a distracted pupil, and no doubt she would better grasp their meaning. Still…" he trailed off, captivated once more by the esoteric carvings on the wooden ball.

"Still?" I prompted.

"I believe I can decipher just enough. You see, lad—" a gnarled finger pointed to one of the wooden panels, where a tiny owl was depicted next to some indecipherable script—"this etching refers to the 'firstborn.' Well, that's simple enough, isn't it?" He applied some pressure to the panel and dragged it backwards—to my surprise, the little sliver of wood retracted neatly, unlocking itself from the neighboring panels. The captain looked and me and grinned. "Can you guess what comes next?"

"We just have to find the next panel," I said, becoming fascinated despite myself. "And then the next one after that." I'm afraid to say that I was rather neglecting my mission in light of this unexpectedly interesting development. "Did the cook teach you a simple sequence of numbers in this strange language?"

"Nothing so easy as that, but I believe that each symbol is *representative* of a number, if you can work it out. Let's try the panel right next to the first one." He pushed down on a bit of wood marked with a tiny representation of the Earth; nothing happened. "Now why do you suppose that is?"

For a moment I was confounded—but then the answer came to me. "Because the Earth is the *third* planet in the solar system."

"Precisely—so that will be the third panel to unlock."

So it proved. And in this manner, Captain Carrig busied himself with opening the wooden device's many locking mechanisms. I cannot pretend that I understood much of the puzzle; the remaining clues were far more cryptic than the single example which I had been able to solve. And while a few of them were based on various pictograms engraved into its wooden surface, most of the globe's panels were decorated with foreign script instead. The captain may have named himself a distracted pupil, but it was clear to me that he had learned a great deal from Old Cedar. Although he had a few false starts (and a few instances of frustrated cursing), he was able to work the device down to its last handful of panels within the space of about thirty or forty minutes. After a time, my mind started to wander, and I found a convenient seat to rest my legs and watch him work. The captain muttered to himself all the while, occasionally sounding out a word which sounded less like a genuine language and more like the guttural vocalization of some wild beast. I began to grow nervous; our situation was characterized by no small urgency, and I did not like to think how much time we were wasting. But at last the riddle was beaten; the captain turned to me with a look of triumph. I got to my feet, feeling a sudden rush of anticipation and apprehension.

"Only a single panel remains," he said quietly.

"What do you suppose it contains?" I breathed.

"Haven't you already guessed?"

At that moment, there was a tremendous rapping upon the cabin door. The captain's reaction was instantaneous: his upper lip drew back in a feral snarl, and he clutched the wooden device jealously to his chest. His eyes seemed lit from within by a preternatural fire. As for me, my heart lurched suddenly within my own chest—could the mutiny already be underway? What had become of my friends on deck?

"Who goes there?" the captain barked.

"Open this damned door," came the booming timbre of Mr. Verne. I breathed a sigh of relief, even as the muffled sound of voices arguing could be heard from the other side of the door. William was making some protest or other in a plaintive sort of voice, but he was overridden by the brook-no-objections tone of the Frenchman. Finally the placating tones of Mr. Clark Russell intervened, and it was that man who spoke next.

"Gordon," he said. "Are you in there—and are you safe? Has the captain harmed you?"

"I am safe."

"For God's sake, man," spat the captain. "What kind of man

do you think I am?"

"The kind who will listen to reason, I hope," said the Englishman. "Now please open this door; we've much to discuss and only a very short time in which to do it."

The captain stayed fast, so I took it upon myself to unlatch the door and swing it wide. The captain glared at me but made no move to intervene. I think maybe he would have tried, if it weren't for the wooden sphere still in his grasp. Even as Mr. Verne, Mr. Clark Russell, and William made their way into the cabin, his eyes kept darting between the three visitors and the queer object in his hands. But wait—a fourth figure now stepped into the cabin's interior before closing the door behind him. It was the doctor!

"Captain Carrig," said that man. "Mr. Clark Russell took it upon himself to rouse me from the passengers' quarters. He's made the situation plain to me, and the time to act is upon us. Now I understand that we have come a long way, and at great personal—I say, what's that in your hands?" The doctor took a step forward, retrieving his monocle from where it dangled near his stout belly and fitting it to his eye. "Why, that's *das verbotene relikt*—it is from the wreck!" he voice rose in consternation. "I thought we agreed that the risk was now too high?"

"What do you know of this?" demanded Mr. Verne.

But the doctor ignored him.

"Glen," he entreated, dropping any pretense of formality. "We brought an army to rescue a single soul. But she is *lost*." He laid hold of the captain's arms, and the captain made no move to shake him free. I wondered what history existed between them to allow for such an impropriety. "You selected me for my expertise," the doctor continued, "and I have rendered it to the best of my ability. Allow me to render another piece of advice: this goes too far. You cannot take revenge upon a dead man."

But the captain's eyes still smoldered. "I do not seek revenge upon any *man*, living or dead. But I will lay my grievance at the feet of the Father Ocean, if I must, and I will knock down any doors that stand before me. You stood at my side once, Mr. -----, and I would see you stand there again." He looked at each of us in turn. "Do any of the rest of you have the courage to stand with me now?"

"So be it," said the doctor. He dropped his hands from the

captain's arms and stepped back. He looked unutterably weary. "If this is the path you've chosen, I see that I cannot sway you from it. But I will not follow you to my own death."

"For the love of God, man!" shouted Mr. Verne, who had evidently had enough of this melodrama. He took a menacing step toward the skipper. But Captain Carrig leaped backwards lightly, eyes flashing. He transferred the wooden globe to his left hand and raised the index finger of his right. With a spark of intuition, I realized that he intended to slide back the final panel, revealing whatever it was that the clever puzzle had been designed to conceal. Suddenly I felt very afraid of what lay inside. I opened my mouth to give voice to my objection, but it was already too late—the final latch was depressed with an audible *click,* the panel began to retract, and a great many things happened at once.

First: a clear tone sounded, as of a bell or chime ringing through a forest glade at dawn. Mr. Verne stopped in his tracks, freezing in place with the rest of us now caught in the midst of this peculiar drama in the captain's cabin. The chime seemed to pierce me to my very core. I cannot speak for the others, but I felt a rush of contradictory emotions run through me, one succeeding another: elation, betrayal, hope, and an infinite, overwhelming sadness. I watched as tears ran unchecked down William's open face and a look which I can only describe as *haunted* settled itself into the lines of Mr. Clark Russell's aged countenance. All the while, the sound of the bell lingered in the air, and for a moment I somehow imagined that I stood upon the edge of a wood. The grass was wet with morning dew, and the clear chime did not quite serve to eclipse the sound of surf breaking upon some unseen shore. In my mind's own eye, I was given to understand that I stood between two opposites, and I felt the inexorable pull of each. Even now I cannot account for this unfathomable impression—I offer it to the reader only upon its own merits.

Second: the "greatest treasure" of Roger Lundamere opened. With all of its wooden locks disengaged, the spherical container unfurled, splitting neatly into two halves to reveal its prize: a flower of ethereal lightness and beauty. Its translucent purple petals were fringed with the purest white; its golden stamen faintly glittered with iridescent pollen. The flower seemed to burst undiminished from its wooden prison, where the deprivation of light and oxygen had somehow failed to rob it of its vitality. Seen with the echoes of the strange chime still resounding in my ears, the sight fairly took away my breath. Indeed, the very atmosphere around the flower now seemed to shimmer with what appeared for all the world to be sparkling flecks of gold or shining motes of gilded dust. The darkness of the cabin was chased away; here was Life, here was Light, here was Knowledge. Had I not been utterly hypnotized by the sound of the bell and the visions which it conjured, I believe I may have fallen to my knees in worship.

Third: as though in a dream, I saw the heavy figure of the doctor take one hesitant step forward—and then another. I cannot say whether it was a mere trick of my own perception or some unknown agency exerting itself upon his mobility, but his movements were slow and halting as he advanced toward the captain in a haze of shimmering radiance. For indeed, the air around the flower—and, by extension, the captain—was now glittering with iridescent particles to such an extent that I could hardly make out the man's rapt face. They had even begun to make a sort of buzzing sound that I heard not with my ears, but rather within my head.

But this did not impede the doctor. Struggling forward as though he labored to walk underwater, the large man laid hold of the wooden device—and he wrested it from the captain's grip. And then, with an unspeakable sense of devastation welling in my breast, I could do nothing but watch as that man cast the device to the ground! I cried out in anguish, and all manner of unkind thoughts flashed through my mind—my fists clenched and I imagined that if I had killed once, it was perhaps not beyond me to kill again—before the doctor raised one leg and brought his boot to bear upon the round little puzzle of such breathtaking cunning and ingenuity. It splintered into pieces there at the doctor's feet, and I felt its crack rend my heart in twain. I became distantly aware that I was moaning softly, and I felt the salt of tears upon my lips—but the doctor only lifted his foot again and crushed the purple flower beneath his heel, grinding it into the floor of the cabin with a savage, heartless twist. Its petals seemed to wilt instantaneously, and the brilliant luminosity in the atmosphere was snuffed out as though it had never been. I thought that a piece of my soul went with it—how could man look upon the divine and then expect to go on living? Emotions played across the captain's face in a mirror of my own: his rapture and ecstasy were transformed into the bleakest loss and the blackest rage. I thought that he would become violent—and I had more than half a mind to join him.

Fourth, and last: with a great crash, the door to the cabin was flung open! I turned in some confusion—the little room had become my entire world, you see, and I could not conceive that anything outside its bounds could still exist. I'm afraid I was brought back down to earth rather quickly, though: standing in the doorway, of course, was Mr. Fairchild. Who else could it have been? And with the crew at his back and a knife in his fist, he presented a forbidding aspect indeed. But even this rogue was given pause when he took his first step into the cabin and his eyes adjusted to the light. This was scarcely to be wondered at—who could have been expected to make sense of this scene? The six of us stood in a loose circle; tears streaked all of our faces; the floor was littered with the detritus of the foreign spherical device; and a tangible, external sense of *something* still lingered in the air. I could see a sense of fascination creeping across Mr. Fairchild's face, and for one hopeful moment I thought that he might waver in his purpose.

But the quartermaster shook his head, dispelling whatever influence had threatened to take hold of him. "Carrig," he announced. "We mean to take the ship. I can see by the presence of the boys that you've been forewarned. That suits me just fine; any fool can see they weren't to be trusted. Now I will deal with you all alike."

Despite the thick atmosphere of confusion which still reigned in the cabin, some flicker of opposition roused itself in Mr. Verne. "Do you threaten me?" the writer demanded. "You with that little knife? I'll pin it to your neck like a brooch before I'm through." The Frenchman took a step forward, and the quartermaster seemed taken aback by this show of unbridled vehemence. But it was clear that he could not now be deterred at this late stage of the game. He brandished the knife in front of him to halt Mr. Verne's advance.

"Take care, old man," Mr. Fairchild said. "My threat is not to your lives, unless that is your preference. Note that you are sorely outnumbered." He gestured with his free hand to the men milling about at his back. Mr. Harris edged his way into the room, leering at us. Mr. Lawrence stood just behind him, looking impassive. I could even see the towering frame of Mr. Derrick looming above the rest of his shipmates, although I could not read his expression. "We propose only to shut you in the cabin. I will assign a guard to provide for you. We are returning to port; you will be released when we make berth."

"You ungrateful curs," spat the captain. "I'll see each and every one of you arrested." In a flash, he turned and retrieved a pistol from a shelf near his writing desk. He moved with a speed that I had heretofore not suspected. "Those of you as I leave alive, you understand." He aimed the pistol squarely at the quartermaster, who blanched.

"No harm will come to you," came the steady voice of Mr. Derrick. The carpenter shouldered his way through the crowd to stand beside the quartermaster. I couldn't help but think that the leader of the mutiny cut a poor figure next to the massive man. The latter now cast an apologetic look at the captain. "I beg you, captain: stand down," he said. "The Lord knows I've little enough taste for this sort of thing, but the men have spoken. We will not choose to die on weird seas for a lost cause we cannot understand. Now, I know something of your character, and I understand that you feel your pride is damaged here. But it need not be so." He paused, seeming to collect his thoughts. "Any leader of men can take an even greater pride in providing for the safety of those in his charge, and it is no cause for shame to see the light of reason."

"We are not unsympathetic to your cause," said Mr. Clark Russell sternly—and quickly. I thought that he wanted to get in the next word before the notorious philosopher became too carried away with his own monologue. "But a ship needs its captain. Would you make this man"—he gestured at Mr. Fairchild—"your leader? I really do not think he has the stuff needed for it."

"And who would you have us choose, you doddering old fool?" snarled Mr. Fairchild. "Do you fancy the job for yourself?"

"Hardly," said Mr. Clark Russell with an exasperated sort of snort—although the reader will come to see how he assumed that mantle within a relatively short period of time, and how he did so with both grace and humility. "A ship's captain should be a man of principle, though, and I should say that rather disqualifies you from the running."

"Never mind all that," said the captain briskly, before Mr. Fairchild had the opportunity to object. "There's no sense in arguing." He sat down heavily upon his bunk. Incredibly, all of the fight seemed to leach from him before my very eyes. "What's the use, Clark Russell?" he said baldly. He made a futile sort of gesture at the scraps of wooden puzzle at his feet, and then he looked up at his angry crew. "My last hope is lost. Your betrayal is as nothing after the betrayals I have already faced this night." He looked at the doctor, who refused to meet the captain's eyes.

Mr. Fairchild hesitated, seeming suddenly unsure of himself. No doubt he had not expected such sudden capitulation. The men looked askance at each other. They nervously fingered the various weapons—axes, pins, and other instruments both sharp and blunt—which they carried in their hands. But the captain was not done.

"You will not convince me to abandon my post as your captain," he said, "neither by persuasion nor by force. But I will not oppose you." With slumped shoulders, Captain Carrig flagged a tired hand at the helmsman, who still stood motionless in the doorway. "Chart a course to Nantucket, Mr. Lawrence." In his voice was none of the old fire, and something in my soul cried out to see this lively man reduced to despondency. But I suppressed the feeling; there would be plenty of time to mourn the captain's broken spirit when we were safely ashore in Nantucket.

IN WHICH THE DOCTOR TELLS A CURIOUS TALE

"See how elastic our prejudices grow when once love comes to bend them."
-Herman Melville, *Moby-Dick or, The Whale*

"I do think the captain handled that rather well," said William. The mutineers had now dispersed, and the two of us remained in the cabin with the writers and the doctor. The crew had taken the captain with them to begin altering the ship's course, you see; they were not content to delay even a moment. I understood that the captain was to be placed under a constant guard, but he would retain his freedom of movement. That concession had not been made without contention, of course—Mr. Fairchild had been disposed to lock Captain Carrig in his cabin with the rest of us. But the cooler head of Mr. Clark Russell ultimately prevailed; the writer made a strong case for the captain's usefulness. I am happy to say that even Mr. Derrick lent his voice to support the Englishman's argument. As for the rest of the crew, their relief at a peaceful solution was plain to see—although part of me wondered whether Mr. Fairchild only went along with them in order to prevent himself from losing face.

"How so?" I asked my young friend. "It seemed to me that he surrendered utterly."

"Not at all," said William. "While he consented to their demands, he managed to retain his life and his liberty—not to mention his status. I think it was rather neatly done."

"Hmm," said Mr. Verne. "I wonder. Was it the shrewd maneuver of a man with his back to the wall? Or was it just an admission of futility from a man who simply no longer cares? I think we had best keep an eye on our captain. I shouldn't wonder if he throws himself over the rail before we ever see Nantucket."

"Surely not!" protested the doctor with unexpected passion.

Mr. Verne arched one bushy eyebrow. "I do not say that he will, Mr. -----; only that he may." He cracked a rare smile. "I daresay speculation of the captain's philosophy is better suited to that great big carpenter, at any rate."

"However it was, I hate to see him in the clutches of those villains," I said. "They fell in line quickly enough when it was clear that the captain did not mean to contest them, but I fear they are capable of still further treachery."

"It may be for the best," Mr. Verne said. "After all, it is better to meet a tiger on the plain than a serpent in the grass. The captain knows this; you may depend upon it. The men have revealed themselves for what they are, and now we can deal with them accordingly—which is to say that we will continue to use them for their abilities, without extending any of our trust."

Mr. Clark Russell grunted his agreement. "In other words, lad, we'll let them steer us for home—but we'll keep an eye upon them."

It would have to do; I saw no other plan that would both see us home and preserve our life and limb. And so while the crew of the *Melville* busied themselves with raising sails for Nantucket, the five of us remained in the cabin to spend the evening chatting quietly amongst ourselves. Sleep was certainly out of the question after the tumultuous events of the past day—and the tempers of the writers, at least, still burned brightly. With nothing else to occupy my time, I took this opportunity to sweep the scraps of Roger Lundamere's wooden globe into a little pile, frowning at them as I worked. Already the impression of divinity that had gripped me so strongly when the flower was unveiled had begun to fade. Even the tiny withered petals—for such was all that remained of the beautiful purple blossom—failed to rouse any particular emotion within me. I wondered at this. Had it all been within my head? Had I been subject to a momentary lapse of sanity? But no, that could not be; I did not think I had taken leave of my senses to such a radical extent, and I had seen the other men enthralled by its power and hypnotism, just as I had been. But if it *had* been real, what then? What did it portend for our futures? For the very nature of reality itself?

"What troubles you?" asked the doctor.

"Besides our general state of affairs, you mean?" I joked. I became aware that I had been staring into space, but I had some difficulty putting my thoughts into words. "I don't really understand any of this," I said finally. "I'm as happy as the next man to put this episode behind us, but I can't help feeling that we've left things unfinished. There is a story here that's only half-told."

My words were not calculated to pique the interest of the writers in the room, exactly, but it should come as no surprise to learn that they murmured agreement with this sentiment. Emboldened, I continued: "I feel that something very nearly happened here, but I cannot understand what it was. I felt that things would come to a head very quickly indeed if the doctor"—I nodded at him—"had not intervened. Part of me wishes that you had not done so."

"Yes," said Mr. Verne slowly. "That was a singular act. How would one know to destroy the device—and why should it be necessary?"

Singled out in this manner, the doctor appeared to grow uncomfortable. He fussed with his monocle. In another man, this would have been an affectation; with the doctor, it appeared to be no more than a nervous habit. "Very well," said the doctor at some length. "I can see that an explanation is warranted. Furthermore, it appears that none of us are inclined to rest, and it may be that my tale will pass the hours of idleness which still remain to us. But do not look to me for answers to the questions you have posed, *junge*. My information will not by itself bring this story to its conclusion. For that, you must turn elsewhere. I can only tell you the part I have played in this greater drama—such as it is."

"I understand," I said quietly. I found a comfortable spot on the floor and leaned my head against the wall. I could feel the rocking of the ship and hear the creaking of her timbers as the men brought her around. I toyed with the broken shards of the wooden puzzle, turning them about in my hands as the doctor launched into his narration. And what a narration it was! I have done my best to reproduce its particulars here as I remember them. Undoubtedly the reader will marvel at some of its more astonishing elements. I can only trust that those who have accompanied me thus far in my recollections will extend their patience far enough to see the doctor's remarkable story told in full. It is not the first extraordinary account to be recorded in my memoir—nor, I am sad to say, will it be the last.

"I am a doctor," said the doctor, "but I am not the type of doctor which you had perhaps assumed. My practice is not in medicine; I am a *biologe.* But my expertise does not belong to the animal kingdom; instead I specialize in the fields *von pilzen und schimmel*—what you would call, ah, molds and fungi. I am of no great renown even within the rather limited sphere of this profession, I am sorry to say, but my work and publications have attained some small measure of respect. And I am not unknown in the lecture halls of Hanover and Hamburg, though only scarcely do I have occasion to leave the northern academic circuit. It was on one such occasion in January last when I was called upon to deliver a talk in *München*[42].

"You will comprehend, of course, the opportunity that such an invitation represented to me. The lecture was to be held at the *Ludwig-Maximilians-Universität,* where a series of presentations concerning the newest developments on the frontier of modern science were scheduled. My own presentation was intended to reveal my latest discovery: a novel species of eukaryotic microorganism. The circumstances surrounding its discovery I shall explain in due course; suffice it to say for now that it was an exciting opportunity which I could not afford to ignore. Advance notice of the lectures and their anticipated content was published, of course, and soon thereafter I began to receive correspondence from medical professionals inviting me to collaborate with them. You see, there was some interest in studying my discovery with regard to its potential to be developed as a disease-prevention agent.

"I am ashamed to admit that I did not respond to these aspiring colleagues—in the fullness of my pride, I preferred to unveil my discovery to the world as its sole proprietor; only subsequently would I consider associating my work with others. However, there was a single correspondent whose proposal was sufficiently *seltsam* as to capture my interest. I very nearly tossed his letter away with the others, but for its unusual provenance. You

---

[42] i.e., Munich.

see, all of the other letters I disdained originated with respected institutions: universities, medical facilities, and the like. This one appeared to come from a private gentleman. It was an unusual exception, but its contents were even stranger.

"The writer identified himself as an anonymous man of limited means, and he professed to be someone with no ambition of achieving prestige by associating himself with my discovery. Rather, he was full of questions about the discovery itself: where had I found this new species? What were the circumstances of its discovery? Did it possess any properties which I had heretofore found difficult to explain? Had I brought the sample into contact with any other form of organic matter? Again I was tempted to dispose of this lunatic correspondence without reply—what strange questions he asked! But as it turned out, I had *not* previously thought to expose my sample to any foreign biological material. I surmised that I might as well satisfy my curiosity on this point before doing away with the whole affair.

"Well, gentlemen, I must emphasize that my experiment produced astonishing results. Never before had I been gladder of the scientist's *kleiderschrank*: his gloves, his gown, his goggles! Never before was a man so amply rewarded for exercising even the most rudimentary of cautions. I think that the boy understands that danger to which I allude—the rest of you must demonstrate a little more patience. Know that your anxiety to learn more could not hope to match my own. I wrote back to my unknown correspondent in a veritable fever, demanding answers: what had prompted him to suggest such an experiment? What did he already know of my discovery?

"As the calendar turned inexorably to the appointed date of my lecture, our correspondence blossomed into a free exchange of ideas such as I have never before experienced. Here was a soul who, if he lacked my scientific discipline and training, was at least possessed of an enquiring mind! Here was a man who was unbound by the restraint of modern academic schools of thought! This came as something of a revelation to me. I had lived my life within the strict confines of academia, you understand, and it is no exaggeration to say that to be freed of these proverbial chains came as something of a revelation. You see, I began to share the results of my experiments with him—in fragments, at first, but eventually in full. His insights into the problems I encountered were remarkable; his mental acuity was such that he was able to propose ingenious solutions which should have frustrated the most accomplished of scholars. Driven by his encouragement, I increased the scope of my studies and even began to revise the agenda for my impending lecture.

"At some point it occurred to me that my correspondent could not remain anonymous forever. Indeed, it became my most ardent desire that he would consent to attend my now-imminent presentation at *München*, where he could see firsthand the fruits of our shared labors. I wrote to him to suggest such a plan; I even went so far as to offer to pay his expenses, as I had been given to understand that he was not a wealthy fellow. To my dismay, my invitation went unanswered. I could not account for this unprecedented development—had I presumed too much familiarity with someone who so closely guarded his identity? I was thrown into a fair state of disarray, and my nerves were all a jumble. As each day brought no new letter from the postman, I even began to doubt whether I should give my presentation in the first place. Surely the general public could not understand its incredible implications! I realized what a rare correspondent I had found—someone with both the power of observation and the freedom of thought necessary to allow for radical conclusions to be drawn.

"But I was able to muster my courage from some unknown reservoir of *entschlossenheit*, and I gathered the necessary materials for my lecture. On the day itself, I was able to approach the stage with my old confidence. I was received with polite applause from an audience of respected academics and youthful students alike. I had returned to my element, and if the topic of my discussion was somewhat more dramatic than usual, what of it? I trusted in the soundness of my research, even if it had been conducted with the assistance of an absentee layman. And so I plunged into my rehearsed oration, describing the nature of my discovery to my captive listeners—and if I glossed over the specific circumstances surrounding the discovery itself, well, perhaps you will come to understand why.

"After introducing my topic, I finally arrived at the more spectacular part of what I had by now come to view as my performance of the evening. I had traveled with one of my laboratory colleagues, one Dr. Sauer, whom I had risked bringing into my confidences. I rather fancy myself a shrewd judge of character, and my estimation of Dr. Sauer was not incorrect—she proved admirably capable of maintaining the strictest of confidences, and she did not shirk from her duties even when the subject of our experiments became very grim indeed. I only regret that she did not share my passion for the work. But I see that I get ahead of myself—a terrible habit, gentlemen, but one which I find is dreadfully difficult to break.

"As I readied my audience for an element they had not been prepared to expect—a practical demonstration—I asked Dr. Sauer to please bring out two carts which had as yet remained backstage. She gave me a brisk sort of nod and retrieved the requested materials. On each wheeled cart was a small glass tank. One contained a single live cricket; the other, a live mouse. She moved the carts to the edge of the stage near my lectern, where our audience could best glimpse their contents. The occupants of the tank seemed small and insignificant under the bright lights.

"'Shall we begin?' Dr. Sauer asked.

"'At your leisure,' I affirmed.

"From within her laboratory coat—you see, we had both donned our safety gowns for this demonstration, and it was not for mere effect—she withdrew a small vial and held it up in one gloved hand. From within, a softly pulsing purple substance could be seen. Our audience had grown silent with anticipation. Standing at the lectern, I narrated her subsequent movements:

"'My colleague will now place *der pilzen* first with the *insekt.*' Even as I spoke, she neatly emptied the contents of the vial into the first enclosure. The substance evacuated its container like a small amount of jelly, striking the floor of the tank near the cricket. It quivered there on the glass, and then a very curious thing happened. As the *insekt* approached the substance with its antennae wriggling, a small filament or growth extended from the substance to meet the insect's own probing apparatus. What happened next you may have already deduced: the purple growth appeared to squirm across the tank, bridging the gap between it and the insect and enveloping the cricket as a snake will entwine around its prey.

"'Ten seconds,' said Dr. Sauer.

"'My colleague refers to the amount of time which has

elapsed since our demonstration began,' I explained. As we watched, the cricket became entirely consumed by the stuff. It hopped madly about the tank and left a number of purple streaks against the glass.

"'Twenty seconds,' said Dr. Sauer.

"'The consumption of the host is now nearly complete; however, those of you in the front rows may be able to discern how the *insekt* still struggles against its parasitic attacker. The length of this struggle varies from one subject to another—even now you will see that its efforts begin to slow—but my research has indicated that the process is generally complete within—'

"'Forty-five seconds,' said Dr. Sauer.

"I bowed modestly in her direction, enjoying the performance. '*Meine damen und herren,* there you have it: before your very eyes, you have witnessed what I believe to be an entirely unique phenomenon within the natural kingdoms of this earth. Now, before I allow myself to speculate as to the agency by which this substance operates, allow me to introduce one further peculiarity. My colleague will now place a second sample of the microorganism into the next tank; please note that this sample is no greater in volume than the first.'

"Dr. Sauer held up the second vial obligingly. With a sharp twist of her wrist, she emptied it into the tank which housed the rodent. This inquisitive creature immediately approached the purple substance, its little nose twitching. As before, a questing filament rose from the fungus. It first gripped the rodent's nose, and then it *expanded* to encompass the entirety of the creature's head.

"'Ten seconds,' said Dr. Sauer.

"Well, gentlemen, I need not belabor the point. Suffice it to say that as with the cricket, so too with the mouse. The curious point is this: the total time required for the rodent to be killed by the fungus was a mere forty seconds. Further experiments have borne out this trend: a rat was consumed in only thirty-seven seconds, and a hare within just twenty-nine. I have tested various hypotheses and have so far been unable to satisfactorily explain this paradox. But it seems a consistent feature of the moss that the larger its victim's mass, the faster its transformation."

The doctor sat back and mopped his brow. It seemed that

recounting this unusual history had produced some agitation in him.

"This moss," I said. "It is the substance which infested the *Veronica*."

"The very same," the doctor confirmed. "And the experiments which I have described to you have been confirmed by the death of that sailor—Craft, I think he was called. In any case, he was entombed within its growth as neatly as any laboratory rat—and far more quickly."

"Not to mention the rest of that ship's crew," I remembered.

"That's all well and good," said Mr. Verne dismissively. "Let's say that I accept your bizarre story on its face; it's not the first tall tale I've been asked to swallow on this ship. But why destroy that strange purple flower? You had given us to understand that we would see your motive clearly when you finished your tale."

The doctor hesitated, clearly uncomfortable. I think now that he was reluctant to stray from the world he knew: rational explanations, scientific deductions, and quantifiable observations. However horrible, his experiments could be reproduced, and they generated a consistent set of data. His next statement would leave all that behind. But finally he spoke: "It was the color of the flower," he said. "Never before had I perceived such a hue, but once. It is a shade which I do not believe exists in nature—except in the form of that infernal fungus."

"Do you mean to say that the fungus *comes* from the flower?" said William.

"I would not say so," the doctor replied. "I am only willing to go so far as to guess that they are somehow associated. But how could something so terrible derive from something so beautiful? And make no mistake, gentlemen: it was a thing of beauty."

Mr. Verne snorted. "I thought you were a scientist, man. In nature, beauty goes hand-in-hand with danger."

"What was the nature of your discovery? You have not revealed the manner in which you found this substance," said Mr. Clark Russell. Until now, the Englishman had seemed content to listen quietly, absorbing the doctor's tale without speaking. Now it fell to him to keep the story on track. The doctor nodded at him gratefully, plainly relieved to get on with it.

"I will come to that presently. First I must tell how things stood after my public demonstration was complete. I don't mind saying that it made quite an impression upon my audience, and I was called upon to answer a considerable number of questions. Most were quite banal, of course—and not moreso from the students in the room than from my professional colleagues, who ought to have known better. But I received one question from a gentleman which gave me some pause. Here was a well-dressed fellow, and no mistake. But when he stood to deliver his question, I couldn't help but notice that his tuxedo was too small by half—his cuffs did not reach even to his wrists. And while it was evident that he had made some effort to tame his unruly hair, already it had begun to escape its bonds—and what color! Never before had I seen such a fiery hue. All told, he gave the impression of a wild brute forced into civilization for some unthinkable purpose.

"But this notion was swept aside when he spoke. His manner of speech was somewhat rougher than that to which I had been accustomed in my field, you understand. But the probing nature of his questions demonstrated that he had followed my lecture closely and had grasped the reach of its implications. I will not trouble you with the technical particulars of his query; suffice it to say that he wanted to know how I had transported the sample safely to the university. He wanted to know the precise grade of the glass vials in which it was housed; he wanted to know whether we had traveled by private coach; he wanted to know about the condition of German roads and whether the sample might also be transported by water. It was an unaccountable line of questioning which also managed to become vaguely offensive.

"'You may rest assured, sir,' I said, 'that my colleague and I have adhered to the strictest precautions when handling and transporting this organism. No samples have yet been made available to other researchers, and thus there is no fear of the substance endangering anyone. Quite aside from safety considerations, you see, there are also certain proprietary matters to resolve with regard to its discovery.'

"Unexpectedly, this made the man laugh—it was a loud, abrasive sound. 'Discovery, indeed,' he said. 'And pray tell: how was it discovered?'

"I now found myself fairly floundering upon the stage. I had expertly fielded dozens of questions about the effects of the organism, the methods of my experiments, and the *ethik* of working with a substance so volatile. But this man had single-handedly rendered me speechless! I was at a loss to understand his effect on me. Was it his accusatory nature? Was it his liveliness and vigor, so at odds with the decorum and restraint of academia? However it was, I intuitively understood that the situation had the potential to put my carefully composed professional persona—and maybe my very reputation—at sudden risk.

"'Perhaps the gentleman would do us the honor of consulting us privately,' said Dr. Sauer, neatly rescuing me from this strange predicament. She gave a brisk nod in his general direction and then swept a hand over the audience, demonstrating that many eager hands were yet raised. 'We wouldn't wish to deny any of our other attendees the opportunity to make themselves heard.'

"'Of course,' the man said, sitting down abruptly.

The questions which followed from the rest of the audience were of the usual type, although I relied more heavily than usual upon Dr. Sauer to get through them. It was some time before I regained my equilibrium—and it did not last for long. You will not be surprised to learn, I think, that just as soon as the conference let out, we found the man waiting for us. I felt a flurry of nerves as he approached us outside of the campus hall, but undercutting my nerves was a thin thread of anger. I was ready to lay into him, you see, for causing what I perceived as a disruption to my carefully rehearsed performance. Perhaps sensing this, Dr. Sauer laid a cautionary hand upon my forearm. But as the man approached, he forestalled me with an unexpected apology.

"'I must beg your forgiveness for my behavior,' he said. He took my hand in both of his and pumped it jovially. 'But I had to see what kind of stuff you were made of.'

"'I beg your pardon?' I don't mind admitting that I was fairly bemused by this abrupt change of tack.

"'After all, you can't really read a man's character from his letters,' the wild-looking fellow said with a glint of humor in his eyes. 'My name is Glen Carrig, and I have been your mysterious correspondent for some time now.' While I stared at him open-mouthed, he turned to my colleague and bowed low from the waist in an old-fashioned sort of gesture. 'Ma'am.'

"'Doctor, you mean to say,' she said. Her voice was clipped.

"'But of course—Dr. Sauer, isn't it? Yes, I believe our mutual friend has mentioned you once or twice in his letters. Rather a curious decision to bring you into the fold, as it were, wouldn't you say? These are, ah, delicate matters. But then he could hardly be expected to handle things on his own, could he? And I'm afraid to say that I haven't precisely made myself available to participate in his studies.' Incredibly, he winked in my general direction. I thought I detected the smell of spirits upon his breath.

"Well, gentlemen, it is useless to describe the effect that this encounter had begun to work upon me. Now that his identity was revealed, I was forced to reconcile my firsthand impression of the man against the impression I had already formed from the letters he had written. Needless to say, he did not match my expectations in the least. I was surprised to find a man so energetic and well-formed—but so unpolished! I knew there was an active mind behind his rough exterior, but at the moment it was difficult to see. In spite of everything, though—and I fear this reflects rather badly upon my pride—my predominant response to this revelation was to be insulted. Had I not invited him to my lecture, and had he not chosen to ignore my invitation? To accost me now in this jocular manner was to show a level of disrespect which I was unprepared to tolerate. I began to actually feel my face flushing red with anger.

"However, the man you know as your *kapitän* managed to preempt me yet again. Though I do not think that he has shown this facet of his personality to any of you gathered here today, he is not a man without certain charms. 'And of course you are owed further apologies for my failure to continue our correspondence,' he said smoothly. He cast a sideways glance at Dr. Sauer. 'I was unfortunately preoccupied with investigations of a certain, ah, sensitive nature…which required the full investment of my time. There are particulars of these investigations which I should like to discuss, should you find yourself able to forgive my poor social graces.'

"Now, you will have already gathered that I did not turn him away; else I would not be sitting here before you to tell my tale. But my tale has already grown long, and I think that morning is nearly upon us. Therefore I will speed us along to its conclusion, such as it is. We agreed to meet privately at my hotel, whereupon he might reveal to me the purpose of his visit—for he had made it quite plain that the opportunity to observe my lecture, while valuable, was not what had truly drawn him to my country.

"'Did you not wonder at the method by which your 'discovery' was made available to you?' he finally asked me when we had gathered in the privacy of my rented room.

"And now we come to it, gentlemen: that which I have been so reluctant to reveal. Even now, see how I cling to my pride! But I suppose it's no use prevaricating. I did not really discover the microorganism, not in any real sense of the word. Nor was its entry into my life especially dramatic; it simply arrived in the post, in the form of an unmarked package with no return address. The fungus itself was packed in straw and triple-sealed in redundant glass containers within this package, and it was accompanied by a handwritten note which stated only that I must under no circumstances come into direct contact with the substance enclosed therein. The note went on to say that the properties of the organism may prove to be novel enough to alter the course of my professional career.

"If it seems unlikely that I would have embraced this unexpected windfall in the manner I have described, you must understand only that the world of academia is one of naked ambition, and such a boon was not to be disregarded out of hand. But never did I expect to be confronted about the true nature of this discovery. I had concocted a vague story about harvesting the mold in the wilds of Bohemia that was sufficient to publish the results of my work. I trusted that I could rely upon the professional discretion of my peers to let matters rest there.

"And so I was wary when I said to him: 'what do you know of it?'

"'More than any other, save yourself,' he returned with another of those lecherous winks. 'It was me who sent it to you.'

"'What!' I demanded. 'That cannot be possible!'

"'I should rather say that it was not really me—but a certain, ah, colleague of mine, whose acquaintance I expect you'll be making shortly.' His expression grew suddenly serious, and he raised a callused hand to hold off my bewildered sputtering. 'It may be that I owe you a third apology this night. If I have deceived you, please understand that I only did so at great need. And do not make the mistake of thinking that our correspondence has been anything but genuine. You see, it is of the utmost importance that together we come to understand the nature of this peculiar substance.

"'I am undertaking a sort of mission,' he continued. He laid a hand over my own and leaned closer, giving the effect of taking me into his confidences. 'I am looking for a person who is dear to me; someone who has gone missing. You must understand that I do not speak of a kidnapping. Agencies are at work here with which the authorities are not equipped to grapple. Instead I have had no choice but to take it upon myself to delve into certain old worlds—and old words. I have made inquiries into particular esoteric matters—I do not think I need say more on this point. Only understand that in this manner, my colleague and I were able to come across the organism which is now in your possession. I have reason to believe that my dear one's fate is tied up with it. I hope that you can understand now why we sought the expertise of a qualified scientist to examine the properties of this organism. We need to know what we're up against, as the saying goes, if we're to have any chance of success at all.'

"'Who is the missing person?' I demanded, seizing upon the only element of the story which could perhaps be substantiated. But as I spoke, I was shocked to see the man's eyes welling with unshed tears.

"'She is my sister,' he said in the barest whisper. 'And I fear she is lost.'

"I laid a hand upon his arm. Pity and empathy coursed through me like a great wave. I forgot my anger at being used. I set aside my bewilderment at his unaccountable story. You see, another sentiment had now risen to the surface of my constitution. Relief. You may scarcely credit this response, but I was relieved to learn that the missing woman was only his sister. And as I was enveloped in this rush of emotion, so too was your captain. His tears spilled from his eyes, and his body began to shudder with suppressed sobs. I leaned in to wrap him in a consoling embrace, and he took me into his arms. I do not think I shall say what happened there next, for some confidences were not meant to be betrayed. But upon the next morning, I agreed to serve as the

Melville's doctor, to the best of my limited ability."

As he told his story, the doctor had continued to play absentmindedly with his monocle. Now he popped it back in place and stared at us defiantly, daring any of us to challenge him. But for several long moments, no one spoke. I believe we were all too busy digesting the doctor's long, strange chronicle. For my own part, the most shocking part of the doctor's tale did not pertain to the experiments which that man practiced upon the deadly moss. Had I not already seen its terrible, carnivorous proclivities for myself? Nor was I especially troubled by the nature or extent of the relationship between the doctor and the captain. This was trivial in light of the incredible events which had so recently taken place before my very eyes. Instead, I simply marveled at the idea that Captain Carrig was capable of impassioned elocution; of vulnerability; of affection; of anything, in short, but impatience and obstinacy. I remembered how the captain had read aloud the contents of his sister's letter. How bitter he had now become! I realized that the doctor had known a different man—maybe a better man. I wondered if that man would ever be seen again.

"'Old worlds, and old words,'" said William thoughtfully, breaking the silence of the cabin. "That was what Captain Carrig said?"

The doctor nodded. "You will have surmised that his colleague was the woman you know as Old Cedar. I believe the captain acted according to her advice. And I don't rightly know where he found the woman, or what kind of person she really was, but make no mistake, she was no mere cook. If some 'old world' did exist in the proverbial shadows, Old Cedar could have led him there. Count upon it."

"As for 'old words,' I think I can take a guess," I said. "The captain told me that the cook was well-versed in some obscure tongue. She taught the captain just enough of this language to allow him to open the wooden puzzle." I held up a broken splinter of the device to emphasize my point. "I think that much of this riddle rests upon the shoulders of Old Cedar. Never before have I so strongly lamented her demise."

"Maybe it does—but this brings us no closer to an understanding," said Mr. Verne abruptly, clapping his hands and rising from where he had sat in the corner to listen to the doctor's tale.

"I am not sure that I *want* to understand," said Mr. Clark Russell. "Plainly these folk have brought an evil upon us. And the only way to work out of a ship's timbers the ill-luck that's been put into them by what's magical and hellish, is for a minister of religion to come aboard, call all hands to prayer, and ask of the Lord a blessing on the ship."

"We don't even have a cook," said the Frenchman dryly. "I think you'll find it difficult to conjure up a minister. But do not look at me so angrily, Clark Russell. I do not disagree with you in principle. The fact of the matter is that we were deceived into boarding this ship upon false pretenses and under what have proven to be very dangerous circumstances. I will not render judgment upon whether these circumstances are supernatural. There is danger enough in the behavior of the ship's men. But I had thought that the blame rested solely with the captain. Now I see the doctor must accept his measure of responsibility for this subterfuge, too."

"What would you have us do?" William said timidly. "Mutiny against the mutineers? We are already sailing home."

Mr. Verne waved a hand. "Nothing like that, lad. I only mean to make it clear that the doctor will share in the legal consequences waiting for the captain when we make berth."

"Now listen here," said the doctor. "I have played my part in this game, and I will make no excuses for my behavior. Have I not already confessed to blind ambition, pride, and arrogance? I will face the consequences of my actions as any man must. But I will not allow you to besmirch the captain's good name. What he has done, he has done for love. Never was there a more noble pursuit!"

"Sit down and settle down, man," growled Mr. Verne. "Or I'll put you down myself."

"*Mein Gott!* Is that the way of it, then?" shouted the doctor. Leaping forward, he seized a letter opener from the captain's desk and brandished it wildly before him. Mr. Verne stumbled backwards and reached for a weapon of his own. But the desk was full of nothing but maps and papers. He seized upon the only instrument to hand: a heavy-bound book from one of the captain's shelves. He held it up to fend off the doctor's undisciplined strokes.

Well, this was shaping up to be a fine confrontation! The doctor was some years younger than the Frenchman, to be sure, but I think I have already described the poor state of his physical condition. While Mr. Verne was the older man, he was full of a certain vigor which I felt sure the doctor would be unable to match. But I was not prepared to stand witness to more violence this day, even if it were to be wrought with books and stationery tools. I grit my teeth and prepared to intervene if it proved to be necessary; I did not relish the thought of placing myself in opposition to one of my greatest heroes. It was therefore to my tremendous relief that I was spared this moral dilemma when the cabin door was suddenly thrown wide.

Captain Carrig rushed into the cabin and only looked at the two men getting ready to fight, his expression alternating between urgency and bewilderment. Over his shoulder, the crewman who had been assigned to guard the captain appeared equally mystified. Under different circumstances, their baffled faces would have been amusing.

"Verne! -----! What is this nonsense?"

The doctor tried to explain, but the captain would have none of it.

"Never mind that," he said sternly. "That is quite enough skulking and arguing in the darkness. I've come to bring you all out on deck. Daybreak is upon us, and there is something which demands your attention."

TELLS HOW A STRANGE MIST ENVELOPED THE *MELVILLE* AND OF THE SUBSEQUENT HORRORS WHICH BEFELL HER CREW

"All are born with halters round their necks."
-Herman Melville, *Moby-Dick or, The Whale*

As we followed the captain and his guard out to the main deck, I saw how the men had prepared the ship for the onset of daybreak. The galley had been transformed into a laundry; stockings and mittens were laid out to dry, whilst all manner of lighter clothing and gear was strung along the adjacent rigging to take advantage of the wind and sun. The morning was still overcast and the daylight was obscured by a low mist, but the heat would be brutal when the sun broke through, and I suspected it would not be long before the clothing was dry. I wondered what Old Cedar would make of this change—but then I remembered that she was in no position to object.

We marched behind the captain past the galley and all the way to wheel, where Mr. Lawrence stood on duty. Now that the ship had been outfitted with canvas and was under full sail, she clipped along through the water at some speed. The helmsman nodded at our approach, and we drew to a halt. None of us returned the nod; instead, Mr. Verne turned to the captain with an impatient sort of pivot. He still clutched the book in his hand, and I should not have wondered if he had meant to strike the captain with it.

"Well, what is it?" he said. "I see nothing amiss."

The answer came not from the captain, but from the helmsman.

"It wasn't long before daybreak when I sent 'Husky' Folsom up into the rigging to see what he could see." If I have not mentioned this sailor by name before now, this is because there is very little to say about him. You may have surmised, of course, that he was not a particularly small man. Therefore his nickname amongst the crew was a foregone conclusion. I craned my neck to see whether the big fellow was still clinging to the lines, but what the helmsman said next made me look back at him sharply. "After about an hour, he hailed the deck from the topsail-yard to say that he had sighted a mass of land on the horizon."

"But we cannot be so close to Nantucket as that," I said.

"Nothing like that, lad," said the captain. "Husky's as fool as the rest of this lot. It's a distant wave, I'll wager. A wave can show black from this distance. Most of these men before the mast, for all their skill—and they know how to brace a sail well enough, I'll admit—understand very little of the trade which is their livelihood."

I'm sure there was something to be said for the captain's wisdom; he had certainly led the crew this far and had proved to be a sharp judge of the mariner's character. But I could not help thinking that he was still harboring some bitterness for the so-recent rebellion which had cost him the command of his ship—in effect if not in name.

And yet even if his words were an uncontested truth, I should think they rather illustrate those most admirable qualities of the seaman. To brave the greatest gales; to perch aloft in the towering rigging amongst breakers as tall as the ship herself; to endure months of lonely, hard labor, and all without understanding how a course is charted or how the captain navigates his ship across the sea? It shows a sort of steadfastness which is unmatched among men ashore—and yet it may even have its echo there, for that matter. For so do we all go about our trades—and who among us can pretend to understand all of life's machinations?

Of course, it was neither my place nor my particular inclination to jump to the defense of the mutineers. And in any case, a more pressing element of our situation presently became apparent.

"So it was a wave, then," said Mr. Clark Russell. "What would you have us see, if not the presence of land? The sea is all but draped in a featureless fog, in point of fact. I cannot distinguish any particular point of interest."

"That *is* the point of interest, as it turns out," said Mr.

Lawrence. He removed a spyglass from the interior of his jacket and passed it to the author. I recognized it as the captain's property and was reminded of the mutiny all over again. But Mr. Clark Russell accepted the spyglass and fitted it to his eye as he stepped to the rail.

"Very well," he said. "Where would you have me look?"

The helmsman gave a rare chuckle. "North, south, east, or west," he said cryptically. "I don't expect these landsmen here to comprehend what they're looking at, but I'm told that you know something of the sea.[43] That bank of fog—do you see the manner by which it advances?"

Mr. Clark Russell gave a start. "Its speed is astounding! What phenomenon is this? At such a rate, we'll be—"

"Come on, man." Mr. Verne snatched the spyglass from him and stood there staring at the mist for some time. But I did not need its powers of magnification to see for myself what had so startled the writers: a thick, dense mist was encroaching upon the *Melville* from all sides. When we first exited the cabin, I had thought it nothing but morning fog to be burned away with the action of the rising sun. But as it crept upon us with a rapidity that even now is hard for me to believe, I began to suspect that it portended something—well, something not quite natural.

"What causes this fog to plague us in such a manner?" I said. "Can we sail under these conditions?"

"It's no more than a vagrancy of nature," said the helmsman with his usual composure. "It will be of no consequence to our navigation. You may rest assured upon that point. I'm a better helm than that, and I will rely upon our charts to see us home. But even so…I've seen nothing like it in all my years at sea."

"Hmm," said Mr. Verne. "The approach of the great phenomena of nature excites vague uneasiness in the heart of every sentient being, even in the most strong-minded." He cast a look at the captain as he spoke, and I wondered what he was trying to communicate. But it was Mr. Clark Russell who responded first.

"It's a queer thing, and no mistake," he said. "But I see no reason that the fog should necessarily portend any great calamity. I

[43] William Clark Russell served in the United Kingdom's Merchant Navy for eight years, beginning at the tender age of 13.

thank you, Mr. Carrig, for bringing this to our attention—but I am inclined to agree with the helmsman's verdict."

Would that he had been right! How different our voyage may have been! What loss of life could even now have been prevented, if only we had taken the time to prepare for what was coming? But nature is wont to unravel the wisdom of even the most learned men—to say nothing of the dire circumstances when agencies other than the natural may be at work.

And so the hours passed, and the unaccountable mist drew nearer, beginning to wrap itself around the ship like a cloak. Whether we were really unaware of our danger or only willfully ignorant of its imminence, we elected to pass the next few hours at the rail, engaged in that philosophical species of conversation which came so naturally to Mr. Verne and Mr. Clark Russell. William and I were rarely consulted during these proceedings, but we did not begrudge our company this neglect. This was what I had shipped for, after all: to be privy to the creative process of these great minds—to say nothing of the article which I still hoped to write, even after everything that had happened. In its own fashion, this was not an unpleasant manner in which to while away the morning hours; the inscrutable atmosphere even lent an air of romanticism and mystery to the writers' conversation. I'm sorry to say that the captain had quickly lost interest in their dialogue and moved off to check on various elements of the ship, always with his chaperone in tow. It seemed that even under armed guard, he would not be divorced from the performance of his duties. This left the four of us unsupervised by the mutineers, although it must be stated that there was precious little to do with our newfound freedom.

By noontime, though, the mist had enveloped us completely. Even when the sun should have stood at its zenith in the sky, it remained invisible to us. Indeed, it became all too easy to imagine that we sailed now in perpetual twilight. I looked up into the rigging and was a little surprised to learn that I could not quite make out the topmost spars of the ship's masts, for they were utterly obscured by the swirling, opaque vapors which now dominated the atmosphere. I began to grow concerned, despite the relative equanimity of my comrades, and it occurred to me that I had seen neither heads nor tails of the crew for some time now. I must also admit that I was still troubled by what William and I had done to the unfortunate Mr. Allen. Thoughts of what must have been his terrible final moments recurred to me without warning, and I began to feel a potent admixture of guilt and uneasiness. So I took it upon myself to go and speak with the helmsman. I did not imagine what kind of update he would be able to provide, but any information would be more than I currently possessed—and I would welcome the distraction from my interior thoughts.

As I stepped away from the rail, I was astonished to observe that the mist had now grown so thick as to permeate the ship itself. I could only just discern the shape of Mr. Lawrence standing at the wheel. I looked back once as I approached him. William and the two authors had become as mere silhouettes in the fog: ghostly shapes without definition or substance. But the helmsman must have noted the sound of my approach, for he called to me through the murk, singing out to discover who approached him. I identified myself and did not wonder to hear that my own voice shook.

"Ah, the writer," said the quiet helmsman. "Although it occurs to me as that label might stand in for any number of men on this particular ship."

"Where is the captain?"

"Back in his cabin, I should say. Even now I don't think he quite grasps the state of things. He is a professional meddler, that one." He said this without malice. "We had to fairly march him back to his quarters."

"And where is the crew?" I knew that I wouldn't be able to see them in so close an atmosphere, but it seemed unnaturally quiet on deck. Surely I should have heard the shouts of the men at work.

"They are belowdecks, by and large," said the helmsman. "You've been chatting at the rail for some time—I sent them away an hour past. It seems they cannot abide this queer mist. They were beginning to grow…restless."

"But don't you need all hands to man the ship under these conditions?"

Mr. Lawrence grunted. "I can sail the ship well enough on my own. I brought her through that storm, didn't I?" But then he paused. "There's something to what you say, though. Lord knows I could use a man to serve as lookout. I'm not worried about running aground—there's no land here, despite what that fool Husky might have said. But there's a very real danger of striking a reef or shoal in weather this close, and we should be hard put upon to effect repairs with morale so low." He peered at me closely. "I think you've already paid one visit to the crow's nest? I'd be much obliged if you'd consent to a second performance. Just tell me where this pall of cloud starts to grow thin, and I'll point our prow in that direction."

The reader may be surprised to learn that I did not object to the helmsman's request. I had already climbed the rigging once, after all, and under wetter and more dangerous conditions, to boot. This would be a timely opportunity to divorce my mind from its tortured ruminations on guilt and distress: an active body, I think, is perhaps the only cure for an active mind.

So once again I hauled myself from rope to rope, climbing higher and higher into a strange world of huge canvas sheets and taut, trembling lines. But there was no wind, no rain, and no sound to accompany my second adventure into the shrouds and stays of the mainmast. As I carefully navigated that no-man's land between the main topmast stay and the lower main topgallant[44], the occluding mist pressed closely about me. I could feel the slickness of the wood and rope where the atmosphere had condensed from vapor to water and rendered each step more treacherous than the last. I risked a glance at my feet and was chagrined to discover that the deck was now completely obscured by eddying curls of mist, like the exhalations of some terrible beast. And as above, so below: the crow's nest itself was invisible to me; a destination whose existence I could trust but could not verify.

At length, I did reach the little structure just above the top platform of the mast. Perched aloft there like the bird for which the feature was named, I turned carefully in a circle to look out over the sea, my clenched fingers white against the basket. But it was a sea of fog which met my eyes—extending in all directions like a featureless plain, alternately translucent and opaque, a totality of obfuscation which deadened all sound and vision. But wait—not all sound! With a suddenness that nearly caused me to topple from the mast in alarm, a horrible howling cry resounded from

---

[44] About halfway up the mainmast, where handholds would be comparatively few and far between.

somewhere in the shadows below me. Even as I steadied myself against the mast, the howl was cut short and replaced by what sounded like nothing so much as the clashing of metal and the splintering of wood. And so with a shout of dismay, I launched myself from the crow's nest and began to effect a hurried descent through the ropes, slipping one hand under another and fairly vaulting through the rigging at a reckless speed, throwing caution to the proverbial wind.

"Mr. Lawrence!" I yelled upon reaching the main stay, where I paused to collect my bearings, lest I inadvertently tumble into some deadly conflict raging on deck. I should have been able to see the helmsman by now, but there was no response from the churning mist which even now screened the ship itself from my eyes. And the clashing, clattering din which had drawn me from the crow's nest had now ceased altogether. I hung in place for several long moments, my arms rapidly tiring, while a stray breeze blew tendrils of fog about my unshaven face. Beads of moisture clung to my eyebrows and lashes; I shook my head with cowardly indecision and scattered the drops into the void below me.

Finally I determined that I had no choice but to fully descend to the deck and make what investigations I could. Dropping my heels to sheets, I made my way to the ship's wheel by memory. The miasma on board had now grown so impenetrable as to render visual navigation an impossibility. Fortunately, I had now spent enough time on the ship that finding my way posed no great challenge. And I think I even handled it rather well when I arrived at the wheel and saw its silhouette turning lazily on its own—now left, now right—in slow half-revolutions. It had been utterly abandoned; the helmsman was nowhere to be seen. I considered taking the wheel for myself, but only briefly; I knew nothing of sailing and doubted whether I even had the strength required to bring the wheel under the control of my arms.

"Mr. Lawrence!" I called again into the fog. But the sound of my voice did not carry; it was as though it were seized by the mist and smothered the very instant it escaped my lungs. I felt suddenly breathless.

But my query must have reached at least one pair of ears, for without warning the limber form of William materialized just a few yards from my position. I was inordinately relieved to see him;

I don't think that I had realized, until that moment, just how tightly the queer atmosphere and inexplicable sounds of battle had wound my nerves—to say nothing of my lonely and taxing climb to the crow's nest. I clasped William warmly on the shoulder. Any grievances I had nursed about being forced into the murder of Mr. Allen were forgotten.

"My friend," I said. "Where is everyone? Did you hear that screaming?"

"The writers returned to the passengers' cabin some time ago," William said. "I daresay they'll have a lot to write about." He attempted to smile but swallowed nervously instead. "I did hear the scream, and the row which followed. I cannot say whence it came, but as there are no men on deck…"

"The forecastle?" I said.

"It's as good a place to search as any," he allowed.

Well, I need hardly say how little I relished the idea of returning to the sailors' quarters. I was quickly developing a negative association with the very idea of the forecastle. First there was that dark and haunted chamber on board the *Veronica,* into which I had plunged not once but twice. Then there was the *Melville*'s own forecastle, where the idea of mutiny had been conceived and where unspeakable violence had already occurred. But there was nothing else for it; the unaccountable absence of the crew had to be resolved. We would need the men to get us through this unnatural weather, I thought, even if I did not especially delight in their company.

And so we made our way to the bow and the little hatch leading to the forecastle. I stooped to open it but paused in the act. I looked at William. "Do you think we ought to fetch the writers?"

William considered. "I don't think so. They are stout men, and I would like to have them in my corner, but I think this calls for more delicate work. We are entering close quarters where I should value the ability to maneuver quickly and quietly over having strength in numbers."

I nodded; it was well reasoned. "And what about the captain?"

William's countenance darkened. "Even were he unguarded, I would not bring him into this business."

"Why do you say that?"

"To tell you the truth," he said, hesitating, "I think the captain is still struggling with everything that's happened. I would not really trust his judgment."

Surprised at such a candid response, I said: "How do you mean?"

"Well, Captain Carrig has brought Mr. Verne and Mr. Clark Russell aboard, as it turns out, for his own ends. He intended to rely upon their expertise in the pursuit of his missing sister. I don't think I need to tell you what a harebrained scheme that was. But after the episode with the derelict and its sequel—a mutiny—I think he may now be driven to his wit's end."

As he said this, I noticed for the first time the pallor of his complexion. But this was hardly to be wondered at; the events of the previous day were surely enough to unman any sailor—let alone a cabin boy. And we did not know what awaited us in the forecastle, after all. I can only say that I, at least, felt a potent presentiment of dread and anxiety. But I nodded to William and attempted to swallow my own doubts. I think this is the best that any one of us can do in this life: plagued by uncertainty, we can only press on. The alternative is to surrender to fear and indecision. Ah, but here's the rub: which is worse? The fear itself—or the confirmation of one's fears? I'm sorry to say that I had the dubious honor of experiencing both.

For presently I opened the door to the forecastle and crept down the short stairs with William at my back. And as I stepped into the perpetual gloom, I discovered to my horror that the forecastle had become as a charnel house. Unmoving forms were scattered about the floor; dark stains shone dully in the lamplight. Bones stuck out here and there, white as the keys of the piano in the Green Pelican. The corpses were not whole, but had been quartered into diverse pieces and strewn about like so many bits of refuse. There was no smell. There was no sound. I stood there frozen in place, choking back a sudden surge of bile, and made a terrible sort of eye contact with the disembodied head of Mr. Lawrence where it rested beneath a gently swaying sailor's hammock. His eyes were open, and there was blood upon his lips. His head had been severed at the neck, and it was not a clean cut. A bit of windpipe protruded from the ragged wound. Nearby I spotted a large facedown corpse which could only have belonged to Husky Folsom. His head was still attached, but it had been bludgeoned beyond recognition. My eyes then fell upon the leering grin and vacant eyes of Mr. Harris, the boatswain. He was slumped against the wall to my left and appeared wholly intact but for the carpenter's adze protruding from his belly. He had been spitted like a boar; blood still shone wetly upon the buttons of his coat, and his arms were broken and twisted.

And have you not already guessed the architect of this unrestrained madness? Standing with his back to us at the far corner of the forecastle was the unmistakable figure of Mr. Derrick. In his right hand was clutched a wide-bladed carpenter's axe, now greased with gore and little fragments of flesh. He was painted in shadow, and his shoulders were slumped. His head hung down, and he shifted his weight from one side to the other, leaning back and forth with the rocking of the ship. He looked for all the world like some apocalyptic woodsman, delivered from the furthest reaches of hell expressly to butcher the entire crew of the *Melville.* For that is what he had done—and we had just stepped into his slaughterhouse.

William's fingers dug into my arm as he took in the terrible scene from over my shoulder. His breath hitched in his throat—and the carpenter heard him. With a dreadful slowness of movement, Mr. Derrick turned in our direction. His wet hair obscured his face, but I could see in the flickering light that his clothes were spattered with blood. Then he took a step forward, and I saw something which even now I cannot explain. You see, the unaccountable mist which had pervaded the atmosphere had begun to permeate even the sailors' berths. But it was as yet a general sort of haziness; an intangible dimness rather than anything of substance. But this was not true of the air surrounding the carpenter's head. Thin whirls of fog churned about his temples, spinning around his face and—yes, it was true—*into his ears.* After everything that has happened to me, I cannot say that I am troubled overmuch by the alleged sin which is blasphemy—but I hope my reader will forgive the comparison which occurred to me next. For as Mr. Derrick took a lurching step in my direction and the little rings of mist moved with him, I thought it looked like he wore a crown of shifting, translucent thorns. And why not? Jesus, too, was a carpenter.

But even upon the cross I do not think that the Christ ever

looked upon man with such anguish. Mr. Derrick now raised his head; blood dripped from the ends of his wet hair; and he cast upon me an expression of total hopelessness and grief. Tears cascaded down pale, grimy cheeks. I have written before of faces transformed by emotion. This is not a literary device; the carpenter was unrecognizable.

"It's…it's in my head," this stranger said. Though we were separated by mere yards, his voice came to me as from across a great gulf or chasm. I realized that we were now separated by entire worlds. The carpenter made a futile little gesture with his left hand as he took another step forward, half-raising it to point at the roiling atmosphere still pouring into and out of his ears. His right hand still grasped the weapon with which he had wrought such terrible destruction.

"Help me," Mr. Derrick sobbed.

"We must go to him," said William in a strained whisper. He took a half-step forward, hands outstretched as though he would simultaneously comfort the carpenter and ward off the strokes of his axe.

"We must flee," I said. I placed a restraining hand on my friend's arm, pressing him to remain in the spot where he stood. Being a proper member of the crew, William was my superior in rank, if not in age, and in truth he need not have felt any compulsion to obey my order. But matters of rank and file have the tendency to fall away in the presence of mortal danger. And make no mistake—though he had handled me with kindness, though he entreated our aid now, approaching the carpenter would be tantamount to suicide. Here in the semidarkness of the sailors' hammocks and chests and bones where the air fairly thrummed with a lethal sort of energy, I knew that the carpenter would cut us down as quickly as he had the rest of the crew.

"Please," Mr. Derrick now begged. He took another step forward. But even as he pleaded for our assistance, he hefted the axe in his right hand. "The choice was taken from me," he said, his voice querulous. "It's in my head, and it's taken it from me."

Well, things were coming to a head now. The carpenter was rapidly closing the distance between us, even with his halting movements. It was time to escape—or to risk becoming embroiled in a confrontation which could not end well for either William or myself, unarmed as we were. But I would make one more attempt; I owed Mr. Derrick at least that much. I held out my hands.

"You have a choice now, man!" I said. "Lay down that weapon."

But the carpenter only shook his head sadly and continued to advance. His arm—and the axe with it—crept higher. I could plainly see that he meant to bring it down with tremendous force upon whichever of us was foolish enough to stand in front of him. I grabbed hold of William's collar and began to drag him back to the stairs. Mr. Derrick paused, looking confused at our flight. "Where are you going?" he cried. "Don't abandon me to this thing."

But abandon him we did. Keeping my eyes on the carpenter, I shoved William up the stairs behind me. He opened the hatch to the main deck; the forecastle should by rights have been flooded with daylight now, but instead a mass of swirling fog forced its way past us into the dark chamber. As it rolled beyond the hammocks and gathered around the carpenter's feet, I saw his look of despondency reach new depths. His hands fell to his sides, and he wailed. It was an unearthly, ungodly sound with nothing human in it. I followed William to the deck and shut the door to the forecastle upon his terrible cry.

"We must block the door," said William. He was panting for breath.

But I was frozen, hunched over with my hands on my knees. I could not move. I was overcome with horror, and the blood was pounding in my temples. I could scarcely even hear my friend's voice over the sound of my own heart. Grisly scenes of the nightmare belowdecks continued to flash through my mind. I saw repeated images of the carpenter laying about with his axe, rending the limbs of his friends and comrades. I even thought I heard the cries of the men as they collapsed beneath the prodigious force of his blows. And I could not stop the memory of the carpenter's final cry as the mists closed in on him in the darkness; I thought the sound of it might linger in my head for the rest of my days. Never before had I imagined that such loss and torture could reverberate from a human throat.

Not for the first time, it fell to my young friend to rouse me from my despair. "Come on," William urged. "I don't think we can expect him to stay down there." I stood slowly, recovering my composure. I did not trust myself to speak yet, so I simply nodded. William's plan was a good one; if we could prevent the carpenter's reentry onto the deck, we could prevent more violence from occurring until we were able to devise a plan to deal with him. It would perhaps have been more prudent for one of us to stand guard at the hatch, but we could not bear the thought of separating and losing each other in the dense fog which had now fully settled over the *Melville*. So we set off together into the murk, roving about the deck in some desperation and looking for an object which could serve the purpose of blocking the door.

This is how we blundered directly into Mr. Verne and Mr. Clark Russell. You may be sure that they gave me a good start, emerging abruptly from the shadows without a sound—although I suppose we must have done the same to them. I almost turned to flee in my surprise, but the Frenchman's hands fell upon on my shoulders and held me in place. Irritation flashed across his face, but then he perceived our state of distress. His features softened as Mr. Clark Russell likewise blocked William's movement. My friend had not attempted to escape the writers, but he seemed intent on pursuing his quest with a single-minded purpose. His eyes wandered across the deck, still looking for something with which to barricade the forecastle.

"Well, boy? What ails you?" Mr. Verne demanded in his characteristically stentorian voice.

"There are none left living," I managed to gasp out. The author must have seen the truth by the stricken quality of my expression, for he did not ask me to clarify what must have been an astonishing statement. Instead he turned to William for confirmation, and while the boy remained silent, what Mr. Verne read on his face must have satisfied him as to the veracity of my report. He exchanged glances with Mr. Clark Russell before tightening his grip on my shoulders. Then they began to march us forcibly off into the fog.

"Where are we going?" I protested.

"We have to—" began William.

"We go to see the captain," said Mr. Clark Russell grimly. His tone brooked no argument. And so I am sorry to say that our errand was left incomplete; the door to the forecastle remained unsealed. It was a negligence which we would presently have cause to regret, even if our minds were now turned to another purpose. For we approached the captain's cabin more quickly than I would have believed; but then, there was both agency and urgency in the advance of the writers. They had not seen the terrible violence wrought by the carpenter, but they must have heard the cacophony which followed in its wake. And while I could not begin to guess what aid they now sought from a deposed skipper, perhaps it was as simple a motive as finding strength and solidarity with anyone still drawing breath on this ship.

But how had things come to this terrible juncture? Just yesterday the men had sung in unison and pulled together to work the pumps. Now that camaraderie was gone; now the men themselves were gone! I felt the dissolution of all my hope and optimism, and I thought that I could sink no lower—little did I know what frightful surprises fate still held in store for me.

As it turned out, the seaman assigned to guard the captain's cabin was grateful to see us, and it was immediately apparent that he was very much on edge. He fingered his blunt weapon nervously and bobbed his head in eager assent when Mr. Verne demanded entry. His eyes darted nervously across the mist-shrouded deck as he stepped aside to let us pass. But as we stepped through the narrow aperture of the cabin door, he plucked at my sleeve.

"Do you know what happened?" he said. "Where are the men?"

I hesitated. I had read enough fiction to recognize the dangers of losing morale in a crisis. But didn't this man also deserve to know the truth? "Something has happened belowdecks," I said. He looked confused and worried at this admittedly evasive response. "Something bad," I clarified. "The men are…gone. I'm sorry, but I can say no more. I think that at least you are relieved of guard duty."

"This ship is cursed," he said with a shiver.

Well, I had nothing to say to that. It was a thought which had also occurred to me over and over again during the course of the past day. But I didn't like hearing it aloud. So I pushed past him and entered the cabin. Inside, the captain sat on his bunk, his head hanging down. The inexplicable fog had penetrated even these private quarters, making his form appear indistinct and ethereal.

He looked up at us as we entered the little room. It seemed that the mist could diminish even this fearsome man's presence. His fiery mane of hair was dulled to the shade of dying embers. His face, so often splotched red with passion, was colorless. He seemed somehow less than real. And when he spoke, there was but a trace of the customary authority in his voice.

"I don't suppose you've come with any good news," he said.

"I'm afraid not," Mr. Verne said brusquely.

"Out with it, then. What was that great noise? I'm afraid my, ah, stalwart guard did not permit me to investigate." There, at least, was a hint of the wryness which so often characterized his temperament.

But Mr. Verne only snorted. "A stiff breeze would knock that man over."

"He won't trouble you anymore, in any case," I said.

"What do you mean?" said the captain.

Only a short time ago, I would have quailed before such an imperious demand from authority. Consider it, then, a mark of my trauma and exhaustion that I did not so much as stutter when I replied. "Only that this man was following orders," I said. "And there are none left now to issue these orders."

The captain's eyebrows shot into his hair. "What is he on about? Make yourselves plain, now. I've suffered enough mystery—and misery—to last me a lifetime. Get on with it, or get out of my cabin. Where are the men?"

"Let the boy tell you," Mr. Verne responded with a pointed look in my direction. "He's made a fine start of it, and it would do you credit to exercise a little patience."

"They are dead," I said baldly, scarcely knowing how else to frame the matter.

"Dead?" Captain Carrig's face was beginning to redden. It was only the mark of consternation and anger, but it made him look that much more like his old self. His hands were clenched into fists. "How can that be?"

"The carpenter has…slain them," I said.

"That cannot be!" the captain said. "He is a peaceful fellow." And then, as though he were working himself around to consider the idea: "All of them were slain by Mr. Derrick?"

"Call it not Mr. Derrick," I said. "The man showed me

kindness, and I would not have his memory tainted by association with whatever evil has now come here to roost." I hesitated. "But yes, that's the way of it: all of them, save your guard."

I saw that my words served to bring a little more color to the captain's countenance. But while his eyes were animated now with mounting emotion, I saw no sign of disbelief or shock. He did not ask me precisely how the men had met their end. He did not ask what became of the carpenter. And I did not see any indication that he was experiencing the panic which had infected myself and William. Beside me, the cabin boy was still trembling with anxiety—but the captain maintained what composure he had.

"Where is the doctor?" he said quietly.

"You expected this," Mr. Clark Russell said suddenly, arriving at the same conclusion which had only just occurred to me. Accusation was plain in his voice. "You've brought something upon us. It has to do with this fog, doesn't it?"

"Where is the doctor?" the captain repeated.

"For God's sake, man," I pleaded. "They are beyond the care of any doctor. If you know what it is which plagues us, I beg you to make a clean breast of it."

"Where—is—he?" Each word was drawn to its fullest length.

"Enough!" roared Mr. Verne. And suddenly he was between the captain and the rest of us, his considerable stature serving to physically interrupt this fruitless back-and-forth. The Frenchman jabbed a finger at Mr. Clark Russell without looking away from the captain. "Answer him!" he said. "What do you know of this?"

And then the captain stood, too. He was no less imposing than Mr. Verne; they were of about the same height and not dissimilar in build. But where Mr. Verne was confused and frightened, the captain had already accepted our situation. He turned a peculiar expression onto each of us in turn. I had the impression that in both a literal and figurative sense of the phrase, he was looking down upon us all. And when he spoke, his tone suggested that he was only telling us something we should have already known.

"That which took *her*…has come for us," he said.

"Then you have led it to us," Mr. Verne said, and I saw with alarm that his hands were curling into fists. But if the captain's flushed face were any indication, he too was on the verge of violence. Each man now raised his fists, prepared to strike. But this was no time for argument amongst ourselves! An atrocity had been committed belowdecks, an atrocity which I felt sure had somehow been perpetrated by the fog which even now continued to gather and thicken, engulfing the ship. We had to act now; any delay on our parts could mean the loss of our chances to escape unharmed! So for the second time in less than a day, and in the very same room, no less, I prepared to wade into the fray to restrain Mr. Verne.

To my great relief, it transpired that I was not alone in this train of thought. Presently Mr. Clark Russell stepped forward and laid a hand on Mr. Verne's shoulder. He shook his head when he spoke.

"There will be opportunity enough to assign blame, should we make it through the afternoon," the Englishman said. His voice was reserved, but I noticed that a pistol had appeared in his good hand. The threat was implicit.

Well, neither the Frenchman nor the captain could fail to see the sense of this good advice. Though reluctant, they each lowered their arms to their sides. But Mr. Clark Russell was taking no chances; he moved between the two men and addressed the captain directly, speaking mere inches from his face.

"Mr. Carrig," he said. "You should not have retrieved that infernal device from the derelict." It was not a question, but a statement. "Even I can follow the basic principles of cause and effect, and it seems to me that this thick atmosphere only began to settle upon us after you opened this object and exposed what was inside. But what's done is done—at least that's what I've been told—and now we must focus on the question of survival."

The captain considered Mr. Clark Russell with narrowed eyes. Perhaps because the Englishman approached with rationality instead of anger (as Mr. Verne had done), he consented to hear the man out. Or perhaps he now recognized that we had reached a state of genuine crisis—and that he had only a finite number of allies with which to address this crisis. However it was, finally the captain laughed.

"Well, this is a fine thing," he said. "The mutineers are all dead, but it seems as though I shall not be restored to my command!" His laughter faded. "But it will be as you say, Clark

Russell. Let us get about the business of surviving."

Mr. Verne scowled, but Mr. Clark Russell allowed himself a small chuckle. "Very good," he said, and he clapped the captain once on the shoulder before turning to face the rest of us. "Gordon," he said, "get that man from the doorway. We'll take anyone still living with us when we go."

"You cannot mean for us to leave the ship?" William said.

But it was the captain who answered. "He's right, lad. We'll take one of the boats. I believe the *Melville* has been *marked*, if you take my meaning, and I should not like to be aboard when that which is responsible for destroying the *Veronica* comes to call. But we may be able to escape unnoticed if we move swiftly and put some distance between us and the ship."

"But we shall be lost in this terrible fog!" protested William.

While they argued the relative merits of this escape plan, I obeyed Mr. Clark Russell's orders and went to the door to retrieve the captain's guard. But when I swung the door open upon its well-oiled hinges, that man was nowhere to be seen. There was nothing but an impenetrable wall of slate-gray fog to meet my prying eyes. The atmosphere was thicker and denser than ever; I could see not fully three feet in front of me.

And it was then, with my vision all but robbed by this unnatural miasma, that I began to detect something far more ominous: a sound. From somewhere across the deck and over the rail, I heard the unmistakable splashing of water. But it was not the little sort of splash that poor Mr. Allen had made when we tossed him comatose into the sea; this was a great and terrible roiling which made me think of a whale breaching the surface of the ocean. And then the ship began to move.

I fell suddenly forward as the *Melville*'s bow pitched upward; I would have tipped directly onto my face had Mr. Verne not caught me by the collar of my shirt and held me upright. He had fallen against the doorframe and remained standing; bracing himself, he hauled me back into the cabin and tossed me bodily against the wall. The whole world was askew. I looked around at the frightened faces of the survivors. Mr. Clark Russell and Captain Carrig had fallen against the captain's bunk. William sat bewildered on the floor where had fallen, holding himself in place with his legs outstretched against the wall.

"What just happened?" said Mr. Clark Russell.

But then the ship rocked again, plunging backwards toward her stern. The five of us were thrown against the cabin's far wall. With a great deal of cursing and shouting, we landed in various states of disarray. I struck my head against the side of the captain's writing desk; for a moment my vision swam, and I remembered that I was supposed to have suffered a concussion. But this seemed like it was a lifetime ago, and it was the least of my worries now. I could see that panic was beginning to infect the cabin; even William had suddenly come around to the idea of escaping.

"We must go now!" he shouted.

"I'm afraid it's too late," the captain said. His voice was small. "They have already arrived."

THE WRECK OF THE MELVILLE

"Consider, once more, the universal cannibalism of the sea; all whose creatures prey upon each other, carrying on eternal war since the world began."
-Herman Melville, *Moby-Dick or, The Whale*

Even as the captain made his terrible pronouncement, a new sound began to ring throughout the fog and to filter through the wooden walls of the cabin. I can best describe this sound as the chittering or chirping of a rodent—only writ large beyond all reason. The volume of the sound suggested that it originated with something of such size that my mind's eye shied away from even beginning to guess the kind of creature which could produce it. William clapped his hands over his ears as the sound stretched and elongated into a shrill kind of keening noise; despite its high pitch, it reverberated with a contradictory deepness which I could feel in my chest like a bass drum. It was a terrible thing; a thing not of this world. But what came next was worse, because it was something which I *could* identify: the rending and tearing of wood. The ship presently rocked anew, pitching back and forth in violent shudders as whatever unspeakable things had landed upon her deck now started the business of bringing the *Melville* to her ruin.

For all his faults, his lies, and his deceptions, I cannot denigrate the captain's actions in the face of this unprecedented catastrophe. He got to his feet, riding out the forceful shudders of the ship with the legs of a man accustomed to life at sea. With loose, balanced movements, he strode to the corner of the cabin and retrieved a small sea-chest from beneath another set of shelves. And as he knelt to open this chest, a modest cache of weaponry was revealed to us: two small pistols and what appeared to be an antique sabre. The captain retrieved one of the pistols for himself and tossed the other to Mr. Verne. As for the sword, he held it out to me with his eyebrows raised. I rose to accept it from his grasp, but a tremor struck the ship just as another of those cataclysmic screeches rang out. The noise filled my head, and I stumbled forward.

“Careful now,” the captain said. Incredibly, he was smiling. Some men thrive on crisis; was the captain one of this kind?

I took the sabre by its grip and hefted its weight in my hand. It was utterly alien to me, but I supposed that its operation was simple enough. I would like to say that it gave me comfort, but I’m afraid it only reinforced the idea that we were all in extraordinary danger. Even now, I was still troubled over the murder of Mr. Allen; the fact that he would almost certainly have been killed in the forecastle anyway did little to assuage my guilt. And so I resolved that I would utilize my new weapon only at great need—in the last defenses of my life or the lives of my friends.

Thus armed, the five of us moved to the cabin door. No weapon had been found for William, and I was especially determined to protect him, if it came to that.

“Our plan has not changed,” said Mr. Clark Russell. “I do not know what awaits us out there—unless the captain can shed any light upon the question—no? Well, it hardly matters. We will march directly to one of the boats. You will follow my lead and we will move closely together. If we come across any of the crew, we will bring them with us. If we do not, we will not go searching for them. It is plain to me that to linger on this ship will mean our deaths.”

It was about as good a plan as could be devised under the circumstances. My reader will recall that the *Melville* had four boats, each suspended by tackles and hooked to davits fastened to the ship’s sides. I guessed that we could reach one of them in a matter of minutes—provided that we were not lost in the fog, and that we were not caught by whatever entities were cracking the ship into broken fragments as they loosed their horrible, screeching cries into the premature twilight of the mist. It was a gamble, to be sure. And there was an additional complication which I had not foreseen.

“I will not leave without the doctor,” the captain said presently.

Mr. Clark Russell took a long, hard look at Captain Carrig. Whatever he saw there must have been enough to convince him that arguing would be an exercise in futility which would only cost us more time. He nodded stiffly. "I'm not happy about it," the Englishman said. "But we'll go to the passengers' quarters first."

"Should we prepare the boat while you look for him?" I asked.

Mr. Clark Russell shook his head. "We stay together. I won't go so far as to say that there's safety in numbers, because I don't know what we're about to run up against on the other side of this door. But I will say that sticking together represents our best chance." As if to underscore the writer's pronouncement, there came from beyond the door a great crashing din. The entire ship shuddered.

"The mainmast goes," said Captain Carrig in a voice utterly devoid of emotion. "The *Melville* flounders, and its captain has failed. We shall all of us drown." What color had returned to his cheeks was now gone entirely. When he spoke, his voice was fled of all command; for a brief moment it was simplicity itself to see the boy he must once have been; a boy filled with love and concern for the safety of his sister, and little else. He stared ahead with a naked emptiness in his countenance which was altogether more frightening than any fit of rage he had previously displayed.

"I don't think so—not yet, at any rate," said Mr. Verne. "Now pull yourselves together and let's get moving—step lively, now." The writer was the first to walk through the door, leading us to a scene more terrible than I, at least, could have imagined.

You see, the captain's cabin was situated at the aft end of the ship. As we left these quarters, I became aware that the source of the crashing and keening was virtually over our heads—it was no wonder the ship had shaken so violently! I spun around in sudden terror, straining to pierce the soupy atmosphere with my eyes. And then I saw it—or thought I did. I could discern only snatches of a colossal form looming through the mist. It was a shadow cloaked in shadow, alternately glimpsed and hidden as the layers of fog shifted with a light breeze rippling though the sails. I garnered a fleeting impression of a great domed hump, like the curvature of a turtle's shell, perched upon the ship's stern. This was a mammoth, sloping shape which reached nearly to the top of the mizzenmast;

its outermost edges became invisible in the fog. But the gargantuan monstrosity was not comprised solely of its arching shell: curling through the mist were what I can only describe as writhing, twisting appendages, greater in length than two men laid head to toe. There were dozens of these reaching arms; in a great crash of horror, I realized that my terrible guess had been correct. Whatever this leviathan was, it was tearing the entire ship apart piece by piece—and it was using these appendages to do the job!

Even as I watched, a great chunk of the rail was torn from its moorings and sent hurtling through the air past our heads. I flinched as it crashed somewhere behind us amidships, sending chunks of splintered wood careening across the deck.

"What…is it?" William cried.

"The end of the world," said the captain.

"Let's keep moving," said Mr. Clark Russell.

The passengers' quarters were nothing so glamorous as the captain's cabin or even the writers' quarters. In point of fact, the doctor was actually staying in steerage: a sort of cargo hold on the lower deck. It was not an enviable class of accommodation, and by-and-large I think I may have had the better deal in the forecastle. At least, I would have done—but I had spied a few personal accoutrements in the captain's cabin which led me to believe that the doctor may have been spending rather more of his time in that berth. But that is neither here nor there, and it was to steerage that we now marched with weapons drawn, clustered about each other in a tight formation as we moved across the deck in the shadow of the nigh-invisible wailing *presence* which threatened to eclipse all coherent action and thought.

But we never made it to steerage, for it pains me to say that Captain Carrig was correct: the mainmast was destroyed. The great towering structure of wood and canvas had collapsed upon the deck, broken off just above the main stay. It had wreaked tremendous havoc upon the deck in its fall; the sheets were broken and splintered, the rail obliterated. Great tears were rent in the fabric of the sails, and the netting was warped and snarled hopelessly. It would be impossible to move any farther across the deck without becoming entangled and mired in this mess.

But even as I looked upon this devastation in dismay, I saw the author of its destruction: another of the terrible, nameless *things* had landed near the foremast. Its reaching tentacles flashed intermittently through the fog, toying with the wreckage of the mast. All at once I understood why the ship had been rocked from end to end: it must have been the weight of these dreadful entities alternately striking the deck as they made their landing. And now there was one of them on either side of us! To make matters worse, their terrible cries had now ratcheted into a cacophony that rendered clear thought impossible. I felt surrounded. I spun in a circle, uncertain where even to point the blade of my sabre.

But then another cry rang out: a sound full of lament which I had heard once before in the cabin of the *Veronica.* It was the captain, for he had made another discovery: pinned beneath the massive weight of the fallen mast was the doctor! The rotund man groaned feebly at our approach; I could scarcely hear him over the incredible din caused by the ghastly actions of the half-glimpsed monsters. The poor fellow was trapped by his ankles; incredibly, he was otherwise unhurt. But he did not seem to be fully conscious, and his lower extremities were ruined; even I could see at once that he would never walk again. This did not stop the captain, who bent at the knees and began hopelessly straining at the mast.

"It is futile," barked Mr. Verne.

"He's right," Mr. Clark Russell said. "He is done for, Mr. Carrig."

I felt a wash of disgust, even for my own heroes. To give up now would be to condemn this man to death. Even if it were an exercise in futility, even if the world were crashing down around our ears, I could not abandon the doctor now. I knelt next to the captain and lent my own small strength to his efforts. Beside me, William did the same. With a heavy sigh that I could hear even over the sound of the creatures busy at their godless work at either end of the ship, Mr. Verne finally consented to join us. Mr. Clark Russell did not, for he took it upon himself to guard us with his pistol while we struggled in vain against the weight of the mast. I pulled with all of my power, until I felt myself go faint and my vision wavered. But finally we were forced to abandon our efforts; the strength of ten more men would have been wasted in such an impossible task. I sank back onto my heels to recover my breath.

"What can we do now?" I gasped.

"Would that we had the carpenter's tools," panted William. "Perhaps we could cut him free."

The captain opened his mouth to reply, but it was then that the doctor stirred. "Glen," he said. From where he lie prone on the ground, he pointed over our shoulders.

"Who goes there!" shouted Mr. Clark Russell. He fired a shot into the air as a sort of warning. For a shadow was now dragging itself to us from out of an obscurity of mist. As it stumbled into our proximity, this spectre resolved into the shape of a man: it was Mr. Derrick—and oh, how I regretted that we had not sealed him in the forecastle! The carpenter moved in a manner most unnatural, owing to his twisted and misshapen legs, which were surely broken. Had he inflicted these terrible wounds upon himself? An axe was still gripped in his hand, after all. But his neck was broken also, and his head now hung at an impossible angle. The carpenter's mouth was open, trailing blood. When he spoke, he was unable to properly articulate his words. I have done my best to reproduce his words here as I understood them.

"I tried to stop it," the carpenter said. "But I couldn't stop it, captain." His voice was wetter and slower than I had ever heard it. "And it's a curious thing: I think I am no longer among the living."

"What wickedness is this?" said Mr. Clark Russell, aghast.

"The Father Ocean comes to call," Mr. Derrick said. "Do you sense His approach? I think your sister heard that thunder."

Well, I'm sorry to say that we all stood more or less frozen as Mr. Derrick drew near, stunned by the man's broken appearance and inscrutable words. Would that we had halted his progress! Only the captain stepped forward, a heartrending convergence of fascination and hope writ large across his face. He stood before the shattered carpenter, his hands limp at his sides. His pistol dropped from nerveless fingers to land forgotten upon the deck.

"What do you know of her?" the captain asked softly.

"He knows nothing of your sister!" Mr. Verne shouted—though for my own part, I was not so sure. It seemed to me that despite the limited visibility afforded by the dim light and swirling fog, I saw clearly into the carpenter's eyes—and they swam with secrets from some realm beyond this one. Even as this occurred to me, the strangled voice of the carpenter rang out to reinforce my fears—and to draw Mr. Carrig further into its net.

"Her name was Colleen, wasn't it?" the carpenter said slowly. "He has taken her. But He comes now, and all Struggle will cease." As he spoke, I thought I heard the distant sound of thunder rolling somewhere above the fog, and I went cold all over.

But it seemed as though Mr. Verne had heard enough. Brooking no further argument and waiting for no man's permission, the Frenchman seized this moment to step past the rest of us and to place his pistol directly against the carpenter's chest.

What happened next I can scarcely credit. It was a frenzy of unpredictable violence: Mr. Verne fired his pistol once, twice. The carpenter doubled over with the force of the impacts, but he did not fall. Blood spilled across the deck as Mr. Verne kept firing, but the hammer in his pistol clicked; it was empty. The carpenter straightened to his full stature and raised his axe high above his head. With his other hand he pushed Captain Carrig aside; the captain stumbled and nearly fell. And then the axe came whistling down—but its target was neither the captain nor Mr. Verne.

With a sickening sound I doubt that I shall ever forget, the weapon lodged itself in the doctor's back. That worthy cried out in shock and in pain—and the captain's response was immediate. He closed with the carpenter, wresting him away from the fallen form of the doctor and pushing him backwards over the ruins of the mainmast. They collapsed into a heap, one on top of the other. The captain seized hold of the carpenter's throat and pushed him bodily into the debris of spars and rigging. The carpenter made no sound as he was driven into the wreckage.

"Look out!" William shouted. A note of terror in his voice caught my attention, and I risked looking away from the deadly struggle between the two big men. And it was a good thing I did: for at the prow of the ship, the second of the unimaginably colossal shelled entities had turned its attentions to the foremast. As the creature dragged itself across the deck with the strength of its questing appendages, I was at last able to get a good look at the nature of its form emerging from the fog.

And this is what I saw: a tremendous, curved, cream-colored shell scraping high against the sails. It had already reduced the outer and inner jibs to shreds. The shell appeared to be smooth in texture and was striated with markings not unlike the stripes on a tiger's pelt. The shell was longer on its bottom; where it terminated on top, a bony sort of plate extended to protect an enormous, staring eye. Its gaze swept right past me, and I felt a new species of horror—but it appeared that I was beneath its notice. It was an unthinking, unseeing eye that was bent only on destruction. And just past this bloodshot, swiveling globe was its mouth, or at least what served as its mouth: a mass of writhing tentacles that stretched and reached to grasp at the ship, drawing the behemoth's bulk across the deck. Its shell made an awful scouring as it progressed, ripping chunks from the sheets. Seeing it so clearly was a revelation of the worst kind; it was a totality of horror and impossibility. But now, at least, we could also put a name to it.

"A nautilus," breathed Mr. Verne in a voice full of awe.

But this was no time for wonder. Even as he spoke, two of the oversized cephalopods' wet appendages wrapped themselves around the foremast. With a flash of intuition, I realized that we stood directly in the path of danger—not from the nautilus itself, but from the mast itself. And the destruction of the foremast was effected more quickly than I ever could have believed. With a terrible crack, the great structure of wood and canvas which allowed us to ply the seas came tumbling down. My recollection of what came next is fuzzy and indistinct; I can reassemble the details now only because William was able to report them to me. I must have acted from instinct: rushing forward, I seized the captain by the back of his shirt. He was still caught in the mess of the collapsed mainmast, pummeling the carpenter for all he was worth. I dragged him backwards and to his feet—and not a moment too soon. The upper half of the foremast collided with the deck in a great crashing rumble; I squeezed my eyes shut against an apocalypse of splinters and debris. When I opened them, I saw that the entire deck had caved in on itself. The ship was already flooding with water, and Mr. Derrick was buried, crushed beneath the weight of the mast. Such was the second and final death of the *Melville*'s carpenter and would-be philosopher. And so too did the doctor perish, if the carpenter's axe had not already killed him; for he was now lost in the collapse below. Even the great nautilus itself sunk into the crater it had made; it thrashed about in the flooding, ruined compartments which were all that remained of the *Melville*'s hold. Its keening cry sounded louder than ever, and its writhing arms snaked along the sides of the hole to grasp at anything they could reach.

Mr. Clark Russell ushered us away from the edge and from the blind appendages of the beast. “We cannot reach the boats at the bow of the ship any longer,” he said. I thought this was rather obvious, but it did serve to bring all of us back to our present need: to focus on our survival. “We go back to the stern,” he continued, “and we take one of the two boats remaining there.”

“Another beast lies in that direction,” said William. His face was pale and bleeding where he had been struck by a flying chunk of wood. “We cannot hope to reach them safely.”

Mr. Clark Russell peered into the churning mist at the ship’s aft. The monstrous creature there had not yet managed to destroy the mizzenmast, but I knew it was only a question of time. When the Englishman spoke again, his voice was grim. “It’s a slim possibility of survival, I’ll admit, but I should take that possibility over the certainty of our demise. We must rely upon the grace of God to escape with our lives.”

“God’s got little enough to do with it,” Captain Carrig snarled. His face was streaked with tears and purpled with bruises, but there was something of his old spirit in his voice. “We must rely upon our own devices now. To the boats!”

No one dared to argue, and as a group we advanced at a rapid-yet-cautious pace across the deck toward the first of the two boats which were accessible to us. As we crossed the length of the ship, I wondered at the wisdom of moving closer to one of the monsters. But what choice did we have? Mr. Clark Russell’s mouth was set into a thin, hard line. Mr. Verne looked determined but tired. The captain looked ready to throttle the nautilus with his bare hands. It was only in William’s countenance that I found the mirror of my own emotions: trepidation and worry.

We arrived at the first boat without incident, but we discovered to our chagrin that it had met with much the same fate as the mainmast and foremast. It still hung askew from one of its tackles, but its hull was punctured with a multitude of rents and tears. It was clear at a glance that the boat would be utterly unseaworthy—in point of fact, it was a poor skeleton which could scarcely be called a frame, to say nothing of a boat. The sense of hopelessness which had been raging within me ever since my encounter with Mr. Derrick in the forecastle threatened to reach a new pitch; and yet I was surprised to discover a voice within me that responded not with panic but with a calm species of resignation.

It seemed to me that it was the same dissatisfied voice which had been so unhappy with the banality of life on shore—the very voice, in other words, which had led me into these dire circumstances in the first place. But that voice was no longer a malcontent: bereft of ennui and wanderlust, having finally led me into events which completely eclipsed the relative mundanity of my life as I had once known it, that voice seemed to say only: *Here you are.* I thought of the carpenter, of the doctor—indeed, of the entire crew. In contrast to them all, I still drew breath. I determined anew to do my utmost to survive.

"One chance yet remains," the captain muttered as we approached the last of the boats which we would be able to reach: our final hope to escape the *Melville* before she sunk to the ocean's floor. Though the boat was marred by a series of scratches and gouges which spoke to the attention of the nautilus, there seemed to be no catastrophic damage which would prevent its utilization. In effect, the boat was whole.

"She is in better shape than the others," Mr. Clark Russell allowed in a dry voice, "though it remains to be seen whether she shall survive wind and wave."

"The dangers of wind and wave are not those which we have most to dread," said Mr. Verne. He surveyed the boat with a critical eye before turning his head in the direction of the mizzenmast, where the shadowy form of the first nautilus could still be glimpsed; it gnawed and chewed at the increasingly fragmented wood. It was clear that this apparition weighed heavily upon Mr. Verne's mind.

"And yet they may sink us as surely as any monster," returned Mr. Clark Russell, following the Frenchman's gaze before turning his head to lock eyes with his colleague. "And it seems we have little enough choice in the matter. Even if these creatures were to withdraw—which I should not count upon—we've taken on too much water. We'll be underwater within the hour."

"Then we go," said Mr. Verne simply.

We approached the boat; Mr. Clark Russell boosted William inside first. We had no water, no victuals, and no supplies of which to speak. We could not hope to last two days upon the open sea. But neither could we hope to last the hour here. And so for my part, I was ready to abandon the ship to her fate. But it seemed that the *Melville* was not quite done with us. For with a shout, two figures suddenly came running from the fog. With a start, I recognized the first as that crewman who had been assigned to function as the captain's guard in the wake of the mutiny. The second was none other than the quartermaster—Mr. Fairchild! As I watched, that treacherous fellow looked about frantically and bolted for the ruins of the mainmast, where he crouched down to conceal himself from discovery. The other sailor was not so lucky.

With a sudden lurching movement, the monster that looked like a nautilus hauled itself forward, emerging fully from the mist. The captain's guard stopped in his tracks, as though he were hypnotized by this unthinkable sight. And as the creature was revealed in all of its terrible grandeur, its size was such that it suggested a feature of the landscape—the rounded slope of a mountain, perhaps, rather than any living animal. But I was quickly disabused of this notion, and the poor sailor was forced to confront his doom.

I found myself consumed with a base loathing as I witnessed the carapace of the beast *unfold*, the plates of segmented armor shielding its eye now *opening* to release the cache of writhing, crawling appendages which served for its arms. Unspooling themselves from its great mewling maw at newfound lengths, the tentacles reached for the nameless sailor in a groping sort of unseeing madness. That man tried in vain to lose himself amongst the wreckage of the mainmast as Mr. Fairchild had done, but he was unable to escape. This unfortunate was seized about his knees by two of the terrible appendages; in desperation, he clung to a line still attached to the mast. The monstrous tentacles tried to reel him in, and for just one hopeful moment it appeared that their strength would prove insufficient to the task. The sailor's forearms strained with the effort of anchoring himself against the monster's pull. The cords of his neck stood out in stark relief against the whiteness of his skin; this image remains indelibly imprinted upon my mind as the last effort of my own subconscious to shield me from the recollection of what happened next. For despite his valiant effort, the man was torn asunder at the legs. Viscera spattered across the deck, and the doomed sailor's sudden howl rose above even the high-pitched keening coming from the creature itself.

To my surprise, the man's severed legs—which had been sharply rent at the calves—were immediately discarded by the monster's reaching arms. These appendages then did something I did not expect. They *dropped* from the cephalopod's gaping cavity and fell onto the deck itself, where they began to thrash about under their own control, coiling and uncoiling like so many distended white worms. To my mounting horror, I watched them enter into a sort of feeding frenzy and splash about in the expanding reservoir of blood that was swiftly flooding from the stumps of the poor sailor's ruined limbs. Perceiving that the man himself was for the moment being ignored by the monstrosities, I took a half-step forward with some unformed thought of rescue beginning to take shape in my mind.

I was halted in mid-step by the restraining hands of both Mr. Verne and Mr. Clark Russell on either of my arms. I looked back at them urgently; I can only guess what a wild-eyed countenance I must have presented, and I can only marvel at their sustained cool-headedness in the midst of this calamitous nightmare. Both men are renowned today as authors; I wonder that they are not better heralded as heroes.

But there were no heroics that could alter the circumstances of the sailor whose life was ebbing out before our eyes. Indeed, one of the crawling abominations, now greatly swollen with blood, presently turned its attentions to the man himself. As Mr. Verne climbed into the boat, his movements hampered by the stiffness of his bad leg, I saw a great maw open at one of its tapered ends; like a monstrous leech, it affixed itself to the bloodied stumps of the sailor's limbs. An unspeakable sucking sound rolled across the deck, its echoes amplified by the acoustics of broken wood and sail. If this attack brought any new pain, the man hardly reacted; his struggles had grown weaker, his screams reduced to moans of despair. His death-grip upon the line slackened, and he was pulled across the deck as the sound of feeding intensified.

I fear that I made a poor witness to this soul's sacrifice as the disembodied arm of the nautilus now swelled in size and began to consume the sailor like a snake. I realized that the appendage must digest its prey through some slow acidic process of dissolution. I tried to shake the idea from my mind—but once intuited, I could not shed this terrible knowledge. The thought of the prolonged suffering this would entail was too much to bear—I could hope only that the sailor under attack would exsanguinate before he could suffer such a dreadful fate. I turned my head as the bile rose in my throat.

But the captain did not turn from this unprecedented exhibition of terror and violence. Instead he brandished his pistol before him and took a step towards the fray.

"Mr. Fairchild!" he shouted.

There was no response; understandably, the quartermaster must have been too scared to risk giving up his location.

"For God's sake, man!" the captain swore. He fired a shot into the air, perhaps intending to startle the quartermaster into showing himself. And if this were his goal, it worked: a pale face rose above the splintered rubble of the deck, looking confused and frightened.

The captain turned back to me and nodded. "Lad," he said. "The others are already in the boat. Join them, and get out of here. I will send Mr. Fairchild to join you presently."

I hesitated to comply with these instructions. "Captain, please. Do not throw your life away for that ungrateful scoundrel. Leave him to his fate." I am not proud of these words, but I resolved to tell the truth when I put my pen to the page—and this was the truth of it. You see, I cannot claim any special quality of character, and cowardice was my constant companion. But I am happy to say that Captain Carrig, at least, was made of nobler and better stuff.

"He is a scoundrel," the captain admitted, "but he is still a member of my crew." And then his face, which had been drawn together in determination and anger, suddenly relaxed. He looked at me now with openness and honesty. "And lad—what more do I have to live for? My sister? The doctor? No, let my life buy you the time required to make good your escape. You may rest assured that I will sell it dearly enough."

And the captain made a fine picture indeed as he strode unhurried to the shrieking nautilus, like a hero marching to war in a Renaissance painting. The monster keened excitedly at his approach, thrashing those of its tentacles which were still connected to its mouth. The captain stepped around the appendages which had already been loosed upon the deck; as one reached for him, he dispatched it with a well-placed shot to its midsection. But I don't think he so much as looked at it; he had eyes only for the gargantuan monstrosity itself. I realized that this was the culmination of his personal vendetta. After all, what fate had befallen the *Veronica*, where the captain's sister had met her end? What monstrosity had its crew battled in the ruins of that ship's forecastle? I thought I was looking at it now, and I can only guess that the captain must have thought the same. For he tread now with confidence to within a few paces of the monster itself, his pistol aimed squarely at the flailing limbs which obscured its maw. I thought I could see a grim smile fixed upon his countenance; for him, it had all come to this.

"Mr. Fairchild!" the captain roared. "Get to the boat!"

The quartermaster emerged from hiding and looked about him. True to his nature, he uttered not a word of thanks—but he obeyed. He scrambled across the deck, slipping and nearly falling prey to one of the grasping tentacles as he stumbled. But he found his feet and leaped from harm's way just before the abomination could seize him. In moments he was at my side and attempting to scramble into the boat. The crawling, squirming appendages on deck followed in his wake, beginning to inch their way towards me. I stared, transfixed. I was now the last of us still standing at the rail. Mr. Verne and Mr. Clark Russell had already hauled the quartermaster into the boat; now they waited only for me.

"Gordon!" William called.

But I could not look away, for Captain Carrig was making his last stand. The tentacles of the nautilus reached for him, and the reports of his pistol rolled across the deck. Smoke from the weapon roiled about his smiling face. Where they had been struck, the grasping arms of the beast flinched away. But he had only a few shots, and the monster's arms were legion. The result of this terrible confrontation was a foregone conclusion. With an escalating sense of dread, I saw the limbs of the nautilus grab hold of the captain's ankles, wrists, and neck. What happened next I hesitate to describe. The monster *pulled*—and the captain was ripped apart in an explosion of gore. Even as his head was torn from his shoulders, he screamed—and there was nothing save animal terror and pain in his cry. The captain had marched to his death with assurance and poise, but there could be no such dignity in death. It is a base thing, an ugly thing, and it strips all the refinements of civilization even from the best of us.

But then, a new terror: with the dismemberment of the captain complete, the monster's tentacles parted to reveal a sucking mouth which opened and closed ineffectually at the air. Would I now be forced to watch as the captain was consumed? But no—instead, the creature's mouth spewed forth a tremendous quantity of purple moss! I gasped in shock and recognition as it vomited onto the deck, the thick substance cascading from the monstrosity's maw like a luminous waterfall from an unknowable planet. And when this all-too-familiar substance made contact with the deck, it began to take on a life of its own, quivering and shaking as it moved across the ruined ship in search of life to consume. I felt sick all over again as I saw one questing lump of the fungus come across a piece of the captain's right arm. The pistol was still gripped in his hand. The purple mold quickly began to knit itself together, forming a shroud over this organic material to better effect its digestion. That the doctor had been right, I now witnessed firsthand: with an object this large, the process was enacted with astounding rapidity. As I watched, I perceived that the moss had begun to attack even the tentacles which still crawled about the deck. I knew that I would soon be caught in the midst of this cannibalistic orgy—but somehow there was no immediacy to this realization. It did not seem to have any direct bearing on me—was I not doomed regardless? I recognize this now as symptomatic of shock.

"Gordon!" William said again.

This time his voice reached me, and I did not ignore his call. With the arrival of the ravenous moss, the destruction of the *Melville* was complete. There was nothing here for me. With some lingering reluctance—and an altogether larger measure of relief—I accepted my friend's outstretched hand and allowed myself to be helped into the boat. And as Mr. Verne and Mr. Clark Russell lowered it into the churning waters of the sea below, I turned my head from the splintering wood, gibbering monsters, and creeping violet substance which had sealed the ship's terrible fate.

I did not look back.

TELLS OF AN ENCOUNTER UPON THE OPEN SEA

"As your craft glides along, what strange monsters float by. Elsewhere was never seen their like. And nowhere are they found in the books of the naturalists."
-Herman Melville, *Mardi, and a Voyage Thither*

Those who have not sailed the ocean cannot hope to understand its immensity. Much has been written about the character of the open water, and by many a more accomplished writer than I have turned out to be. It will suffice to say that the enormity of the sea was merely imposing from the relative safety of our three-masted ship; from the boat, it was a thing of existential terror. While the fog persisted, we were spared from the full extent of this impression. But as we drifted farther and farther from the wreck of the *Melville,* the mist began to thin at last. What was revealed was an endless horizon of still water the color of slate, stretching in all directions as far as the eye could see. We were but a speck upon this great expanse; no more than a mote of dust in the eye of what Old Cedar would have called the Father Ocean.

We had escaped the devastation of the *Melville* with our lives, you understand, but our troubles were not over. As I have already said, we set out upon the open sea with no provisions: we had no food, no blankets, and very little in the way of weaponry. Our arsenal consisted of no more than Mr. Clark Russell's pistol and our own oars. And to echo Coleridge, we were surrounded by water—but there was not a drop to drink.[45] The only mercy our situation afforded us was that the sight of the *Melville* herself was quickly lost in an opaque wall of fog as we rowed away with all of

[45] A reference to Samuel Taylor Coleridge's 1798 long-form poem, *The Rime of the Ancient Mariner.*

the strength left in our tired limbs. But it was some time before the ghostly cries of the godless nautili faded beyond our hearing. I sat in the back of the boat and shivered as these thin wails pierced the wet and dismal atmosphere. I was unable to erase the recollection of bloodshed, suffering, and death from my mind, and I'm afraid to say that I made but little effort to help us pull away from the ruins of the ship. I began to suspect that I had become numb to all sensation.

But when the mist began to recede, drawing back its curtain from the flat vastness of the Atlantic, I knew I had been wrong. For my heart quailed to face such an uncaring breadth of sea from the precarious little boat. When had any of us last eaten? How long would it be before we began to feel the first terrible pangs of thirst? Even if we were not capsized by a passing wave, we had precious little hope of surviving longer than a few days. And what if we were discovered by another of the monsters which had already destroyed our much larger ship? They would make quick work of the boat. I looked at each of my fellow survivors: Mr. Verne, Mr. Clark Russell, William, and Mr. Fairchild. Was it possible that we would even turn on each other? Mr. Fairchild, at least, had already done so once. Of what further treachery was he capable?

The terror and anxiety was too much for me. I could not continue to function with my nerves wound so tautly, and at some point I simply collapsed into a state of unconsciousness. My memories of sleep are peppered with the indistinct voices of my shipmates: the authoritative tones of Mr. Clark Russell, the gruff responses of Mr. Verne, and the wheedling timbre of Mr. Fairchild. Their voices rose and fell as I drifted in and out of awareness. Only William remained silent; at least, I have no memory of hearing him speak. Perhaps he too was overwhelmed with the hopelessness of our situation.

However it was, when I next awoke, the sun was setting over the still waters to the east[46]. Its reflection on the ocean was a thing of beauty, but it made no impression upon me. I doubted whether my eyes would see aught but misery and despair wherever they

[46] This could be a simple mistake on the part of the author—or it could be our first indication that the boat has already sailed into strange waters.

looked from this point henceforth. As I slowly brought my attention to bear upon my immediate surroundings, I realized that the writers were discussing the loss of the ship while Mr. Fairchild and William dozed fitfully, their heads tipped forward onto their chests.

"Did you see what spouted from that creature's mouth?" Mr. Clark Russell said.

"Indeed," said Mr. Verne. "Is it that of which the doctor spoke?"

"I cannot say," came Mr. Clark Russell's slow reply. "Was he truthful with us? I seems to me that we have encountered one deception after another—and each with worse consequences than the last."

"It is the same," I confirmed. My sudden intrusion into the conversation startled the men, but no more than the sound of my own voice startled me. It sounded rusty and unused. But I persisted: "It is the same substance which we encountered on the derelict. You did not see it there, but you may consider that to be a stroke of rare good fortune. I have now encountered it twice, and never again will be too soon."

"Yes, well," said Mr. Verne. "I should say we've seen the last of it, in any case."

"How can you be certain?" I said, suppressing a violent shudder. "Those monsters could reappear at any moment." Needless to say, I did not relish the thought.

"I shouldn't think so," Mr. Clark Russell said. "As I told the captain, it seems to me that whatever was brought upon us was summoned only after the device from the derelict was activated. As the doctor was clever enough to destroy it utterly, I cannot see that they will pursue us. No, gentleman, I think we've washed our hands of the supernatural. We must now contend with the dangers of wind and wave"—he nodded at Mr. Verne—"and I think that will keep us busy enough."

Would that he had been right! For to this learned man's credit, his reasoning was sound enough. But little could he know that we had already strayed beyond the sight of God. The captain recognized this as early as our failed mission aboard the *Veronica*, but I'm sorry to say that the rest of us still clung to an irrational hope. As for myself, I was exhausted well beyond the point of reason. This short conversation was enough to deplete what little energy I had, and I soon found myself dropping back into what small comforts I could find in oblivion.

When I opened my groggy eyes, it was to a flurry of activity in the little boat. The thin, watery light of day had already begun to suffuse the atmosphere; I had slept through the night. And as I peered about me, I saw that William and Mr. Clark Russell were stretching a piece of torn canvas sail across the boat's stern. Catching my questioning eye, the Englishman deigned to explain.

"My design is to catch rainwater," he said. "I've no idea how long we'll be at sea, lad, but we must drink—and soon." Once they had the scrap of sail stretched tightly in place, William loosened the ropes at Mr. Clark Russell's instruction and allowed the canvas to sag in the middle. I saw at once that this would serve as a catchment where the water would collect. It also appeared that the canvas was rigged at sufficient elevation to provide a spot of shade for at least one man during the hottest part of the day. Presently William returned to his seat, whereupon he took hold of a second piece of canvas and began scraping at it with a sharp piece of metal.

"Surely a sail with holes cut into it will not answer to your purpose?" I said. I was troubled to hear that my voice had not improved; if anything, it sounded more strained and broken than the night before.

"Mr. Clark Russell says that the canvas retains too much salt," William explained. "Our rainwater will be as briny as the sea if we allow it to collect in an untreated sail." He held up the little scrap of metal. "This is hardly the tool for the job, but it's the best we can manage under the circumstances. And anyway, Mr. Verne's got some ideas of his own."

I turned my attention to the Frenchman, who was sitting cross-legged in the bow of the boat, sewing up a bit of salvaged netting with blistered fingers. He welcomed the chance to shed some light on his efforts: "Mr. Clark Russell is of the opinion that fresh water can be supplemented with small quantities of seawater without adverse effect. I myself am not so certain, and I should have welcomed the doctor's judgment on the matter—it's a pity he didn't survive. Nonetheless, I'm not one to take any unnecessary chances, nor to venture all of my eggs in a single basket."

"But what can you hope to accomplish with a net?"

Mr. Verne cocked an eyebrow at me. "We've been through a lot, lad, but I thought you were sharper than that." He gestured to port, where Mr. Fairchild was diligently attaching a second piece of netting to the side of the boat using one of its hooks. When it was clear that I still failed to understand, Mr. Verne shook his head. "We're fishing," he finally explained, smiling. "It may be the sole task with which the quartermaster can be trusted."

"That may hold off starvation," I admitted. "But how can it provide for our thirst?" I knew that my mind was addled with tension and weariness, but I did not think I had taken complete leave of my senses.

Mr. Verne grinned. "With any luck, you'll find out presently. You won't like it, but you'll find out."

Having thus made what preparations for our survival that could be made, there was nothing for it but to wait: to wait, and to scour the horizon with our eyes for any sign of rescue. Naturally, the men fell to conversation.

"Have you ever seen a sea so unnaturally still?" Mr. Clark Russell mused. For my own part, I thought the calmness of the water was a relief after the nightmare on board the *Melville.* But Mr. Verne only studied the Englishman without speaking. At length, Mr. Clark Russell continued: "And did you see the stars last night? I have never previously experienced such a feeling of quiet disturbance. In its way, it was worse than the attack upon the ship."

"What about the stars?" I said, feeling a rush of sudden alertness.

Mr. Clark Russell looked at me without speaking; his eyes were troubled by some unfathomable emotion. It was an uncomfortable silence that was only broken by Mr. Verne.

"Never mind all that," he said. "We have everything needed to survive our sojourn upon these waves—and that which we do not have, we have the brains necessary to procure." He spoke with confidence, but I had the feeling that it was only for my benefit.

"Surely there is something more we can do," I said. "Even if we will not die of thirst—which, by the way, is something of which I am hardly convinced—we face all the dangers of the sea. We are likely as not to be destroyed by a passing wave!" I heard my strained voice growing shrill but was unable to bring it under control.

"In the presence of Nature's grand convulsions, man is powerless," Mr. Verne said by way of reply, accompanying this blasé statement with the slightest inclination of his shoulders. "There is no sense worrying about that which we cannot control."

But flashes of those terrible entities, those grotesque shapes which hunched over the ship as they rent it to pieces with flailing limbs, rose involuntarily before my eyes. I suppressed a shudder and pushed these recollections forcibly from my mind. I would pretend that the *Melville's* demise had been the result of a gale and nothing more. It was a fiction, to be sure, but I thought that if I could avoid thinking about the terrible reality, I would be able to go on living. Such is the facility of the mind: it will leap with avidity to consume the basest lie in any attempt to preserve one's last shred of sanity. It is only now, as I put my pen to paper, that I allow myself to recall what my eyes revealed to me on the previous day, though I tremble with the remembrance and the pen shakes in my hand.

Presently, however, I was spared further rumination on these grisly thoughts.

"A fish!" came a sudden voice.

We all turned in the quartermaster's direction; he was fumbling with the net hooked to the side of the boat.

"Don't let it slip through," cautioned Mr. Verne—unnecessarily, I thought. But when Mr. Fairchild finally managed to extract the slippery creature, it very nearly did tumble from his grasp. At last he brought it under control and presented it to the Frenchman, who seemed to have been designated as our chief fisherman. The big man took hold of the fish in one hand, frowning. "I had not thought to catch one so quickly," he said, "and our supplies are limited. Clark Russell—your tobacco jar?"

The Englishman dug about in his coat pockets for a moment before producing the requested object. It was a small container, and I could not see what Mr. Verne planned to do with it. But then he popped the lid from the jar with his free thumb and upended its contents over the side of the boat. Mr. Clark Russell shouted a surprised objection, but it was too late—the dried leaves of tobacco fell in a clump into the gray sea. Mr. Verne knocked the jar once or twice against the side of the boat. Then he muttered: "Well, seeing as I have no knife," and he folded the fish in twain. I heard its brittle bones break. And then he did something unexpected: he held the fish over the empty tobacco jar and squeezed the fish with all of the strength in his hand. A thin, yellow liquid trickled from the fish and into the jar.

When the well had run dry, so to speak, Mr. Verne passed the container to William first, who then handed it to me. Each man was permitted a small amount of the suspicious liquid before passing it to the next in line. Well, this was a good trick, I thought. I can't say that the drink went down easily, and my stomach made a clenching sort of protest against this unfamiliar and decidedly unpalatable intrusion. The combined flavor of raw fish and dried tobacco is not one which I can recommend. But the liquid was not tainted with salt, and I experienced the first flush of relief in my parched throat. I had not realized just how thirsty I had already become.

And for the first time since escaping the wreck of our ship, I began to feel something like the faint stirrings of hope. It occurred to me that maybe the captain had been on to something when he recruited these men, after all. His methods were duplicitous, to be sure, but maybe there was something to the idea itself. I watched Mr. Verne take up another stray scrap of metal and begin to carve up the flesh of our catch for consumption; I watched Mr. Clark Russell finish arranging the second piece of canvas which was to provide the better part of our drinking water. Captain Carrig had identified these two men as experts in survival, and I now realized that he had been correct in his estimation. They had written many tales of shipwreck and subsequent privation, and they had become intimately familiar with the strategies we needed to practice to endure. And so I allowed myself to hope that the two authors had developed the skills and knowledge needed to see us through these dire straits. Was it possible that we could hold out long enough to be rescued?

With my thirst appeased, if not satisfied, I settled back into as comfortable a position as could be managed under the canvas. This would be as good a place as any to wait out the day, I supposed, although I knew I would be expected to rotate with the others so as to afford each man the opportunity of obtaining relief from the sun.

I resolved to offer William the next rotation, but before I knew it, I had passed once again into unconsciousness.

I was awoken only by an unexpected shout. Alarmed, I jumped to my feet and stared about me in confusion. I had been dreaming of the *Melville*, you see—I had been in the forecastle, and Mr. Derrick was there. He had been smoking a pipe and telling me a story about what it was like to die. To be plunged into sudden wakefulness came as a shock, and my consternation was exacerbated by the fact that somehow the sun had already begun to set on the distant horizon. For a moment I could not remember where I stood, and it would have been no wonder had I stumbled directly over the side. But William placed a steadying hand on my shoulder and pointed over the starboard side of the boat.

"It's a man!" he called out.

I peered into the gathering twilight as the other men stood to better examine the accuracy of William's claim. Sure enough, there appeared to be a single forlorn figure clinging to a wooden piece of flotsam. Presently he drifted in our direction, paddling weakly with one arm as he drew nearer to our little boat. I did not immediately recognize the man, and his face was hidden owing to the position he had adopted upon the little bit of wreckage which had proved to be his salvation.

When he was within reach, Mr. Clark Russell leaned over the side of the boat and extended one of the oars for the sailor to grasp. The poor fellow took hold of the proffered oar and was summarily pulled within our reach.

"By the grace of the Almighty," the man panted. "I dared not hope you were anything more than an hallucination."

"How did you survive?" said Mr. Clark Russell. As he spoke, he clasped the man's raw, chapped hands and began to pull him over the side of the boat. But the unfortunate sailor never had the chance to answer—a sudden shot rang out over the still waters, and the man tumbled from Mr. Clark Russell's grasp to splash back into the ocean. I turned in shock to behold none other than Mr. Fairchild! He was poised upon the side of the boat, where he had leaned out to fire upon his hapless victim; the pistol still smoked in his hands.

Mr. Verne rounded on him in fury. "What have you done!" he demanded.

"Only that which needed doing, even if none of you has the heart for it," the quartermaster said haughtily. "We've caught but a single fish in two full days upon the sea—and no rainwater. If you think to stretch that between six men, you're more fool than I thought. Another hungry mouth is the very last thing we can afford."

I think Mr. Fairchild would have said more, but he was interrupted by Mr. Verne's fist crashing into the side of his face. The quartermaster crumpled to the deck, and the small boat rocked with the impact. As he fell, the pistol slipped from his grasp and tumbled into the sea. Mr. Fairchild made no attempt to recover it; he lay upon the deck and did not stir.

"He's gone," said William, but he did not mean the quartermaster. The cabin boy and Mr. Clark Russell had been trying in vain to rescue the sailor from his doom. A thin trail of blood muddied the dark water, but there was no sign of the man himself.

"We ought to toss this villain over the side to join him," Mr. Verne said. "How did he get hold of the pistol?"

Mr. Clark Russell patted his jacket, and a look of chagrin swiftly passed across his face. "He must have stolen it from my pocket."

To my surprise, I saw that William had begun to strip to his smallclothes. "What are you doing?"

"I'm going in for the gun. It can't have gone far."

But Mr. Clark Russell stayed him: "Never mind that," he said. "A few shots would have done us precious little good anyway. And I do not trust these waters." He exchanged glances with Mr. Verne. "Indulge an old man, lad—stick to the boat."

William looked bemused, but he obeyed. And so we continued to drift upon the featureless sea as the dark of night settled over the world. As we sat in silence, one man standing watch in turns as the others made some effort to sleep, I reflected upon the words of Mr. Fairchild. Was there some terrible wisdom in his statement? Or was he just a murderer—twice over now? I turned these thoughts over and over in my mind in the fuzziness of half-sleep, where the unreal and the real lose their definition and become indistinguishable. I could not slip fully into the relief of unconsciousness; the emptiness of my stomach and the terrible dryness of my throat were a constant distraction. Mr. Fairchild had said that one fish could not be shared by six men; I thought that it was scarcely any better divided between five. We would need sustenance soon—and we would need water sooner.

At some point in the night William shook my shoulder, and I gave up the attempt to fall asleep as a bad job. "Are you awake?" he said. "I am uneasy."

"Oh, he's harmless enough without a pistol," I said. I was not excited about the prospect of this conversation. The blood in my temples was pounding in a terrible fashion. And even with my voice pitched low so as not to wake the others, each spoken word pained my cracked and parched throat, and my tongue was swollen in my mouth. "Would that we could tie him up, but we lack even a bit of rope."

"It is not Mr. Fairchild which concerns me," William said.

"What, then?" I rather wished that he would get to the point of it.

But instead of replying, my young friend merely pointed a finger above our heads to indicate the night sky. With a sigh, I turned my eyes to the heavens. And a glorious sight it was! Even in a state of dehydrated stupor, I could appreciate the sparkling magnificence of ten thousand stars shimmering against a backdrop of purest black: a moonless night. It was the sort of undiminished splendor which is rarely seen in the world today, and its exquisite beauty was almost enough to make me forget my discomfort—for a moment. But I saw nothing especially troubling in it, and I said as much to William. I'm afraid that I did not sound very charitable.

"Look more closely," he said patiently. "We are as yet still in the northern hemisphere, where the northern circumpolar constellations can be seen each month of the year. So tell me: where is Ursa Major? Where is Cassiopeia?"

I rubbed the sleep from my eyes and peered more closely at the sprawl of stars overhead, forcing my exhaustion-addled mind to make sense of this vast field of disparate, twinkling lights. As I stared, I felt a sort of dull surprise steal over me. William was correct! I could not identify the constellations he named. Indeed, the entirety of the heavens appeared utterly unfamiliar to me. A chill ran down my back. What could this portend?

"Where is Cepheus? And do you see Auriga's chariot?"

William continued.

I held up my hand in the starlight. "Your point is made, but I cannot see what to make *of* it." I placed a hand upon William's forehead, and then upon my own. "We have had neither sufficient food nor sufficient water. Let us call it a shared delusion born of fever. We must do what we can to repair our bodies. Things will look better in the morning."

But my friend was not satisfied with this suggestion. "This is real, Gordon. Things will only look better in the morning because we cannot see the stars by the light of day."

"Then what do you propose?" I said, my irritation finally cracking through. "Shall I fly up and rearrange the stars for you?"

William shrunk back, chagrined and embarrassed. I felt a hot flush of shame, and I was glad that he could not see my face in the darkness. But I made no attempt to reconcile with him, choosing instead to withdraw into myself and seek what solace I could find in sleep. This is the way by which desperation and hardship can drive a wedge between even the closest of friends. And there was another thing, after all: I did not like what I had seen in that alien night sky, and I preferred to close my eyes against it.

Things did look better in the morning, after a fashion, but our situation on the whole was not improved. Mr. Verne's nets had captured another two fish for us, but they were pale and sickly things from which very little moisture could be obtained. Their raw flesh tasted as though it had already turned, and even the meager portion divided amongst five men sat poorly in our stomachs. To make matters worse, there had been no sign of rain, and so Mr. Clark Russell's water collection scheme had not yet had its chance to provide for us. The skies were just as clear as they had been on the previous night, and we drifted upon the open sea under a hot and broiling sun. We took turns sheltering from its glare beneath the shade of the canvas, but this was a temporary relief only. Each of us had already begun to suffer cracked lips and blistered skin from the combined effects of the sun and our shared lack of water. It would not be long, I thought, before we found ourselves in a very desperate situation indeed.

So it was perhaps a good thing that we were attacked now rather than later, before what remained of our strength could wane altogether. The assault began sometime after noon, I think, although all conceits of time had quickly grown meaningless under the relentless monotony of our unchanging circumstances. The first sign of the incident was a boiling of water just off the boat's bow. I was unlucky enough to be standing watch at just that moment; while our watch was relaxed somewhat during the day, one man was at least nominally designated to scan the horizon for signs of land or sail. This was my appointed duty during the hour in question, and I performed it well enough: I called out to Mr. Verne and Mr. Clark Russell, jabbing a finger over the rail to show where the water had begun to bubble and roil with the action of some unknown agent.

Mr. Verne leaped to my side, causing our boat to sway with the sudden violence of his movement. In his hands was clasped one of the boat's oars, and his knuckles were white. His face was ashen but determined. "What I wouldn't give for that pistol now, eh?" he muttered.

And when the first tentacle snaked above the waterline in front of us and groped blindly for the prow of our boat, every fiber of my being cried out in agreement with him. It seemed that the nautilus had found us, after all, and thought I had better get about the business of resigning myself to death. But not Mr. Verne; he lashed out with the oar, striking the tentacle where it had now curled around the gunwhale. Its reaction was immediate; the questing limb recoiled and drew back beneath the surface, where the water began to churn anew.

As did my hope for survival.

But a second tentacle was bolder, and it did not come alone. Three or four of the long arms rose simultaneously from the sea to creep along the edges of the boat. As they wound their way towards us, I realized that these tentacles were not the same as those which the nautilus had employed to such devastating effect just a few short days ago. Instead of the smooth texture of those arms, these were equipped with round, pulsating discs which latched onto the sides of the boat with adhesive suction. These queer grasping saucers winked like miniature eyes as they roved over the boat, clenching and unclenching as the tentacles themselves extended from the water. This was not a nautilus at all—it was a devilfish![47] But even as I made this anatomical distinction, I also realized that the creature's arms were long enough and wide enough to encircle us completely, should we allow them.

Well, this would not do. I seized an oar from Mr. Fairchild, who sat open-mouthed in the stern, and I began beating back the monster's advances in synchrony with Mr. Verne. Behind us, Mr. Clark Russell pulled the quartermaster and cabin boy into the middle of the boat to best avoid the fray. And what a fray it was! The arms of the beast lashed the air around us like a cat[48], and it was all I could manage to stay their advances—which presently escalated into an outright assault. The tentacles slammed against the deck; our oars collided against the wet flesh with a hollow slapping sound. The arms continued to withdraw when we struck them, but they grew more daring and pulled back more slowly, as though the devilfish was beginning to intuit that we were powerless to cause it any real harm. It was a stalemate that could only end in our destruction.

With each swipe of the oversized oar, I felt the weakness of my limbs and knew that I could not keep up this defensive effort indefinitely. I leaned more heavily into each stroke, counting upon the weight of my body to deliver the force which my arms could no longer generate. But this was a temporary measure: I began to stagger, and it was not long before one of the creature's arms wrapped itself around my calf and pulled me swiftly to the deck. I shouted as I fell, but I struck my head. My vision became suddenly indistinct, and I felt myself lifted somehow. I knew that the devilfish intended to hoist me into the air—the better to devour me.

Mr. Verne shouted something, and Mr. Clark Russell reached for my flailing arms as I was pulled away from the boat—but the arthritic fingers of his right hand could not clasp me with sufficient strength, and I was fairly ripped away from him and brought to dangle over the water like a fisherman's lure.

---

[47] The term "devilfish" was historically applied to stonefish and rays but was most commonly understood to refer to a large octopus or squid. The shared feature of these genetically distinct animals is no more than their menacing or alien appearance.

[48] i.e., cat o' nine tails.

It is useless to explain the panic which suffused my entire being at this moment. Time seemed to have slowed nearly to a standstill, and my terror intensified with each labored beat of my galloping heart. Beneath me, the waters foamed in agitation as the devilfish breached the surface with its head. Suspended in the air, I had the time to observe how the tentacles joined the beast's head in a mass of webbing. In this base was a rapidly widening aperture that served for a mouth; it was ringed with teeth that looked like nothing so much as the blades of fine razors—but given the exaggerated size of the monster, I was not surprised to see as it pulled me in that they were in fact more closely akin to paring knives. The mouth grew impossibly wide as the monster's tentacles lowered me to within its reach, and for an unaccountable moment I was reminded of the way in which Captain Carrig's precious flower had unfurled within the darkness of his cabin. But where there had been beauty and luminescence, here there was nothing but darkness and death.

Even now I cannot account for the presence of mind which allowed me to practice an almost unconscious form of self defense. As I was drawn to my doom, I became dimly aware that the boat's oar was still clasped in my hands. Before the creature could deposit me bodily into the blackness of its yawning mouth, I brought the oar to bear upon it with all of the strength I could muster. My previous attacks had been like swinging an oversized bat; my effort now more closely resembled the last-ditch exertions of an exhausted javelinier. At least I had the force of gravity working in my favor, and I think that is what really did the trick: the flat paddle of my oar plunged into the creature's mouth, and the devilfish closed its snapping jaws around the wood. Even as the oar itself splintered and cracked, I strove to drive it more forcefully into my target. The creature's eyes, heretofore hidden in the wet folds of its skin, suddenly popped open to register surprise and pain. I had a moment of surprise myself, for I had not suspected the creature to possess eyes which could convey such unbridled, sentient menace—and then I was dropped into the water, and my weapon tumbled from my grasp.

The next several minutes of my beleaguered existence were a jumbled confusion. There was shock as I hit the cold water and plunged beneath its surface. There was fear as the lashing tentacles of the devilfish stirred the water around me. There was panic as I struggled to bring my body to the surface, and there was also pain as my lungs spasmed for want of air—but these sensations soon grew somehow distant and unimportant. For paramount amongst the notions which gripped my mind and body was fatigue. My small reservoir of strength had been depleted in my attack on the beast, and I could summon neither the energy nor the motivation to make a serious go at reaching the surface. This was not merely exhaustion of the body, you see; it was exhaustion of the spirit. We had come so far, and I had avoided death more times than I could count; but it seemed that death would not rest until it had sought me out. Was it not better to surrender now than to struggle in vain? Even as I mused on these dark thoughts in a detached sort of fashion, bits and pieces of the boat drifted past me through the water. Over the pounding of the waves in my ears, I thought I even heard some evidence of the destruction which was surely being enacted over my head. I took a slow comfort in this. My friends would be joining me soon, and our shared labors would finally come to an end. My lungs gave a final contraction, and I smiled. Even as I reflexively inhaled a mouth full of water, I found myself looking forward to the prospect of rest.

It was then that I was hauled from the water. My head broke the surface, and my reemergence into an atmosphere comprised of life-giving oxygen was perhaps even more shocking than being deprived of it in the first place. Coughing and sputtering and with my eyes stinging with salt, I could not make immediate sense of this change in my circumstances. Only slowly did my senses return to me, and I could see that my rescuer was none other than William. He floated beside me in the water, our weight supported by a chunk of wood which could only have come from the boat itself. The sea around us was littered with wreckage, and Mr. Verne and Mr. Clark Russell floundered in the water nearby. They reached desperately for any bits of flotsam which would support them. Of Mr. Fairchild there was no sign—but then I saw him paddling over to the authors. He seemed at ease in the water, which is not usual in a sailor, but I was pleased to see that he was at least trying to help the older men. But the significance of these observations paled in comparison to a far greater concern: the presence of the devilfish.

"What happened?" I said when I had managed at last to expel a great quantity of water from my lungs. "Where is the beast?"

"It fled," William said. "But not before taking out its frustrations upon the boat." He grinned rather desperately. "You must have given it a grave insult, indeed."

"Maybe I did." I thought that the creature was unlikely to forget us soon, at any rate. "But it's a wonder that none of us were lost."

"That is a premature statement," William said, his face sobering. "In case you haven't noticed, our situation has not improved."

As if to make a liar of him, a sudden voice rang out over this scene of destruction: "Land!" This unexpected pronouncement was made by Mr. Clark Russell, and he was pointing wildly over my shoulder. I turned so quickly that I nearly managed to capsize both myself and my savior, but fortunately William had the presence of mind to stabilize our crude raft as we surveyed the object of Mr. Clark Russell's attention. I have to admit that I was not impressed. There was but a fleck of darkness in the far distance, and I had to squint to see it. I remembered what Captain Carrig had told me about the way by which a distant wave can trick the untrained eye—but then, Mr. Clark Russell had spent plenty of time at sea. He should know better.

"Are you certain?" I said doubtfully. "It doesn't look like much to me."

"Nothing is certain, lad," Mr. Clark Russell said. "But I'd wager my life upon it: that's land, and no mistake."

"You *will* wager your life upon it," said Mr. Fairchild. "And all of our lives, to boot."

"I have not solicited your input, rogue," said Mr. Clark Russell. "You are free to swim in any direction you choose. For the rest of us, I cannot see as we have any other choice."

"If we swim to that spot," the quartermaster pressed, "it will cost us what little energy we have left. We will perish more quickly if we exhaust our stamina now."

"And your proposed alternative is to wait and do nothing?" said Mr. Verne. He sounded exasperated.

"To wait for a passing ship," Mr. Fairchild clarified. "To wait for rescue."

"We are not likely to encounter another ship," said Mr. Clark Russell slowly. He hesitated and exchanged glances with Mr. Verne, shifting his weight on the bobbing plank which supported him in the water. "There are certain…indications that we have sailed beyond conventional shipping lanes."

"What do you mean to say?" said Mr. Fairchild. There was a combative and dangerous edge to his voice even in these dire straits.

"Only that I would preserve our lives if I can," said Mr. Clark Russell. "And I believe that making landfall represents the best opportunity to do so."

The five of us settled into a weary sort of debate. I didn't like to admit it, but I understood the merits of Mr. Fairchild's argument. In a survival situation, the conservation of endurance takes on an element of supreme importance. If we had any chance to hold out as long as possible in the absence of food or water, it would be critical to restrict the expenditure of our energy. But what use was life without hope? And that indistinct smudge of land represented the possibility of respite from our travails. Furthermore, Mr. Clark Russell was convinced that to wait for rescue would only prolong our suffering and end in a slower, more painful death. I remembered the alien aspect of the unfamiliar stars in the night sky and determined that he was on to something: wherever we had strayed, we could not rely upon a chance encounter with another ship to save us. And so I lent my own voice in support of Mr. Clark Russell. At length, his sentiment carried the day. Mr. Fairchild reluctantly fell in line, and we began the long, slow paddle towards the speck of land on which we had determined to pin all of our hopes.

And what first appeared as nothing more than a speck on the horizon soon resolved into the unmistakable manifestation of a great mass of land: Mr. Clark Russell had been right! Within the hour, this coastline grew to encompass my entire field of vision. Indeed, we seemed to be drawing closer to that sudden shore in a fashion altogether more rapid than the trivial paddling of our exhausted arms could allow. For my own part, though, I was not troubled by this impossibility. After all, our deliverance was in sight! I had been willing to embrace my own demise just a short while ago, but now I was transformed by hope and the prospect of rest. I cannot say that my tired limbs were renewed with life, but for the first time in some days I now experienced a genuine sensation of relief. If we seemed to arrive at the shoreline more quickly than I could credit, I was willing to suspend my disbelief.

The island—if an island it was—began to dominate the scene. As we swam, I gathered some vague impression of large rocks and spindly trees. The shoreline appeared to ascend to a rounded hillock which hid any further features of the landscape from my view. I'm afraid this was rather the extent of my observations as we propelled ourselves into the shallows; I found myself altogether preoccupied with the simple task of staying afloat, which had become more difficult as time wore on and my muscles grew unresponsive. Moreover, I was so ecstatic at the mere sight of land that I thought my heart would burst in my chest. Whatever island we had found, it was somewhere our little party would be able to plant our feet, and that alone would be as good as salvation! Visions of breadfruit and springs of water danced through my delirious brain. I understood that even if Mr. Clark Russell were right and we could not expect to be rescued, at least our immediate troubles were over: the weirdness and terror we had experienced must surely now come to an end.

How wrong I was.

IN WHICH WE SEEK REFUGE ON A HITHERTO UNDISCOVERED ISLAND

"From obvious prudential considerations the Pacific has been principally sailed over in known tracts, and this is the reason why new islands are still occasionally discovered by exploring ships…indeed, considerable portions still remain wholly unexplored."
-Herman Melville, *Omoo*

Stumbling fatigued through the surf that crashed ashore on this desolate stretch of beach, I am afraid to say that the group of us did not make for a very pretty picture. I was wearied to the point of exhaustion and led poor William by the hand; neither of us had the energy even to raise our heads to survey the land which we hoped would be our deliverance. We concentrated instead only upon placing one foot in front of another—and an arduous enough task we found it. But we clung to life and hope with a desperate sort of zeal, supporting each other as we drew free of the water at last. I suppose that however miserable the nature of life gets to be, the human spirit is loath to give it up—and none in our party now differed on this basic principle.

Behind us came a grim-faced Mr. Verne, limping through the water with a scowl and keeping a stern eye upon Mr. Fairchild beside him. Only Mr. Clark Russell showed any real degree of vigor in his bones; he was the last to break free of the waves and step ashore, it must be said, but I attribute his slow progress rather to his incredulity at our surroundings than to any deficiency of energy—for it must also be said that he remained standing when the rest of us had sunk to our knees in the sand, gasping for breath. This indefatigable mariner only placed a hand to his brow so as to shield his eyes from the glare of the sun, and surveyed the land upon which we had been so fortunate—or unfortunate—to find ourselves.

Following the line of his gaze, I observed that we had come ashore upon a narrow crescent of rocky beach. The sand was exceptionally dark in color and was peppered with a startling variety of small sharp rocks, which glistened queerly in the sun and which made me rather glad for my boots. Kneeling in the surf, I was dismayed to realize that we would find little shelter from the hot sun on this shoreline. There were trees here, to be sure, and they stretched to a prodigious height above our lowly position—but they were an exotic species which I could not identify. Tall and thin with unusually pale bark, they were nothing like the leafy conifers and deciduous trees of home, and they cast no shade. There was nothing exceptional about them in any way, but their very unfamiliarity reinforced to me the disconcerting idea that we had landed very far from home indeed. Other than a few shining boulders scattered here and there across the sand, the beach was entirely devoid of any other distinguishing features.

"Our first object must be to obtain water," pronounced the ever-practical Mr. Clark Russell. "We'll need to climb that hill just beyond the encroach of the tide in order to get the lay of the land. Yet I should say that no man will wander alone if you gentleman are willing to do me the very great honor of accepting me as your captain."

I must explain that in a state of shipwreck, common practice dictates that all contracts and articles which have been signed by the crew are assumed to enter into a state of implicit dissolution. Therefore it is no guarantee that the men will have any use for a captain's authority—much less the election of a new captain. Let it therefore be understood as a testament to the trust we placed in this singular man that his earnest supplication was answered with hearty agreement from all of us—save for Mr. Fairchild. The erstwhile quartermaster muttered under his breath, but it seemed he was unwilling to openly dissent. After all, the first mutiny had not exactly worked out to his advantage. Mr. Clark Russell, however, was a stout judge of character, and the grumblings of the rascal did not go unnoticed. The Englishman met Mr. Verne's eye, and an unspoken thought seemed to pass between the two men.

"I won't let him stray from my sight," growled Mr. Verne.

"Then I shall search for water with one of the boys," Mr. Clark Russell said. "The rest of you must take this opportunity to find what rest you can in the shade of one of these great rocks. Our next moves will depend upon what I discover at the summit of that hillock."

"I will go," I volunteered, and I gestured to the prostrate form of William upon the ground. He was wild-eyed and breathing shallowly. "I am older and perhaps less spent than my friend."

My reader must understand that this proposition did not stem from any sense of nobility or self-sacrifice—or bravery. Indeed, I even surprised myself by speaking up. But I was convinced that I would be rather more useful than poor William, who was so clearly at his wit's end. And it was critical that this mission should succeed; without fresh water, none of us were long for this world. Well, there it is—I acted from self-interest. And yet I dare you to show me the man or woman who has not done so now and then. At least I took some comfort in knowing that my efforts, should they prove successful, would benefit all of us.

My suggestion was met with approval by Mr. Clark Russell, and he gestured that we should embark upon our explorations at once. We began to walk up the increasing grade of the hill, and the sand soon turned to soil beneath our feet. Mr. Clark Russell bent to scoop up a handful of it, letting it run through his fingers. The soil itself was soft and fine, but it too was an amalgamation of dirt and rock. Like the sharp bits of stone mixed into the sand, these rocks shone faintly in the waning daylight. It was as though they had been dipped in oil. This was curious to me. My reader may remember that I enjoyed the benefit of a first-rate overseas education, and so I was acquainted with the basic principles of ecology. I knew that such thin, rocky soil was unlikely to support an abundant array of vegetation; this explained the presence of the sickly trees as the only foliage on the beach. But how to account for the profusion of these glistening rocks? Even the bigger boulders scattered about the beach fairly shone with a similar luster.

"Do you think we will find water?" I asked. I decided that, like our newly-elected captain, I would focus on goals which could be achieved. There was no use puzzling over the inexplicable.

"I cannot say," Mr. Clark Russell said. His words came

slowly, as though he gave each of them special consideration. "But I think we shall survive for a short time, at least."

"For a short time only?" I said. We had been walking for just under an hour, to the best of my estimation, and I paused to wipe sweat from my brow. I was surprised to observe that my body was still capable of producing moisture.

Mr. Clark Russell stopped with me, taking the opportunity to catch his breath. I remembered that despite his incredible stamina, he was significantly older than me.[49] "I hesitated to speak openly in front of the cabin boy, but you're a stout enough lad." He eyed me critically. "We may find food and water to sustain us," Mr. Clark Russell continued, "but we are only postponing the inevitable. What use is life without hope of rescue? I, for one, do not care to spend the last of my days after the manner of a Selkirk."[50]

Well, it was not so long ago that I had been ready to give up on life altogether. Tossed into the water by the terrible devilfish and divested of oxygen, I had been prepared to accept my fate; it had even promised to come as a relief to my tired body. But what a difference a few short hours can make! With my feet once again upon solid ground, I found that my spirits had rallied. Even while suffering from a profound lack of sustenance and water—or perhaps because of it—I found the courage to lead where Mr. Clark Russell faltered.

"'If at every instant we may perish, so at every instant we may be saved,'" I said.

Mr. Clark Russell looked up, startled. "You are well-read, at that," he said in an appraising tone. "I wonder what Mr. Verne would say to so casual an invocation of his own words?"

"I should hope he would be flattered," I answered honestly. "But that's neither here nor there, and we've got work to do. We had better get to it." Without waiting for his response, I continued to ascend the hill before us. Mr. Clark Russell fell into line behind

---

[49] William Clark Russell was only 46 in 1890; not a spring chicken, but hardly an old man.

[50] The sailor Alexander Selkirk was marooned on an island in the South Pacific in 1704. He survived for approximately four years before being rescued. His story is widely accepted as the inspiration for Daniel Defoe's *Robinson Crusoe* (1719).

me. I think he was chuckling to himself, but he did not object to my taking charge. As we climbed in elevation, there was a gradual respite from the heat and humidity of the beach. There was even something of a breeze blowing about the hilltop. Mr. Clark Russell called for another rest when we were perhaps ten minutes from the summit. I wanted to push on, feeling invigorated by the exercise and eager to learn what we could see from the crest of the hill. But I recognized that I was trekking without any reserve of energy; taking time to rest was the correct decision.

When he had recovered his breath, Mr. Clark Russell spoke for the first time since our previous break. "I wonder at only one thing, Gordon."

"What is that?"

"You quoted Mr. Verne. I must ask: would none of my own passages have suited your purpose?"

Surprised, I looked at him. Despite Mr. Clark Russell's cracked and weathered exterior, not to mention the dire conditions in which we now found ourselves, writ upon his face was a look of such frank jealousy that I began to laugh aloud. After a moment, the venerable author joined in with me, and our voices rang throughout this wasteland of rock and sand, seeming to make it that much more hospitable—even if only for a fleeting moment. It was good to laugh; I could not recall the last time I had had reason to do so.

With our spirits thus temporarily buoyed, we made the final push to the summit of the hill. As we climbed, the beach grew distant beneath us. I could see the far-off forms of our companions scurrying about the shore, but the distance and the darkness of the sand made it difficult to distinguish what they were about. And as we finally crested the hill, I no longer had any eyes for what lie behind me; the vision that spread out before us commanded the entirety of my attention. I cannot hope to convey the sense of scale which characterized this unexpected scene, and I'm sorry to say that my facility with the English language is insufficient to communicate the extent of its awful grandeur. But I did once have the ambition to become a writer, and so I suppose that I must write:

Standing at the top of the hillock with a cooling breeze playing about our temples, Mr. Clark Russell and I now occupied the highest point on our little island. What spread out before us and below us was a blasted heath of rock and stone, stretching all the way to the farthest reaches of the island, where a short beach was washed with the pounding of the tides, audible even at this distance. This scorched landscape was at least two hundred feet below us, and it was a wasteland. I experienced a sudden sensation of misery; there was scarcely a tree to be seen, and nothing whatsoever in the way of fresh water or game. This land which had promised deliverance had only emptiness and lifelessness to offer. But if I have yet to describe its most distinguishing feature, this is only because I had no small difficulty in bringing myself to an understanding of what it represented.

"I…I can make no sense of this," I said to Mr. Clark Russell.

"Are you certain?" the Englishman said. If, like me, he had experienced the feeling of all his hopes crashing down around him, he disguised it well. I believe he even meant to transform this moment into an opportunity for instruction. "Did you study nothing in the way of geology at university?"

"Do you mean to suggest that we are looking at the evidence of volcanic activity? I suppose that would account for the general devastation of the landscape. But while the rocks here are curious enough—have you noticed their particular coloration?—I do not see any evidence of igneous material."[51]

"Not volcanic activity," said Mr. Clark Russell.

Well, I suppose I had better make myself plain. The object of our attention was an enormous crater which occupied the approximate center of the barren ground which represented the greater part of the island. It looked like some great hand had simply scooped a colossal amount of earth from the island, leaving a tremendous black cavity in the wake of its passage. The sides of the depression sloped towards this opening. Its size was a tricky thing to judge from our distant vantage point; I guessed that the entire feature must be several hundred feet in circumference. But if this phenomenon were not volcanic in nature, how then to account for the ruin of the landscape?

And then I understood.

"Aha," I said at last. "We are looking at the site where an asteroid—or perhaps a meteor—has collided with the island. But

[51] i.e., volcanic rocks.

where is the celestial body itself?"

For once, Mr. Clark Russell had no immediate rejoinder. I had stumped him: if my guess was correct, where was the meteorite now? I stared into the crater itself; like the pupil of an eye, its black gaze seemed to somehow draw me in. I felt its allure even from such a great distance, and I was suddenly glad that we had ventured no closer. What secrets did it hold within that empty stare? I wanted to know—and I wanted nothing to do with it.

"Wherever it is," Mr. Clark Russell finally said, "It's not likely to answer to our need for water, is it?" He looked around the blasted heath, roving over the boulder-strewn rubble with restless eyes. "We can make a more thorough exploration in the morning, but I'm afraid that our present circumstances are as dire as they were upon the boat. I cannot see that this island will provide for us."

"Can we not rely upon the sea?" I said. "Surely we can fashion some fishing implements from the fibers of the trees on the beach."

"Not for any great length of time," the author said. "Verne's method to obtain potable water from the innards of a fish has its merits, I suppose, but it's only a temporary measure. I fear we're already at the limit of our endurance. If we don't find water by this time tomorrow, lad, we'd better dig graves before we build fishing rods."

And so we began the long trek back to the beach in diminished spirits. For the second time in a day, I decided to make my peace with my own mortality. The struggle for life was the human condition, maybe, but I had just about had my fill of it. I resolved that I would find a comfortable place to sit on the sand, where there were not too many of those queer shining rocks, and that I would watch the play of light and shadow on the water as the sun set over the open sea. There I would pass into the relief of slumber—and if I did not wake in soft light of the morning, what of it? The nagging voice in my head which had led me to this point would be satisfied, I thought, with such a conclusion.

But as though the thought had summoned the thing, this very voice intoned loudly and without warning in my fatigued mind to prove otherwise.

"And your friends?" it said. "Are you content to leave them to their fates—even the cabin boy? I wonder how he should take your death."

"Our fates are shared," I said—not aloud, you understand, lest Mr. Clark Russell think I had been entirely divested of my sanity. No, this was a conversation which took place entirely within my addled psyche, and it was an exhausting affair. I had not heard from this voice in some time, and I had forgotten just how combative it could be.

"Precisely," it now said. "Should you give yourself over to a quiet death, do you not also consign your friends to the same?" Incredibly, the voice was smug.

"My death will mean only that there is one less mouth to feed," I protested. "And in any case, I should think my friends would prefer a quiet death to a violent one. And no man here is responsible for the decisions of another."

"Save for the man you selected as your captain," the voice said. "Don't you owe a duty to him? Remember his song: *these men must all pull together*."

This gave me pause. Mr. Clark Russell had truly inspired the men during the terrible storm, and I was no exception. Perhaps there was something to this argument. But then I realized that, inspired or not, those men were no more. Cooperation had failed to preserve their lives, even with the relative wealth of resources on board the *Melville*. How could cooperation save us now in our extremity of deprivation?

"No, I think it is hopeless," I said at length. "I will argue no more."

"Well," the voice said. "If you really want to give up the ghost, I suppose that's your prerogative. But if you would have a full belly tonight instead, take a look around you now."

"What do you mean to say?" I demanded.

But the voice had gone silent. I stopped walking in frustration, looking around me as though the island itself could shed some light upon this last cryptic remark. Mr. Clark Russell ran up against me and swore softly to himself. Dusk had settled over the island with remarkable rapidity, you see, and our footing had begun to grow treacherous. I thought it would be a fine thing indeed if that damned voice distracted me to the point of tripping over one of those stones and cracking my head upon the ground.

Despite myself, I smiled—and then I saw what the voice must have meant for me to see.

It was a low and creeping thing, crouched at the base of one of the thin trees which sprouted irregularly from the hill. Its pelt was red in complexion, and its fur was clumped and matted. A profusion of tiny tusks sprouted from its flat face, and it made a quiet chittering noise as it turned its gaze upon us. It was no larger than a small dog, and it most closely resembled the rodent called the capybara which is said to inhabit tropical regions of the Americas. It did not appear unduly alarmed by our sudden arrival. Mr. Clark Russell did not see it, and he began to ask me why I had stopped walking. I silenced him with a sharp motion of my hand, indicating that quiet was now of the utmost importance.

"Gordon," the Englishman whispered presently into my ear. "That creature has but a single eye."

I did not respond; I only shook my head at him. I did not care what the animal looked like. Ever so slowly, I knelt to the ground, never releasing the furry thing from my sights. My hand groped through the dirt until it settled upon that object which I sought: one of the sharp, glittering rocks which littered the hillside. I ran a thumb along its edge and determined that it would serve for my purposes if only I could put a little strength behind it. I gathered my legs beneath me and prepared to spring—but then I felt the old mariner's hand fall upon my shoulder. I looked at him, and he shook his head at me.

"Wait," he mouthed silently.

I clenched my teeth in frustration as he started walking forward again—he would give up the whole game! But with supreme nonchalance, Mr. Clark Russell took a wide berth around the noisy little animal, which turned its horned head to watch him pass. When it seemed that he represented no threat, the thing looked back at me. Was there curiosity in its single eye? It was disconcerting, to say the least, but I thought that there would be time to examine it with regard to ecology if only we could succeed in bagging it first. And I was about ready to try my luck without Mr. Clark Russell—what had delayed him? I could no longer see him in the gathering gloom, and I did not even really know what he intended to do.

But then a tremendous whooping shout resounded over the

slope, and the Englishman himself came sprinting between the trees. The creature's reaction was instantaneous: it bolted with the speed and agility which mankind too must once have possessed, but which it has lost in long eons of evolution. Now I saw the genius of Mr. Clark Russell's plan: never would I have been fast enough to chase the animal down. But if it were driven into my arms, there would be a chance.

I shuffled sideways to anticipate its course, but the little animal changed direction without so much as a pause and very nearly flew right past me. With every bit of energy left in my body, I leaped in its direction as it drew near—and we collided with tremendous force! My one hundred fifty pounds struck its fifteen, and I wrapped my left arm about the animal reflexively as I brought the jagged bit of stone to bear upon it with my right.

Mr. Clark Russell later told me that our struggle was a comedy of errors. I can only say that I partook of it in utter desperation: it is not an exaggeration to say that our very futures hinged upon its outcome. The animal and I began to roll down the hill with the force of our exertions, scattering rocks and flinging soil into the air as we went. I tried to reach its neck, but the creature tossed its head and scored my arm with its pointed tusks. I brought us to a stop with my feet and held its head back with my left hand, exposing its throat at last—but the fur about this part of its anatomy was too thick to allow for a clean death with my imperfect weapon. And so I'm sorry to say that I had no alternative but to bludgeon the strange little rodent to death with the rock. It was not a pretty sight, but at least it did not take long. When I finished the job and climbed shakily to my feet, I did not know whether the blood which now colored my dirty clothes had originated with the beast or had been spilled from my own veins.

When I had recovered my breath, I retrieved the animal by the scruff of its neck and began to trudge back towards the beach.

But Mr. Clark Russell stopped me, taking the rodent from me and clapping me upon the back. His face was serious, but amusement danced in his tired eyes. "Well done, lad. I daresay you've just saved us all."

Let it be understood as a mark of my exhaustion that even this praise from one of my foremost heroes could not penetrate the fugue which now enveloped me. I stumbled back to the shore in a muddled state of mind, and I have no substantive recollection of the return journey. But when we arrived, we discovered that our landing spot upon the beach had been utterly transformed. Mr. Verne and Mr. Fairchild greeted us in great spirits; for the very first time, I thought that the smile on Mr. Fairchild's face might even have been genuine. The reason for their unexpected cheer was immediately apparent.

You see, the men had not been idle! As we approached, Mr. Verne thrust a small wooden cup into my hands. I marveled at its construction; it appeared to have been carved from the pale flesh of the island's only species of tree. But I was more concerned with its contents. I turned the cup in my hand, peering at the rippling surface of the liquid held within it. Mr. Verne nodded at me to give it a try, and so I did. To my surprise and delight, I was rewarded with the taste of water! It had neither the unwholesome flavor of the liquid squeezed from the fish of the sea nor the salty tang of rainwater squeezed from our own clothes. It was clear, sweet, and clean—and I savored it more than I can begin to say. I drained the wooden vessel at a single go.

"Where did you come across water?" Mr. Clark Russell said, wiping his lips as he finished a cup of his own.

"Each of these queer trees contains a reservoir of water," Mr. Verne explained. "I believe they are a species especially suited to a desert environment. The same tree has provided the cup from which you drink."

"But how did you think to try this? And by what method did you extract the water?" Mr. Clark Russell said.

I did not hear the Frenchman's answer; I was distracted to learn that the discovery of water did not represent the sole extent of our friends' labors. Incredibly, the men had also managed to ignite a fire! It was a small and rather paltry affair, but under the circumstances it seemed the most captivating vision I could have dreamed. The fire had been built within a small pit dug into the sand; the walls of this excavation were about two feet apart and served to seal in the heat of the flames. The men had placed a ring of shining rocks around the perimeter of the hole. For fuel, they had scavenged what remained of the boat's wreckage which had floated ashore alongside us. Some needles and fronds harvested from the tall trees had answered the purpose of tinder; I could see a pile of them drying near the fire to be used in the future. I wondered that the wet wood would burn at all, but I could not imagine how the fire had been started in the first place.

"How did you manage to generate a flame?" I asked.

The Frenchman's eyes twinkled merrily. "We've been blessed with a sunny day, at least," he said. "I was able to dry out Clark Russell's matches on one of those strange rocks sitting in the sun; it was quite hot to the touch. I had to go through just about all of them before finding one which could be lit, it's true, but I think the result rather speaks for itself. The trick will be to keep the thing burning. I've laid out what little wood remains to us to keep it dry, but I fear we may have to sacrifice some of our own clothes to the flame—we'll be naked savages before the sun sets on the morrow." He even managed to laugh at the prospect.

Well, I could not find it in myself to share his mirth—I did not see how the fire could last more than a few hours. But I did feel a small surge of pride when Mr. Clark Russell deposited the body of the rodent onto the sand before the fire. Its red pelt shone dully in the dancing flames. "Tonight we dine courtesy of Gordon. Don't ask me what it is, but it looks as though it's got some meat on its bones."

Suddenly Mr. Fairchild produced a knife; the firelight caught the sheen of its blade and drew my eye. I stumbled backwards in alarm and very nearly fell into the fire, but Mr. Verne only gave another of his dry chuckles. "Don't worry, lad. It seems our quartermaster had another trick up his sleeve, and I've no doubt that he meant some mischief with it. God knows I could've used it to cut up our fish, and I can't think why else he should have kept it to himself. But it turns out that we should not have been able to access any water without his little surprise—nor should we have had any device from which to drink it. So it was rather a stroke of good fortune in the end. And I daresay he knows how to gut a rodent, too—eh, Fairchild?"

"He certainly gutted the mate well enough," William said darkly. I had not noticed his arrival, but I nodded in agreement with him. Mr. Taggart had actually been stabbed in the neck, in point of fact, but my friend's sentiment was at least accurate in spirit. I was not predisposed to trust the quartermaster after everything he had done.

"Now, now," Mr. Clark Russell said. "I'll have none of that. Each man here has cause to regret his mistakes. Henceforth that is all behind us. If you have consented to follow me as your captain, consider this your first order: we will work together to survive. Now, then: quartermaster? Get busy preparing our meal, and be careful not to lose all of its blood in the sand. We'll have a need for any liquid we can capture, and I don't think we can count upon finding many more of these creatures."

The quartermaster obeyed at once; it seemed he had been tamed, at least for the nonce. He spread a bit of fabric onto the ground—it must have been torn from his own jacket. He anchored its four corners to the earth with rocks and pushed the center of the fabric into the sand so that the animal's blood would pool into the cloth. Then he turned his attentions to the animal itself, and I saw that he was not a novice butcher. This should not be wondered at—rare is the sailor who has not dabbled in many trades. But while Mr. Fairchild busied himself with this grisly task, I took another sip of water and sat myself down by the fire. With the sun below the horizon, the air had grown chill.

"Is it safe to eat?" William asked, taking a seat beside me.

"It will be safer than starving, at any rate," I said.

"I'm thinking particularly of parasites and disease," he said softly. "It did not escape my notice that this animal possesses certain physical features which are…not typical of mammals."

"They are not typical of any life on the earth, so far as I am aware," said Mr. Verne, sitting down heavily next to us. "The creature is an aberration. I should not expect to encounter its kind again."

"What factors could have led it to evolve a single eye?" I mused. "Natural selection would seem to favor the development of two eyes and their associated benefits: the ability to perceive three dimensions and to distinguish a sense of depth."

"Don't speak to me of evolution," Mr. Verne said with a little wave of his hand.[52] "Least of all in a place such as this, where the

---

[52] Verne's views on evolution as a whole were neither mainstream nor classically Darwinian. I would direct the interested reader to his book *The Village in the Treetops* (1901), as it provides several illustrative examples of his philosophy.

only evolution which has occurred has been to develop those characteristics least hospitable to the human animal."

That was rather the point of the process, I thought—to evolve those adaptations which would ensure survival against other hostile species. But I was simply too tired to argue, and the coppery tang of the rodent's blood had already set my stomach to growling. We spoke of evolution, but what of devolution? If I grew hungry at the prospect of raw flesh, was I not already becoming something of a beast myself?

But these ruminations were cut mercifully short by the arrival of Mr. Fairchild with our meal. He had spitted the carcass on a length of wood; I thought it might have come from one of the boat's paddles. As he settled the animal's body over the flames to roast, I wondered what we would do when our meager supply of this wood was depleted. It would not be long, now, and there was no question of keeping it lit until such a time as rescue arrived. But I supposed that was a worry for another time; my thoughts were soon dominated by the tantalizing aromas of our meal.

I will spare the reader a lengthy account of how this strange little animal tasted. I will say only that it was not unpleasant, if rather leaner than I had anticipated. But if one has never experienced true hunger, then one cannot imagine the sensation of breaking that involuntary fast. Life returned to my limbs more quickly than I should have believed; it was as though a reprieve had been granted, and I felt a new affection for my comrades around me. Had I really been resigned to death—not once, but twice—just hours ago? If ever the condition of poverty seemed mired in hopelessness, I realized, it was no wonder: sustenance was the basis of all life. I had been born into relative privilege, but here was my first taste of the other side of that coin.

Mr. Clark Russell laid aside some of the roasted flesh to be eaten at a later time in case we could not capture another meal. As we freely consumed the remainder, he told the others of the sight which we had glimpsed at the crest of the hill: the enormous crater which could only have been the product of a meteor or asteroid striking the earth. I noticed that Mr. Verne took a particular interest in its description, and it was not long before he announced his intentions.

"Tomorrow I shall explore this crater," the Frenchman said.

"What do you hope to discover there?" Mr. Clark Russell was looking at him with narrowed eyes, as though he guessed some hidden purpose.

"I cannot say," Mr. Verne said slowly. "But this is a small island, and we must explore it in its entirety. I mean to descend into this crater and discover what lies therein, if this is possible. We may find some resources needed to effect our survival. We may even find a nest of the creatures which you and the boy have discovered."

"Allow me to be perfectly clear," said Mr. Clark Russell. "This is not one of your stories.[53] This is not an adventure to enjoy before returning to the comforts of civilization. This is a matter of life and death."

Mr. Verne grew red in the face, and opened his mouth to protest—but Mr. Clark Russell preempted him.

"That is why I will permit this," the Englishman said. "I agree that any chance of survival must be investigated to its fullest extent. But you will not go alone; I will send Gordon with you. He has proven his mettle and may be of some use to you."

Mr. Verne sat back, mollified. "Very well."

"That's settled, then," Mr. Clark Russell confirmed. "Now I suggest that we all catch what sleep we can. Quartermaster: build up the fire, there. I don't think we should have any need for a watch this night. I have laid eyes upon the length and breadth of this island, and I am satisfied that we are alone here."

Accordingly, we made ourselves as comfortable as possible upon the sand. I swept some of the sharp rocks out of my way; as I did, I noticed that William had moved off towards the shoreline. I understood his reluctance to retire; I too was restless. And so with my belly sated and the other men starting to nod off around the warmth of the fire, I brought myself to my feet and stretched. Whether a watch were truly needed or not, I felt sure that it was important to at least determine where exactly William had gone. It would not do to become separated in these unknown environs.

I did not have to wander far. William sat alone at the edge of the water, facing the dark expanse of the waves; a reflection of

---

[53] I cannot help but think of Verne's *A Journey into the Interior of the Earth* (1864); it's likely that Clark Russell was thinking along the same lines.

firelight danced on the back of his ripped jacket. As I approached, I saw that he held in his hands an unexpected object: my missing journal! I felt a brief flare of jealousy that he should have found it and kept it from me, before realizing that my missing notes from the outset of the *Melville*'s journey were hardly the most pressing of our concerns under our present circumstances. And it appeared that William was clutching the little book very tightly as his pen traced a scrawl across a blank page; I don't think I could have stood to take it from him.

"What are you writing, William?" I asked softly.

"Muddled yarns of grim things."

I perceived at once that the mind of my young friend had begun to unravel. Poor, altruistic William! I reconsidered taking the book from his hands, but now I also had to take into account the state of his sanity. Perhaps the journal represented his only method of coping with the desperate straits into which we had fallen. His eyes flickered across the page seemingly at random; could he even hope to see what he was writing in the gathering of twilight?

I resolved at that moment that I would do whatever necessary to effect our rescue, if only for the sake of my eternally optimistic friend. He had welcomed me aboard the *Melville* with no motive of his own—something which could not be said for any of my other companions, neither living nor dead, though I held them in the highest esteem. I could not imagine how our imminent adventure into the crater of the island could lead us to rescue, but if the opportunity arose, I determined that I would at least see that William found his way home.

I made my way back to the fire and stared into its flames, occasionally poking at its glowing embers as dusk rolled slowly into blackest night.

TELLS OF OUR EXPEDITION INTO THE IMPACT CRATER, AND OF THE DISCOVERIES WE MADE THERE

"We may have civilized bodies and yet barbarous souls. We are blind to the real sights of this world; deaf to its voice; and dead to its death."
-Herman Melville, *Redburn: His First Voyage*

"Words of human tongue are inadequate to describe the discoveries of him who ventures into the deep abysses of earth," said Mr. Verne. We stood upon an outcrop of rock near the top of the hill, and the tremendous impact crater had only just been revealed to us in the light of the breaking dawn. As this dry wasteland of cracked boulders was washed with the rising sun, I perceived that no light penetrated the black hole of the crater itself. Once again my gaze was drawn there; I felt a pull which could not be rationalized—but neither could it be denied.

"This island is both bigger and smaller than I had imagined," said Mr. Fairchild. The quartermaster had also been assigned to accompany us, you see. Mr. Clark Russell had determined that three bodies were better than two, and that he had things in hand well enough at the beach, in any case. Mr. Fairchild had brought along his knife, of course, but it was now tucked safely into Mr. Verne's belt.

"I have come to expect nonsense from you," the Frenchman now said. "But that is an especially empty statement." Surveying the scene before us, Mr. Verne took this opportunity to catch his breath after our strenuous climb to the top of the hill. Otherwise I don't think he would have responded at all.

"I mean only to say that I can see all the way to the farthest shore," the quartermaster said, sounding slighted. "And yet this wilderness before us seems unaccountably vast."

Mr. Verne only snorted, but I thought I understood what the quartermaster meant. The island had been large enough, after all, to weather the impact of a meteor or an asteroid without being destroyed entirely. And yet…I looked askance at Mr. Fairchild. Could he really be trusted to accompany us into the unknown? He had given me no reason to suspect that he had ever acted in good faith. I would have to keep an eye on him, even if his weapon had already been confiscated.

"You'd be dead without him," the voice in my head stated.

I didn't bother to reply—it had a point, after all. It was only by the grace of Mr. Fairchild's knife that we had been able to obtain water. And while we had no canteens or flasks to bring any water with us on this little expedition, I thought we were tough enough to last a few hours without a drink. "Let's get on with it."

We made our way down the opposite slope of the hill, which was far more treacherous than the ascent. The hillside was littered with rock and scree, and each step threatened to send our feet skidding out beneath us. Slipping, I sent a small landslide of pebbles and stones cascading down the incline before me; the commotion startled two of the island's small rodents, which bolted from cover and darted across our path to disappear behind a larger boulder. I caught my balance and asked Mr. Verne to supply me with the knife; I thought perhaps I could capture one of them. But he did not give it to me, and he did not look at me—he stared only at the crater ahead. I thought I detected hunger in his eyes.

"There will be time for hunting later," he said. "For now we have been assigned an objective, and I mean to complete it."

I wondered at the wisdom of that. I thought our objective was rather vague, and the promise of sustenance was surely more concrete and important than casting about an empty hole. And as I have said: I did not like the look of that hole. But I'm sorry to say that Mr. Verne didn't stick around to argue the point; he moved ahead of me, and I had to hasten to catch him up.

The ground soon leveled into a flat, broad plain: the blasted heath which I had first identified on the evening prior. With the sun now rising in the sky, the morning quickly grew hot. Sunlight reflected from the large shining boulders, making us squint against the glare. There were many of them deposited across the field; as we passed one, I took a closer look at its surface. When I stood unmoving before it, the great rock did not look like anything especially remarkable. But with each step I took, colors danced and shimmered across its glossy face like translucent glass. Each new angle brought forth unexpected hues and shades as though they bubbled from the heart of stone within. It should have been mesmerizing, but I was disconcerted. Something about these colors did not seem quite right; it was almost as though this action of light did not belong in the natural world. I did not linger, and I tried not to look too closely at the next boulders we passed.

At length we reached the crater itself. The hole which marked the site of impact occupied the center of a steep declivity; its sides sloped to the great crack in the earth at a precipitous degree. We drew to a halt upon its rim and stared wordlessly into that black fissure. I cannot speak for the other men, but I felt its hold on me intensify. I even began to think that Mr. Verne was right, after all: entering this cavity was our true purpose here. Matters of obtaining food or water—indeed, matters of life and death—seemed somehow paltry in the face of this terrible rent in the crust of the earth. I could not imagine why this should be, but I had the distinct impression that I would find answers here.

Mr. Verne bent at the knee to better examine the depth of the crater. To my surprise, it was more shallow than I had expected. By clinging to its edge and lowering ourselves backwards into the hole, our feet would only be forced to drop eight or nine feet. The potential for injury was present, of course, but I had almost expected to find the obstacle insurmountable. But how then to account for the near-total absence of light in a cavity that was not, as it turned out, so very deep? Maybe I would not find answers here, after all—maybe there would be only more questions.

Well, there was only one way to find out. A startled, wordless objection escaped Mr. Verne's lips as I swung myself over the lip of the hole and let my legs dangle into the darkness—but he did not try to stop me. I stretched out my feet, ensuring that I had the smallest possible drop to endure. And then I let go. The fall was short enough, but the impact was jarring nonetheless. The shock of striking the ground radiated through my calves; I toppled forward and only just caught myself upon the palms of my hands. Though the light filtering in from the midmorning sky above me was dim, and though my eyes were still adjusting to their new environment,

I could see at once that many small fragments of rock had become embedded in the skin of my hands.

"Well, boy?" Mr. Verne called down. "What do you see?"

"Very little," I answered truthfully.

But as my eyes grew accustomed to the dimness of the crater, I perceived that I stood at the center of a wide chamber which had been blasted into the rock. Along its outer walls, I thought I detected the openings of tunnels which branched off here and there like the shoots of a vine. The best comparison I can draw is to say that it felt not unlike being plunged into an oversized rabbit's warren—but no rabbit ever made its home in this singular labyrinth of tunnels, which shone faintly with the same alien fluorescence which characterized the boulders and rocks strewn about the exterior of the island. For it was the light of the shining rock which allowed me to distinguish my surroundings, you see, and it was with a growing sense of disquiet that I realized that stepping into one of the branching passages would bring me into a world fully enveloped by that faint luminosity.

Mr. Verne and Mr. Fairchild landed beside me in the crater with consecutive heavy thumps. Dusting himself off, the Frenchman looked about him with an appraising eye. At his side, the quartermaster looked uncomfortable; his hands fidgeted at his belt, twitching nervously.

Mr. Verne was equanimous enough. "We've found ourselves in a queer place, and no mistake."

"I don't care for it," Mr. Fairchild said. "Something about that light makes me shiver. This hole looked black as night from above, but here the very walls are glowing."

"Where do they lead, I wonder?" I said. Despite my trepidation, I was fascinated by the prospect of following these tunnels. I took a hesitant step towards the nearest of them—and as I did so, a strange thought rose unbidden to my mind. Entering the mouth of the tunnel felt akin to walking willfully into the throat of a great and terrible beast. But I pushed this thought aside; I had already seen great and terrible beasts in the flesh, and they did not look like this. I trailed a single finger along the wall of rock at the aperture of the passage. When the tissue of my finger did not promptly melt from my bones, I took heart, and I advanced. But my progress was arrested by the strong grip of Mr. Verne's hand upon my arm.

"Be careful where you step, lad."

He pointed at my feet, and I saw that a furrow of blooming moss trailed neatly down the center of the passage which I had been about to explore. Its color was indistinct in the dim shine of the crater's unearthly light, but it was unmistakably the very same substance which had dogged our steps since we first encountered the derelict which had served as the final resting place of the captain's sister. This, I think, is where I lost hope for the last time. You see, even if we were fated to perish of thirst or starvation, I thought we had at least escaped the supernatural weirdness that had been the doom of the *Melville.* Instead, it seemed that it had followed us here—or else we had ventured unwittingly into its very heart. This latter impression was presently reinforced by the next words of the quartermaster.

"I say, what is this?" said Mr. Fairchild. His tone was quavering and hushed—I would almost have called it reverent—but it echoed in the cavernous space of the crater. I turned to see the object of his query, stepping carefully away from the line of fungus which traced the grotto's floor. He was bent at the waist, studying something which rested on the earthen floor very near to the center of the chamber. It did not look very big, and I was ready to dismiss it as just one more rock amongst many—but then I took a closer look.

For it seemed that our troublesome quartermaster had discovered something of very great import indeed. Despite my studies, I am no expert in the sciences and am certainly not qualified to distinguish between a meteor, a meteorite, or an asteroid. The distinction between these various objects of heavenly origin is no doubt fiercely debated amongst their enthusiasts—for my part, I was overwhelmed with awe simply to stand before this chunk of stone which had once hurtled between the stars in the vastness of untold galaxies. All at once I understood Mr. Fairchild's rapturous tone; as had first happened to me when Captain Carrig unveiled the radiant flower of Roger Lundamere from its cryptic housing, I once again experienced a sudden compulsion to fall to my knees in worship. Lest I be accused of exaggerating in the pursuit of dramatic effect, I will not linger over this unfathomable notion. I will only say that I was utterly captivated until Mr. Verne approached to examine the object for himself.

"It's full of holes," the Frenchman said. His voice served to return me to my senses. I shook my head to clear it, and I saw that he was not mistaken. The meteorite itself was no larger in size than any of the boulders we had already come across, but it was pockmarked with small apertures, leading in turn to a network of miniature tunnels running throughout the entirety of its interior. Furthermore, the meteorite shone faintly with an ethereal glow, not unlike the walls of the tunnels branching off from the very cavern in which we now stood. It was as though this ghostly light could only shine at a distance from the meteorite itself; as though the object sucked the very light from the atmosphere around it. Was this why the crater had seemed so dark from the surface of the island? And just like that, I had a startling revelation all at once.

"I'll be damned," I said softly. Even speaking in the presence of the object felt somehow sacrilegious, to say nothing of cursing, but I was not able to keep my surprise to myself. "The rocks all over this island—the queer light which suffuses the very tunnels before us—I believe this is their source."

Mr. Fairchild said nothing; he only cocked his head at the meteorite as though he were listening to it. Mr. Verne was slow to reply, but eventually he nodded in the dimness. "I do think you're on to something, Gordon. We may be looking at a small fragment of the original meteor; it's possible that the remainder was scattered all over this place, inside and out. The impact must have been truly cataclysmic; it's a wonder that any life survived on this island at all."

But I'm afraid to say that this was not even the most salient feature of this mysterious remnant of mineral from space. For if it were the sourcc of thc eerie light, it was also the source of the deadly moss: from each of the meteorite's tiny holes, a thick channel of the substance poured forth to squirm down its glossy surface. These lines merged on the floor of the passage with subtly trembling filaments and tiny blooms, where they joined together to create trails leading off into the glowing tunnels which surrounded us. It was one of these very trails upon which I had nearly tread and had been saved at the last minute by Mr. Verne's timely intervention.

"This is whence it grows," I said. "This stuff is truly not of this world."

"But this substance originated with the monsters which destroyed our ship," said Mr. Fairchild. "I saw it with my own eyes."

"I would have said the same," Mr. Verne mused. "Is it possible that such a singular substance can spring forth from two unique sources? Would that the doctor were present to lend us his diagnosis—I believe he was the most qualified amongst us to solve this riddle."

"If we step carefully," I said, "we may be able to solve it for ourselves." This was another of those reckless impulses to which I am occasionally disposed. My reader will by now have recognized this streak in my temperament, but in this instance I believe there was something more to it. As I have said, I had really nothing left now in the way of hope. This island was clearly not capable of sustaining our lives for any length of time, and on our expedition to find rescue we had instead stumbled into a nest of the creeping fungus which had already killed so many men. But if I were really meant to die in this place, I thought that perhaps I could satisfy my intellectual curiosity before being consigned to my fate.

"I propose that we follow one of these trails," I said, "and see where it leads."

But Mr. Verne objected. "It is too dark, and it would be far too easy to come into contact with this stuff by mistake. And anyway, our purpose here is to find something which we can use to effect our rescue—I hardly think it likely that this substance will aid us in that endeavor." He finished with an air of finality; he trusted that his pronouncement was as good as law. But I was no longer quite so worried about winning his approval, and I was rather more inclined to act according to my own whims.

"I thought your purpose was to explore this place to its fullest?" I countered. Then, stepping carefully over the fungus which undulated along the corridor, I did not wait for his response. I had been overtaken by something—I will not call it fatalism, because my entire life had been dominated by a struggle against what fate had determined for me. Why else should I be here? But I suppose the sentiment I experienced now did have something in common with that philosophy; the distinction was that mine was not a passive acceptance of my fate. Rather, I intended to march to my doom with such zest and zeal as I could muster, if my doom would have me.

Well, thank goodness for cooler heads. Mr. Verne hastened after me, grumbling all the way, and it's a good thing that he did. Else I cannot say into what trouble I should have blundered! But I will come to that presently—for the moment I fairly danced through the soft light of the passage which twisted and turned throughout the underground interior of this strange island. There were times when I should have slowed my progress through the darkness; side tunnels sprouted from the main thoroughfare here and there. But instead I plunged recklessly ahead, only dimly aware of the manic grin which had affixed itself to my face somewhere along the way. At length, Mr. Verne caught me up and chastised me for my lack of caution.

"What are you thinking, boy?" he hissed. "You'll get us all killed here."

"You needn't have followed me."

"Stuff and nonsense." He snorted. "The only thing more foolish than venturing off into this maze without a plan would be to split up first." He cast a glance behind us. "Although the quartermaster is lagging behind somewhat."

"Wait for him," I said. "You'll know where to find me."

Mr. Verne grabbed hold of my collar and shook me, hard. "Snap out of it, lad." His voice was stern, but his eyes were not unkind. "I won't lose you down here."

Unperturbed, I removed his hands from my shirt. "I don't mean to wait around for death to catch me up." I was still smiling. "If it means to have me, then I'll meet it with my head high. Captain Carrig did the same, and it did him credit."

"It did him *nothing*," Mr. Verne said. Now he sounded contemptuous. "There is no honor in death, Gordon. There *can* be honor in life, but only if you do not throw it away without need."

I have to admit that this gave me pause; hadn't I thought the same when I actually saw the captain die? It was a grisly scene, with very little in the way of honor about it. But then, what was my alternative? To cower afraid in the darkness? To return to the surface and die of thirst in the sun? The grin faltered on my face, but my resolve did not falter. No, I would keep marching; to turn back would be to submit to a longer and slower species of death.

By the time I had made my decision, Mr. Fairchild drew abreast of us. He hopped from one foot to another with exaggerated caution, trying to steer himself as far away from the moss as possible. The substance had not diminished as it progressed along the tunnel, and his vigilance was a timely reminder of its ever-present danger.

"What are you arguing about?" he snapped. "We've come this far, and I don't see any sense in stopping just when it looks as though we've reached the end."

Mr. Verne and I turned in unison; to my surprise, the quartermaster was right! Our tunnel stretched still farther into the blackness ahead, but I thought I could discern a pale gathering of ambient light somewhere in the far distance. It did not have the dreamlike quality of the glow which coursed through the rock, and there was no mistaking it: this was daylight. I allowed myself to match the slower pace of the other two men as we continued towards the tunnel's end, and it transpired that visibility seemed to improve with every step. There is little to say about this quiet journey from the darkness to the light—even our conversation fell away as we anticipated returning to the open air—but it was not swift. Only after some time did we reach the mouth of the tunnel; it did indeed open into the fullness of daylight, and my eyes were fairly blinded by the sudden and overwhelming whiteness of the sun.

When my unsuspecting eyes finally adjusted to the natural light of day, I could scarcely believe the scene which they revealed to me. The tunnel had deposited us onto a swathe of beach, you see; doubtless the other passages which honeycombed the subterranean maze beneath the island would have led us to still more. But none could have contained a sight so shocking as this; even now I wonder that I did not go mad at the mere sight of it. And as it turned out, one amongst us was not so lucky—but it will not do to get ahead of myself. First I must show my reader what we had discovered.

As elsewhere on the island, the dark sand here was mixed with the sharp fragments of rock which I now believed to have originated with the meteor which lay somewhere behind us in the darkness. Boulders were arrayed here and there across this expanse, offering scant shade from the relentless sun overhead. The beach itself sloped to the waterline some three or four hundred yards before us. The moss which we had followed through the cave—and here in the sunlight, I was able to confirm that it was the same impossibly purple hue which had wreathed the decks of the *Veronica*—coursed in more or less a straight line all the way to the water's edge. Or rather, it would have done, were it not for the animals which fairly churned from the surf to lap at it with the greed and fervor of long-starved dogs. I do believe my heart actually stopped beating when I laid my eyes upon them and recognized them for what they were.

The foremost creature amongst them emerged fully from the waves as we watched, entering a world of oxygen which it was never meant to inhabit. It pulled itself along the sand with the strength of the limbs which sprouted from its mouth; its shell scraped and bounced over the rocks as it crawled towards the terrible fungus which had drawn it from the sea. It had not yet reached the size of those demons which had destroyed the *Melville* and was only perhaps the size of one of those German automobiles[54]; but it was quite large enough to instill a very real and preternaturally awful sense of terror in each of us. For this was the nautilus—the very species which had risen from the fog to demolish the *Melville* timber by timber! And it was not alone; its fellows followed behind it in an untidy row. They were not of uniform size; most were smaller than the first of their kind, but one or two of their number were even larger. My fevered mind counted perhaps twelve or thirteen in all, and a busy brood they were: they clustered around the thickly growing moss and sucked it into their mouths with an audible slurping. They jostled together as they fed; their shells knocked together with a sound which called to mind the collision of colossal billiard balls.

Mr. Fairchild began to whimper with panic, but I found myself fascinated. I had expected to march towards my doom, and I had little doubt that these monsters would make quick work of us, given so much as half a chance—but I wanted to understand what I

[54] Carl Benz developed the first practical automobile in 1885; to modern eyes, this vehicle would have most closely resembled a motorized stagecoach and was over eight feet long.

was seeing before I died. And just as Captain Carrig had solved the riddle of Roger Lundamere's infernal device, certain elements of the puzzle were now sliding into place in my mind. I recognized now that the purple moss was an alien growth: something delivered from the very stars themselves. It flowed forth from this island where the meteor had chanced to strike, and here it had found a willing host. These creatures ingested the dread substance and were transformed utterly. The *Melville* had run across their path, and its subsequent destruction was no more than a foregone conclusion. But how to account for the singular effect that the moss appeared to have on the monsters?

"Why does it not destroy them?" I mused. "We have seen its effect upon other living organisms. If the doctor's principle holds true, they should be consumed in a matter of minutes. Instead they seem to relish the stuff."

"They must represent the single species in all of the ocean which is immune to the action of this substance," said. Mr. Verne. He shook his head as if to clear it and suppressed a shudder. "I think fate has shown us what we ought not to have seen."

As though to underscore his words, the nearest nautilus seemed suddenly to notice our presence. We had only just emerged from the mouth of the cave and were sheltered by an overhanging lip of rock; nonetheless, our conversation must have caught its attention. One of the beast's great wet eyes rolled in our direction, and it stopped feeding to evaluate our unexpected intrusion into its territory. When it began to emit a terrible keening cry which I remembered all too well, I knew the game was up. The hour appointed for our doom had arrived. The other creatures snapped to attention all at once, abandoning their feast to stare in our direction with unthinking malevolence.

"It's time we get moving," said Mr. Verne.

"Why?" I said. "Here's as good a place as any to die."

The Frenchman looked ready to strike me, but he was distracted by the quartermaster. Mr. Fairchild made the sign of the cross over his chest with a shaking hand. "Only the Father Ocean can deliver us now."

"What did you say?" said Mr. Verne quickly. "That is not the first time I have heard that name."

But the quartermaster did not reply; instead, he turned and

bolted back into the darkness of the tunnel from which we had come. And it appeared that he had thrown caution to the wind; where he had first stepped carefully around the growing moss, he now flew with reckless abandon.

"Go after him, Gordon," Mr. Verne urged me. "You are younger and you are faster; I will follow behind. I daresay those creatures will not be able to pursue us into the narrow confines of these caves, at any rate."

Well, I had been ready to meet my maker, and I was not pleased at the prospect of delaying that appointment in order to chase after Mr. Fairchild, of all people. But I knew better than to argue with Mr. Verne when he had that look on his face. I had known him for no more than a few weeks, but I think I was sufficiently acquainted with his character to gauge how such an argument would end.

So I turned without a word and chased the quartermaster through the tunnel with all I could manage in the way of haste. I was grateful that the moss followed a straight path through the passage; it was easy enough to place my feet to either side of it as I ran through the darkness. Even if I were ready to die, you see, I did not relish the thought of perishing by slow suffocation as the alien substance knitted itself over the entirety of my corporeal body. As I followed him through the warren of twisting paths beneath the island, I could only just discern the flitting figure of the quartermaster in the eerie glow emanating from the walls around us. I worried that he would take one of the side passages and that we would become lost, but it seemed that he was content to follow the same course we had initially tread.

And that way led to one place only: the crater itself, where the strange meteorite had come to rest after its unfathomably long journey through the coldness of space. My steps slowed as I entered into this larger chamber. I beheld Mr. Fairchild at once; to my surprise, he was approaching the celestial object itself. Even at this distance I felt its magnetic pull, along with that mounting sense of reverence not unlike the sensation one might experience when stepping into one of the great old churches of continental Europe. But if this were a church, it was not built to house any holy relic—and only one mad villain had come to kneel before its altar.

“Mr. Fairchild!” I said. My words sounded slow and muffled, and he did not heed them.

The quartermaster dropped to his knees in front of the great chunk of rock. His legs landed squarely in churning rivulets of purple fungus; even as I watched, transparent little filaments reached up from the substance to grip at the fabric of his trousers. The moss established little footholds in the cloth, as it were, and began to envelop his legs with remarkable swiftness.

“Mr. Fairchild!” I called again, taking a half-step towards him. His fate was sealed, so far as I could tell—there would be no rescuing him from the grip of the alien moss, and I did not intend to try. But I wanted to know what had passed through his mind; what had led him to this terrible juncture? “What have you done?”

I did not really expect him to answer, so it was with a dim sense of surprise that I watched his face turn to regard me with wild eyes. “Those things on the beach,” he said. His voice was soft. “Did you not hear their cries?”

“The howls of unthinking beasts—what of them?”

“They were the words of the Father Ocean Himself.” The moss had now reached the seat of his pants. “And in them I heard my instructions. He will deliver me, you see—this is how I must reach him.”

“Who is the Father Ocean?” I demanded. In that moment, it seemed that everything hinged upon the answer to that question.

But before he could make himself plain, the quartermaster turned away from me. And to my shock and horror, he reached out and took hold of the meteor with both hands! Its reaction was instantaneous, and I realized all at once that this was not a piece of insensate stone. It *responded* to his touch, and new channels of purple fungus poured forth from its innermost hidden recesses. The moss surged up his arms like a swarm of eager bees tasting honey of heretofore unsuspected sweetness; it wrapped around his torso and reached beneath his coat like a sly lover; it extended even to his neck and began to envelop him as completely as the Egyptians once enveloped their dead in wrappings of cloth. And then something happened which I can scarcely bring myself to describe.

The moss entered into his eyes, his nostrils, even his ears. The quartermaster opened his mouth to scream, but he made no sound—for the substance gushed into that orifice and flooded it utterly. His head was transformed into a mask of churning violet; the moss had established a direct conduit with the meteor, and as I stood mesmerized with horror, it spewed forth more and more of its terrible product. I thought the quartermaster's head would explode with the sheer force of this unthinkable inundation. But in his final moments, Mr. Fairchild somehow got to his feet, wresting himself from the terrible communion into which he had entered. He now stumbled in my direction, looking like he had been dipped bodily into a great pool of the stuff. Threads and strands of it were entwining themselves together in his hair, and it seemed that this was the final nail in his coffin—with one last muffled groan, the quartermaster ceased his struggles and collapsed onto the ground, passing at last from this life and into whichever form of existence might next await his arrival.

It is useless to describe the effect of this scene upon me. Never before had I experienced greater consternation; it was as though my entire consciousness was wiped clean and replaced with a blank slate. I was senseless, staring, oblivious of my surroundings. The moss could have sought me out then and there, and I would have been powerless to stop it; I was powerless to flee. I could not rely even upon that goading voice in my head which had occasionally led me safely from dangerous situations. But that voice had not gone silent—it was screaming. The sound was white heat in my brain; my vision became indistinct, and I think I should have fainted were it not for an exterior provocation.

You see, what finally released me from my inaction and prompted my unthinking flight from the crater was an external noise. And as this sound slowly filtered into my consciousness and took the form of words which my overwrought mind struggled to comprehend, I understood that its source was the meteor which rested just past the fallen corpse of the quartermaster. I cannot say how this understanding was given to me; only that once it was glimpsed, the insight was complete and was not to be denied. Somehow the object was communicating with me, and I became aware of a vast and terrible intelligence behind the sound. The words themselves were whispers which reached only to the fringes of my consciousness, eluding my grasp—or perhaps it was that I shied away from their full import, resisting their pull. For I recognized these words for the whispers of the Father Ocean, and I surmised that their soft susurration must have been what drove the quartermaster to his final lapse of sanity. And if the Father Ocean was speaking to me now from that alien rock, did that mean that I had been identified as His next acolyte? Though I could not discern the words themselves, His voice was sibilant and pleading. I thought that if I allowed myself to listen, I might begin to understand His meaning—and that this act would represent the beginning of a capitulation from which I would not, could not recover. But the whispers *insisted* to be heard, and I stood rooted to the spot in an agony of indecision.

And then that restless old voice made its return at last, drowning out the terrible entreaties of the Father Ocean—if that is what they were. Its familiar nagging intonations, previously maddening, now came as a tremendous relief. My reader will readily imagine how eagerly I seized upon this intrusion, clinging to its presence as a drowning man will cling to a raft. The voice had stopped screaming, and if there were now something of desperation in its timbre, at least it came to me in my hour of need.

"Is this how you will die?" it asked me.

"I cannot escape," I said. "I think He has hold of me."

"Then die," the voice said. "But first tell me this: even in death, don't you long for something different? Something *more?*"

Well, this was an old refrain, and no mistake. But somehow the sentiment resonated with that stubborn streak which characterized my bolder moments. It gave me the strength I needed to resist, and I determined that I would not yield to whatever strange entity meant to seize me in its grasp. I knew that I would die here, and my reader has seen how I had more or less come to terms with that idea—but I did not mean to be *taken.*

And so I fled. I cannot now say which route I followed through the caverns beneath the island, taking turns at random, and it is truly a divine miracle that I was ever able to retrace my steps. But my mind was plunged into darkness, and so it was only natural that my animal body should follow suit. I fled the light of the meteor, the fluorescent violet moss, and the glow which emanated from the very walls of this dreadful cathedral. I entered into black places beneath the earth, and all memory of light passed from my mind.

IN WHICH I MEET THE SOLE SURVIVOR OF THE *FOUNDLING*

"He looked strange enough to me, then, to have come from the moon; and he was full of stories about that distant country."
-Herman Melville, *Redburn: His First Voyage*

It was in a state of supreme disorientation and confusion that I finally emerged from this Stygian nightmare, stepping at last into a dazzling arena of light. It was only natural sunlight, but it reflected upon the glossy surfaces of shining boulders and sparkling rocks to blind my eyes. Squinting, I stumbled into the open air, taking deep and grateful breaths of the fresh oxygen which suffused the atmosphere. It came as a tremendous relief after the cloying darkness of the tunnels adjacent to the impact crater. It took considerable time for my eyes to adjust to the sudden change, of course; I cannot say how long I had spent in darkness. And when they did, I did not really believe what I was seeing. I could no longer attribute any hallucinations to starvation and thirst, it was true, but could this be some delusion born of terror and exhaustion? You see, the sight which met my eyes was so unexpected as to defy belief: it was another person standing on the beach!

She stood with her back to me, gazing out at the boundless ocean. The wind played about her dark hair, blowing it back over her shoulder to ripple with the salt breeze of the sea. Her hands hung loosely at her sides. Her attire was curious; it was evident at a glance that she came from a position of privilege. She wore Turkish trousers and a dark coat which buttoned snugly at the waist; the fabric was exceptional, and it was clearly tailored to her exact specifications. But her coat was torn, and her trousers were stained with salt and with mud. This, more than anything, convinced me that she must be real: these little details which spoke of hardship and struggle.

I found myself hesitant to approach her. How long had it been since I had laid eyes upon a woman? Surely not more than a few weeks—and yet it felt like a lifetime. And there was something more: I was afraid. Her appearance suggested that she had been on this island for some time, and she had not been rescued. This did not bode well for our own prospects. I had a half-formed thought of creeping back into the tunnels unseen; if I did not acknowledge her presence, I could hold onto some vain hope of salvation. But coward as I was, even I could not deprive another soul of what I imagined to be her only chance at contact with another human in this bleak wilderness.

"Pardon me," I said haltingly.

She turned swiftly, her hair whipping to pass in front of her face. Her eyes flashed, and she advanced towards me with a speed and determination which I could scarcely credit. I jumped backwards in alarm, suddenly convinced that she meant to do me harm. But she only seized me by the arm and stared intently at my face. I had the disconcerting impression that she was drinking me in, somehow, as though this one glimpse of another person would have to serve for the rest of her days, and she meant to make the most of it.

"Who are you?" she demanded.

"My—my name is Gordon."

"Have you come here to find me?"

Oh, how I wished I could answer her in the affirmative! It was clear that she wanted—needed—confirmation. She needed to know that she had not been forgotten, that the sun still rose and fell beyond these shores, that I had the power to return her whence she came. I knew nothing of her yet, and less of her situation, but I swear by these first impressions: the desperation and hope in her eyes could not be misread. But of course I could offer her no solace. I knew not who she was, and I had not come for her. I could not save her, for I could not even save myself. I found that I was at a loss for words.

"But no, of course you haven't," she said upon reflection, when I failed to answer her. Her face fell, and my heart cried out. "How could you have? After all, I do not think He means to let me go."

"Who are you?" I asked. "Who keeps you here?"

"My name is Lydia," she said softly. She removed her hand from me, letting it fall to her side once more. "I am the last survivor of the *Foundling.* As for who keeps me here…well, if you are truly here too, and you are not a creation of my own invention, I think you know Him well enough—though you may not know Him by His name."

"The *Foundling*," I repeated, seizing for the moment upon that information which seemed most immediately digestible. "She was your ship?"

"She is my ship."

"I do not see her."

She smiled for the first time since our conversation began. "Do you know what a foundling is, Gordon?" She did not wait for my response. "The name refers to a child who is abandoned at birth before being discovered and raised by another."

"It seems rather an inauspicious name for your ship."

"It suits me well enough." She shrugged. "I was an orphan at birth, and so too will I be an orphan at death, I think. The question is this: who has found me? And who has found you?"

"I'm afraid I don't understand your meaning."

"Whence did you set sail?" she said, suddenly changing tack. "How did you come to these far shores, and where is your own ship?"

"We sailed from Nantucket," I said slowly. "But we encountered some troubles along the way, and there are only a few of us left now. I'm sorry to say that our ship was wrecked, and we survived long enough to reach this island only by an extraordinary intervention of divine providence."

"Hmm," said Lydia. "I wonder at that last point. Nevertheless, your tale already hints at certain particulars which fascinate me. Nantucket, did you say? I don't believe I am familiar with it. You had better make yourself comfortable, Gordon. I am going to ask you to tell me your story."

Well, my story did not take long to tell, and my reader is already acquainted with its specifics. Needless to say, when the tale turned to its darkest hour—both literally and figuratively—I struggled to make myself plain. How could I convey the whispers which had resounded in my head? How to describe the sense of consciousness and evil which had fairly radiated from an unthinking rock? How, in short, to finish my account without coming across as nothing more than a desperate lunatic? My reader will not be surprised to learn that it is a problem with which I have grappled once again, as I set my pen upon the page to recount its particulars here for posterity. And I can only imagine that I made rather a poor job of it, then as now; the events of the last few weeks were all but incomprehensible even to myself. How could a stranger hope to understand them?

It was therefore with some surprise that I observed the manner in which Lydia absorbed this information. She nodded to herself as I elucidated one development or another, asking pointed questions which suggested to me that she could almost have guessed what I would say next. Other elements of my recollection were met with a considered frown, as though what she heard displeased her—but it did not appear to surprise her. In point of fact, this is the principal impression which I must convey: at no juncture did my interlocutor express anything whatsoever in the way of surprise, doubt, or disbelief. Any one of these reactions would have been as natural as breathing. In the preceding pages I have told a tale which I would expect none to credit without first setting aside their own skepticism—but this woman accepted it readily. What was I to make of this?

When I had finished my little speech, the sun had passed its noontime zenith and was just beginning its descent towards the horizon. Its rays caught the scattered bits of meteorite strewn about the beach and sparkled. Lydia took my hand in hers.

"So it is as I surmised: you too have incurred the wrath of the Father Ocean." She gave my hand a gentle squeeze; it was a gesture of consolation.

"What do you mean by that?" I was beginning to believe that everything we had experienced—all of our grief and loss—hinged upon that oft-invoked entity. But I had come no closer to understanding what He was. Nor did I not comprehend how so many disparate persons appeared to be intimately familiar with His name. It was a riddle, and no mistake—but bear with me a little while longer, my reader, and I will yet have the occasion to make everything as plain as I can.

But not just yet:

"I think that it is not for me to say." Lydia smiled sadly and shook her head, releasing my hand from her cool grip. "I do not fully understand it myself, you see. But unless I am much mistaken, I think we shall both discover the answer to your question for ourselves in a very short time indeed."

"But you must tell me," I pleaded. "If there is anything you can tell me which may allow my friends to survive in this place, I must know."

She arched an eyebrow. "You do not speak of your own survival."

"I have abandoned that cause."

She sighed. "Well, Gordon, perhaps our fates are intertwined, after all. Very well. I will tell you what I know. But it is not a short tale, and I think that its implications will not make you comfortable." She cleared her throat. "Nevertheless, I shall begin by introducing myself in full: my name is Lydia Cheves, and I am a cartographer by trade. I have worked in this field for no small number of years and have attained an unimpeachable reputation within my small circle of peers—such as they are.

"I was living and working in the French city of Dubois when I was approached by one Mr. Boucher. This man introduced himself as the captain of a ship called the *Foundling*, and it was his ardent desire that I should join his expedition as its principal cartographer and translator. You see, much of my work involves the translation of foreign maps—the British and Spanish have long been pioneers in exploration and colonization, and my skills have been called upon to assist the *Marine Nationale*[55] by providing reliable records of those regions which they have not had the privilege to discover firsthand. In any case, it appeared that Mr. Boucher had come across a map pointing to a territory which had not yet been claimed by any country. I was dubious; the year was 1850[56]. What unclaimed territory could possibly exist in the

[55] The French Navy.

[56] According to its first chapter, this memoir describes events which took place in 1890. It seems inconceivable that Lydia Cheves could have been stranded for 40 years; I can only leave the reader to draw their own conclusions on this point.

modern era?

“Nevertheless, Mr. Boucher was insistent. Evidently his goal was to reach this place and declare it in the name of France. It was a noble goal, and it stirred some feeling of patriotism in my breast—though I discovered in the fullness of time that his purpose was not so noble, after all. But first I was put to work in the translation and revision of the maps which Mr. Boucher had been able to obtain. They were a fascinating series of documents of great antiquity, and I engrossed myself eagerly in the work. I wondered at their provenance, but the captain was curiously mum on this subject, and no amount of persuasion would alter his disposition. And so I took the only recourse left me to assuage my curiosity: I disobeyed Mr. Boucher, and I took these maps and documents to a source of my own.

“There is an old woman in Dubois—or there was, at any rate. She was something of a historian, but she did not operate in academic circles, you understand. Her chosen field lay in the realm of folklore and that traditional wisdom which has fallen out of favor during the inexorable march of modernity. She had helped me once or twice before in the translation of certain obscure French dialects. Now, I had discovered one or two cryptic references in the margins of Mr. Boucher’s maps which led me to believe that perhaps she would be able to help me once again. And so I knocked on her door one cold morning in late September with a sheaf full of the captain’s documents wrapped neatly and tucked within my handbag.

“If I was nervous to meet her, Gordon, I assure you that it was perfectly natural. She was not a welcoming figure, you understand; her appearance alone would be sufficient to set you quaking in your boots. Her stature was large, but she had shrunken somewhat with old age, and she gave the impression of a hunchback. She had one clear blue eye and one blind, sightless orb in place of its counterpart—but do not think for a second that she ever missed a trick. All together, she presented a frightening aspect indeed, and I’m sorry to say that her brusque mannerisms did not win her many friends. Had she the misfortune to be born in an earlier era, I should not have wondered to find her stoned for a witch. But I was not one to be put off by appearances, you understand—not when I was seeking answers.

"And so she brought me into her home, and we entered into an examination and discussion of the maps which I had brought with me. I shall not bother you with the particulars of this conversation; they would be of interest only to the linguist or cartographer. I will say only that it was immediately evident to me that this old woman recognized these documents, or else identified something in them which troubled her greatly. The little drawings I had discovered in the margins of the maps seemed especially vexatious to her—but when I asked her about them, she clammed right up. She demanded to know how I had come across these documents; I explained what little I knew, telling her about my assignation to the *Foundling* and of its captain's errand. Well, never before had I seen her become so uncommunicative! I found myself bundled into my cloak and deposited upon her doorstep almost before I knew that I had been dismissed! So great was her agitation that she was even ready to shut the door on me—but then a queer look passed across her face.

"'Go and see this Mr. Boucher of yours,' she told me. 'But do not let on that we have spoken; only return these maps to him at once. You have heard the adage: nothing ventured, nothing gained? Turn the phrase on its head, Miss Cheves; if you venture to this place with that man, you will lose everything.'

"And then the door really was shut on me, and I was left alone on her stoop with the chill wind of late September playing about my ankles. Well, Gordon, you can scarcely imagine the state of confusion into which I had been plunged! I am not a superstitious woman—at least, I was not—and although the old woman's words troubled me, I was not about to be put off from a lucrative opportunity for employment. Moreover, we were scheduled to depart in just one week's time, and I did not imagine that Mr. Boucher would be able to find a suitable replacement for his expedition. Abandoning the venture now would only harm my professional reputation. Nevertheless, I thought I would take some modicum of caution in hand and offer him the opportunity to defend himself against the old woman's accusations.

"I inquired after Mr. Boucher at his offices in the shipping district of Dubois, but his clerk informed me that the captain was to be found aboard the *Foundling* herself. Evidently there were many preparations to be made before our imminent departure, and the captain had taken to spending each day and most nights on the vessel in order to outfit her for our expedition. The guard at the marina gave me some trouble, and I was prepared to put him in his place—but the name of Mr. Boucher did the job for me. He became politeness itself and escorted me directly to where the *Foundling* was berthed, but he refused to step aboard. It seemed that the good captain had a professional reputation of his own.

"The deck of the great ship was very busy when I arrived, with many men hauling cargo to and fro in a flurry of activity. Many a curious glance was cast in my general direction, but the workmen averted their gaze as one and did not speak to me. As I approached the captain's cabin, I saw four of the fellows wrestling with a very curious object: it was a great cauldron of shining metal, stoppered with something very much like the cork of an oversized bottle of wine. I was here on a mission, you must understand, and my personality is not the type to be diverted by any old distraction—but this was a curiosity which captured my attention. I approached the workmen presently.

"'I say, what is that device?' I asked them.

"'Begging your pardon, ma'am,' was the unsatisfactory reply.

"'He'll have our hides,' grumbled another of the men as they moved hurriedly past me. 'I told you we never should have taken it from its crate.'

"'It's too damned heavy,' the first man said.

"But then they passed from earshot and I was left to contemplate this bizarre—not to mention very rude—exchange. I found myself considering this puzzle as I reached the captain's cabin, and it was to this state of distraction which I must attribute my slowness to actually knock upon the door. Well, this was a stroke of good fortune at last. As I stood there like a contemplative statue with my fist raised in the air, I detected the sound of voices inside. I risked a quick look around me; I should not like to have been caught in the act of eavesdropping. But none of the workmen paid me any heed; indeed, it was almost as though they were going to great lengths to avoid looking at me. Well, that suited me just fine. I inched closer to the cabin door to hear what I could.

"'No, no,' came a voice which I recognized straightaway as belonging to Mr. Boucher himself. 'It is being moved belowdecks as we speak.'

"'How can you be sure it will serve to contain the stuff?' said a second voice. It had a thin, wheedling sort of timbre which I found disagreeable at once. 'By all accounts it is a corrosive substance which multiplies with great speed; I should not like to think what would happen should it come into contact with the ship herself.'

"'I should say it's a little late for doubts now, Mr. Baudelaire,' the captain said. 'I have been given every assurance that our vessel—in both senses of the word—will do the job. Focus on the reward which awaits us when we bring the stuff back to port and only do your duty as my mate in the interim.' He gave a throaty little snort which did very little credit to his character. 'In any case, I have more reservations about the woman I've been forced to employ. She's trouble, and no mistake.'

"My heart gave a little lurch, and I leaned closer to the door. My ear was met with the unpleasant sound of Mr. Baudelaire—who appeared to be the ship's mate—chuckling dryly to himself. It was a sound which I have only heard once or twice since that time, but it never failed to send a shiver along my spine. What he said next was even more chilling.

"'Never give her a second thought,' the villain said. 'I can follow the Father Ocean's instructions as well as the next man. If she can really get us to the source of this stuff, her purpose will be served. Her journey will end with a knife in the back just as surely as ours will end with riches beyond imagination.'

"Gordon, you cannot hope to understand the emotions which now inflamed my spirit! Suffice it to say that I did not meet with the captain that day. I fled from the ship in a bewilderment of consternation and fury. How dare this man seek out my expertise only to betray me! Putting aside the cryptic nature of their conversation, it was the indignity of personal insult which weighed most heavily upon me. I stalked from the marina in a blind rage, paying little attention to where my feet carried me. Let them find their uncharted island without me, I thought. Whatever they were after, they would have a hard time of it without their maps! I retrieved the documents from my bag and squeezed them in my hand. I was determined to tear them into fragments and scatter them over the ocean itself. Then I would return to that old woman and demand to learn just how she had known of this imminent betrayal, using whatever force was necessary to extract her confession.

"But when I took hold of the maps in my hand, I noticed for the first time that my steps had now taken me far from the water's edge. A small stand of vegetation existed on the fringes of the shipping district, you understand, and it was in this miniature forest which I now found myself. In my rush of anger I had failed to notice just how far I had walked. It was a peaceful enough glade, though, and I found myself a comfortable spot to sit and mull over the unfortunate and shameful position into which I had nearly been thrust. My face flushed with embarrassment when I realized just how neatly I had been used; doubtless the men would have thought very little of leaving me dead on some unknown shore whilst they sailed away with their fortune firmly in hand. Now they would be lucky to find their 'unclaimed territory' in the first place.

"I was just on the verge of rending the maps to shreds here in this small woodland when a sudden hush fell over the scene. I had become accustomed to the trilling of birds and the chirruping of crickets, and the cessation of all this usual noise made an immediate impression upon me. I looked around me with alertness, if not serious alarm—while the environs of coastal Dubois can hardly be described as wild, I reasoned it was possible that some dangerous beast could still linger here and there upon the fringes of civilization. One reads of just such a story now and then in the press. But what I spied approaching me between two thin and barren trees was not a predator, but an herbivore: a great Black Goat, to be precise. Its matted, filthy hair could not dim the gloss of its coat, and the confidence with which it approached me suggested that it felt no fear of the human animal. Each footfall of the Goat was silence itself, but I thought I could taste something foreign upon its breath as it drew nearer with every snorting exhalation. If this is a baffling description of the animal, I can offer none better. I can only say that it had one additional salient feature which I have thus far neglected to mention.

"You see, Gordon, this creature—which seemed to me to straddle the boundary between the human world and the animal, the domestic and the wild—did not have the face of a goat. It had the face of a woman—my own face! I stared as it approached, and Mr. Boucher's maps fell to the ground from my nerveless fingers. I think that some of the pages would have blown away with the wind off the water, but even that coastal breeze seemed to have fallen away in the presence of my visitor. My eyes roved over the reflected image of my own face: the thin arch of my own lips, the sweep of my own high brow, the gentle curve of my own chin. Finally my eyes looked into their own twins, and while the Goat did not speak—I think I should have started screaming and never stopped if it did—a great many words began to pass between us.

"I cannot pretend that what transpired between us resembled in any substantive way a real conversation; that is, a give and take of ideas between two equals. There was no suggestion of equality in this exchange. No, Gordon, this was a simple transmission of instructions, and to pretend otherwise would be to betray the very reality of my experience. For even now, when so much of our journey across the sea seems but a dim memory, this encounter remains vivid and somehow vital. I cannot reproduce the instructions exactly as they were given to me; I do not think I could so much as speak the language in which they were conveyed. But I will strive to give you some impression of what I was told.

"You see, Gordon, the conversation which I had chanced to overhear between Mr. Boucher and his mate was only the beginning of a very sordid plot indeed. I was now given to understand that their machinations went much further and that their ultimate goal was far more sinister. Someone or something called the Father Ocean had reached out to them, you understand, and He had intimated that they would discover a substance of great power on the far shore which was to be their destination. It was Mr. Boucher's intent to take hold of this substance and return it to France, whereupon he would be rewarded handsomely in some predetermined manner. Well, Mr. Boucher went to work right away, and he commissioned a sort of sealed metal basin in which to transport the stuff—this was the vessel which I had seen so recently for myself. The expedition of the *Foundling* was subsequently put together in great haste to go and fetch what he meant to put inside it. It was only natural that the captain would approach me to assist him in this endeavor when his navigator proved insufficient to the task of leading them.

"But the Black Goat led me to believe that this substance would produce nothing but devastation and loss once introduced to civilization. And so, though I sailed to my own death, it meant for me to sail with these men. I was to be its saboteur, you understand, and I was assigned to do anything within my power to ensure that these men never achieved their goal. You will not be surprised to learn that I resisted this imperative—who would do otherwise? I had learned of the men's subterfuge only at the last moment, and it was a stroke of great fortune that I had the opportunity to avoid such a nasty fate.

"But the creature which spoke to me that day was unaccountably persuasive. At length I was swayed to consider its command. I am not and have never been a woman of faith, Gordon, but there was something unmistakably Divine about this creature. Though I now nurse a bitter grievance against it, I will not deny that it exerted an influence over my autonomy that was beyond the realm of the prosaic. And so I returned to the *Foundling* on the appointed date, and I pretended that all was well. I translated the maps and notes of long-deceased navigators, and I led Mr. Boucher to the place where he meant to carry out his errand. But as I have said, I had an errand of my own. Now, it will not do to linger upon this gruesome task; suffice it to say that I was given the tools which I needed to do the job.

"And that is how I came to stand before you here and now. That is also why none of the men of the *Foundling* stand here with me. I carried out my task, you understand; I performed the terrible duty which was assigned to me. I have no special regrets, unless it is to say that I should have slain the men before we ever reached this place. For now it seems to me that I have been abandoned here—I saw the Black Goat one more time only, Gordon, and it was on this very isle. You see, I had managed to eke out a stark sort of living by subsisting on what little remained of the ship's provisions and elsewise relying upon the occasional bounty of the sea. I clothed myself in the apparel of dead men and walked the beach by day; I took shelter on the *Foundling* at night and when storms raged in the skies. I cannot say how much time elapsed in this manner, but it must have been months, if not years. I had begun to grow thin, and I knew that this arrangement could not continue indefinitely. It was then that the Black Goat finally deigned to make its appearance.

"It showed itself to me one morning on the shore—it almost

seems as though it was only this very morning, but that cannot very well be possible. It was standing between two of the queer trees which populate this island, and I recognized it at once. But for its bestial body, after all, it was akin to looking into a mirror. It is useless to describe the anger which suffused my being at the sight of it; remember that I placed the blame for my ruin directly upon its hairy shoulders. I had taken to carrying a knife from the *Foundling* in my belt as I wandered the island—I believe it had formerly belonged to the mate, Mr. Baudelaire—and I now seized this knife in my fist and chased after the Goat with no small gusto. If I had been brought here to commit murder, you see, then I reasoned that perhaps I had one more victim to strike from my list.

"Well, it led me a very merry chase indeed. You will understand my surprise when it fled directly into one of the dark tunnels which pass beneath the surface of this place. I had thus far neglected to explore these caverns, for I hesitated to become lost in what was surely a subterranean labyrinth of unknown dimensions. But on this morning I felt no such compunction. I plunged into the dark with murder in my heart, and I chased after the Black Goat with what vigor remained to me.

"At some point along the way I lost sight of my quarry—and is that any wonder? Who could hope to navigate this warren without a light? And so I was left to roam in dark places for many hours; time seemed to fold in upon itself, and it was only at length that I discerned any light beyond that which suffuses the rock itself in this strange place beneath the earth. I emerged at last onto the very shore upon which we now stand; I would insist that I arrived here this afternoon, but for the fact that I could swear in the same breath that I have been waiting here for many weeks."

Lydia let out a long breath. She looked confused, but it was clear that confiding in me had lifted a burden from her shoulders. "Doubtless you will have many reasons to question the veracity of the tale I have told you," she said. "But I now believe that the Black Goat led me to this spot because it knew that you would be coming. If that is too much for you believe, you may add it to the list of the outrageous fabrications which you are almost certainly compiling in your mind, even if you have not yet spoken them aloud."

"Yours is not the first such story I have been told," I said slowly. But even compared with the triumphs and tribulations of Colleen Carrig, Roger Lundamere, and the *Melville*'s own doctor, the account of Lydia Cheves was marvelous in the extreme. It took me some time to produce a cogent response. "You are already acquainted with the circumstances of my own arrival upon this island," I began. "I think we can agree that the dreadful algal bloom which destroyed my ship and which now runs through the heart of this place is the very same substance which your Mr. Boucher pursued. Certainly its very nature answers to the description of 'devastation and loss' which you have given it. But the parallels between our lives run still deeper. You see, I too have been told of the Black Goat, though I am happy to say that I have not seen its face for myself. The story I was told matches your own with an uncanny precision; and so I cannot doubt you on that particular point. As for the Father Ocean, I have heard His name often enough—even if I do not understand who He is or why everyone but me seems to be so well acquainted with Him. Therefore I cannot discredit you on this point, either.

"But there is a third point on which our shared experiences would appear to rest," I continued. "I too have encountered an inscrutable sort of person who answers to the description of your old woman—the one whom you consulted about your maps?" When Lydia nodded eagerly, I went on. "I knew this person, or else someone very like her, as the cook assigned to the *Melville*. This person was known to me only by the name of 'Old Cedar.' And though it becomes apparent to me now only with the clarity of hindsight, I believe this person set both of us on a path which now appears to have led us to a state of ruin and despair."

"You do see, Gordon!" Lydia said. Her voice was full of unmitigated relief. "I was right to place my trust in you. But your experiences have confirmed that which I have long suspected: we are only the playthings of higher entities. I had no choice but to join the *Foundling*, not really—and I believe you had no choice but to board that ship of your own. Free will is an illusion, and it is just as well that you did not speak of your own survival. You have not heard the voice of the Father Ocean, but I'm afraid that will soon change. For what must be done next has now become plain to me, though I hesitate to lay responsibility for the task at your feet."

"What must be done next?" I said, puzzled. "Do you refer to

the means by which we are to leave this island?"

Lydia Cheves looked at me with pity in her eyes, but she did not respond at once. Instead she slipped a hand into the folds of her once-fine coat and retrieved a creased bundle of paper from an inside pocket. She gave me a significant look and then began to unfold it. From where I stood, I could see that the first page was adorned with sketches and diagrams. There was also writing, though it did not appear to be in the English language, and there were runes and glyphs which called to mind the cabalistic symbols which had decorated the device which Captain Carrig had retrieved from the cabin of the derelict. I perceived that this document could only be one of the maps to which Lydia had alluded in the course of her tale; in other words, this page was directly responsible for her current state of misery and solitude. I wondered that she had not already burnt it or tossed it into the ocean.

"I said that I hesitate to assign this responsibility to you," Lydia said, drawing a long breath. "You have already been used by the people in your life and the forces which have come to meddle in it, and it is not right that anyone should ask more of you. But that is not why I hesitate."

"What do you mean to say?" I demanded.

"I am reluctant to trust you," she said simply, "because I don't know whether you are capable of rising to meet this burden. Am I correct to guess that you cannot read these words? Can you infer meaning from the formulas which decorate the margins of this page? There is no need to answer me—how could you? But you must understand. I am beginning to sense that my own purpose has been fulfilled, and I do not think that I shall be capable of taking your place." She held her hand up to the lowering sun and turned it over, peering at her fingers. "So I will do my utmost to prepare you for what I believe you will encounter when you return to the object which lies at the center of these tunnels."

"Why would I ever return there?" I said. "The meteor is the source of the moss, and it is where our quartermaster met his end. I cannot see that there is any purpose in revisiting that place." I trust that my reader will understand that it is not a boast to say that I was unafraid to venture back into those passages. Remember that I had abandoned any concerns regarding matters of my own life or death. No, my protest was far more pedestrian: I simply did not see the point.

"You care for your friends," Lydia said quietly. "I understand that you have given up hope for yourself, and perhaps that is for the best. I do not think you can survive what must follow. Certainly your quartermaster did not. But what about your companions? I detected the care with which you spoke of your cabin boy, and I am much mistaken if you do not fairly revere the authors with whom you have sailed so far. You see, Gordon, I have reason to believe that if you know the way, you can establish a sort of *contact* prior to the moment of death. You must learn to look past delusion and obfuscation—and it will be a narrow window of opportunity. But if you would save your friends, I believe that I can help you."

As she answered me, a sad sort of smile rose to her lips, and her voice grew somber. She smoothed the paper in her hands and began to read from it. Her words took on a lilting quality, and I understood that the incantation which follows represented a verse of poetry. I do not doubt that it required both skill and artistry to preserve its rhyme scheme in translation. The rhythms and cadence of her speech rose and fell as she recited these words, inflecting each of them with the unmistakable resonance of mourning. I don't mind saying that the melancholic timbre of this composition pulled keenly at my heartstrings. Even now I have only to close my eyes to hear her voice and her words. I give them now:

Timeless Mother, Aged Father; men crawl at their feet
'Neath the waves, upon the tides; never should they meet.
Beyond the sea, beyond the stars; this thing has come to call
Man has not reckoned with its kind; not ever since the Fall.
Here truth and lies are all one kind; not with one eye nor two
Can Man perceive the grim designs of the master of the Blue.
'Tis but one chance to make your mark; to meet Him face-to-face.
Leave pride behind you; bring your wits and plead your case.
A bargain must be struck; a hard price must be paid
Only blood will pay for blood; else He shalln't be swayed.
Waver not from your purpose; here you must hold firm
Lest the Ocean's Father bring you lower than the basest worm.

To find His altar, hit upon the center of this labyrinth
Lay your hands upon it now; kneel before its plinth.
Abandon hold of all attachments; leave yourself behind
No greater fate can Man attain; no worse prize can he find.

"I understand," I said—and I thought that I did. At least I knew what was now expected of me.

A single tear rolled down Lydia's face as she concluded, folding the paper neatly and returning it to the pocket of her coat. "Then you must go," she said. Her voice was steady, but she did not meet my eye. "I do not know whether your errand is urgent, but it seems to me that one should not delay decisive action in a case such as yours. The nerve fades in the waiting, you understand."

"What will you do?"

"I will wait for what comes next. I do not think it will be long. But I have told you that I was an orphan at birth, and now you know that I have slain my companions to the last man. I did what was asked of me and no more, but it is only just that I should pass from this world alone."

"Not alone," I said quietly. I reached for her hand and felt her fingers interlacing with my own. She had taken my hand when I told her my own story, but this was somehow different. Her skin was cool, and I found a comfort and realness in her touch which I had not experienced since the day we sailed from Nantucket. It was only then that I really knew just how ardently I had missed a sense of authenticity and truth; it had been so long since I had a touchstone with reality. So I looked at her, and though her face remained impassive, I thought I saw a smile return to her eyes. It was a sad smile, and no mistake, but I was pleased to see some restoration of her good humor. But this was a fleeting thing, and it was only moments before the touch of her skin began to feel somehow insubstantial against my own. She blinked in surprise; to my confusion, she seemed to *flicker* somehow. Before my very eyes, she seemed to grow indistinct. I put a hand to my forehead, feeling faint. Was it possible that even now I was experiencing a recurrence of my concussive symptoms?

"I am going back now," she said. "To face I know not what."

"Where are you going?" I said. I heard the desperation in my voice but was powerless to suppress it. My vision blurred with tears even as her corporeal form began to fade and become translucent. You see, I had already surmised the answer to my question: she was going to wherever it was that Mr. Fairchild had gone. "Fight Him!" I cried. "Do not let Him take you."

I cannot say why I was so affected by this development. The entire episode had now taken on the cast of unreality, but that was nothing so new to me. I had experienced enough weirdness and terror by now that this latest impossibility playing out before my eyes should hardly have daunted me. No, this was something else: the scene was tragic somehow. It seemed profoundly unfair that someone could survive the expedition of the *Foundling* only to be taken away now. I railed against this development—but it seemed that I was powerless to intervene.

"It is not the Father Ocean who takes me," she now said. Even her voice had begun to waver, and I had to listen closely to distinguish her words. "It is the firstborn who will show me the way." Incredibly, she sounded pleased, like a child who has received an unexpected gift when she expected only punishment.

And then she was gone. The beach was empty save for a few boulders and one pale tree. Her disappearing act was complete, and it was as though she had never been. I stood alone in the hot sunlight of late afternoon. The waves crashed against the shore, ceaseless and uncaring. Where they struck the sand, little bits of stone flashed and shone with uncanny fluorescence. There was no sound but that of water and of wind to mark the passage of the sun's descending arc across the sky.

I sat myself down on this desolation of shining rock and burning sand, and I wept.

THE ARCHITECT OF THE EVENING TIDE

"We incline to think that God cannot explain His own secrets, and that He would like a little information upon certain points Himself."
-Herman Melville, *private correspondence*

There is nothing in the scripture of man which answers to my experience with that meteor, and there is naught in the English language which could serve to furnish an adequate description of what transpired when I laid my hands upon its pockmarked surface. I have written much about my increasingly cavalier attitude towards my own death, and I would forgive the reader for believing that I now pursued this course in order to seek my final oblivion. I cannot stress strongly enough the essential wrongness of this idea. It is true that I had no reason to expect that I should survive my forthcoming ordeal, but my intentions were noble. If by my sacrifice I might save Mr. Verne, Mr. Clark Russell, and especially William, then I had no alternative but to proceed as Lydia Cheves had directed me.

It was this frame of mind which informed my return journey through those eerie halls of quiet stone. Though I marched to my doom, I stepped carefully: it would not do to succumb to the moss running along the ground here before I reached my ultimate goal. And when I arrived at the chamber where the strange rock had so abruptly terminated its journey through the cosmos, I did not hesitate. If I allowed myself to stop and think of my family, my career—indeed my very life—I would lose the courage necessary to proceed. It was as Lydia had said: the nerve fades in the waiting.

And so I gripped the meteorite with both hands, and it was as though a bolt of lightning coursed at once through my entire being. My arms spasmed and jerked, and I would have pulled away were it not for an electric force which seemed to bind my flesh to stone. I watched with a distant species of fascination as my hands were enveloped with that purple slime; it quivered like a jelly, flowing forth from every nook and cranny in the rock as though it had scented new prey after some interminable fast.

Within seconds my arms were consumed to their elbows, just as though I had donned an especially ostentatious pair of violet gloves. But the moss did not cease its action at my elbows. It advanced to my shoulders; crawled along my skin; slid beneath my shirtsleeves and slipped past my belt. The deadly substance tasted my flesh and penetrated every orifice; it consumed me utterly. And when it reached my head and knitted itself together over my very eyes, I believe I passed from this world at last—and glimpsed an entirely new reality altogether.

I must beg my reader to forgive the manner in which I have chosen to recount this episode, for I know no better method by which to convey its eddies and whirls; its circuitous nature; its very nonlinearity. I have therefore reduced it to its most straightforward form—but it must be understood that this encounter most closely resembled a religious experience. If this smacks of indulgence, know at least that it is no mere artifice: in this hopeless place beneath the earth, I believe that I slipped the bonds of mortality and entered into discourse with something akin to the divine—and I know of no other way to achieve the distance necessary to convey the strangeness of this incident.

But first there was only darkness, you see: darkness, and a sort of howling wind which seemed to encompass the whole of the universe. In the density of this sound could be detected muffled voices which were somehow familiar to me. These voices were sharp and incensed, and I believe they meant to accuse me of some slight or betrayal. I heard the voice of my father, the voice of my mother, and the voices of the departed: Mr. Derrick, Mr. Allen, even Mr. Fairchild. Were their grievances valid? Had I abandoned them, wronged them? I strained to discern their words from the wind which consumed my world, hoping even now that I could perhaps reach them and strive to make what amends I could—and then I remembered the warning of Lydia Cheves.

This, then, was the delusion and obfuscation of which she had spoken; this was the false path that would lead me astray—to perish as Mr. Fairchild had done, haunted to the last by my own regret. And so I turned my back on these voices, though it tore my heart to ignore their desperate cries. No sooner had I done so than they fell away into the wind and simply ceased to be. I was alone now, you see—alone in an eternity of darkness. But at last I perceived a light in that void, as a single lantern will dispel the gloom of night upon a country road. I oriented myself in its direction, seeking the warmth and comfort promised by its welcoming glow. But as I approached, it grew brighter and brighter—distressingly so. Presently I wished to close my eyes against it; its very sharpness seemed somehow to risk the total erasure of all coherent thought. But I could not close my eyes. Instead—and I cannot quite account for the queerness of this impression—I *opened* them. This is when I became myself; this is when I ceased to be.

***

I awoke to perceive the unmistakable trill of morning birdsong. This sound filtered through my ears to reach my conscious mind only gradually; it was so far removed from my last memory as to be rendered an absurdity. But the familiar sound did not represent the only change in my circumstances. Beneath my outstretched palms lay the soft mattress of grass in springtime, faintly damp with the first flush of dew at dawn. I flexed my fingers, relishing the welcome sensation of something so wonderfully normal even whilst wondering at its sudden appearance. Gone was the cold alien rock of the caverns beneath the island; gone too was the purple moss which had enveloped the entirety of my body. I almost thought that I could lie here indefinitely, so acute was the relief I experienced at finding myself free of that substance which dwelt in those dark chambers. But then another sound rang out over the din of chirruping birds, and it demanded my attention. Moreover, it was a sound which I faintly recognized: the tolling of a clear bell, its crystalline chime piercing even to the inmost recesses of my jumbled confusion of thoughts.

I pushed myself into a seated position, knuckling at my bleary eyes. As the world came into focus about me, I recognized that I was situated within a forest glade. A faint light suffused the atmosphere, but it was no more than the light of daybreak; there was not a single shining boulder or rock to be seen. My sudden movement startled several animals into flight; I saw amongst them one or two of the strange little rodents which had so recently served as sustenance for both myself and my shipwrecked companions. They scattered into a verdant screen of lush undergrowth, quickly obscured within a tangle of green leaves and vines. But I had little attention to spare for them; my concentration was rather preoccupied with that animal which did *not* flee. Instead it drew nearer with a dignified sort of gait, stepping carefully, almost daintily, and stopping to survey me at a respectful distance. Even in the midst of my bewilderment and displacement, I felt a thrill of recognition course through me. I had not imagined that I would have occasion to lay my eyes upon this creature.

And have you guessed its identity? I have resolved to keep no secrets, and I suppose there is no reason to be coy: it was the Black Goat, and its face was my own. I stared in fascination, even as a sense of reverence crept over me. My eyes gazed into their own reflection; my unshaven face and unkempt hair were mirrored here before me in a perfect reproduction of my appearance. Distantly, I recalled the account of Colleen Carrig and her reluctance to look upon its countenance; I remembered how Lydia Cheves had done so and had subsequently been led to her own doom—or something very like it. But for my own part, I detected no particular malice in this creature's presence. It occurred to me that the Black Goat was neither an agent of the devil nor some pagan symbol of virility, as he was commonly depicted. He was only a messenger; and he must have a message to impart to me—else he should not have appeared.

So I stood, determined to meet him as an equal—and as I rose, I detected for the first time the crash of the ocean somewhere behind me. Its sound was terribly familiar, and I began to suspect that I had not left the island, after all. The idea was not especially comforting, but I pushed it out of mind for the moment.

"Where now do I find myself?" I demanded presently of the animal which bore my likeness. "And where is the Father Ocean? I have business with him, you understand—and this is not what I had expected to find when I took hold of that rock."

As I spoke, that strange chime resounded again throughout

the forest. The Black Goat cocked his head, allowing the sound to pass before responding. Its call gently diminished into ghostly echoes, overlaid with a cascade of birdsong. Only then did he speak; and I was pleased to observe that the sound of his voice did not drive me mad.

"You have been spared that audience," the creature said.

Its voice, too, was my own—but I found that there was no terror in that knowledge. I thought I was beginning to understand why the goat was given to wear the face of its beholder. It was a tool of persuasion, you see, meant to remove some of the instinctive fear with which all mortals must regard that which exists beyond the confines of life and death. By all accounts it should not have worked, but it did—as it must have worked on many men and women before me.

"Come with me," it said simply.

I need hardly explain why I obeyed—what other recourse existed to me? So it transpired that the Black Goat plunged into the forest, and I followed in his wake. Wet leaves slapped against my trousers as we drew beneath a canopy of tall trees. They were colossal things, bearing no resemblance at all to the sickly specimens which inhabited the island as I knew it. We followed no path, for none existed; my guide twisted and turned between the great trunks seemingly at random, or else answering to the whims of a directive to which I was not privy. At times he would stop and listen to the peal of that bell tolling intermittently throughout the wood before continuing on his course, and I began to wonder whether he were not following that sound to its source.

Our wanderings lasted long, as I could not count the time, neither in minutes nor in hours. Suffice it to say that at last we drew up before an especially dense wall of foliage. The Black Goat nodded at me to precede him into its interior, but I hesitated. What might be waiting for us behind this opaque curtain of greenery? Then, too, there was the sound of the ocean, audible even now after we had traversed what must have been miles of strange wilderness. I lingered, listening to the distant surf crashing against an unknown shore. As once before, I had the idea that I was standing poised between the pull of two opposites. I turned my head to look behind me.

"We do not go that way," the Black Goat said softly. "That is now His domain."

Contrary to what the beast must have supposed, this was almost sufficient to make me turn back in earnest. I had meant to confront the Father Ocean, after all, and I was still not sure what to make of the idea that I had been "spared" the opportunity to do so. Did my destiny lie in that forbidden direction? I rather think I would have given it serious consideration even now, but for a sudden intervention: the bell chimed again, and it was far closer than at any time previous. And so I parted the snarl of vines which stood in my path, and I stepped into a small clearing sheltered amongst what must have been the tallest trees in all the wood.

What waited for me there in the precise center of that dell was something which I had not looked to find: it was that luminous purple flower, that greatest treasure of Roger Lundamere and Glen Carrig alike, and it was restored now to all of its former glory. Its silken petals filled the air with a perfumed radiance, and the stalk which now bound it to the earth glowed faintly with a delicate luminosity. The air itself was charged with shimmering particles of gold; as they danced around me, I felt a very great weight lifted from my shoulders. Helpless to do otherwise, I found myself stepping into its sphere of influence and inhaling deeply an atmosphere which I had thought chased from the world forever. I had the impression that the flower recognized me—recognized me, and welcomed me home.

"How can this be?" I asked of my guide. I could hear the angst and consternation ripping through the fabric of my own voice. "It was destroyed—I saw how the doctor's shoes crushed it and snuffed out its light. My soul wept to see its splendor ruined—for how could it be anything but an evil to grind such beauty into dust?"

The Black Goat drew himself abreast of me, and in his eyes—my eyes—was sadness. "It has not yet been destroyed," he said softly. "Look more closely."

I peered into the heart of the flower, where seemed to dwell an exquisite amalgamation of light and truth. The divine chime sounded once more, and I perceived that it came from the blossom itself. It was then that a vision—or rather a series of visions, for their number was three—began to unspool before my wondering eyes, and I was made to witness very many things in what seemed to be only a very short period of time. I felt a wash of sudden vertigo as this epicenter of light shifted and changed, revealing a series of mutable images which have since made me question all that I had previously known of reason and reality. Though I fear I am unequal to the task, I shall endeavor to describe them to the best of my ability.

The first vision showed to me a scene which could only have existed in some far distant time, before even the advent of recorded history. Indeed, I should not have been surprised to learn that it represented events which took place before the birth of Man himself. This much I was able to ascertain both from the general wildness of the landscape which stretched to the horizon and from the nature of the beasts which stalked its fringes—never before had such massive creatures shared the earth with the human species. I rather think I may have been the first soul afforded the privilege to look upon them in the flesh as they moved amongst a riot of tropical foliage—but they were not the most remarkable facet of this first vision. For in the jungle grove which spread before me grew that same purple blossom: younger, and perhaps wilder, and more magnificent in its resplendent brilliance than I should have dared to imagine. It bathed the entire forest in a shining radiance to such an extent that it was almost difficult to behold with my own eyes. I began to understand that I was looking upon this place in its undimmed infancy—and that it may even have been the infancy of the world itself.

It was at this moment, more or less, that an unexpected shadow fell over the tranquility of this place without warning, and my field of vision shifted somehow to encompass the entire cerulean dome of the sky. A new creature was arriving, you understand, and in its arrival I sensed a kinship to this place and to the flower which grew here. They were of the same kind; I scarcely know how else to frame the matter. If my reader understands nothing else from the revelations I have undertaken to relate here, he must understand this: the entrance of this entity upon the scene changed everything.

At first I gathered only a vague impression of wings spreading wide; golden motes of light scattered like dust from shimmering feathers. As the creature alighted upon one of the enormous trees which characterized this place, I perceived that it was embodied in the form of a great Owl—though even now I recognized that it was only a representation. The creature's wings seemed to cast all the earth in benevolent shadow; its head turned as did the globe upon its axis, and I should not have wondered if its flexing talons should have proven capable of holding the entire world within their grasp. Presently it cast its wide-eyed gaze upon me, and I gasped aloud to behold all of the midnight firmament reflected in its eyes. Stars wheeled and danced within its stare; planets revolved in their orbits between unaccountable reaches of cold space. I looked into this unknowable intelligence and something within me flinched away—even as I felt drawn into its depths.

Thus ended the first vision.

It faded in the manner of a slowly dissolving dream, leaving behind only a swirl of translucent imagery churning within the heart of the purple blossom. Slowly I became aware of my own body once again, and of my companion standing silently beside me. Whether he had shared the vision I cannot say; certainly it seems assured that he understood something of what I had witnessed.

"What was that creature?" I murmured. I recognized only dimly that I had spoken aloud, and I was frankly surprised when the Black Goat actually responded—and with more directness than he had been previously inclined to show.

"She is the firstborn, the Architect of the Evening Tide. The ocean advances and withdraws at her beck and call; mountains rise and fall according to her whims. Or at least they did—before He came." The Black Goat lifted one hairy leg in a human sort of gesture which was really quite surreal to witness, pointing one cloven hoof at the flower. I understood that he meant for me to look into the flower once more; there was plainly still further information to learn. And so I bent at the waist to peer closely at what was next to come.

The second vision was night. The perspective which was opened before me was such that I could perceive the island in its entirety: the island, and the vault of unfamiliar stars which hung uneasily overhead in a greasy arc of glittering light. Ah, but they were not entirely unfamiliar, at that. Had I not seen them once before, after all? I remembered William's fright at their sudden appearance in the night sky as we drifted upon the open sea, and I recalled how I had chided him roughly with the sort of impatience which could have been born only from my own deep-seated terror. Well, he had been right to fear—for what emerged next from this foreign welkin was sufficient to freeze the very marrow of my bones. The central feature of this vision was now made manifest, you see: it was nothing less than the appearance of the Father Ocean Himself. And as this vision resolved from black night to dim dawn, I beheld Him at last in all of His dreadful grandeur.

I can describe this spectre only as a slowly rolling bank of blackest cloud, its colossal dimensions beyond rational thought, beyond comprehension, beyond even imagination—and certainly beyond my ability to depict in the fullness of its terrible majesty. Lightning flashed and flickered within the heart of this roiling form as it descended from some far distance between the stars to settle itself like a heavy cloak upon the horizon of the terrestrial world. Tendrils of fog and arms of swirling vapor extended from the main body of this apparition, reaching out to grasp the world itself—to swallow it and make it His own. Mountains were struck down as I watched; entire continents were broken at a glance; it seemed an inescapable conclusion that the sum of existence itself could not fail to collapse beneath the weight of His cold fury. All would be consumed in an empty void of storm cloud and mist—even this forest and the divine blossom which it served to shelter.

But as it turned out, He was not unopposed. The Architect of the Evening Tide rose to contest him, even as I watched with equal parts rapture and horror, and the conflict which presently raged within the skies themselves took on a character which is fit to describe only in Biblical proportions. Black skies and bursts of lightning clashed with gusts of wind thrown from tremendous wingbeats. She who was the master of the seas moved to defend them from the Father Ocean, and that interloper worked to destroy Her utterly. With lurches alternating between clarity and the maddening ambiguity of dreams, I saw that each wounded the other. At great length, the Father Ocean put out one of Her eyes, leaving it dead and dark; the sprawl of stars within that great orb fell still and cold. But the Father Ocean too was stayed, reduced at last with the expenditure of His fury to an incorporeal mist which could exert its influence upon the world—but which could no longer act directly against it. He had taken the sea from Her, but He could not take that radiant bloom; could not extinguish that spark of life which grew only in this place and made it unique amongst all of the worlds scattered across the length and breadth of the universe.

Thus ended the second vision.

"She halted His advance," I said. I suppose I meant it as a sort of question, although I cannot now imagine what kind of answer I might have expected.

With the conclusion of this second vision, I had found myself returned once more to the grove whence grew the sacred flower. I was beginning to understand something of its nature—and I understood that the flower as I saw it now did not necessarily represent the flower as it currently was. The evidence of my own eyes was not to be denied, after all: the doctor had broken the flower beyond repair. And so while the Black Goat had intimated that the flower was not *yet* destroyed, I thought I had finally gathered his meaning upon this point. I am not ready to say that the course of time had been reversed, precisely, but at least it seemed apparent to me that the place in which I now found myself existed independently of time. If this seems too much to credit, you may rest assured that reading about it now can scarcely compare to actually experiencing the same.

"It was a species of stalemate," confirmed the Black Goat.

"You speak in the past tense," I said. "What then has changed?" That I should have seized upon this detail in the face of the larger cosmogonic revelation which had been thrust upon me seems now remarkable. I think I must have grasped at the only facet of the experience which I was able to comprehend.

But my strange companion only nodded at the flower once more; if an answer existed, plainly I was meant to discover it for myself. I met the messenger's eyes for what turned out to be the last time, and in them I thought that I read a wary breed of encouragement. Well, why not? I had come this far.

The third and last vision was faster and looser than its predecessors, and it appeared on its face to represent a far greater scope and span of time. Years, decades, centuries passed in the blink of an eye—and I was no more than their silent observer. The great beasts which once guarded this place passed into oblivion. Countless forms of life rose and fell before my eyes, slipping from prosperity into obscurity along with all that came before them. Ships began to ply the seas, and the world was transformed not by the hand of the Father Ocean, but by the works of Man. All the while the stalemate between the Father Ocean and the Architect of the Evening Tide persisted, with neither holding an advantage over the other. The industry of Man grew unabated; they scurried about the earth unaware of those forces which hung poised above their necks like the headsman's axe. Little skirmishes broke out here and there, of course, for the Father Ocean never stopped scheming. But always He was stymied in His efforts—always this sacred object that was the wellspring of creation was protected by the uninterrupted vigilance of the firstborn and Her messengers—until He seized upon an idea.

For the Father Ocean had grown cunning, and if He had lost power over the earth, He had not lost influence over the stars whence He came. And when He called down that celestial rock from the void and brought it to bear upon the earth, I saw it flicker with a dubious fire as it burned through the atmosphere of the world and hurtled towards its target. The firstborn was powerless to prevent its arrival; She had been bested at last, outmaneuvered by the madness and cleverness of Her enemy. And so She took the only recourse which remained to Her: She sent the lotus away from this place and passed it into the hands of Man. And when the Father Ocean's missile struck the soil of this place and transformed it utterly, it nevertheless failed to achieve its object.

Those men who now held the flower knew not what treasure they carried, to be sure, but across generations they sensed enough of its import and its significance to see that it was preserved. I was now privileged to witness for myself the rise of that society which grew to care for it, with all of its disparate temples and little shrines. And I saw a number of familiar faces initiated into their ranks.

First came the saga of the *Foundling*; the particulars of this story were known to me already, and I have related them in the preceding chapter to the best of my ability. My reader will recall how the Father Ocean had employed recruits of His own to bring the destructive power of the alien fungus to the mainland where the secret flower was hidden. He will recall, too, how this plan was foiled by the intervention of Lydia Cheves. However, it must be said that I did glean one new piece of information from this vision: the location of the *Foundling* herself. I saw how the nefarious Captain Boucher had guided her to this island; how he had steered her safely into a sheltered cove before he had been so summarily dispatched along with the rest of his crew.

Of this episode I will say no more; you must understand only that the Father Ocean had been foiled again, and that His rage had reached unprecedented heights in the wake of His defeat. The Architect of the Evening Tide saw now that it was time to act. I cannot really say how this was made clear to me, for I perceived only broken glimpses of the events related herein—but I was given to understand that if the flower were returned to the land of its birth, that place would be cleansed of the fungus which had corrupted it. The sacred bloom itself would be in danger again, but no more could that foreign moss be used as a weapon against civilization itself. And so with the help of Her messengers, the firstborn began to move again.

When Roger Lundamere entered into the equation, there could be no question of his identity. His story, too, has more or less already been told, but I must stress the sense of unreality which I experienced upon seeing his face for myself. Colleen Carrig, too, was known to me: she was the very image of her brother writ in feminine form, and I could see at a glance that she acted with the same rashness and vigor which had characterized the late captain. I learned furthermore that Roger Lundamere was no villain, in the end; indeed, he was tasked personally with bringing the flower home.

I need not recount the multitude of ways in which Roger Lundamere's errand ended in failure. Suffice it to say that when his part was played, so began my own: the voyage of the *Melville,* and her subsequent ruin. I was presently forced to relive my own adventures in rapid succession; images flashed before my eyes one after another, and I was powerless to close my eyes against them.

And so I traipsed to the top of Sankaty Head with the blind assurance of my own untested abilities; I descended into the forecastle of the derelict in a crescendo of fear; I committed murder in conspiracy with he who had become my closest friend. I fled the monsters which now attacked our ship; I suffered in a fugue of hunger and thirst as we drifted beneath strange skies; and I laid my hands upon an object which had once been sent from them. But for all the death and loss which had characterized my journey, none featured more heavily in this vision than the destruction of the flower. You see, I understood now that the *Melville* really did have a purpose, even if her captain had not known its essential nature for himself. She had been called to recover the flower from the frozen hands of Roger Lundamere's corpse—to recover it, and to bring it home. And she had failed.

Thus ended the third vision.

What came next came only after I had at last wrenched my gaze from the swirling light of the flower's interior. I was troubled, you see, for I knew now that the flower really was gone. The place where I had met the Black Goat had once existed, and maybe in a certain way it still existed out of time itself, but it was no more than an occluded reflection of what once had been. And so when I did look away, I was not altogether surprised to find that I had not returned to that place; indeed, it so transpired that I had gazed upon its radiance for the last time. Instead I was delivered once more to that black abyss which was characterized only by an all-consuming wind and by a single shining light. My spirits sank as the knowledge of my whereabouts occurred to me with a dreadful sort of finality; was I returned to death, after all?

But here was something new: even as I peered into the intensity of its glare, that light resolved into the shape of a single eye—and it was an eye which I recognized. The entirety of the cosmos was encapsulated within its glow; stars flickered and flashed across a universe written in miniature, and I realized that I was in the presence of the Architect of the Evening Tide once more—even as Her alien intelligence looked back at me and beheld, I am quite sure, everything which could be known about me. My thoughts were laid bare; every doubt and insecurity was quite plain to Her. I felt compelled to speak, to defend myself against this unprecedented admixture of intimacy and intrusion—but as it turned out, there was really no question of mounting an objection.

I raised my head to meet Her gaze more fully, you understand, and it was then that my ego fell away at last. Please do not interpret this statement to mean only that I became aware of my own insignificance in the face of the divine. That was part of it, and no mistake, but it will not serve to furnish the impression which I now seek to convey above all else. I must be clear on this point even if I have been clear on precious little of that which has preceded it: meeting the gaze of the firstborn caused the last vestiges of my own sense of self to be ripped away and cast into the wind of that black chasm which surrounded me. I have since recovered them, or very nearly so, but at this moment in time I was not myself any longer—or I was not *only* myself. My reader will discover presently that the information I received was intended not for an individual, but for the entire human race. I have therefore elected to represent the exchange which followed as a simple Dialogue; if in so doing I have exceeded the bounds of credibility, I can say only that my experience must stand on its own merits.

MAN: What are you? And who is the Father Ocean? I have seen you both for myself now, but I am no closer to an understanding.

NOT-MAN: I am the stars; He is the dark between them. Diametrically we are opposed; long has He sought to take your world from me and long have I striven to preserve it from His grasp. But this is no more.

MAN: Your conflict is over, then.

NOT-MAN: The spark of life has been snuffed out; both of us must withdraw. Our impasse is broken; victory goes to neither. The world is now Man's to make in his own image. You will be left to your own devices to succeed or to fail; I cannot say which is the more likely.

MAN: Am I to die, then? Have I died already?

NOT-MAN: I will remove that substance which now pervades your living body. Do not begrudge it wholly; it is only by its action that you exist now beyond yourself. But my remedy will not be complete; it is the last curse of the Father Ocean, and you will carry it for the remainder of your days.

(The single eye of the firstborn begins now to dim. The scattered stars and spinning planets reflected across its glassy surface now recede, leaving behind only a deep pool of stunning blue rimmed with a lingering golden glow, which suggests somehow the last light of a setting sun.)

MAN: But who am I? It is a curious thing, but I seem to have fallen away from myself in some fashion. Can you help me? I cannot really say why I was meant to speak with you in the first place.

FIRSTBORN: You are Gordon. Return now to yourself and what life remains to you.

So I did.

IN WHICH I OFFER A FEW FINAL REFLECTIONS

"Is it not natural, after all, for the heart to be assailed by a thousand apprehensions as we near the end of any enterprise?"
-Jules Verne, *An Antarctic Mystery*

Happy tales are short in the telling; such it was with our escape and subsequent rescue. Suffice it to say that with the help of the firstborn's visions, I was able to locate the cove where the *Foundling* was moored. There were many queer qualities to this ship which would take many more pages to describe; not least amongst them were the unusual notes in the ship's log, which referred to ports of entry whose names I could neither identify nor pronounce. But that is neither here nor there; my reader need only know that I wasted no time in assembling what remained of my party. Mr. Verne, Mr. Clark Russell, and William were the very picture of ecstasy when they saw the condition of the *Foundling.* They were also fairly brimming over with questions which I could not very well answer. I put them off as best as I was able, explaining that I had stumbled upon the discovery of the ship whilst fleeing from the horrors of the nautilus on the beach. Of Mr. Fairchild's demise I had no need to dissemble; the evidence of his fate was plain enough for my companions to read for themselves.

Well, it was a difficult business to set sail with so small a crew, and we met with no few adventures on our return from the desolate shores of that unspeakable place. I had no reason to doubt the wisdom of the Architect of the Evening Tide—but if the Father Ocean were withdrawing from the world, His monsters had not yet received this latest intelligence. We had more than one narrow escape, and I don't mind saying that there were a few more instances during which I imagined that I might not make it back to Nantucket, after all. To read of them I must direct you to such stories as "The Sea Serpent" and "The Voice in the Night:"[57] though our names have been removed from the narratives, these examples will serve to show you the sort of travails we faced. They may also serve to give you a happier ending than the one which I'm afraid I must soon deliver.

You see, at last we come to it. I am sorry to say that I cannot in good faith conclude my missive here without revealing just how badly things turned out for me in the end. In the months and years which followed our adventures, I began to be assailed by doubts about why I had been spared by the Architect of the Evening Tide. My friends went on to flourish in their professional careers, but I found myself left behind to grapple with the burden of my experiences. I was troubled, you see, by my encounter with the divine. It weighed upon me in such a manner as I had not expected. Many a man or woman has sought evidence of a world beyond this one; to them, I say: turn back! For life is little more than an empty husk, devoid of all reward and sensation, once one has laid eyes upon a heavenly Truth and been forced to turn away. Or so it began to seem, as I started to lose interest in the world and those who peopled it.

My reader can rest assured, at least, that I did my part to ensure that no more lives were lost to the terrible machinations of the Father Ocean or the strange things He had loosed upon this world. When we arrived safely in Nantucket, I took it upon myself to contact Dr. Sauer, with whom the *Melville*'s doctor had worked so closely to study the moss which ultimately proved to be (after a manner of speaking) his own doom. This was no simple task, for I knew only the most cursory information concerning her identity, and it transpired that I was eventually obliged to travel to Germany to plead my case to her. The reader can only imagine how little I was inclined to embark upon another transatlantic voyage—but after my singular audience described in the preceding chapter, I felt it was my responsibility to address these concerns for myself.

---

[57] *The Sea Serpent* by Jules Verne (1901) and "The Voice in the Night" by William Hope Hodgson (1907). I can only guess at the relationship between the former and the adventures of this memoir; certainly it is a suggestive title to choose from Verne's canon. There is less mystery about the relevance of the latter selection: its story tells of a fungus which consumes and absorbs human bodies.

This was a most delicate business. When I reached Dr. Sauer, I had to make it plain that her colleague would not be returning to Germany without divulging any details which would open an inquiry into the nature of his disappearance. More importantly, I urged her to destroy any remaining samples of the purple moss which had been the subject of their terrible experiments. I was dismayed to discover that she was not initially sympathetic to my overtures; she was a true academic, you see, and the pursuit of knowledge was paramount to her understanding of life. At length I was driven to commit a most rash act: I seized a scalpel from a table on which her tools were arrayed, and I made a small incision on the inside of my left forearm. I fairly thrust the open wound beneath her eye (ensuring that she first donned a pair of goggles, of course) to show her that mingled with my crimson blood was a thin trickle of that brilliant alien fungus. She peered at this substance beneath a magnification lens, and she grew very quiet indeed.

"How do you yet draw breath?"

"That is beside the point, but if any samples of this substance were to escape your collection, I do not think that others would be so fortunate."

Well, this convinced her at last. She promised to destroy what samples were left to her at once; but I resolved to stay until this task was accomplished. We gathered the materials together and transported them (with no small amount of caution) to the university's incinerator. This was a machine poised on the very cutting edge of science, and Dr. Sauer assured me with great confidence that no remainder of the fungus could possibly survive its action. The device was outfitted with a little window by which a spectator could watch its flames. We stood side-by-side and bore witness to the final destruction of the alien fungus. As it blackened and shriveled in the unrelenting heat of the machine, small tendrils reached out from the heart of the stuff, just as though they were trying in vain to escape their doom. Did the fungus have its own memory, after a fashion? Did it recall even now those fires which must have burned bright around the meteor as it was delivered to earth, penetrating the atmosphere of the world to land upon the isle where the spark of life was born? If this seems an impossible flight of fancy, I would only remind you that I have seen stranger things.

With this objective satisfied, I thought that I could now begin to settle into a more pedestrian sort of life. Perhaps I would renew my efforts to find employment within the field of journalism. But I quickly discovered that this occupation no longer held any attraction for me. How could I bring myself to report upon the news of the day? It seemed bland and somehow trite, leached of significance in the face of those greater events to which I had already borne witness.

Instead I turned to the docks, where I busied myself in the task of working with my hands. This helped for a time; the restorative effects of exercise and sunlight are not to be denied. But as I grew familiar with my work and gradually developed the skills of a laborer, my mind was freed to reflect upon the experiences of my life once again. A restlessness grew within me over the years which followed, and I returned over and over again to the question of why I had been allowed to escape from the clutches of the Father Ocean. Had I been spared for some particular purpose? What use was whiling away the hours of my life in meaningless toil? And whence did this restlessness derive? Now and then I would think of the alien life that coursed within my blood, and I knew that I could not sustain the fiction of an ordinary existence for all the rest of my days.

At length, I decided that the only thing for it was to contact Old Cedar. I can already hear the objections of my reader: but she was lost at sea! Well, I was not so sure. I had begun to devise a certain theory about the *Melville*'s cook, you see. First and foremost, I remembered how one sailor had reported that the old woman flew off into the rain during the storm which presaged the ship's doom—just like a bird. Had I not seen another bird, in a manner of speaking? Second, who could forget the peculiar condition of her occluded eye? For what had once seemed only to be a physical impairment now took on a new significance. I recalled the eyes of the firstborn: one light, one dark. One swam with the possibilities of vibrancy and life, while the other must have seen only bereavement and despair. Was this what Old Cedar saw when she looked upon the world? Plainly some connection existed between the cook and the Architect of the Evening Tide. If one existed outside of time, who was to say the other did not?

Discovering her last known whereabouts was no easy feat. I began my inquiries with Dr. Sauer. My reader may recall that the

Melville's doctor knew something of Old Cedar; it only stood to reason that his colleague might also remember this unusual personage. Alas, she was of very little help. Still disturbed by the carnivorous moss which even now pulsed through my veins, she was reluctant to correspond further with me. She was willing to say only that she could recall the old woman's name arising in connection with some mention of "Old Europe."

Fortunately, this sparked the memory I needed to proceed with my investigations. I remembered what little Lydia Cheves had told me of her own old woman: namely, that she was a historian specializing in old and forgotten folklore. The chief obstacle was that Lydia had told me that the woman resided in the French city of Dubois. I could locate no such municipality; but then, I was developing a theory about this, too. Had not the Black Goat escorted me beyond the confines of linear time? I thought that maybe there once *was* a Dubois. And if my search were necessarily limited to the realm which I occupied, I nevertheless had the time and the money required to look for it.

In the course of pursuing this task, I finally grew to understand what Captain Carrig had meant when he referred to the "disreputable places" in which he had roamed when searching for his sister. My research likewise brought me into the company of many an unsavory character, as I made appointments within the lecture halls of discredited universities and visited the homes of disgraced clergy. But they held little enough terror for me; having looked upon both the blasphemous and the divine, what had I to fear from common man, however nefarious his intent? And they held no special interest for me, at any rate: they were amateurs, in point of fact, who had dared only to dabble in the occult. Their scant knowledge could not compete with my firsthand experience.

But at last my efforts were rewarded with a morsel of credible information: the woman I sought was to be found in a suburb of the French city Avignon. It was in a state of great excitement that I traveled there. The city was best known for its multitude of churches, containing an uncommonly great number of hallowed religious artifacts. Had she chosen this place of residence for its proximity to the sacred; the celestial? My anticipation increased: idleness had not suited me, and my heart quickened at the thought that I might yet discover more answers to the mysteries which had now plagued my fate for so long.

But this was not to be. You see, I inquired after her whereabouts from the moment I arrived in that town which once answered to the name of Dubois. I went from one door to another, describing my quarry to the best of my ability to those puzzled souls who answered my knocks.

"You cannot fail to remember her once you have seen her," I said to one. "I need know only where she resides."

I even went so far as to visit the chapels of Avignon, reasoning that if she were truly connected to the divine as I suspected, then it would be there that she would be found. Failing that, I took the opposite tack: I began haunting the cemeteries and mortuaries of the city. It was a morbid task, but then my own mind had turned to darkness in view of my failure to find her.

It was in this manner that I found myself in the churchyard of a small parish upon a dark night; the moon was little more than a sliver in the night sky, and the air was unseasonably chill. I wandered aimlessly between the headstones as I had in so many other cemeteries; I was given over to despair. My movements had become slow and dragging, and I daresay I must have looked a wraith to the grizzled old sexton who first spotted me sometime after two or three o'clock in the morning.

"I say," he said. "Who goes there?"

I caught an impression of narrowed eyes behind the fellow's lantern; his coat whipped about his ankles as he advanced towards me. But he drew up suddenly when he saw the state into which I had fallen; it had been some days since I had availed myself of rest and proper ablutions. Plainly the man was now questioning the wisdom of approaching me in the dead of night in so secluded a locale. I smiled in what I hoped was a disarming expression rather than a mad leer; I held up my hands to show that I was unarmed and meant the old caretaker no harm.

"I'm sorry if I startled you," I said. I was now grateful for the time I had spent with Mr. Verne; while I would never be fluent in the tongue, I possessed enough facility with the French language to make myself understood. The sexton scowled, quickly recovering his composure when he heard the relative youthfulness inherent to my voice and recognized the slightness of my stature.

"If you're to apologize," he said, "then apologize for

trespassing—and be on your way. I'd just as soon not hassle myself with reporting another vagrant to the police." He was already beginning to turn away, trusting that I would heed his warning and find some other churchyard in which to linger. But something in his words gave me pause, and I was not prepared to walk away until I had satisfied my curiosity on a certain point.

"Excuse me, sir," I said. "'Another' vagrant, did you say?"

He turned around, and I was surprised to see only resignation upon his face, where I had expected to find exasperation. He sighed audibly and shook his head, but I knew that the gesture was meant for himself. I waited silently, allowing him to work through the conflicting emotions which now passed across his countenance. Finally he nodded.

"Come on, then," he said. He took another step and motioned for me to follow.

"Come where?"

"You're looking for *her*, aren't you? Same as all the others, unless I miss my guess." He gave a dry chuckle. "Oh, does that surprise you? Thought you were on to something special, did you? Well, I don't know where they all come from, lad, but she must've been someone extraordinary to inspire such long-lasting devotion. I should say it's been nigh on fifty years, now." He cleared his throat. "I'll show you the way, but do this much for me: be quick about your errand." He looked me up and down. "And see the pastor in the morning. I daresay you could use a meal—and a bath."

Mystified, I followed the sexton into an older and darker part of the churchyard. Here the old trees grew taller and obscured the weak light of the moon; here the gravestones were larger and more ornate. Small tombs had been erected here and there to serve as the final resting places of those privileged few who were not content to lie in the ground with the common men and women of the earth. I wondered vaguely whether their bodies were preserved in their houses of marble—or were they too subsumed into the earth, returned now to dust and to dirt? These grim thoughts were my only accompaniment as our path wound and meandered to the farthest reaches of the cemetery; the sexton did not speak. But at last we reached our destination: it was no more than a curiously plain headstone, marked with a brief inscription.

"Well, there you are." The caretaker held out his lantern to illuminate the script which had been carved into the slate. As I knelt to examine it, I observed that a multitude of objects had been scattered at the base of the stone: an old rosary; a candle worn to its nub; a little stone fetish worked into the approximate likeness of an owl. This last caused a pang of bittersweet recognition to flare briefly within my heart. But I knew that I could not spare the time to inspect these disparate offerings; the caretaker had made it very plain that his patience was finite. So I focused my attention upon the headstone itself. There was not much to see; its inscription consisted of no more than a single verse. I reproduce it here:

Look not for me upon this earth;
I have gone like wind, like breath;
As we met upon your birth;
so too shall we meet in death.

It is useless to describe the despair which suffused my soul when I comprehended the meaning of these words. Here, then, was the end of my quest. There would be no answers; no deliverance from the doubts which plagued me. If Old Cedar could not be found in this world, where then would I turn? I trust I need not explain why I did not accept the sexton's offer to meet with the chapel's pastor. What solace could such a man offer me? What promises of salvation and eternal life could satisfy the longing in a soul which had already glimpsed eternity for itself?

But I will not linger upon this memory or its consequences; not yet. I would prefer to leave my reader with one final recollection of happiness and camaraderie before we come to the end at last. And so now I will step back in time, as it were, and relate a conversation which took place at the Green Pelican shortly after my friends and I were returned safely to Nantucket. Let it stand to represent all such happier times; it was the last occasion upon which I ever laid eyes upon the three of my friends all together. Indeed, it was the last time I sat down with any one of them to break bread at the same table.

A hot and bright day had given way to a warm and pleasant night; the windows of the little inn were open to invite a freshening breeze. It was a stark contrast to the last time I had sat at one of these tables. But some things, at least, were the same: the matron who worked behind the bar frowned at us and at the general wildness of our appearance. I have no reason to believe that she could have recognized me, changed as I was both inside and out. Her severe eyes roved over our little party in an effort to determine whether we might represent trouble; the familiarity of this expression made me smile. And when Mr. Verne returned from her company to press a mug of ale into my hand, I was reminded forcibly of the memory of the late Mr. Derrick, who had done the same not so very long ago.

"Gentlemen," said Mr. Clark Russell when we had all seated ourselves around the table. "To the *Melville* and her captain." He raised his glass.

"And to her crew," I added. "I will not say that they were good men one and all, but they seem somehow very dear to me now."

Our glasses clinked together; ale spilled onto the table. I relished the burn of the alcohol in my throat as I swallowed, suppressing the thought of the last substance which had torn a fiery course through the entirety of my anatomy. We drank in companionable silence, each man reflecting on his own thoughts. William looked especially pensive as he sipped from his glass. I cannot say whether he had ever previously had occasion to fall in his cups, as the saying goes, but none could deny him the right to do so now if such was his choice. I laid a hand upon his shoulder and smiled at him, feeling our mutual warmth and friendship more acutely than at any time since the discovery of the *Foundling*. Shaken from his reverie, he smiled back at me. But it was not long before more serious matters had to be addressed—this was not purely a social call.

"Next week I shall return to England," said Mr. Clark Russell, setting his empty cup on the wooden surface before him and spinning it idly between his calloused fingers. "We had better set our stories straight."

"What do you mean?" William looked suddenly alarmed.

"I should think it obvious," snorted Mr. Verne. He sounded impatient; I am sorry to say that our recent escapades had done very little to curb his famous temper. "We cannot very well go about spreading stories of monsters and mutinies, can we?"

"There will be questions," I said. "The matter of the *Melville*'s voyage was public record; I need not remind you that I was to share it with the world."

"Let me handle any matters of public record," said Mr. Clark Russell. "I have some experience with the press."[58]

"That's settled, then," said Mr. Verne. "Now, let us move on to more pleasant matters. Gordon—I believe I have heard that you are something of a musician?"

"You're joking, surely?" I nearly dropped my glass in surprise. Perhaps I had been too rash to suggest that his humor had not improved.

"I have heard him play," said William. "He is quite good."

This, too, was surprising—I had not known that the cabin boy was present in the Green Pelican on that first fateful evening. Just how oblivious had I been to my surroundings? Well, I had been rather desperate to ingratiate myself to the crew. My focus had been single-minded, to be sure. So despite myself, I smiled. I set down my drink and cracked my knuckles, flexing my fingers theatrically.

"Go on, then," said Mr. Clark Russell, now grinning back at me.

I approached the piano willingly enough; the only question was which tune to play. But really, wasn't it obvious? Only one melody would serve. As I slid onto the bench, I positioned my fingers over the keys and toyed with the first few notes of that university song which I had once played on this very same piano. Of course, this new occasion demanded new lyrics. This was a prodigious challenge; it would be flattery to suggest that I was any kind of poet. Nonetheless, words which were more or less appropriate soon sprang to my lips with an unexpected sort of inspiration. I give them presently:

O'er water, crest and trough,
Come hear my tale and dare ye not scoff!
All over wide seas, from one shore to the next,

---

[58] As noted previously, Clark Russell was a regular columnist for *The Daily Telegraph*. Presumably he was able to manipulate his influence with the industry to suppress or censor any records of the *Melville*.

We met with strange beasts and sailed past doomed wrecks.
We suffered black despair, that curse of mortality;
As we ran up against scenes of surpassing brutality.
But neither hunger nor thirst could turn us away;
Bonds forged in blood hold true to this day.
We passed together through death and debris;
I sing this song now with my friends all beside me.

The entirety of this memoir contains no sentiment so essentially true as that which was expressed in my song. If it seems too saccharine, the reader must recognize that those who have not toiled together in black weather upon a roiling sea cannot hope to understand the bond which is formed between men in such extreme circumstances—to say nothing of those supernatural challenges which we met and over which we triumphed. Indeed, as I transcribe these words today, the faces of my friends appear before my tired eyes just as though they stood before me. And if they are blurred with tears, what of it? I would know these smiling faces whatsoever the nature of the veil which is soon to separate us.

For however strong the bond between the four of us had grown, it could not hope to overcome the changes which have befallen me in the subsequent years. As I searched in vain for answers to my fate on the other side of the ocean, my friends carried on with their lives. As I floundered in despair, they rose to new heights of success and acclaim. Now, I do not mean to say that they did not suffer—for I followed the literary output of my friends with rapt attention. I saw that they too, in their particular ways, were steadfastly engaged in dealing with the traumas which had beset our journey aboard the *Melville.* Each new work of fiction contained some recognizable element of our travels together. I hoped that it gave them some satisfaction; some sense of working the terror and wonder from their bones. I hoped that it gave them rest.

Alas, I have found no such rest. The fungus surges now in my blood, you see. It has been content to lie dormant these past many years, biding its time whilst I labored at the pretense of a normal life and wasted my days in an ineffectual hunt for some elusive truth of cosmic significance. But no longer. Even now as I gather this rope in my hands, I feel its relentless action: it beats with its own pulse, entirely independent of the regular rhythms of my heart. I suppose I should have expected something along these lines; after all, I had been told that I would carry this burden for the rest of my days. But what would happen if I let this infection run its course? Would the moss simply burst the fragile bonds of my blood vessels at last, consuming me wholly as it has consumed so many other men before me? Or would it have something more nefarious in store for me? It is the last curse of the Father Ocean, after all—even if that entity has departed this world, I cannot guess what havoc might be wreaked by the tools He left behind.

Well, I do not intend to wait and see what transpires. I have tested the fit of this coiled loop, and the accuracy of my measurements are rewarded—it is snug. Did I not say that I have become something of a skilled craftsman? And after all, what sailor could have failed to learn how to tie a knot? This, then, is my ultimate purpose in putting the pen to the page: I do not wish to pass from this world without leaving an account behind me. This memoir represents both the best and the worst of my life. I cannot predict whether it shall be published; I would not betray the wishes of my dearest friends whilst any of them still live. And if my reader has gathered any sense of my character throughout the preceding pages, it will be understood that I do not pursue this course lightly.

But neither will I entertain the eventuality of a gruesome death accompanied only by the lingering melancholy of dim memory. If the Father Ocean means to claim me after all these years, I will not make Him wait any longer. I can only hope that I might be privileged with one final encounter with the Architect of the Evening Tide as I move from this reality to the next. She spared me once, and while I do not believe it rests within Her power to do so again, I should very much like to look upon Her countenance once more. The inscription upon Old Cedar's headstone gives me hope that this wish is not in vain.

But even more than this last wish, the innermost desire of my secret heart is that I might hear *that* voice once more before I go: that voice which once goaded me onto an adventure the likes of which I could never have imagined—and which preserved me against all odds to see its conclusion.

I have not heard *that* voice in years.

About the Author

Mark Smeltz is an author of fiction and nonfiction whose work is inspired by a relentless fascination with the far-flung corners of the world and the mysteries that rest just beneath the surface. When he's not parked behind the keyboard, plugging away at another tale of terror and suspense, he can be found in the game reserves of Africa or the foothills of the Himalayas, exploring the intersection of nature and culture, which ultimately lies at the heart of everything he writes. He lives in Pittsburgh, PA, with his wife and a ragtag assortment of badly behaved cats and dogs.

https://marksmeltz.portfoliobox.net

www.ingramcontent.com/pod-product-compliance
Lightning Source LLC
Chambersburg PA
CBHW051139030726
47504CB00004B/944
9781944045807